The legacy of John Polidori

The legacy of John Polidori

The Romantic vampire and its progeny

Edited by
Sam George and Bill Hughes

MANCHESTER UNIVERSITY PRESS

Copyright © Manchester University Press 2024

While copyright in the volume as a whole is vested in Manchester University Press, copyright in individual chapters belongs to their respective authors, and no chapter may be reproduced wholly or in part without the express permission in writing of both author and publisher.

Published by Manchester University Press
Oxford Road, Manchester, M13 9PL

www.manchesteruniversitypress.co.uk

British Library Cataloguing-in-Publication Data
A catalogue record for this book is available from the British Library

ISBN 978 1 5261 6638 8 hardback

First published 2024

The publisher has no responsibility for the persistence or accuracy of URLs for any external or third-party internet websites referred to in this book, and does not guarantee that any content on such websites is, or will remain, accurate or appropriate.

Typeset by Newgen Publishing UK

Frontispiece. *John William Polidori*, by F. G. Gainsford, oil on canvas (*c.* 1816). NPG 991. © National Portrait Gallery, London.

For Marcus Sedgwick (1968–2022)

'*I will live seven times, and I will look for you and love you in every life.*'
(Midwinterblood, 2011)

Contents

List of figures	ix
Notes on contributors	xi
Foreword: Polidori revisited – Christopher Frayling	xvi
Acknowledgements	xxi
Chronology	xxiv

Part I: The birth of *The Vampyre*

1 Introduction – Sam George and Bill Hughes	3
2 Phantasmagoria: Polidori's *The Vampyre* from theatricals to vampire-slaying kits – Sam George	23
3 A séance in Bristol Gardens: Reassessing *The Vampyre* – Fabio Camilletti	48
4 Byromania: Polidori, fandom and the Romantic vampire's celebrity origins – Harriet Fletcher	64
5 Rebellion, treachery, and glamour: Lady Caroline Lamb's *Glenarvon*, Polidori, and the progress of the Romantic vampire – Bill Hughes	81
6 Sexual contagions: Romantic vampirism and tuberculosis; or, 'I should like to die of a consumption' – Marcus Sedgwick	106
7 *The Vampyre*, Aubrey, and *Frankenstein* – Nick Groom	123

Part II: The legacy of *The Vampyre*

8 From lord to slave: Revolt and parasitism in Uriah Derick D'Arcy's *The Black Vampyre* – Sam George and Bill Hughes	143
9 'But if thine eye be evil': Tropes of vision in the rise of the modern vampire – Ivan Phillips	167
10 'Knowledge is a fatal thing'; or, from fatal whispers to vampire songs: Breaking Polidori's oath in The Vampire Chronicles and *Byzantium* – Sorcha Ní Fhlainn	186

11 'The deadly hue of his face': The genesis of the vampiric
   gentleman and his deadly beauty; or, how Lord Ruthven
   became Edward Cullen – Kaja Franck   202
12 Vampensteins from Villa Diodati: The assimilation
   of pseudo-science in twenty-first-century vampire fiction
   – Jillian Wingfield   217
Afterword: St Pancras Old Church and the mystery
of Polidori's grave – Sam George   233

Appendix 1 John William Polidori, *The Vampyre*   240
Appendix 2 George, Lord Byron, 'A Fragment'   268
References   273
Index   292

Figures

Every reasonable attempt has been made to obtain permission to reproduce copyright images. If any proper acknowledgement has not been included in the caption of each image, copyright holders are invited to contact the author via Manchester University Press.

Frontispiece *John William Polidori*, by F. G. Gainsford, oil on canvas, circa 1816. NPG 991. © National Portrait Gallery, London.　v
2.1　Playbill: J. R. Planché, *The Vampire*, English Opera House (1820).　30
2.2　'Dance of the Sorcerers', from Marion Fulgence and Charles William Quinn, *The Wonders of Optics* (New York: C. Scribner & co, 1869), p. 198.　32
2.3　T. P. Cooke as the Vampire, Mrs Chatterley as Lady Margaret.　37
5.1　*Lord Byron*, by Richard Westall (1813). NPG 4243. © National Portrait Gallery, London.　82
5.2　Thomas Phillips, *Lady Caroline Lamb* (oil on canvas). CTS336396. The Devonshire Collections, Chatsworth. Reproduced by permission of Chatsworth Settlement Trustees/Bridgeman Images.　84
5.3　'The English Vampire', in *The Irish Post* [Dublin]: [Richard Barratt], 7 November 1885. Reproduced courtesy of the National Library of Ireland.　94
5.4　Cover of Lady Caroline Lamb, *Glenarvon* [1816], Empress Gothic (New York: Curtis Books, 1973).　99
9.1　F. Gilbert's cover for the popular edition of *The Vampyre* (London: John Dicks, 1884).　178
9.2　Opening page of *Varney, the Vampire* (London: Edward Lloyd, 1845). Artist unknown.　180

A.1 St Pancras Old Church exterior. © Sam George. 234
A.2 *Memento mori*, St Pancras Old Church. © Sam George. 234
A.3 Church motto, St Pancras Old Church. © Sam George. 235
A.4 The Hardy Tree, St Pancras Old Church. © Sam George. 236
A.5 Mary Wollstonecraft Godwin's tomb, St Pancras Old Church. © Sam George. 237

Notes on contributors

Fabio Camilletti is Professor of Italian Literature at the University of Warwick. He has worked extensively on European Romanticism and the Gothic from a transnational perspective, particularly focusing on Anglo-Italian writers such as Dante Gabriel Rossetti (*Beatrice nell'inferno di Londra* (Da Libreria Studio Bosazzi, 2005); *The Portrait of Beatrice* (Notre Dame University Press, 2019)) and John Polidori (John Polidori and Lord Byron, *Vampiri e altri parassiti*, ed. and trans. by Fabio Camilletti (Nova Delphi, 2019)). He is currently finalising, together with Maximiliaan van Woudenberg, the first complete English edition of *Fantasmagoriana*, and working on a monograph on Italian occulture from the 1940s through the 1970s.

Harriet Fletcher is Lecturer in Media and Communication at Anglia Ruskin University. Her research explores the intersections of celebrity and the Gothic in literature, media, and popular culture. Her first monograph is under contract with Bloomsbury Academic, with the working title *Gothic Celebrity: Fame and Immortality from Lord Byron to Lady Gaga*. Elsewhere, she has published on Andy Warhol's Gothic portraits in a special issue of *Celebrity Studies*. She has further interests in feminist media studies and horror studies, with forthcoming publications on ageing Hollywood actresses in Gothic television and the star images of Britney Spears and Megan Fox.

Kaja Franck is Lecturer in English Literature and Creative Writing at the University of Hertfordshire. She is a researcher on the Open Graves, Open Minds project. Her latest research project, Danse Macabre, explores the Gothic quality of ballet and other dance forms, and her thesis looked at the literary werewolf as an eco-Gothic monster. She has published on the depiction of wolves and werewolves in *Dracula* and in young adult fiction in *Werewolves, Wolves and the Gothic* (ed. by Robert McKay and John Miller,

University of Wales Press, 2017) and *In the Company of Wolves: Wolves, Werewolves, and Wild Children* (ed. by Sam George and Bill Hughes, Manchester University Press, 2020). Most recently, she has written about werewolves, gender, and race in 'Ginger Snaps Back' for *Gothic Studies* (22:1 (March 2020), 64–80), on the wilderness in *The Palgrave Handbook of Contemporary Gothic* (ed. by Clive Bloom, Palgrave, 2020), and has co-authored a chapter on contemporary werewolves for *Twenty-First-Century Gothic* (ed. by Maisha Wester and Xavier Aldana-Reyes, Edinburgh University Press, 2021).

Sir Christopher Frayling was the first to bring vampires into the academy with his groundbreaking study of *Vampyres* (Gollancz, 1978; Faber & Faber, 1990; Thames and Hudson, 2016; Thames and Hudson, 2022). His classic four-part TV series *Nightmare: The Birth of Horror* (prod. by Letitia Knight, 1996) similarly brought Gothic horror into the mainstream. He is an award-winning broadcaster and writer. He was Rector of London's Royal College of Art (1996–2009), Chairman of Arts Council England, and Professor of Cultural History at the Royal College of Art for over thirty years (and is now Professor Emeritus). Christopher was knighted in 2000 for 'services to art and design education'. He collaborated with Open Graves, Open Minds on the Bram Stoker Centenary celebrations and has been a keynote speaker at three of our events: 'Bram Stoker Symposium' (2012), 'In the Company of Wolves' (2015), and the 'Polidori Vampyre' symposium (2019). His mammoth book *Vampire Cinema: The First Hundred Years* was published by Reel Art Press in 2022.

Sam George is Associate Professor of Research at the University of Hertfordshire and Convenor of the Open Graves, Open Minds project (OGOM). She has published over ten articles on natural history, together with a monograph, *Botany, Sexuality and Women's Writing* (Manchester University Press, 2007). In 2010 she founded with Dr Bill Hughes the Gothic research group OGOM. Following OGOM's international conference on vampires, Sam developed the first postgraduate module on vampire studies in the UK, exciting the interest of the national and international press. She is now a leading spokesperson for the literary vampire. Her interviews have appeared in newspapers from *The Guardian* and *The Independent* to *The Sydney Morning Herald*, *The South China Post*, and *The Wall Street Journal*. She has amassed over 292,374 reads for her feature articles on vampires alone. In 2022 she recorded an obituary of Anne Rice for BBC Radio 4's *The Last Word* and was a guest on *In Our Time* on BBC Radio 4 with Melvyn Bragg (on John Polidori's *The Vampyre*). Her work with OGOM has led to several co-edited publications with Dr Bill Hughes: *Representations* of *Vampires and the Undead* (Manchester University Press, 2012), *In the Company of Wolves* (Manchester University Press, 2020), and the in-progress collection *Gothic Encounters with Enchantment and the Faerie Realm in Literature and Culture*. Sam co-edited the first ever issue of *Gothic Studies* on 'Vampires' with Bill Hughes in 2013 (15:1) and 'Werewolves' in 2019 (21:1). Having written on British werewolves in the journal *Gothic Studies* and Japanese mermaids in the *Critical Quarterly*, she is focusing her new research on the intersection between folklore and the Gothic. She is currently completing a monograph on the folklore and cultural history of the shadow, developing the *Cambridge Companion to the Vampire* and writing *Gothic Fairies: A History* for Bloomsbury.

Nick Groom is Professor of Literature in English at the University of Macau and has previously held positions at the Universities of Oxford, Bristol, Stanford, Chicago, and Exeter. He is well known for his work on the Gothic, which includes the monographs *The Gothic: A Very Short Introduction* (Oxford University Press, 2012) and *The Vampire: A New History* (Yale University Press, 2018; revised edition 2020), scholarly editions of novels such as Matthew Lewis's *The Monk* (Oxford University Press, 2016) and Mary Shelley's *Frankenstein* (Oxford University Press, 2018), and many essays and articles on subjects ranging from the politics of punctuation in Gothic texts to the lyrical sources of singer-songwriter Nick Cave. He has an article on the publication of *The Vampyre* in *Romanticism* (28:1 (April 2022), 46–59). Among his other books are studies of literature and forgery (*The Forger's Shadow*, Picador, 2003), national identity (*The Union Jack*, Atlantic, 2006; revised edition 2017), environmentalism (*The Seasons*, Atlantic, 2013; revised edition 2014), and J. R. R. Tolkien (*Twenty-First-Century Tolkien*, Atlantic, 2022; revised edition 2023). His next book is a newly edited collection of pre-*Dracula* vampire tales for Oxford University Press.

Bill Hughes is co-convenor, with Dr Sam George, of the Open Graves, Open Minds: Vampires and the Undead in Modern Culture Project at the University of Hertfordshire. He is co-editor (with George) of *Open Graves, Open Minds: Vampires and the Undead from the Enlightenment to the Present* (Manchester University Press, 2013), *In the Company of Wolves: Wolves, Werewolves, and Wild Children* (Manchester University Press, 2020), and 'Ill met by moonlight': *Gothic Encounters with Enchantment and the Faerie Realm in Literature and Culture* (forthcoming). Bill is completing a monograph on contemporary paranormal romance and young adult Gothic from the perspectives of formalism, genre, and critical theory. His essays on this topic have appeared in books from *Werewolves, Wolves and the*

Gothic (University of Wales Press, 2017) to *Young Adult Gothic Fiction* (University of Wales Press, 2021). Elsewhere, Bill has published widely on communicative reason and the interrelation of the dialogue genre and English novels of the long eighteenth century: 'Enlightenment Fact, Orientalist Fantasy: Dialogues of Colonial Encounter in Sydney Owenson's *The Missionary* (1811)' (*Wenshan Review of Literature and Culture*, 17:1 (2023), 147–72) and '"Base and Degenerate Language": Genre and Rational Voices in John Thelwall's *The Daughter of Adoption*' (forthcoming). This apparently disparate research is not unfocused; it has at its core concerns with the Enlightenment as viewed through the Frankfurt School and the Marxist tradition.

Sorcha Ní Fhlainn is Reader in Film Studies and American Studies, and a founding member of the Manchester Centre for Gothic Studies, at Manchester Metropolitan University. Ní Fhlainn has published widely in the fields of Gothic and horror studies and popular culture, specialising in monsters, subjectivity, and cultural history. She is the author of *Postmodern Vampires: Film, Fiction and Popular Culture* (Palgrave, 2019). Recent articles and book chapters include an examination of neoliberal horror in *Joker* and the retro 1980s in *Stranger Things*, and the books *Twentieth-Century Gothic*, co-edited with Bernice M. Murphy (Edinburgh University Press, 2022), *Visions of the Vampire*, co-edited with Xavier Aldana Reyes (British Library, 2020), and *Clive Barker: Dark Imaginer* (Manchester University Press, 2017). She has recently curated special issues of the journals *Gothic Studies* (July 2022) and *Horror Studies* (December 2022). She is currently leading a project on the long 1980s onscreen.

Ivan Phillips is Associate Dean in the School of Creative Arts at the University of Hertfordshire. His research interests span such subjects as Romanticism and its contexts, Gothic culture, modernism into postmodernism, twentieth-century poetry and poetics, and experimental fictions from Laurence Sterne to the web. His published work includes articles on poets such as Thomas Chatterton, Dylan Thomas, and David Jones; chapters in Sam George and Bill Hughes, *Open Graves, Open Minds: Representations of Vampires and the Undead from the Enlightenment to the Present Day* (Manchester University Press, 2013) and *In the Company of Wolves: Werewolves, Wolves and Wild Children* (Manchester University Press, 2020); Andrzej Gasiorek and Nathan Waddell, *Wyndham Lewis: A Critical Guide* (University of Edinburgh Press, 2015); Paul Booth, *Doctor Who: Fan Phenomena* (Intellect, 2013); and his monograph *Once Upon A Time Lord: The Myths and Stories of Doctor Who* (Bloomsbury Academic, 2020).

Notes on contributors

Marcus Sedgwick (1968–2022) was an internationally award-winning writer of over forty books for young people and adults, including both fiction and non-fiction. His work has been translated into over thirty languages. He wrote feature articles for papers such as *The Guardian*, *The Independent*, and *The Sunday Times*. He taught creative writing at the Arvon Foundation and Tŷ Newydd and judged numerous book awards, including the Guardian Children's Fiction Prize and the Costa Book Awards. His contributions to OGOM included an essay on the folkloric origins of the vampire in relation to his novel *My Swordhand is Singing* (Orion, 2006) in *Open Graves, Open Minds: Representations of Vampires and the Undead* (Manchester University Press, 2012) and a chapter derived from his interest in wolf children, drawing on his research for the character of 'Mouse' in *The Dark Horse* (2002) for *In the Company of Wolves: Werewolves, Wolves and Wild Children* (Manchester University Press, 2020). He was born in East Kent and lived on a mountainside in the Haute-Savoie in the French Alps, where just once, at dusk, he heard the howl of a lone wolf. Marcus was working on a long-standing project on tuberculosis, melancholia, and the Romantic vampire at the time of his premature death in 2022. He intrigued and delighted audiences with lively and memorable papers based on this research at various OGOM events including 'Polidori: The Romantic Vampyre and its Progeny' (2019), 'Gothic Visions of New Worlds' (2020), and 'Nosferatu at 100' (2022). He is sorely missed.

Jillian Wingfield was awarded her PhD from the University of Hertfordshire in 2019 for a thesis entitled 'Monsters, Dreams, and Discords: Vampire Fiction and Twenty-First Century American Culture'. She has presented her research on the American vampire at various OGOM symposia and conferences. While she has gone on to author material ranging from stage to academia, the undead retain their centrality in her research heart. She is currently involved in secondary-level education, where she enjoys engaging the next generation, some of whom need little persuasion to embrace the Gothic, and most of whom are fascinated by all things vampiric.

Foreword: Polidori revisited

Christopher Frayling

I have always considered the oil painting of Dr John William Polidori by portraitist F. G. (Francis) Gainsford to be strangely moving (see Frontispiece). There he is, a fashionably dashing figure 'with a marked Italian cast of countenance', his dark eyes looking soulfully to the right, his curly black hair and full lips, white wing-collar, and cravat, with a hint of vanity – this is clearly the portrait of a self-conscious young man, one who takes himself seriously – *and* vulnerability; a recent graduate with a glittering professional career ahead of him... 'a handsome, harum scarum young man', as Harriet Martineau was to call him... and yet, only a few months later, it all fell apart. He found himself to be the wrong person in the wrong place in the wrong company at the wrong time of his life. His *Diary* of Lord Byron's colourful adventures on the Continent – which he had hoped to issue with publishers John Murray, but which in the event remained unpublished for the whole of the nineteenth century – reveals instead what it felt like to be on the receiving end of literary snobbery, borderline racism, and clever-clever remarks by a group of very bright, very self-assured, very entitled – and of course very talented – people. *The Vampyre* may have become, over time, the most influential piece of prose literature in the history of mass culture – I once called it 'the first story successfully to fuse the disparate elements of vampirism into a coherent literary genre' – but where Polidori was concerned, it ruined him professionally and personally. He never established copyright, and it earned him in total the princely sum of £30.00. Even his authorship, his paternity of the book, was only recognised obliquely, thanks to the publisher's sleight of hand. He was the light that failed.

The portrait – the only close-up image of Dr Polidori to which we have access – was donated to the National Portrait Gallery in early September 1895 (accession number 991) by Polidori's nephew William Michael Rossetti, the man who eventually published the *Diary* – from an expurgated transcript rather than the original manuscript – in 1911. The painting had evidently been in the Polidori family ever since it left Gainsford's studio:

William Michael inherited it from his aunt, Polidori's unmarried younger sister Charlotte, who had died in January 1890. She was that same elderly lady of severe virtue responsible for censoring 'peccant' passages from her brother's *Diary*. Rossetti went to inspect the portrait in situ – at the National Portrait Gallery's new premises in St Martin's Place off Trafalgar Square – on 4 June 1896, and wrote touchingly in *his* journal, 'how great would have been the delight if my good grandfather [Gaetano Polidori] could have seen that his greatly beloved and lamented John will be there too'. He felt that the painting was on the whole acceptably displayed, but that the light level did not show it off to best advantage. When offering the picture to the Gallery, Rossetti could not at first remember who on earth had painted it ('if I can hit upon the name of the painter of the likeness of Dr Polidori, I will notify it to you'). Aunt Charlotte had thought it might be by a Mr Clover, but she had evidently muddled it up with 'a different and less noticeable' painting. Only in August 1904 – some eight years after the acceptance of the donation – did William Michael Rossetti confirm to the Gallery that the portrait was in fact by F. G. Gainsford. It seemed somehow typical of the whole Polidori saga. The Gallery also accepted Rossetti's brief account of the background to the painting: a line or two about *The Vampyre* followed by the speculation that Polidori, unable to meet his large gaming debts, took his own life in August 1821. These lines remain – unchanged – on the website and background materials published by the National Portrait Gallery, just four lines of text, even though the speculation has since been seriously questioned. Was Polidori a gambler? There seems to be little or no evidence of this, beyond family folklore, unless he was behaving out of character. Did he take his own life? The coroner certainly did not think so, and Polidori was buried in hallowed ground, in St Pancras Old Church's churchyard. He *had* been suffering from severe concussion and cerebral trauma ever since his driving accident of September 1817, which by all accounts impacted on both his mental state and his behaviour. The family speculation was of course believed – with some alacrity – by John Murray and Lord Byron, and it has been uncritically accepted by lazy historians ever since. Again, typical of the whole Polidori saga. Even his biography (Macdonald, 1991) is entitled *Poor Polidori*.

Gainsford, born in Worksop, Nottinghamshire, had enrolled at the Royal Academy Schools in winter 1807 at the age of twenty-three, in the same cohort as William Etty. He'd already set himself up as a professional portraitist, exhibiting six portraits at the Academy in 1805/06, followed by a self-portrait in 1814. A year later, at the RA's Summer Exhibition, he showed two portraits – one of P. E. Ottey, Esq. (a chief clerk at the navy office in Somerset Place) and one of the actress Eliza Walstein (well known on the Dublin stage, and in the process of making a comeback in

London). To judge by the engraved version of the Walstein painting (printed by George Hayer), she too has curly black hair, a soulful sidelong glance to the right, full lips, and a defiant, rather vain, pose – evidently a Gainsford speciality by then. When not exhibiting, Gainsford seems to have earned a reputation of sorts for medical portraits at this time. Two of them are currently in the collection of Sheffield's Teaching Hospitals, and were originally painted for Sheffield Infirmary: the sitters were John Browne, first chairman of the Board, and Robert Ernest MD, house surgeon to the Infirmary. This suggests that the portrait of John William Polidori was commissioned by the family as the portrait of a young, up-and-coming member of the medical profession – which would date it a little earlier than is implied by the Portrait Gallery's 'c. 1816'. The sitter is wearing a formal black garment against a plain brown background, and it looks to be a graduation portrait – perhaps dating from between August 1815 (when his dissertation was examined and accepted by the University of Edinburgh) and November 1815 (when he presented himself in Norwich as 'an Italian poet' – an indication of his changed career priorities by then). Or certainly before mid- to late March 1816, when Polidori – against well-intentioned parental advice – made the fateful decision to become Byron's travelling companion and personal physician. A family portrait, then, commissioned by doting parents to celebrate Polidori's achievement as a graduate in medicine from Edinburgh at the unusually precocious age of nineteen – or, as he himself wrote with pride on his personal copy of the dissertation, to celebrate the day he 'was by imposition of the velvet cap raised to the Degree of Doctor of Medicine'. Gaetano and Anna Maria Polidori may well have thought of the painting as the portrait of a young doctor: the sitter was more likely to have thought of it as the portrait of an artist as a young doctor…

When I was researching my study of the vampires of nineteenth-century literature from Lord Ruthven to Count Dracula in the early 1970s, I had a reproduction of Gainsford's portrait on the wall of my study. In those days, the NPG supplied large black-and-white photographic reproductions, on request, mounted on card. I had been to view the painting itself in the Gallery's offsite storage area – not in the main collection – on a wheeled rack surrounded by portraits in elaborate frames of assorted Regency and Victorian worthies I hadn't heard of. My photographic reproduction was placed above a bookshelf which contained the third issue in book form of Polidori's *The Vampyre* and a photocopy of his Edinburgh dissertation on somnambulism and other trance-like states written in Latin. As my research progressed, I must say I began to feel a certain affinity with the young doctor. I was sometimes patronised by the literary establishment in Cambridge, treated with amused caution by the staff in the round Reading Room at the British Museum, and questioned about my motives by humanities colleagues at the University of Exeter – 'vampires', said one, 'surely the only possible reason for studying them is to attract publicity rather than advance scholarship'. Gothic literature had yet to gain admittance to the Great Tradition – though it was already knocking on the door. All of which explains the dedication contained in the resulting book of *The Vampyre: Lord Ruthven to Count Dracula*, first published in 1978:

> *For Dr John William Polidori, who came too close to great men*
>
> May 28 – Went to Geneva. Introduced to a room where about 8; 2 ladies.
>
> Lord Byron's name was alone mentioned; mine, like a star in the halo of the moon, invisible…
>
> (Polidori's *Diary*)

It also explains why I took that same reproduction to Keats House in Hampstead – on 6 April 2019 – for my contribution to the conference '"Some Curious Disquiet": Polidori, the Byronic Vampire, and Its Progeny', convened by the Open Graves, Open Minds project to commemorate in style the bicentenary of Polidori's *The Vampyre*. The photograph rested on the lectern, when I spoke about 'Polidori Revisited'. The collection of essays in this volume started life at that same very stimulating conference. There were papers on the theatrical versions of *The Vampyre*, on *The Vampyre* as satire, and its relationship with Lady Caroline Lamb's *Glenarvon* and Mary Shelley's *Frankenstein*; as literary vampirism 'and the medical symptoms of pulmonary consumption'; Lord Ruthven on stage and the development of special effects; connections with recent fiction, films, and fan literature; *The Vampyre* and clichés of masculinity, and, by welcome contrast, the legacy of Romantic female fiends; and discussions with a medical historian about the evidence surrounding Polidori's departure from 'this life in a natural way by the visitation of God'.

Polidori's shadow has lengthened very considerably since first I started researching literary vampires all those years ago. His *Diary* has become widely available (1975/1978/2009); he has featured in at least four major films (*Gothic*, 1986; *The Haunted Summer*, 1988; *Rowing with the Wind*, 1988; *Mary Shelley*, 2017) and several novels (I know of twelve); there have been two full-length biographies (Franklin Bishop, 1991; D. L. Macdonald, 1991) and numerous critical editions of *The Vampyre*; even his Edinburgh dissertation has been translated from the Latin (*European Romantic Review*, December 2010). And – perhaps the ultimate accolade – Polidori has appeared in an episode of television's *Doctor Who* (2020).

And this timely volume, aptly titled *The legacy of John Polidori: The Romantic vampire and its progeny*, a scholarly tribute – from a variety of today's perspectives – to a remarkable man. Thomas Moore, in his *Life and*

Letters of Lord Byron (1830), prompted anonymously by Mary Shelley, wrote that '[Polidori's] ambition for distinction far outweighed both his powers and opportunities of attaining it'. This collection of thought-provoking articles, by specialists in their fields, respects his powers while providing plenty of opportunities for his distinction to be celebrated.

Acknowledgements

This book is dedicated to the memory of the writer Marcus Sedgwick (1968–2022), who left this world on 15 November 2022. Marcus was a brilliant and powerful storyteller; he could grip your heart with just one sentence. He never shied away from exploring the dark side of his imagination, and this is what led to his unique collaboration with OGOM. He was involved from its inception, starring at our very first conference, 'Open Graves, Open Minds: Vampires and the Undead in Modern Culture', in 2010. He presented on his journey to Romania to research the folkloric vampire for his novel *My Swordhand is Singing* (2006). We invited him back in 2012, when we hosted our 'Bram Stoker Centenary Symposium' and he staged an 'in conversation' on vampires with Kevin Jackson. In an act of pure inspiration and generosity, he distributed hand-printed copies of his story 'Bram Stoker: Vampire' to all our delegates. Serendipity dictated that he returned for 'The Company of Wolves: Sociality, Animality, and Subjectivity in Literary and Cultural Narratives – Werewolves, Shapeshifters, and Feral Humans' (2015). Sam discovered that they shared a fascination with wolf children, and they co-presented a memorable and meaningful session on the myths of children raised by wolves. Mouse, the wolf child in Marcus's *The Dark Horse*, remains Sam's favourite ever character. Marcus went on to launch aspects of his new research on vampirism and tuberculosis at the '"Some Curious Disquiet": Polidori, the Byronic Vampire, and Its Progeny' (2019) symposium. He delighted us again with his take on 'The Black Vampyre and Other Creations: Gothic Visions of New World' (2020) and his paper for 'Nosferatu at 100: The Vampire as Contagion and Monstrous Outsiders' (2022), which sadly was his last encounter with us. Luckily, his lively talks developed into original essays to three of our books: 'The Elusive Vampire: Folklore and Fiction – Writing *My Swordhand is Singing*', in *Open Graves, Open Minds: Representations of Vampires and the Undead from the Enlightenment to the Present Day* (2013); 'Wolves and Lies: A Writer's Perspective', in *In the Company of Wolves: Werewolves, Wolves and Wild*

Children (2020); and 'Sexual contagions: Vampirism and tuberculosis; or, "I should like to die of a consumption"', in this volume. Sam adopted many of Marcus's books as key texts on her modules at the University of Hertfordshire over the years (*My Swordhand is Singing* for 'Reading the Vampire', *The Dark Horse* for 'Generation Dead: YA Fiction and the Gothic' and *Saint Death* for 'Border Crossings'). And whenever he visited the university to talk to her students, he always mentioned the impact of OGOM on his own writing. One of his finest books, *Midwinterblood* (2011), was, Marcus told us, inspired in part by his collaboration with OGOM:

> Working with OGOM and the team around Dr Sam George has encouraged me to voyage more deeply into the relationship between folklore and fiction, and I can see the result in all my work. It has been consistently inspired, enriched and informed by it ... I strongly see a connection between this work with OGOM and a book I wrote some time later, *Midwinterblood*, perhaps the book for which I am best known. *The Monsters We Deserve* was very influenced by our discussions and my thinking about gothic monsters. One of the central questions ... was inspired by OGOM.

(*Midwinterblood* won the Michael L. Printz Award, America's most prestigious prize for writing for young adults.)

Sam has fond memories of working closely with Marcus for over twelve years, accompanying him to the Edinburgh Festival for a 'Battle of the Books' (*Dracula* versus *Frankenstein*) and to Conway Hall to contribute to an event to celebrate the launch of *The Monsters We Deserve*. We came to know Marcus as a sensitive and engaging companion. His generosity to other writers is well testified to on social media. His passing is a terrible loss.

Sam and Bill would like to thank all of the vampire scholars who presented at the Polidori symposium (Stacey Abbott, Xavier Aldana Reyes, Daisy Butcher, Kaja Franck, Sir Christopher Frayling, Nick Groom, Sorcha Ní Fhlainn, Ivan Phillips, Marcus Sedgwick, Catherine Spooner, Jillian Wingfield, and Gina Wisker). Thank you for contributing to the project; this book would not have developed without you. We are, of course, grateful to all those who contributed such engaging essays for this collection. We would like to give special thanks to Sir Christopher Frayling for providing us with a wonderful Foreword. His dedication to Sam in *The Vampire Cinema: The First Hundred Years* was very touching and was gratefully received. Sam would also like to thank Melvyn Bragg and his producers at BBC4 for inviting her to take part in *In Our Time* on Polidori's *The Vampyre*, following the symposium, together with her co-panellists, Martin Rady and Nick Groom.

Thanks also go to the University of Hertfordshire for contributing to funding the symposium; to the International Gothic Association (IGA) and

British Association for Romantic Studies (BARS) for generously sponsoring postgraduates and Early Career Researchers places; the staff at the Keats House, for their kind hosting of the OGOM project. Thanks also to Father Elston at St Pancras Old Church for assisting with research into Polidori's resting place. We would like to thank Sam's University of Hertfordshire Literature colleagues, particularly Dr Rowland Hughes, for his guidance regarding OGOM research, and Tara and the staff at the UH Research Office for their help with our impact case study on ethical Gothic.

Daisy and Kaja deserve special thanks for their services to OGOM. We are also grateful to all the scholars who have engaged with us over the years on vampiric themes, particularly Stacey Abbott and Catherine Spooner, who have worked with OGOM from its very beginnings – that dialogue has been truly inspirational and has helped form this book.

We want to thank Sarah Rendell of Newgen, and Lianne Slavin, Matthew Frost, Paul Clarke, and their team at Manchester University Press, including our copy-editor Dan Shutt and our anonymous readers, for working so hard on this book. Thanks, Matthew, for overseeing the publishing history of OGOM from its beginnings; we wish you well in your new life.

Thanks, too, to Paul Flewers, Rachey Taylor, Curtis Runstedler, and Sara Williams for valuable assistance with resources and formatting.

Sam would like to thank Jonathan and Willow for their love and support; her father David George, who has been a source of inspiration throughout her life; and her sisters Rowena and Demelza. Her third sister Caroline, though absent, helped form the person she has become. Sam would like to wish her happiness. The youngest members of the family, Lyra and Maria Liliana, have been a joy in these dark times. She would like to thank Angela and Chuck Silverman for the music. Also, Teddy, her ginger feline muse, gone but not forgotten. Finally, Bill, for his humour and kindness, and his generous gifts of books. Thank you for working with me on OGOM and for sharing ideals and ideas over the many years we have supported each other and collaborated on our shared projects. I could not have conceived of OGOM without you.

Bill would like to dedicate this book to the memory of his mother Barbara and father Bernard, and to those of Pete Duxbury, Mavis Fox, and Elizabeth Bostock. He could not have finished this book without the support of his sister Caryl and brother Bob, and the friendship of Sarah and Dave Bartlett, Mel and Liz Fox, Rachey Taylor, Sue Chaplin, Kev Jones, and Martin Green.

Bill owes a huge debt to his feline muses Morticia and Gomez, and the revenant Spike, who reappeared after an Odyssean absence of nearly ten years!

Last, Bill would like to thank Sam for her endless intellectual and emotional companionship.

Chronology

1702	Joseph Pitton de Tournefort, *Voyage to the Levant*
1732	'Political Vampires', in *The Craftsman*
1746	Antoine Augustin Calmet, *Dissertations on the Apparitions of Angels, of Demons and of Spirits, and on Revenants or Vampires of Hungary, of Bohemia, of Moravia and of Silesia*
1795	John William Polidori b.
1797–1800	Samuel Taylor Coleridge, *Christabel*
1801	Robert Southey, *Thalaba the Destroyer*
1804–09	John Polidori attends Ampleforth College
1810–11	Johann August Apel and Friedrich Laun, *Gespensterbuch*
1811–15	John Polidori studies medicine at the University of Edinburgh; graduates as the youngest MD in the university's history. Thesis on somnambulism.
1812	*Fantasmagoriana*, trans. by Jean-Baptiste Benoît Eyriès (from Apel and Laun's *Gespensterbuch*)
1813	*Tales of the Dead*, trans. by Sarah Elizabeth Utterson (from *Fantasmagoriana*)
1813	Lord Byron, *The Giaour*
1816	April: John Polidori appointed physician to Lord Byron and travels with him to Europe
1816	15 June: ghost story writing competition at Villa Diodati
1816	Lord Byron, 'A Fragment'
1816	Lady Caroline Lamb, *Glenarvon*
1816	John Polidori, *On the Punishment of Death*
1818	John Polidori, *An Essay Upon the Source of Positive Pleasure*
1818	Mary Shelley, *Frankenstein*
1819	John Polidori, *Ximines, A Tragedy, and Other Poems*
1819	John Polidori, *The Vampyre*
1819	First French translation of *The Vampyre*
1819	First German translation of *The Vampyre*
1819	John Polidori, *Ernestus Berchtold; or, The Modern Oedipus*
1819	Uriah Dereck D'Arcy, *The Black Vampyre: A Legend of St Domingo*

1820	Cyprien Bérard, *Lord Ruthwen; ou Les Vampires*
1820	Pierre Carmouche, Achile de Jouffroy, and Charles Nodier, *Le Vampire* (play)
1820	James Planché, *The Vampire; Or, The Bride of the Isles* (play)
1821	John Polidori, *The Fall of Angels: A Sacred Poem*
1821	John Polidori, text for Richard Bridgens, *Sketches Illustrative of the Manners of France, Switzerland and Italy*
1821	John William Polidori d.
1822	*The Vampyre* (dramatised in German, Brunswick)
1828	*Der Vampyr* (opera; libretto by Wilhelm August Wohlbrück, music by Heinrich August Marschner)
1828	*Der Vampyr* (opera; libretto by C. M. Heigel, music by Peter Jospeh von Lindpainter)
1845–47	James Malcolm Rymer, *Varney the Vampire*
1851	Alexandre Dumas, *Le Vampire* (play)
1852	Dion Boucicault, *The Phantom [The Vampire]* (play; adaptation of *Le Vampire* (1820), by Carmouche, de Jouffroy, and Nodier)
1872	Sheridan Le Fanu, *Carmilla*
1897	Bram Stoker, *Dracula*

Part I

The birth of *The Vampyre*

1

Introduction

Sam George and Bill Hughes

This collection of essays emerged from the Open Graves, Open Minds project's symposium for the bicentenary of John Polidori's *The Vampyre*, at Keats House, Hampstead, 6–7 April 2019. ' "Some Curious Disquiet": Polidori, the Byronic Vampire, and Its Progeny' brought together OGOM researchers and other eminent vampire scholars in literature and film.[1] The event marked 200 years since the publication of the first prose vampire narrative in English and celebrated the entrance of this Gothic archetype into literature from folklore. Polidori is perhaps the least regarded figure in the history of literary vampirism and his novella, despite its seminal character (Christopher Frayling calls it 'probably the most influential horror story of all time'), has never been the subject of a book-length critical study until now.[2] Our book traces Polidori's bloodsucking progeny and his disquieting legacy in literature and other media. We present new perspectives on both the genesis of *The Vampyre* and its still-flourishing legacy. It is a return to the beginnings of the OGOM project and our vampire research with our foundational conference in 2010, the subsequent edited collection, *Open Graves, Open Minds: Representations of Vampires and the Undead from the Enlightenment to the Present Day* and the first special issue of *Gothic Studies* devoted to vampires (May 2013).[3]

John Polidori's tale *The Vampyre* was published in 1819. It is a commonplace that his vampire emerged out of the same storytelling contest at the Villa Diodati in 1816 that gave birth to that other archetype of the Gothic heritage, Frankenstein's monster. Present at this gathering were Polidori (who was Byron's physician); Mary Godwin, author of *Frankenstein*; Claire Clairmont; Percy Shelley; and (crucially) Lord Byron. Byron's contribution to the contest was an inconclusive fragment about a mysterious man characterised by 'a cureless disquiet'. Polidori took this fragment and turned it into the tale of the vampire Lord Ruthven, preying on the vulnerable women of society. *The Vampyre* was something of a sensation (partially owing to its misattribution to Byron) and spawned stage versions and imitations that were hugely popular.[4] It also very quickly prompted a parody which turned the aristocratic Ruthven into the first vampire of the USA, a revolutionary black slave: Uriah Derick D'Arcy's *The Black Vampyre* of 1819, a text which has, surprisingly, been overlooked in literary studies and the history of the Gothic.[5] A significant moment in our work with the OGOM project has been in arousing public interest in this fascinating text, with Sam George publishing a widely read article and our holding an online event in 2020 as part of the nationwide 'Being Human' festival.[6] This article caused something of a sensation and achieved 59,000 reads and 19,100 shares on Facebook. Our event, too, was attended by over 200 people internationally. Thus, Polidori's legacy of the Romantic vampire is not confined to the immediate aftermath of *The Vampyre*; it can be found still in texts (literary, dramatic, and cinematic) of the twentieth and twenty-first centuries. Polidori's continuing relevance prompted a recent discussion on BBC Radio 4's *In Our Time*, with Melvyn Bragg and guests Sam George, Nick Groom, and Martyn Rady.[7]

Sir Christopher Frayling declares *The Vampyre* to be 'the first story successfully to fuse the disparate elements of vampirism into a coherent literary genre'.[8] This could be qualified; if short political satires and ethnographical enquiries featuring the monster constitute genres, then these had already emerged out of folkloric accounts during the eighteenth century.[9] However, Polidori gave the creature the form that largely persists through subsequent vampire narratives, transforming it from the animalistic monster of the Slavic peasantry to something that can haunt the drawing rooms of Western society, undetected. This figure has become known as the 'Byronic vampire', but this perhaps effaces Polidori's importance.[10] Macdonald and Scherf, in their introduction to the Broadview Press edition of *The Vampyre*, enumerate the distinctive innovations Polidori made to the vampire figure: they are human rather than an animated corpse, they are aristocratic, they are a seducer, and they are a traveller. This last mobility is significant. Among other things, it enables an open ending; the vampire always returns (Polidori was considering a sequel).[11]

Polidori's Lord Ruthven, modelled on Lord Byron via Lady Caroline Lamb's scandalous *Glenarvon* (1818), is aristocratic and sexualised and, though something of a blank canvas, is humanised, bearing the seed of the Romantic vampire that would culminate in various demonic lovers, predatory but eventually even sympathetic as with the contemporary paranormal romance. Thus, the familiar vampires Count Dracula (1897), Anne Rice's Lestat (1976), and the infamously sparkly Edward Cullen of *Twilight* (2005) can all claim to have been his heir.

Our contributors share their research into the many variations on monstrosity and deadly allure spawned by Polidori's textual reincarnation of Byronic glamour. The essays span such fields as literature, bibliographical research, drama, cinema, medicine, the visual arts; they emphasise the background of colonial revolution and racial oppression in the early nineteenth century and the cultural shifts of postmodernity. Together they make a coherent case for the importance of John Polidori's tale and its continuing influence, offering original insights and redeeming 'poor Polidori'. This book rescues him from the neglect he has suffered, revealing him to be an authentic creative force in the origins of vampire literature rather than the parasitical mimic he has frequently been dismissed as.

John Polidori: 'A star in the halo of the moon, invisible'

John William Polidori was born on 7 September 1795 to an Italian émigré father and an English governess mother. He attended Ampleforth School in Yorkshire (1804–09), where he was taught by Benedictine monks, before studying medicine at the University of Edinburgh (1811–15). He graduated as the youngest MD in the university's history; he was just nineteen. His thesis was on somnambulism or *oneirodynia*. His biographer D. L. Macdonald points out that the word *oneirodynia* meant 'nightmare', 'a compound of the Greek *oneiros* (dream) and *odyne* (pain)'.[12] This recalls the famous Fuseli painting *The Nightmare* (1781). What is more significant for researchers in Gothic studies, however, is how the idea of sleepwalking is connected to vampirism in literature. Vampires fill nightmares and induce sleepwalking in their victims; Polidori may be the catalyst for the way somnambulism and vampirism become linked.[13] In Sheridan Le Fanu's *Carmilla* (1871), the title character pretends to suffer from somnambulism; she turns out to be the vampire responsible for her young victim's nightmares. In *Varney the Vampire* (1845–47), Flora Bannerworth sleepwalks into the arms of the nightmarish Varney. This motif is repeated in Bram Stoker's *Dracula*, with Lucy sleepwalking into Dracula's sinister embrace.

In 1816, Polidori became Byron's travelling physician and they ventured to Switzerland (Byron quitted England soon after the separation from his wife) and Geneva, where they meet Percy Shelley, Mary Godwin, and Jane 'Claire' Clairmont. Polidori, who began writing *Ernestus Berchtold; or, The Modern Oedipus* at this point, clearly had literary ambitions of his own, but when Byron fired him, he ended up walking to Italy instead, where he visited his uncle, the physician Luigi Polidori. This is significant because by 1817–18 he appeared to have given up on literature and was practising medicine in Norwich. This turning away from literature was short-lived, however, and in 1819 he published *Ximenes and Other Poems*. In the same year, in London, *The Vampyre* was published without his permission or knowledge.[14] Following the publication of *Ernestus Berchtold* in 1820, he abandoned literature for law and considered entering the priesthood, but in 1821, *The Fall of Angels, A Sacred Poem* was published. Polidori's poetry is not outstanding but, for such a young author, shows promise. Interestingly, it uses vampire imagery on occasion.[15] The sonnets in *Ximenes* were well received.[16]

At this time, he spent about three weeks in Brighton and returned to London weighed down by depression and, reputedly, by gambling debts, where he died in 1821, aged just twenty-five. His family suspected that he taken Prussic acid (hydrogen cyanide) but the verdict asserted that he had 'departed this life in a natural way by visitation of God'.[17] His father was supposedly never able to hear his name again and his sister Frances wrote a painful elegy asking for mercy on her sinful brother (which suggests she thought his death was by suicide).[18] Following the verdict of death by 'visitation from God', Polidori could be laid in consecrated ground and he was buried on 29 August in St Pancras Old Church graveyard. Byron did not learn of Polidori's death until 2 January 1822, when he received a letter from his publisher, John Murray. He showed no sign of mourning or remorse, merely announcing, 'Poor Polidori is gone.' Two years later, Byron himself was dead.

Polidori's sister Frances married the exiled Italian scholar Gabriele Rossetti and thus Polidori posthumously became the uncle of Maria Francesca, Dante Gabriel, William Michael, and Christina Rossetti. William Michael Rossetti published Polidori's journal in 1911 and persuaded the National Portrait Gallery to exhibit his portrait. This shows him to be a romantic-looking man with fine features (see Frontispiece). Polidori was extremely young when he went abroad in April 1816 with Byron, to whom he had been recommended. He was only twenty years of age (Byron being twenty-eight and Shelley twenty-three). Tellingly, William Michael Rossetti writes that Polidori was thought 'too fond of putting himself forward in opposition to Byron and Shelley and too touchy when either of them declined to take up his ideas'.[19] Polidori, then, was not without talent, but he was regarded as precocious and petulant by his contemporaries and associates. 'Poor Polidori' and 'Doctor Polly-Dolly' are just two of the dismissive epithets bestowed on him by Byron and Mary Shelley, and they reflect his marginalisation and ridicule. In her introduction to the 1831 edition of *Frankenstein*, Mary famously criticised 'poor Polidori['s]' 'terrible idea about a skull-headed lady, who was punished for peeping through a keyhole' (his contribution to the story writing at Diodati).[20] Polidori himself describes being completely overshadowed by Byron and Shelley; his name 'was like a star in the halo of the moon, invisible'.[21]

Byron's publisher, John Murray, had offered Polidori a sum of £500 for an account of his forthcoming tour with Byron; he began to keep a journal.

The Vampyre may be seen as being born out of this biographical material, his journeys with Byron, and his observations of the latter's character. *Ernestus Berchtold*, too, scandalously draws on Byron's rumoured affair with his half-sister: it was a Faustian updating of the Oedipus myth and has a theme of incest. In the novel, Julia and her Byronic brother Olivieri are lovers, and so too are Ernestus and Louisa (his sister). The subtitle (*A Modern Oedipus*) echoes Mary Shelley's *Frankenstein; or, The Modern Prometheus*.

The Vampyre: Genesis and publication

The story of the genesis and publication of *The Vampyre* is now very well known. It can be found accompanying most editions of the story and critical texts on vampire literature, though the details have been much qualified and contested. Thus, we only need to supply the following brief precis.

The received account begins with the celebrated ghost story competition of June 1916 at the Villa Diodati, on the shore of Lake Geneva. Polidori was staying there with Byron as his paid companion and physician; the relations between them were strained. The intellectual atmosphere was soon enlivened by the arrival nearby of Percy Shelley, his lover Mary Godwin, and Mary's stepsister Claire Clairmont, then pregnant by Byron. After much philosophical, literary, and scientific debate and on reading the French translation, *Fantasmagoriana*, of a collection of German Gothic tales, they devised a competition where each would write a supernatural story. Mary Shelley famously began *Frankenstein*; Polidori began what would become his 1819 novel *Ernestus Berchthold*; and Byron wrote a fragment which was the seed of Polidori's *The Vampyre*.[22] (James Rieger, however, considers the 'received history' of the story-writing contest to be 'an almost total fabrication' and claims that Mary Shelley's account is completely untrustworthy.)[23]

In 1818, a package was delivered to the periodical *New Monthly Magazine* which contained a scandalous letter describing the supposed goings-on at the Villa Diodati, plus a prose tale – *The Vampyre* – with some other prefatory material. The paratexts suggested that the tale was by Byron and, indeed, the tone of the piece was very Byronic: Goethe later thought it Byron's finest work. The material included an extract of the vampiric moment from the latter's *The Giaour*, and the vampire protagonist was named 'Lord Ruthven' – the very name Lady Caroline Lamb had used to denote her thinly disguised avatar of Byron in her 1816 novel *Glenarvon*. The publisher, Henry Colburn, eager to seize the opportunity for enlarged sales, announced the tale as being by Byron, forcing Polidori to declare himself the true author. Byron denied authorship and published his own fragment as an appendix to *Mazeppa* in 1819. Polidori then announced that he was the author, acknowledging the inspiration found in Byron's piece, claiming that he had been challenged by an anonymous woman to complete it, and denying responsibility for the imposture and for giving it to the publisher. The details of Polidori's involvement and even of the original competition itself have been much questioned.

The tale then appeared in book form and was translated into several European languages, spawning stage adaptations and novelistic sequels across the Continent, while forming the literary vampire as we know it and eventually that of cinema and other media. After its magazine debut, the story was published in book form and went through seven English printings in 1819 alone. It was expanded by Cyprian Bérard in 1820 into a two-volume French novel, *Lord Ruthwen ou les Vampires* (the first vampire novel). After being adapted for the stage the same year by Charles Nodier, Pierre Carmouche, and Achile de Jouffroy, an English adaptation of this was staged by James Robinson Planché; a growing number of vampire theatricals and melodramas were to follow. By 1830, the vampire had been translated into German, Italian, Spanish, and Swedish.[24] We have included the text of *The Vampyre* from the first edition as Appendix 1 in this collection.

Avatars of Polidori

The archetype of Polidori's pale, hypnotic, aristocratic vampire is not his only legacy, though it is of great importance, as this volume will show; nor are the actual adaptations of *The Vampyre*. Polidori himself has an afterlife in film and fiction. This began with *Varney the Vampire*, the Victorian Penny Dreadful. Its creator, James Malcolm Rymer, gleaned many ideas for his plot from Polidori, whose tale had also been revised in a penny illustrated format. Polidori appears as a character, Count Polidori, who tries to force his daughter into marriage with Varney. There is thus a small but interesting niche where Polidori himself has been resurrected as a character in fictional narratives, in film and novels – sometimes as victim, sometimes as vampire, sometimes as vampire hunter. There are fourteen novels at the very least featuring Polidori; they include somewhat trashy vampire romance (Brooklyn Anne's *Bite Me, Your Grace* (2013)); fantasy as alternative history (Tim Powers, *The Stress of Her Regard* (1989)); straightforward reconstruction of the Villa Diodati moment as historical fiction (Anne Edwards, *Haunted Summer* (1972)); 'literary fiction' (Emmanuel Carrère, *Gothic Romance* (1984)); and futuristic science fiction (in Brian Aldiss's *Frankenstein Unbound* (1973) as a hysterical Italian and in Amanda Prantera, *Conversations With Lord Byron on Perversion, 163 Years After His Lordship's Death* (1987)). Some of the novels in Ben Aaronovitch's magical detective series *Rivers of London* feature invented treatises by Polidori on magic.[25] Jeanette Winterson's recent novel *Frankissstein* (2019) traces contemporary concerns with artificial intelligence (AI) and transhumanism back to the genesis of *Frankenstein* as recounted by Mary Shelley, and features Polidori (a touch disparagingly).[26]

He has also featured in films: the wildly excessive (and somewhat defamatory) *Gothic* by Ken Russell (1986) has him played by Timothy Spall as a bloated religious maniac and rejected lover of Byron. Three others are more or less accurate portrayals of Polidori with Byron and the Shelleys: *Haunted Summer* (1988; based on Edwards's novel); *Remando al viento* (1988; English title: *Rowing with the Wind*); and *Mary Shelley* (2017), directed by Haifaa Al-Mansour.[27] James Mason plays him in a 1973 BBC adaptation of *Frankenstein* (*Frankenstein: The True Story* (1973)), with an accompanying novel by Don Bachardy and Christopher Isherwood. He appears in various other media, too: in Howard Brenton's play *Bloody Poetry* (1989) as a voyeur and in an episode of *Doctor Who*.[28]

Polidori's *The Vampyre* played a significant role in the phenomenon of Byromania, yet the crucial accounts downplay this. Biographies of Byron paint a negative picture of the young Polidori; if they mention him at all it is to depict a petulant and quick-tempered upstart with literary pretensions. Thus, these portraits are rarely celebratory or sympathetic. Even his biographer D. L. Macdonald admits that his interest in Polidori is inspired by his failures:

> There are also specific reasons for a specifically biographical interest in Polidori. To put it bluntly, he was so unsuccessful in everything he tried to do – demonstrating the pattern of compulsive failure that Karl Melinger regards as a form of chronic suicide – that he ended up trying an unusually wide variety of different things: medicine, literature, politics, philosophy, law (in particular penology), and religion.[29]

Macdonald perpetuates the stereotype of Polidori as a hapless and ineffectual minor figure, choosing to call his biography *Poor Polidori*. He is a marginal and overlooked figure in accounts of the Byrons and the Shelleys. Fiona MacCarthy's biography of Byron is dismissive of Polidori's 'sub-Byronic' tale, reading it only as derivative and a personal attack.[30] William St Clair's influential and widely read book *The Godwins and the Shelleys* (1989) has no entry for Polidori in the index. Daisy Hay's *Young Romantics* (2010) is a vibrant narrative, yet only has five or six pages out of 364 dedicated to Polidori. She depicts him only from Byron's perspective: he is 'exhausted and more than a little irritated by Polidori'.[31]

Thus there is a legacy, but it has been a far-from-positive one. Our book seeks to challenge this, especially within Gothic studies; Polidori, not Byron, succeeded in founding the entire modern tradition of vampire fiction.[32] We hope that readers will reject the received idea that *The Vampyre* is a mere Byronic pastiche. There have been scathing and malicious attacks on Polidori stemming from his dependence on Byron (Skarda brutally compares him to a 'willing rape victim', which is hard to forget).[33] There are accusations of plagiarism, but it is possible to argue, as Ken Gelder has done, that if Polidori did use material from Byron, he did so 'creatively (even ironically) rather than slavishly'.[34] Skarda's biographical deciphering yields a reductive reading. She sees Polidori's allusions and debts to Byron as authorial incompetence and a failure of imagination; we suggest it is more interesting to read them as fertile intertextuality.

Today, over 200 years since the publication of *The Vampyre*, Polidori lies in St Pancras Old Church in an unmarked grave, uncelebrated in life and unmemorialised in death.[35] Our celebrations to mark the bicentenary of *The Vampyre* in 2019 finally gave Polidori his due. It is intended that this book will further redeem him, and that the dismissive epithet 'Poor Polidori' will be laid to rest.

Interpretations

Despite its brevity, *The Vampyre* is rich with interpretive possibilities, which is why it has become the foundational text for so many other works in the way this collection charts. Critics have drawn attention to such themes as: companionship; social parasitism; democracy; the public and the private; Philhellenism; Romanticism; antiquarianism and modernity; past and present; superstition and credulity; intertextuality; uncertainties and antinomies following the French Revolution; and desire (homoerotic and other). The seduction narrative and the strange attraction of Aubrey to Ruthven inevitably prompt psychoanalytic approaches or other explorations of sexuality. Thus, Mair Rigby sees both *The Vampyre* and Byron's fragment as unsettlingly queer narratives.[36] There is the unspoken homoeroticism between Aubrey and Ruthven but a queerness about the whole history of publication too. *The Vampyre* can be read as a study of the fear of homosexuality and also an unmasking of the heteronormative constraints of society.

There are obvious concerns with class too and the tale may be read as, in part, political satire; historicising analyses bring this to the fore. Christopher Frayling sees forbears of this 'upward social mobility of the vampire' from the aristocracy in the Restoration period but, more crucially, in the persona of Byron.[37] This culminated in *The Vampyre*, which reflected Polidori's conflicted emotions towards Byron, fuelled perhaps by class hostility. Nina Auerbach also observes that the class antagonism between Byron and

Polidori fostered dislike, though she sees the vampire in their texts as an 'equaliser' of class conflict; we think this may miss the irony Ken Gelder observes in Polidori's reworking of Byron's fragment.[38] Polidori was of the professional middle classes; Ruthven is an aristocrat, as was, of course, Byron. Thus, David Punter sees the vampire as representative of a dying class.[39] Erik Butler, however, sees the new literary vampire as 'a reflection of the bourgeoisie's ascendency'.[40] Butler suggests Ruthven may not be a genuine aristocrat; he is something new and qualitatively different. His mobility and protean nature exemplify the modernity of the rising middle classes. For us, Ruthven's solipsistic individualism indicates his bourgeois character: he is 'a man entirely absorbed in himself'.[41] There was a fraction of the aristocracy that aligned itself with bourgeois interests and, in fact, merged with them. The Whiggish crowd of nobility that was part of Byron's circle was associated with this strand. Thus, Ruthven may well be aligned with them. In contrast, Aubrey's affiliation with the romance genre suggests a more archaic strand of aristocracy, free from the utilitarianism of bourgeois modernity. This sense of modernity, as James Uden shows, is imbricated with the antiquarianism in the tale, a feature inherited from Byron's fragment. Aubrey's name recalls that of the seventeenth-century antiquarian John Aubrey, noted for his credulousness. From him, '*The Vampyre* incorporates themes' such as 'the supernatural, credulity and belief, the passion of the antiquary, and the importance of folk traditions'.[42] This feeling for the past is valorised against Ruthven's empty modernity. Aubrey is fascinated by romance yet laughs at the 'idle and horrible fantasies' (251) of folklore. The irony is, of course, that he is caught up in such a narrative.

Thus, genre is involved with power and domination. Troy Boone connects vampire narratives with Sade's novel *Justine* (1791) in a Foucauldian analysis of knowledge and power.[43] He argues that Ruthven consolidates bourgeois power, particularly that of the heterosexual male (though this is surely challenged by the homoerotic undertones of the tale). Not unconnected with the concerns with bourgeois power is the opposition of public to private. For Ahmet Süner, Ruthven is 'a symptom of Aubrey's own vampiric private life that must be brought under the public gaze'.[44] Genre is again involved, with romance being associated by Süner with interiority and the private, opposed to public life. Thus, the novella serves to regulate the tensions between private and public, particularly concerning disruptive sexuality and a critique of the antisocial dangers of interiority. Süner also suggests an affinity between Aubrey and Ruthven that Nick Groom develops further in Chapter 7 of this volume.

Much of the criticism is concerned with genre and intertextuality, considering *The Vampyre* and its involvement with such modes as allegory, romance, realism, Gothic, and 'elegiac romance'.[45] Polidori himself alerts the reader to the importance of genre in the text by repeated references to Aubrey's susceptibility to romance narratives, as: 'He thought, in fine, that the dreams of poets were the realities of life' (247). Thus, an ironic tension is set up between novelistic realism and romance, in a text that could itself be categorised as the latter. The generic reference here also connects with the homoerotic theme mentioned above, since Aubrey 'soon formed [Ruthven] into the hero of a romance' (247). One other important generic relationship is to the travel narrative, already a feature of earlier Gothic. The tale reflects Polidori's commission by John Murray to record Byron's travels. James Uden stresses the importance of the *travelling* vampire in relation to this genre.[46] Polidori's tale takes place during a Grand Tour of Europe, with Greece being the principal locale: *The Vampyre* gothicises the genre of satires on the Grand Tour which flourished in the eighteenth century. The significance of the Greek locale is examined by Álvaro García Marín, who discusses the role played by Polidori in the formation of Greece as both origin of Western modernity and its ethnic Other.[47] Greece is important for Gelder too; he argues that Polidori democratically revises Byron's image of a passive Greece, restoring the *social* aspect of vampire folk beliefs and valorising 'the folk' over the leisured classes.[48]

Plagiarism is a form of intertextuality – a vampiric form, one might say – and the events surrounding the text's publication and attribution have led to accusations of this against Polidori. Skarda has some disparaging remarks about the Bloomian 'anxiety of influence' and the effects of a stronger mind on a weaker one (a relationship pictured, of course, in the tale itself). These are countered by Ken Gelder, who, as we note above, sees not parasitic plagiarism but creative, ironic refashioning.[49] Gavin Budge, like Gelder, sees a 'creative dialogue' with Byron rather than incompetent imitation.[50] He too, while recognising the homoerotic component, pays attention to the clash between aristocratic and middle-class values. This involves the threat of Byronism and wider anxieties about the corrupting effects of sensational fiction. In a like manner, Simon Bainbridge anticipates feminist analyses of the dubious power of romantic fiction.[51] Bainbridge, like many others, draws attention to Polidori's Byronism. He argues that Polidori uses vampirism to represent the threat of Byronic rhetoric to readers, particularly women. In addition, he explores the link between this and doubling, anticipating later Gothic texts of the double.

Carol Senf also emphasises the social criticism, showing how Polidori initiates the use of the vampire as 'a social metaphor' for 'a corrupt society' riddled with parasitism.[52] Elsewhere, Senf praises the story for its reworking of folklore into Gothic, accompanied by realistic detail.[53] It anticipates later novels in the transformation of romance to realism with its emphasis on character rather than plot, using contemporary settings, thus deviating from established Gothic. Similarly, Richard Sharp Astle stresses the encounter in Gothic between novelistic realism and premodern supernaturalism as announced by Walpole in the Preface to *The Castle of Otranto*.[54] In *The Vampyre*, these issues are split geographically between bourgeois London and rural Greece. Bourgeois society and feudalism, rationalism and supernaturalism, novel and romance, are set against each other. There is a hesitation between the rational and the supernatural in the text (reminding us of Todorov's fantastic) and a generic ambivalence that, Astle suggests, may mean the story works better as allegory than realism. This hesitation, argues Astle, is connected with political pessimism following the French Revolution.

Debates over whether a work participates in 'movements' such as Gothic or Romanticism may be fruitless. Nevertheless, placing *The Vampyre* in its literary context can be illuminating. We argue that *The Vampyre*'s indeterminate genre yields a productive friction with other writings and our collection shows its genesis from other texts and modes while generating further texts in its turn. James B. Twitchell situates the vampire in the tradition of literary Romanticism.[55] He praises Polidori's originality in using the vampire to explore intersubjectivity, thus again assimilating it to the realist novel. Jerrold Hogle also associates the tale with Romanticism, discerning a marked shift from the use of Gothic in first-generation Romanticists such as Wordsworth and Coleridge to the second at the storytelling at Diodati.[56] The Gothic mode had rested on a conflict between progressive and regressive forces in society; Wordsworth and Coleridge tried to efface this dialectic. For the writers gathered at Diodati, by contrast, their writing reveals those tensions and the process of attempting to erase them. These tensions spur the fertility of Polidori's tale that makes its legacy possible. According to J. P. Telotte, Polidori challenges ideas in Romanticism of human participation in the natural world.[57] Ruthven's gaze reifies the human beings around him, treating them as victims. (See Ivan Phillips's Chapter 9 in this volume for a further analysis of the gaze.) This again, as with other interpretations, discerns in the text a social critique which also discovers an alternative, participatory vision in Ianthe and in Aubrey's sister. In a further essay, Hogle asks why the hitherto-neglected vampire rises rapidly in Gothic fiction with Polidori and what made it so ubiquitous a symbol.[58] The inherently contradictory mode of Gothic, torn between novelistic naturalism and archaic romance, suits it for expressing the contradictory viewpoints of the rising middle class, looking both backward and forward.

Thus, as this summary shows, part of Polidori's legacy has been to incite a great variety of interpretation of the Romantic vampire in its sociohistorical context, uncovering its literary qualities and subversive force, and paying attention to its formal qualities and relationship to other texts. These very different approaches also reveal the protean nature of Polidori's tale, its generic variety, and this is what made it such a powerful incitement for further texts. The scope of the following essays illustrates this. This collection responds to that body of work, beginning with further interpretations of the genesis of *The Vampyre* and succeeded by a set of essays on the progress of the Romantic vampire, with its origins in Polidori's work constantly in mind.

Overview of the collection

Our collection begins with an essay by Sam George, who explores vampire theatricals, focusing on the stage progeny of Polidori's *The Vampyre*. In 1820, John Robinson Planché adapted Charles Nodier's Parisian dramatisation *Le Vampire* of the same year for the English stage. Focusing on Planché, George argues that the Romantic vampire, and the plays that are its legacy, have a shared origin in phantasmagoria, from the German ghost stories that inspired Byron's vampire fragment at the Villa Diodati, to the spectacular summoning of revenants on stage in Paris. George demonstrates how crucial stage props and effects are to the changing representation of the vampire, registering important shifts. George argues that it was Polidori, not Byron (nor Bram Stoker, the stage manager at The Lyceum), whose work succeeded in founding the stage vampire.

Fabio Camilletti approaches Polidori somewhat obliquely at first, via Spiritualism and the various séances attended by the Rossetti brothers, William Michael and Dante Gabriel, who were nephews of Polidori. This prompts Camilletti to consider three topics: the composition of *The Vampyre*, the history of its publication, and the legacy of Polidori among the Rossettis. Polidori, says Camilletti, observed links between Englishness and the inhuman. Camilletti argues that Polidori's writings, including those on somnambulism, are much concerned with free will and mechanical determinism, evoking too the discussions at the Villa Diodati. He claims that, through Lord Ruthven, Polidori targets Britishness and aristocracy as well as Byron. He also draws on the psychoanalysis of Nicolas Abraham and Maria Torok to show how. from their readings of their uncle's diary, the Rossetti brothers were haunted by family memories, which, in turn, were resurrected in later vampire fictions.

Harriet Fletcher argues that *The Vampyre* uses vampirism as a vehicle for critiquing Lord Byron's literary celebrity, specifically by drawing out the Gothic qualities of Byronic fan culture and the mutual relationship of consumption between Byron and his readers. In doing so, Polidori reconsiders the parameters of the Gothic; by attaching celebrity to the vampire, he reshapes the image of this Gothic trope in Western culture. Fletcher identifies the early nineteenth century as the advent of modern celebrity culture due to the emergence of mass culture, within which the role of Byron and the rise of industrial print culture is paramount. She combines Gothic studies, celebrity studies, and fan studies to develop what she calls 'a Gothic celebrity reading' that draws inspiration from Romantic literary culture. Lord Ruthven is a model of Byron, and, in turn, Aubrey is a model of the Byron fan or 'Byromaniac'.

Bill Hughes shows how, in her 1816 novel *Glenarvon*, Byron's spurned lover Lady Caroline Lamb turned her own attraction–repulsion to the poet into a Gothic and sentimental fiction of amatory seduction and betrayal alongside political revolt. Here, the eponymous Glenarvon is notably Byronic, feeding off Byron's own self-fashioning and Lamb's mimicry of him, while drawing on Milton and Richardson. Glenarvon takes part in the anticolonial Irish Rebellion of 1803, inciting the people with his rhetoric and personal charm. Glenarvon's political persuasiveness is linked to his sexual glamour. Glenarvon's women themselves become Byronic: Byronism is an infection, like vampirism. With all these conflicting forces, Lamb's novel shifts between an anti-Jacobin stance and radicalism. Polidori's revision of Ruthven strips away Lamb's ambivalence but, by clearly marking the aristocratic demon lover as both Byronic and a vampire, inaugurates a literary archetype. Yet many of Ruthven's descendants, in Gothic and paranormal romance, resurrect the alluring mix of rebellion and faithlessness that Lamb depicted and whose progress is traced in this essay.

The original folkloric vampire was a very different notion from its modern conception – at some point in time a transformation occurred, moving the vampire from a repulsive undead peasant-corpse into a sexually alluring, frequently aristocratic supernatural being. John Polidori's *The Vampyre* was the critical culmination of a variety of changing views about who and what a vampire is. In his essay, Marcus Sedgwick considers that a considerable part of this monster-makeover was due to contemporary beliefs about tuberculosis, with which Polidori, as a newly qualified doctor, would have been very familiar, and which he drew on in his recreation of the mythic beast. An implicit intertwining of the natures of the tubercular and the vampire occur, specifically in that certain physical characteristics of the sufferer of late-stage tuberculosis, together with heightened sexuality and sensibility, become at this time permanently attached to the conception of the vampire – such ideas being reinforced by the already current metaphorical use of the word 'vampire' in popular parlance, as well as in medical textbooks.

Nick Groom develops his earlier work on the influence of *The Vampyre* on Mary Shelley's novel *Frankenstein*. Both were conceived at the Villa Diodati during the summer of 1816, and *Frankenstein* has deep affinities with the vampire lore that was evidently aired during conversations between Lord, Byron, Percy Shelley, Mary Godwin (later Shelley), Claire Clairmont, and Polidori. But the influence was also reciprocal, and *Frankenstein* echoes through Polidori's tale in unexpected ways. The character Aubrey has often been seen as a self-portrait of Polidori, while it is generally accepted that the vampire Lord Ruthven is an audacious attack on Byron, who employed Polidori as his personal physician. However, in this essay Groom presents a radical and unsettling close reading of the character of Aubrey, informed by Mary Shelley's presentation of Victor Frankenstein, arguing that the relationship between Aubrey and Ruthven is far more complex and uncanny than has hitherto been recognised.

Sam George and Bill Hughes turn their attention to a little-known yet revelatory descendent of Polidori's vampyre. Uriah Derick D'Arcy (Richard Varick Dey)'s *The Black Vampyre*, a short novella featuring the first Black vampire in literature, was published within months of the US publication of *The Vampyre*. There is a whole story of literary appropriation and intertextuality here which is quite crucial to D'Arcy's text and which depicts literary production itself as vampiric. *The Black Vampyre* is situated in the context of slavery and the slave revolts in Saint-Domingue (now Haiti). The text was written not long after Haiti was the first nation to abolish slavery during its revolution of 1791–1804. George and Hughes show how D'Arcy turns his satire on to contemporary society, where the members of a corrupt commercial elite are now the vampires. D'Arcy very consciously plays with the theme of plagiarism that surrounded Polidori and connects it to the wider vampirism of society. The links *The Black Vampyre* uncovers between racial oppression and a vampiric, commercial society make its resurrection worthwhile.

In his essay, Ivan Phillips explores themes of vision and visibility as they are developed through *The Vampyre*. He examines Polidori's distinctive concern with the imagery of eyes, and with acts of seeing (or not seeing) and being seen (or not being seen), in connection with the evolution of the modern vampire. Phillips understands these motifs through Sigmund Freud's famous essay 'The Uncanny' (1919) as a fantastical challenge to the limits of the human. The vampire, in this sense, enters the fiction of modernity as a threat to stable assumptions about identity, experience, and being. As well as exploring tropes of vision in *The Vampyre*, this essay also considers other texts by Polidori, notably his medical dissertation on sleepwalking and his novel *Ernestus Berchtold*, written at the same time as his vampire story and published in the same year. Ultimately, Phillips argues that the work of this remarkable but neglected writer generates an anatomy of the modern vampire that is still influential today.

The Vampyre initiates two tantalising elements in vampire fiction which continue to inform its postmodern iterations today. The disclosure of a terrible secret and the forbidden, if not downright blasphemous, nature of vampirism itself inform a myriad of vampire confessions in the late twentieth and early twenty-first centuries. Sorcha Ní Fhlainn shows how Polidori's tale incepts several elements that directly inform the literary legacy of Anne Rice and the cinematic vampires of director Neil Jordan. Jordan returns to numerous themes haunting the margins of Polidori's tale and Byron's unfinished vampire 'Fragment'. His own vampire films, *Interview with the Vampire* (1994) and *Byzantium* (2012), meditate on the horrid nature of immortality as a brutal, masculine force which threatens to strip away and destroy all remnants of feeling and feminine influence. These tales also foreground vampire subjectivity as a means to liberate vampires from the torment of their lingering human guilt. These rich and cinematic 'vulgar fictions' disclose an unpaid debt to Polidori's tale, and to its continued influence in contemporary reimaginings of immortality.

Unlike his progeny Count Dracula, Ruthven is able to pass in polite society, making his seductive nature more insidious and damaging. Thus he anticipates the arrival of late-twentieth-century vampires such as Anne Rice's much-lauded sympathetic vampires. Kaja Franck, in her chapter, concentrates on Ruthven's twenty-first-century children, the sparkling vampires of Stephenie Meyer's Twilight novels, through the intersections of gender, the Gothic, and consumerism. Where Polidori's narrative is focalised through Aubrey's increasingly disturbed viewpoint, Meyer's novels usurp the masculine voice, replacing it with the object of the vampire's desire, Bella Swan. Ruthven's 'deadly hue' is replaced by sparkling attraction. Polidori's narrative, and its critique of social mores, is reimagined for a twenty-first-century audience that is attracted to rather than repulsed by the Other. Like Ruthven, the Cullens are at once embedded within and yet permanently removed from their society. However, rather than being symbols of social degradation, they are held up as an aspirational, wholesome family. Franck shows how Meyer's vampires act as reflections of consumerist desire in a society shaped by social media and celebrity culture.

Jillian Wingfield turns to the events at the Villa Diodati in 1816. She shows how, alongside Byron's conjuration and Polidori's later development of the charismatic and aristocratic vampire Lord Ruthven, Mary Shelley shaped the pseudo-science behind her patchwork creature in *Frankenstein*. Since then, the link between these Gothic stalwarts has evolved to a point where, two centuries after Polidori's glamorous parasite was summoned into being, the genre of vampire fiction has soundly assimilated science. This essay discusses the effects of evolutionary manipulation in Justin Cronin's

The Passage (2010) and Octavia Butler's *Fledgling* (2005) as twenty-first-century exemplars of this 'vampensteinian' conjunction of the supernatural and cod science. Through this, Cronin and Butler invite a questioning of genetic modification, otherness, and racial prejudice, upending the aristocratic singularity started by Polidori. Consequently, Wingfield argues that this conjunction suggests the need for a twenty-first-century revision of Gothic taxonomy, amalgamating what has been a Polidorian paradigm into the novel nomenclature of the vampensteinian.

Finally, Sam George's Afterword indulges in a spot of Gothic tourism and investigates John William Polidori's links to St Pancras Old Church, the site of his burial, together with its associations with the group of visionary writers, Mary Wollstonecraft, William Godwin, and Mary and Percy Shelley.

Notes

1 Presenting were: Stacey Abbott, Xavier Aldana Reyes, Daisy Butcher, Kaja Franck, Sir Christopher Frayling, Sam George, Nick Groom, Bill Hughes, Sorcha Ní Fhlainn, Ivan Phillips, Marcus Sedgwick, Catherine Spooner, Jillian Wingfield, and Gina Wisker. 'Polidori Vampyre Symposium 2019', Open Graves, Open Minds www.opengravesopenminds.com/polidori-symposium-2019/ [accessed 9 March 2023]. 'Curious disquiet' was a serendipitous play on the 'cureless disquiet' of Byron's fragment which inspired Polidori (Lord George Byron, 'A Fragment', Appendix 2 in this volume.
2 Christopher Frayling, ed., *Vampyres: Lord Byron to Count Dracula*, 2nd edn (London: Faber & Faber, 1991), p. 107.
3 *Open Graves, Open Minds: Representations of Vampires and the Undead from the Enlightenment to the Present Day*, ed. by Sam George and Bill Hughes (Manchester: Manchester University Press, 2013); *Gothic Studies*, Open Graves, Open Minds: Vampires and the Undead in Modern Culture: Gothic Studies Special Issue, ed. by Sam George and Bill Hughes, 15:1 (May 2013).
4 See Sam George's Chapter 2 in this volume.
5 See our Chapter 8 in this volume for an analysis of this significant text.
6 'America's First Vampire Was Black and Revolutionary – It's Time to Remember Him', *The Conversation*, 30 October 2020 http://theconversation.com/americas-first-vampire-was-black-and-revolutionary-its-time-to-remember-him-149044 [accessed 25 May 2023]. See 'The Black Vampyre and Other Creations: Gothic Visions of New Worlds', 14 November 2020, Open Graves, Open Minds www.opengravesopenminds.com/the-black-vampyre-and-other-creations-2020/ [accessed 25 May 2023].
7 'Polidori's *The Vampyre*', *In Our Time*, BBC Radio 4, 7 April 2022 www.bbc.co.uk/programmes/m00162xz [accessed 26 May 2023].
8 Frayling, *Vampyres*, p. 108.

9 See Sam George and Bill Hughes, 'Introduction', in George and Hughes, *Open Graves, Open Minds*, pp. 1–23 (pp. 7–15).
10 Conrad Aquilina gives a very concise summary of the development of the 'Byronic' vampire from its sources in the ethnography of the Greek *vrykolakas* and the Slavic vampire in Tournefort, Calmet, and elsewhere, through Byron and Polidori to its twentieth- and twenty-first-century avatars ('The Deformed Transformed; Or, from Bloodsucker to Byronic Hero – Polidori and the Literary Vampire', in George and Hughes, *Open Graves, Open Minds*, pp. 24–38).
11 D. L. Macdonald and Kathleen Scherf, 'Introduction', in John William Polidori, *The Vampyre and Ernestus Berchtold; or, The Modern Oedipus*, ed. by D. L. Macdonald and Kathleen Scherf (Peterborough, ON: Broadview Press, 2007), pp. 8–31.
12 D. L. Macdonald, *Poor Polidori: A Critical Biography of the Author of 'The Vampyre'* (Toronto, ON: University of Toronto Press, 1991), p. 35.
13 Anne Stiles, Stanley Finger, and John Bulevich connect Polidori's 1815 thesis on somnambulism, recently translated from the Latin (and included with the article), with Polidori's and other vampire narratives: 'Somnambulism and Trance States in the Works of John William Polidori, Author of *The Vampyre*', *European Romantic Review*, 21:6 (2010), 789–807.
14 This has been challenged by Fabio Camilletti, who also moves the date of composition forward to 1818 (Fabio Camilletti, 'A Note on the Publication History of John Polidori's *The Vampyre*', *Gothic Studies*, 22:3 (2020), 330–43). But see also Nick Groom, 'Polidori's "The Vampyre": Composition, Publication, Deception', *Romanticism*, 28:1 (March 2022), 46–59 and Chapter 7 in this volume; Groom sets the date as 1819.
15 For example, 'and here / Will live a vampire on his son and him, / Sucking in living drops his very blood' (*Ximenes*, I. 2. 185–87).
16 See Macdonald, *Poor Polidori*, pp. 172–73.
17 Henry R. Viets, 'By the Visitation of God: The Death of John William Polidori, M.D. in 1821', *British Medical Journal* (1961), 1773–75, cited in Macdonald, p. 237. See also Nick Groom, 'Thomas Chatterton and the Death of John William Polidori: Copycat or Coincidence?', *Notes and Queries*, 67:4 (2020), 534–36.
18 Macdonald, *Poor Polidori*, p. 238.
19 William Michael Rossetti, 'Introduction', *The Diary of Dr. John William Polidori, 1816: Relating to Byron, Shelley, etc.*, ed. by William Michael Rossetti (London: Elkin Mathews, 1911), p. 5.
20 Mary Shelley, *Frankenstein; or, The Modern Prometheus*, ed. by M. K. Joseph (1831; Oxford: Oxford University Press, 1998), p. 7.
21 John William Polidori, *The Diary of Dr. John William Polidori, 1816: Relating to Byron, Shelley, etc.*, ed. by William Michael Rossetti (London: Elkin Mathews, 1911), 28 May 1816, 'Sécheron', p. 105.
22 Included here as Appendix 2.
23 James Rieger, 'Dr. Polidori and the Genesis of *Frankenstein*', *Studies in English Literature, 1500–1900*, 3:4 (Winter 1963), 461–72 (p. 461). See also Frayling,

Vampyres, pp. 11–17. Rieger also argues that Polidori was an important influence in the genesis of *Frankenstein*.

24 For the history of publication and adaptation, see Henry R. Viets, 'The London Editions of Polidori's *The Vampyre*', *The Papers of the Bibliographical Society of America*, 63:2 (1969), 83–103; and Richard Switzer, 'Lord Ruthwen and the Vampires', *The French Review*, 29:2 (1955), 107–12. For the reception of Byron in Europe, particularly Poland, in conjunction with adaptations of *The Vampyre*, see Monica Coghen, 'Lord Byron and the Metamorphoses of Polidori's Vampyre', *Studia Litteraria: Universitatis Iagellonicae Cracoviensis*, 6 (2011), 29–40 (a melodrama Upíor [*The Vampyre*], a translation of the play by Nodier et al., was staged in Warsaw in 1821). For Planché and other stage adaptations, see Katie Harse, 'Melodrama Hath Charms: Planché's Theatrical Domestication of Polidori's "The Vampyre"', *Journal of Dracula Studies*, 3:1 (2001) https://research.library.kutztown.edu/dracula-studies/vol3/iss1/1; and Ronald E. McFarland, 'The Vampire on Stage: A Study in Adaptations', *Comparative Drama*, 21:1 (1987), 19–33. Jane M. Kubiesa discusses the incarnations of Lord Ruthven in Berard, Nodier, Planché, and so on in terms of the growth of mass production and consumption ('The Many Lives of Lord Ruthven: Somatic Adaptation, Reincarnation and (Mass) Consumption of Polidori's The Vampyre', *Revenant, Vampires: Consuming Monsters and Monstrous Consumption*, 9 (2023), 59–70).

25 The first novel in the sequence is *Rivers of London* (London: Orion, 2011).

26 Thanks to Curtis Runstedler for alerting us to this.

27 See Harvey O'Brien, 'Creation Myth: The Imagining of the Gothic Imagination in the Diodati Tryptich: *Gothic* (1986), *Haunted Summer* (1988), and *Remando al viento* (1988)', *Gothic Studies*, 24:2 (2022), 118–36.

28 'The Haunting of Villa Diodati', *Doctor Who*, 12:8, dir. by Emma Sullivan, writ. by Maxine Alderton (BBC, 16 February 2020).

29 Macdonald, *Poor Polidori*, p. x.

30 Fiona MacCarthy, *Byron: Life and Legend* (London: Faber & Faber, 2003), pp. 293–94.

31 Daisy Hay, *Young Romantics: The Shelleys, Byron and Other Tangled Lives* (London: Bloomsbury, 2011), p. 81.

32 James Twitchell even argues that Byron's Darvell is not a vampire (pp. 114–15).

33 Patricia L. Skarda, 'Vampirism and Plagiarism: Byron's Influence and Polidori's Practice', *Studies in Romanticism*, 28:2 (1989), 249–69 (p. 262).

34 Ken Gelder, *Reading the Vampire* (London: Routledge, 1994), pp. 26–34 (p. 26). For more on the creative interaction between Byron and Polidori, including new archival research, see Matt Beresford, 'The Lord Byron/John Polidori Relationship and the Development of the Early Nineteenth-Century Literary Vampire' (unpublished doctoral thesis, University of Hertfordshire, 2019).

35 See Sam George's Afterword in this volume.

36 '"Prey to Some Cureless Disquiet": Polidori's Queer Vampyre at the Margins of Romanticism', *Romanticism on the Net*, 36–37, 2004.

37 Frayling, *Vampyres*, p. 6.

38 *Our Vampires, Ourselves* (Chicago, IL: University of Chicago Press, 1995), pp. 13–27 (p. 15).
39 David Punter, *The Literature of Terror: A History of Gothic Fictions from 1765 to the Present Day*, 2 vols (Harlow: Longman, 1996), vol. I: *The Gothic Tradition*, pp. 103–05 (p. 104).
40 *Metamorphoses of the Vampire in Literature and Film: Cultural Transformations in Europe, 1732–1933* (Rochester, NY: Camden House, 2010), pp. 85–96 (p. 85).
41 John William Polidori, *The Vampyre*, Appendix 1, pp. 240–67 (p. 247). All further references are to this edition and are given as page numbers in parentheses.
42 'Gothic Fiction, the Grand Tour, and the Seductions of Antiquity: John Polidori's "The Vampyre" (1819)', in *Illusions and Disillusionment: Travel Writing in the Modern Age*, ed. by R. Micallef (Boston, MA: ILEX Foundation, 2018), pp. 60–79 (p. 72).
43 'Mark of the Vampire: Arnod Paole, Sade, Polidori', *Nineteenth-Century Contexts*, 18:4 (1995), 349–66.
44 'The Gothic Horrors of the Private Realm and the Return to the Public in John Polidori's *The Vampyre*', *Moderna Språk*, 1 (2018), 187–200 (p. 190).
45 For Kenneth A. Bruffee, elegiac romance is 'pseudo-autobiography concealed in pseudo-biography' ('Elegiac Romance', *College English*, 32:4 (1971), 465–76 (p. 467)). One of the earliest examples is Byron's 'A Fragment', which he discusses in some detail, and which he compares to Polidori's tale. The bond between hero and narrator in elegiac romance is the grip of the past and the struggle against it is a response to specifically modern questions of identity.
46 James Uden, 'Gothic Fiction, the Grand Tour, and the Seductions of Antiquity: John Polidori's "The Vampyre" (1819)', in *Illusions and Disillusionment: Travel Writing in the Modern Age*, ed. by R. Micallef (Boston, MA: ILEX Foundation, 2018), pp. 60–79.
47 '"The Son of the Vampire": Greek Gothic, or Gothic Greece?', in *Dracula and the Gothic in Literature, Pop Culture and the Arts*, ed. by Isabel Ermida (Leiden and Boston, MA: Brill Rodopi, 2016), pp. 21–44.
48 Gelder, *Reading the Vampire*, p. 34.
49 Gelder, *Reading the Vampire*, pp. 26–34.
50 '"The Vampyre": Romantic Metaphysics and the Aristocratic Other', in *The Gothic Other: Racial and Social Constructions in the Literary Imagination*, ed. by Ruth Bienstock Anolik and Douglas L. Howard (Jefferson, NC: McFarland, 2004), pp. 212–35 (p. 212).
51 'Lord Ruthven's Power: Polidori's "The Vampyre", Doubles, and the Byronic Imagination', *The Byron Journal*, 34:1 (2006), 21–34.
52 *The Vampire in Nineteenth-Century English Literature* (Bowling Green, OH: Bowling Green State University Popular Press, 1988), pp. 33–40 (p. 39).
53 'Polidori's "The Vampyre": Combining the Gothic with Realism', *North Dakota Quarterly*, 56:1 (1988), 197–208.
54 'Ontological Ambiguity and Historical Pessimism in Polidori's *The Vampyre*', *Sphinx: A Magazine of Literature and Society*, 8 (1977), 8–16.

55 *The Living Dead: A Study of the Vampire in Romantic Literature* (Durham, NC: Duke University Press, 1981), pp. 102–16.
56 'Gothic and Second-Generation Romanticism: Lord Byron, P. B. Shelley, John Polidori and Mary Shelley', in *Romantic Gothic: An Edinburgh Companion*, ed. by Angela Wright and Dale Townshend (Edinburgh: Edinburgh University Press, 2015), pp. 112–28.
57 'A Parasitic Perspective: Romantic Participation and Polidori's *The Vampyre*"', in *The Blood Is the Life: Vampires in Literature*, ed. by Leonard G. Heldreth and Mary Pharr (Bowling Green, OH: Bowling Green State University Popular Press, 1999), pp. 9–18.
58 'The Rise of the Gothic Vampire: Disfiguration and Cathexis from Coleridge's "Christabel" to Nodier's *Smarra*', in *Gothic N.E.W.S., Volume I: Literature*, ed. by Max Duparray (Paris: Michel Houdiard, 2004), pp. 48–70.

2

Phantasmagoria: Polidori's *The Vampyre* from theatricals to vampire-slaying kits

Sam George

John William Polidori (1795–1821) took the vampire out of the forests of Eastern Europe, gave him an aristocratic lineage and placed him into the drawing rooms of Romantic-era England. His tale *The Vampyre*, published just over 200 years ago on 1 April 1819, was the first sustained *fictional* treatment of the vampire and completely recast the folklore and mythology on which it drew. The vampire figure abandoned its peasant roots and left its calling card in polite society in London. The story emerged out of the same storytelling contest at the Villa Diodati that gave birth to that other archetype of the Gothic heritage, Frankenstein's monster. Byron's contribution to the contest was an inconclusive fragment about a shadowy man from an ancient family, Augustus Darvell, who is 'prey to some cureless disquiet'.[1] Polidori took this fragment and turned it into the sensational tale of the vampire Lord Ruthven, preying on the vulnerable women of society. After its magazine debut the story was published in book form and went through seven English printings in 1819 alone.[2] It was expanded into a two-volume French novel by Cyprien Bérard, *Lord Ruthwen ou les vampires* (1820), and was adapted for the stage the following year by Jean Charles Emmanuel Nodier (1780–1844) as one of a growing number of vampire theatricals or melodramas inspired by Polidori, such as those by the playwright James Robinson Planché (1796–1880) and others. By 1830, *The Vampyre* had been translated into German, Italian, Spanish, and Swedish.[3]

Despite these imitations and adaptations, 'Poor Polidori' has all but been forgotten and his lively tale has often been dismissed as a crude narrative, written under the influence of a greater, more subtle talent, Byron.[4] And yet it was Polidori, not Byron, who succeeded in founding the entire modern tradition of vampire fiction.

In this chapter, I map the trajectory of Polidori's vampire from page to stage, charting its ascendance in Paris in a horde of Ruthven-inspired theatricals, and its debut in England in performances at The Lyceum. A cult of the supernatural was manifest in the uncanny stage effects that were designed to delight and terrify theatre audiences. These shaped perceptions of the vampire and played an important role in its history and development. I explore the influence of phantasmagoria shows on the staging of this Romantic vampire, together with the innovations that came from Polidori himself.

The vampire prior to Polidori had been a blood-gorged, animalistic monster of the Slavic peasantry. In his study of the origins of vampire lore, *Vampires, Burials and Death*, Paul Barber describes the traditional image of the undead bloodsucker as 'a plump Slavic fellow with long fingernails and a stubbly beard, his mouth and left eye open, his face ruddy and swollen. He wears informal attire – in fact, a linen shroud – and he looks for all the world like a dishevelled peasant.'[5]

Polidori transformed the Eastern European peasant vampire of old into a pale-faced, dead-eyed – but alluring – English aristocrat. This deceiving, dashing and cursed creature was in possession of 'irresistible powers of seduction', haunting the drawing rooms of Western society undetected.[6] This elevation in social rank is not all. Polidori's *The Vampyre* is responsible for several groundbreaking innovations. There seemed never to have been an urban vampire, nor an educated vampire prior to this. Polidori had introduced a predatory sexuality in relation to the vampire. We see for the first time the vampire as rake or libertine, a real 'lady killer': 'The guardians hastened to protect Miss Aubrey; but when they arrived, it was too late. Lord Ruthven had disappeared, and Aubrey's sister had glutted the thirst of a VAMPYRE!'[7]

Lord Ruthven is generally understood to be a satirical portrait of Byron as a seducer of women in polite society. His victims are 'hurled from the pinnacle of unsullied virtue, down to the lowest abyss of infamy and degradation'.[8] This is the image we have of the predatory male vampire. Polidori's vampire, despite being something of a blank canvas, is sexualised and mesmeric, providing a template not only for Count Dracula but for the 'Byronic hero' that features in Gothic romance from pre-Victorian times down to present-day paranormal romances such as *Twilight*'s Edward Cullen. Cullen is a relic of earlier models of vampiric masculinity, further evidence of the long-reaching legacy of Polidori's vampire.[9] As Catherine Spooner has argued, 'Over a period of about 200 years vampires have changed from the grotty living corpses of folklore to witty, sexy, super achievers'; this is wholly Polidori's legacy.[10] The literary and historical importance of Polidori's creation of the aristocratic vampire cannot be overstated. It is a figure later reincarnated as Sir Frances Varney in J. M. Rymer's *Varney the Vampire* (1845–47). After Lord Ruthven, most of the notable vampires are aristocrats: E. T. A. Hoffmann's Countess Aurelia, J. Sheridan Le Fanu's Countess Mircalla Karnstein, Dion Boucicault's Sir Alan Raby, and, of course, Count Dracula.[11]

Thus, Ruthven is responsible for the vampire's association with aristocracy; he also inspired the first vampire novel.[12] It is important to briefly note these prose translations and adaptations in order to record the changes that they make to Polidori's narrative. The first edition in book form of *The Vampyre* was published in 1819 by Sherwood. Following this, Polidori's novella was translated into French by Henri Faber (*Le vampire, nouvelle traduite de l'anglais de Lord Byron* (Paris, 1819)). Then, in February 1820, there followed, under the patronage of Charles Nodier, a very obvious imitation, or rather a continuation, of Polidori's story by Cyprien Bérard, *Lord Ruthwen, ou Les Vampires*.[13] This novel-length extension of Polidori's story is named after his vampire lord, but the plot is entirely new, with the introduction of a benevolent female vampire. In this version the protagonist is named Léonti and he is in pursuit of the monster who has turned his fiancée Bettina into a vampire. Bettina leads Léonti to Ruthwen, who is now Lord Seymour, prime minister of Modena. Richard Switzer, who has documented the changes Bérard makes to Polidori's narrative, summarises the remaining action as follows:

> The people of Modena refuse to believe Léonti's accusation of Ruthwen; instead they arrange the vampire's marriage with the Duke's daughter. When the vampire makes a victim of his bride Léonti challenges him to a duel. After inflicting a mortal blow on his adversary, Léonti kills himself. But since Ruthwen does not die, he is recognized as a vampire.[14]

Polidori's *The Vampyre* had deliberately avoided any sense of closure; his vampire is still at large in the drawing rooms of England. *Lord Ruthwen, ou Les Vampires* is noteworthy for its violent ending in which Ruthwen is ritually executed and exhumed, his heart pierced with hot irons and his eyes gouged out! The destruction of the vampire is informed by an obscure work, cited as *Les prejuges de tous les peoples* by M. Salgues.[15] The methods differ from the received accounts, such as the exhumations of the suspected vampires Peter Plogojovitz or Arnod Paole in Augustine Calmet's *Dissertations sur les apparitions des anges des démons et des esprits*. These vampires were exhumed, staked and their bodies reduced to ashes.[16] Interestingly, *Lord Ruthwen* did not set a precedent for the ritualistic killing of the vampire in the melodramatic stage productions that followed: there, the revenge is usually enacted through mysterious supernatural happenings, curses or avenging angels, and not through human agency. Polidori's Ruthven, responsible for the vampire's Englishness and his aristocratic pedigree, is undoubtedly the model for the stage vampire, to which I now turn.

Vampires on stage

The vogue for the stage vampire began in France; following *Lord Ruthwen* at least four versions of Polidori's story were staged in Paris. The first, Charles Nodier's *Le Vampire*, was performed at La Théâtre de la Port-Saint

Martin on 13 June 1820.[17] This theatre had staged a sensational production of Goethe's *Faust* in which the stage was divided in half, showing both heaven and hell; it was specially equipped for the staging of melodrama and spectacle.[18] Pierre-Luc-Charles Cicéri (1782–1868), the chief designer of Porte Saint-Martin, was the most important stage innovator of the period.[19] The role of Lord Rutven [*sic*] was taken by the actor M. Philippe, who also appeared as Frankenstein's monster in a play co-authored by Nodier; the celebrated Madame Dorval played Malvina.[20]

Nodier, a novelist, scholar and bibliophile, was familiar with the legends of vampires from his travels in Illyria.[21] In the years 1820–22, he published a vampire novella, *Smarra, ou les Démons de la Nuit, conte fantastique* (1821), contributed pieces to an anthology of ghosts and vampires, *Infernalia, Infernaliana* (1822), and played a role in the writing of *Lord Ruthven ou les vampires*.[22] It is significant that he had a romantic attachment to Scotland, favouring Scottish fairy tale landscapes in his own work. *Trilby, ou le lutin d'Argail* [*The Imp of Argyll*] (1822) and *La Fée aux Miettes, conte fantastique* [*The Crumb Fairy*] (1832) are adult fairy tales set in the Western Highlands of Scotland (Sir Walter Scott country). This explains in part why Nodier transports the vampire myth from the Greece of Polidori's story to a Gothicised Scottish island setting. Scotland was appropriately associated with an undead past and uncanny states of being at this time.[23] The Scottish elements have divided critics. Montague Summers, writing in 1929, cites Planché on the recklessness of French dramatists setting the theatrical vampire in Scotland, where the superstition never existed.[24] Roxana Stuart defends Nodier's decision, arguing that for the French, Ruthven was Byron, whose family seat and heritage through his mother was Scottish.[25] *Le Vampire* opens with a discourse on vampires in the Caledonian caves of Staffa; these hellish grottos are the haunts of evil spirits in the play. Fingal's Cave on the coast of this same island would be associated in the minds of the public with James Macpherson's Ossian poems, which were hugely popular in Britain and the rest of Europe.[26]

The drama follows the plot of Polidori's *Vampyre* but with a few notable changes. Lord Rutwen (Ruthven) and Aubray (Aubrey) have been fellow travellers, but the latter has no suspicion of his companion's true nature. In fact, he holds him with the fondest regard. When he was attacked by bandits, he was saved from death by his friend, who had fallen by a single gunshot wound. When Lord Rutwen arrives to claim Malvina's hand, Aubray hails him as his preserver (it is explained that the wound did not after all prove fatal). Aubray eventually realises there is some horrid secret and is carried off by the servants, who fear he has lost his senses, an idea Rutwen encourages. In the final scene, when Rutwen and Malvina approach the altar, Aubray rushes in to intercept the ceremony with a wild cry; the vampire draws his dagger, about to plunge it into Malvina's heart, but when one o'clock strikes his power is gone. Malvina faints into the arms of the housekeeper, Brigitte, and, as thunder rolls, Rutwen is condemned to nothingness. The denouement is bloody and terrifying, an example of the production's Gothic excess:

> Ruthven's raised arm falls. The lightning flashes. The rear of the stage opens revealing the shades of the Vampire victims. They are young women covered by veils.
>
> They pursue him, pointing to their breasts from which blood still flows from the wounds. At that moment, the angel of love crosses the stage in a luminous chariot [...]
>
> Thunder rolls more strongly and lightning strikes the vampire who is consumed. CURTAIN.[27]

The ghostly apparitions of the vampire's victims, veiled and bloody, the fleeting appearance of the luminous chariot of the Angel of Love and the diabolical disappearance of the vampire amid lightning strikes are stage effects indebted to earlier phantasmagoria shows, as I will demonstrate.

Two years later, in 1823, a revival of *Le Vampire* with Philippe and Madame Dorval again thrilled the Porte Saint-Martin theatre audience with a riot of theatrical extravagance. Alexandre Dumas was present at this production and, in his *Memoires* of 1863, recorded the audience's extreme delight at the sepulchral melodrama: 'how the theatre applauded the lean livid mask of the Vampire, how it shuddered at its stealthy steps'.[28] Dumas relates with rare powers of recollection his adventures at this performance. Such was the effect of the stage vampire on his imagination it occupied five chapters. The Gothic excess of the final scene is described with particular vividness; shades come up out of the ground and carry off the vampire, the destroying angel appears in a cloud, lightning flashes and Rutwen is engulfed amid the shades.[29] Dumas went on to use the theme of *Le Vampire* in his own drama of the same name, which was performed at the Ambigu-Comique on 20 December 1851.[30]

Nodier prophesied that his revenant would triumph on the stage:

> *Le Vampire épouvantera, de son horrible amour, les songes des toutes les femmes, et bientôt sans doute, ce monstre encore exhumé prêtera son masque immobile, sa voix sépulcrale, son oeil d'un gris mort [...] tout cet attirail de mélodrame a la Melpoméne des boulevards; et quel succés alors ne lui est pas reserve.*
>
> The Vampire will horrify, with his horrible love, the dreams of all women, and soon, no doubt, this still unearthed monster will lend his motionless mask, his sepulchral voice, his eye of a dead grey [...] all this paraphernalia of

melodrama à la Melpomène of the boulevards; and what success then is not reserved for him.[31]

Yet despite the uproar it created, surprisingly, the vampire drama is overlooked in accounts of the history of the vampire.[32] Only Montague Summers (1880–1948) has given prominence to the nineteenth-century stage vampire:

> Immediately upon the furore created by Nodier's *Le Vampire* at the Porte-Saint-Martin in 1819 vampire plays of every kind from the most luridly sensational to the most farcically ridiculous pressed on to the boards. A contemporary critic cries: 'There is not a theatre in Paris without its vampire! At the Porte-Sant-Martin we have Le Vampire; at the Vaudeville Le Vampire again; at the Variétés *les trois vampires ou la clair de la lune*.'[33]

The fascination with vampire theatricals continued to gain momentum in 1820s Paris. A farce, later attributed to Emile B. L., *Encore un Vampire*, met with considerable success when produced in 1820, as did another vampire burlesque, *Les Etrennes d'un Vampire*, attributed to 'A. Rousseau'.[34] This deliberate reference to the philosopher Jean-Jacques Rousseau (1712–78) playfully draws on his ambiguities regarding evidence for the existence of vampires.[35] The work was sensationally gothicised, and billed as a transcript of a manuscript buried at Père Lachaise cemetery.

Within two days of its opening, the Nodier play was burlesqued in the vaudeville comedy *Le Vampire*, or *Le Vampire Amoureux*, by Eugène Scribe and Mélesville (a pseudonym of Anne H. J. Duveyrier), staged at La Théâtre de Vaudeville, 15 June 1820, and *Les Trois Vampires, ou le clair de la lune*, a farce in one act by Nicholas Brazier, Gabriel De Lurieu and Armand d'Artois.[36] The latter depicts the adventures of M. Gobetout ('gullible'), an avid reader of Byron whose home is invaded by vampires. The play ends in a triple marriage between his daughters and the three vampires. Scribe and Mélesville's play is set in Hungary, which was associated in the public mind with revenants due to the influence of Calmet's *Treatise* on the vampires of Hungary and surrounding regions. By contrast, the French players in *Les Trois Vampires* draw on Polidori's English vampire, explaining to the audience that '*Ils nous viennent d'Angleterre. C'est encore une gentilesse de ces messieurs ils nous font de joliscadeaux!*' ('The vampires they come to us from England. It's another kindness of these gentleman. They give us such nice presents').[37] In London, as I will show, the vampire was adapted as a very British theatrical character.

The Lyceum's cult of the supernatural

James Robinson Planché's *The Vampire, or The Bride of the Isles* opened at the English Opera House in London on 9 August 1820.[38] Planché had drawn heavily on Nodier, having been given the script of *Le Vampire* (which had premiered two months earlier in Paris) by Samuel Arnold.[39] Planché's *Vampire* was similarly followed by a string of imitations: vampire plays by W. T. Moncrieff, Charles Edward Walker and others.[40] There were also two more vampire works by Planché himself, a burletta and an opera, set in Hungary. The burletta, *Giovanni the Vampire*, is noteworthy because it allowed for a comic spoofing of the vampire legend and the vampire was a breeches part played by Mrs Waylett.[41] Planché, who created breeches roles for his fairy tale extravaganzas, deliberately increased the sexual ambiguity of the vampire.[42] The evening's entertainment consisted of sensation, onstage and off. The vampire's attack on stage mirrored the nightly assaults on virtue that appeared in the wings, among audience members and on the streets directly outside the theatre. The playbills represented this air of lurid excitement surrounding the productions and they illuminate the profile the vampire assumed at the time (see Figure 2.1).

The Vampire demonstrates Planché's early skill at adaptation.[43] His theatrical *oeuvre* included melodramas, comedies, farces, burlettas, pantomimes, interludes, vaudevilles, burlesques, extravaganzas, masques and spectacles. He was eventually appointed 'superintendent of the decorative department' at Covent Garden and The Lyceum, where he collaborated with scene painters, machinists, prop makers and costumiers.[44]

The Lyceum's license in 1795 allowed the company to present 'exhibits, entertainments and waxworks'.[45] By 1820, the audiences were mesmerised by The Lyceum's macabre themes and illusions, by the very witchcraft of the theatre, from sophisticated trapdoor work to flying and mechanical artifices of all kinds. The Lyceum's cult of the supernatural was a development from the *fantasmagorie*, fashionable in Paris. The focus on spectacle had obvious implications for the vampire myth, as did the invention of the vampire trapdoor trick, by which the vampire would enter or exit the stage.

The influence of phantasmagoria

Phantasmagoria shows used optical effects to produce sensational dreamlike illusions. They were popular in Europe from the 1790s to the 1830s, most notably the performances of Johann Georg Schrepfer (or Schröpfer; 1738–74), a German necromancer who staged ghost-raising séances using magic lantern projections onto smoke, and Paul Philidor (or Phylidor), a stage magician who was active from 1785 to 1828.[46] Philidor was performing in Britain between 1801 and 1829; he was granted a British patent for his Phantasmagoria on 27 January 1802. Mannoni observes that Philidor would invite prospective audience members to request a slide of a

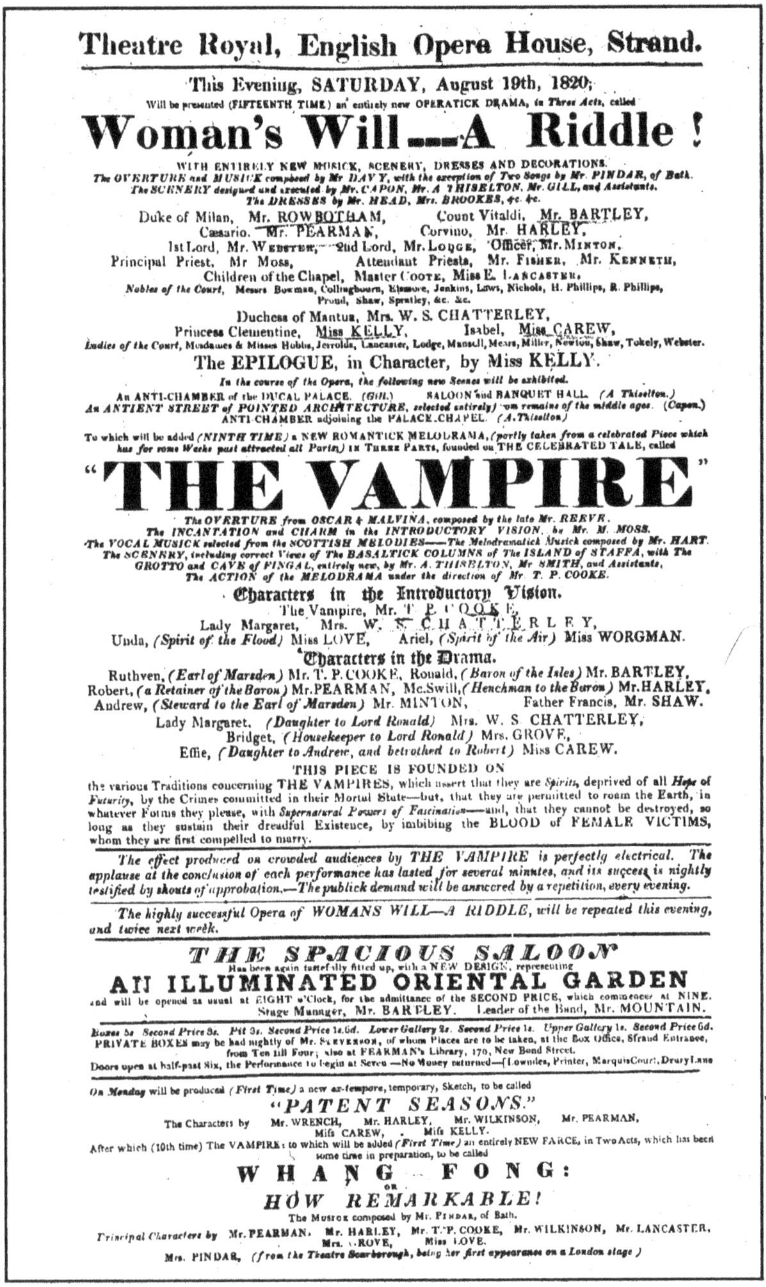

Theatre Royal, English Opera House, Strand.

This Evening, SATURDAY, August 19th, 1820;
Will be presented (FIFTEENTH TIME) an entirely new OPERATICK DRAMA, in Three Acts, called

Woman's Will—A Riddle!

WITH ENTIRELY NEW MUSICK, SCENERY, DRESSES AND DECORATIONS.
The OVERTURE and MUSICK composed by Mr DAVY, with the exception of Two Songs by Mr. PINDAR, of Bath.
The SCENERY designed and executed by Mr. CAPON, Mr. A THISELTON, Mr. GILL, and Assistants.
The DRESSES by Mr. HEAD, Mrs. BROOKES, &c. &c.
Duke of Milan, Mr. ROWBOTHAM, Count Vitaldi, Mr. BARTLEY,
Cesario, Mr. PEARMAN, Corvino, Mr. HARLEY,
1st Lord, Mr. WEBSTER, 2nd Lord, Mr. LODGE, Officer, Mr. MINTON,
Principal Priest, Mr Moss, Attendant Priests, Mr. FISHER, Mr. KENNETH,
Children of the Chapel, Master COOTE, Miss E. LANCASTER,
Nobles of the Court, Messrs Bowman, Collingbourn, Elsmore, Jenkins, Laws, Nichols, H. Phillips, R. Phillips, Proud, Shaw, Spratley, &c. &c.
Duchess of Mantua, Mrs. W. S. CHATTERLEY,
Princess Clementine, Miss KELLY, Isabel, Miss CAREW,
Ladies of the Court, Mesdames & Misses Hobbs, Jerrolds, Lancaster, Lodge, Mansell, Mears, Miller, Newton, Shaw, Tokely, Webster.
The EPILOGUE, in Character, by Miss KELLY.
In the course of the Opera, the following new Scenes will be exhibited.
An ANTI-CHAMBER of the DUCAL PALACE. (Gill.) SALOON and BANQUET HALL. (A Thiselton.)
An ANTIENT STREET of POINTED ARCHITECTURE, selected entirely from remains of the middle ages. (Capon.)
ANTI-CHAMBER adjoining the PALACE-CHAPEL. (A. Thiselton)

To which will be added (NINTH TIME) a NEW ROMANTICK MELODRAMA, (partly taken from a celebrated Piece which has for some Weeks past attracted all Paris) IN THREE PARTS, founded on THE CELEBRATED TALE, called

"THE VAMPIRE"

The OVERTURE from OSCAR & MALVINA, composed by the late Mr. REEVE.
The INCANTATION and CHARM in the INTRODUCTORY VISION, by Mr. M. MOSS.
The VOCAL MUSICK selected from the SCOTTISH MELODIES——The Melodramatick Musick composed by Mr. HART.
The SCENERY, including correct Views of The BASALTICK COLUMNS of The ISLAND of STAFFA, with The GROTTO and CAVE of FINGAL, entirely new, by Mr. A. THISELTON, Mr SMITH, and Assistants,
The ACTION of the MELODRAMA under the direction of Mr T. P. COOKE.

Characters in the Introductory Vision.
The Vampire, Mr. T. P. COOKE,
Lady Margaret, Mrs. W. S. CHATTERLEY,
Unda, (Spirit of the Flood) Miss LOVE, Ariel, (Spirit of the Air) Miss WORGMAN.

Characters in the Drama.
Ruthven, (Earl of Marsden) Mr. T. P. COOKE, Ronald, (Baron of the Isles) Mr. BARTLEY,
Robert, (a Retainer of the Baron) Mr. PEARMAN, Mc.Swill, (Henchman to the Baron) Mr. HARLEY,
Andrew, (Steward to the Earl of Marsden) Mr. MINTON, Father Francis, Mr. SHAW.
Lady Margaret, (Daughter to Lord Ronald) Mrs. W. S. CHATTERLEY,
Bridget, (Housekeeper to Lord Ronald) Mrs. GROVE,
Effie, (Daughter to Andrew, and betrothed to Robert) Miss CAREW.

THIS PIECE IS FOUNDED ON
the various Traditions concerning THE VAMPIRES, which assert that they are Spirits, deprived of all Hope of Futurity, by the Crimes committed in their Mortal State—but, that they are permitted to roam the Earth, in whatever Forms they please, with Supernatural Powers of Fascination——and, that they cannot be destroyed, so long as they sustain their dreadful Existence, by imbibing the BLOOD of FEMALE VICTIMS, whom they are first compelled to marry.

The effect produced on crowded audiences by THE VAMPIRE is perfectly electrical. The applause at the conclusion of each performance has lasted for several minutes, and its success is nightly testified by shouts of approbation.—The publick demand will be answered by a repetition, every evening.

The highly successful Opera of WOMANS WILL—A RIDDLE, will be repeated this evening, and twice next week.

THE SPACIOUS SALOON
Has been again tastefully fitted up, with a NEW DESIGN, representing
AN ILLUMINATED ORIENTAL GARDEN
and will be opened as usual at EIGHT o'Clock, for the admittance of the SECOND PRICE, which commences at NINE.
Stage Manager, Mr. BARTLEY. Leader of the Band, Mr. MOUNTAIN.

Boxes 5s Second Price 3s. Pit 3s. Second Price 1s. 6d. Lower Gallery 2s. Second Price 1s. Upper Gallery 1s. Second Price 6d.
PRIVATE BOXES may be had nightly of Mr. STEVENSON, of whom Places are to be taken, at the Box Office, Strand Entrance, from Ten till Four; also at FEARMAN's Library, 170, New Bond Street.
Doors open at half-past Six, the Performance to begin at Seven.—No Money returned—[Lowndes, Printer, Marquis Court, Drury Lane

On Monday will be produced (First Time) a new ex-tempore, temporary, Sketch, to be called
"PATENT SEASONS."
The Characters by Mr. WRENCH, Mr. HARLEY, Mr. WILKINSON, Mr. PEARMAN, Miss CAREW, Miss KELLY.
After which (10th time) The VAMPIRE: to which will be added (First Time) an entirely NEW FARCE, in Two Acts, which has been some time in preparation, to be called

WHANG FONG:
OR
HOW REMARKABLE!

The Musick composed by Mr. PINDAR, of Bath.
Principal Characters by Mr. PEARMAN, Mr. HARLEY, Mr. T. P. COOKE, Mr. WILKINSON, Mr. LANCASTER, Mrs. GROVE, Miss LOVE.
Mrs. PINDAR, (from the Theatre Scarborough, being her first appearance on a London stage)

Figure 2.1 Playbill: J. R. Planché's *The Vampire*, English Opera House (1820).

deceased loved one which he would prepare in advance of the show.[47] After a fierce storm effect, a lifelike ghost of a dead person known to the audience would rise from the floor and then slowly sink back into the abyss in the ground. It seems likely that this visual effect inspired the development of the stage device known as the vampire trap. Significantly, in October 1801, Philidor set up an exhibition of *Phantasmagoria* at The Lyceum Theatre in London, cementing the links between phantasmagoria and the figure of the vampire forever. The Lyceum, home to the vampire theatre in the 1820s, was the same establishment where Bram Stoker would later become stage manager and business manager to Henry Irving, though it was known as the English Opera House in 1820.[48] It was here that Stoker staged a reading of *Dracula-The-Undead* on 18 May 1897 to seal the copyright of the novel *Dracula*.[49]

Paris is also significant; the Belgian physicist and stage magician Etienne Gaspard Robertson (1763–1837) perfected the optical stage illusion known as *fantasmagorie*, using it to terrify the Parisian public.[50] His memoirs revealed that he had had an interest in the macabre from his early years, and that he believed in werewolves, enchantments, infernal pacts with the devil and even the tombs of vampires.[51] He created scenes that included some degree of motion by modifying and perfecting the use of the magic lantern for illusion. The phantasmagoria (*fantasmagorie*) was distinguished from the magic lantern show: the slides for phantasmagoria were entirely black except for the image to be projected, making them look more ghostly.

Robertson, a gifted artist, painted his own slides, and was able to give them a wonderfully diabolical appearance. Then, instead of displaying images on an obvious fixed background, he projected them onto smoke or a semi-transparent screen. The ghosts and demons were seen to hover in midair. One of his most famous illusions, the 'Dance of Demons or Sorcerers' (see Figure 2.2), employed the method of multiplying shadows and putting them into motion at the same time. An illustration of the phantasmagoria itself, taken from Robertson's own *Mémoires* (1831–33), shows hysteria breaking out among the audience members and a pistol being aimed at the apparitions.

Robertson used disembodied voices to enhance the terrifying experience, including the murmuring and screaming of the spirits ventriloquised by his assistants. His choice of an abandoned, decaying convent as the location for his show demonstrates his debt to the macabre atmosphere of the eighteenth-century Gothic novel. According to Fabio Camilletti, the show, a mixture of lights, images, and sounds, was sold under the name *Fantasmagorie*.[52]

Figure 2.2 'Dance of the Sorcerers', from Marion Fulgence and Charles William Quinn, *The Wonders of Optics* (New York: C. Scribner & co, 1869), p. 198.

The group at the Villa Diodati were fascinated by tales of fantasmagoriana and this was manifested in the story-writing competition of 1816 which spawned the literary vampire. The party read and discussed a volume translated into French from the German entitled *Fantasmagoriana*, which had been published in 1812.[53] Importantly, as Camilletti argues, 'Naming the book *Fantasmagoriana* meant, therefore, to assimilate the experience of reading to Robertson's popular phantasmagoria shows, and to offer the reader a comparable hullabaloo of horrors within the three hundred and more pages that each of the two tomes was made of.'[54] The stories included Friedrich August Schulze's 'La morte fiancée' ('The Corpse Bride'), where an inconstant lover finds himself in the arms of a pale ghost, the spectre of the woman he deserted, and Johann August Ape's 'Le portraits de famille' ('The Family Portraits'), featuring a sinful founder of his race whose miserable doom it was to bestow the kiss of death on all the younger sons of his fated house.[55] However, as Camilletti points out, 'No indication of authors or of original sources was given and readers were invited to think of stories as of embellished versions of real supernatural cases. The title joyfully played with this ambiguity, evoking the kind of shows, popular at the time, which were known as phantasmagorias.'[56] When Polidori read the book of *Fantasmagoriana*, with its themes of revenants and phantoms, returners from beyond the grave and their appearances and disappearances, he could never have anticipated that his own creation, Lord Ruthven, would provide the link between Robertson's *fantasmagorie* and the demonic antics of the stage vampire.

The vampire trap

Polidori's *The Vampyre* and the plays that are its legacy have a shared ancestry in phantasmagoria, seen in the spectacular summoning of demons or revenants on stage. In Planché's *The Vampire, or The Bride of the Isles* (1820), for example, the first scene is a vision where two spirits, Ariel, spirit of the air, and Unda, spirit of the flood, perform various ceremonies to raise the vampire from its tomb or sepulchre and then banish it back again, or force it deeper into hell. *The Recollections and Reflections of J. R. Planché* (1872) confirm that this is the first ever use of the stage device known as the vampire trap: 'The trap, now so well known as "the vampire trap" was invented for this piece, and the final disappearance of the Vampire caused quite a sensation.'[57] The vampire trap allowed the stage vampire to appear and disappear as if by supernatural agency. A similar device known as the 'star trap' had been used for the stage harlequin.[58] Both traps were a source of fascination to stage manager Bram Stoker, who released his own vampire into the world. *The Primrose Path* (1875) draws on his experience as a reviewer for the Dublin theatre.[59] In this story, stage carpenter Jerry O'Sullivan explains the workings of the vampire trap to a female visitor to the theatre; enthralled, she tricks him into standing on it and releases the trap 'so that she might see him shoot up through the opening in the stage'.[60] Stoker's description of the harlequinade, a British comic theatrical genre in which the harlequin and clown play the principal parts, appears in the short story 'The Star Trap' (1908):

> There was a spot light just above it on the bridge, which was intended to make a good show of harlequin and his big jump. The people used to howl with delight as he came rushing up through the trap and when in the air drew up his legs and spread them wide for an instant and then straightened them again as he came down – only bending his knees just as he touched the stage.[61]

The harlequin actor, Henry Mortimer, has his neck broken in a gruesome follow-up scene when the trap fails and his mangled body is flung onto the stage:

> The trap didn't [...] open at once as the harlequin's head touched it. There was a shock and a tearing sound, and the pieces of the star seemed torn about, and some of them were thrown about the stage. And in the middle of them came the coloured and spangled figure that we knew.[62]

For Stoker, the maintenance of the star trap 'wasn't ordinary work; it was life or death'.[63] His fictional accounts of the 'star trap' and 'vampire trap' are terrifying when compared to Montague Summers's tame descriptions. Summers saw the vampire trap as a dull and unsophisticated stage effect consisting of:

> two or more flaps, usually India-rubber, through which the sprite can disappear almost instantly, where he falls into a blanket fixed to the under surface of the stage. As with the star trap, this trap is secured against accidents by placing another piece or *slide*, fitting close beneath when not required, and removed when the prompter's bell gives the signal to make it ready. [64]

There is a lot more to the vampire trap than Summers suggests here, however. Nina Auerbach brings it within the realms of the uncanny and through this we can better understand its debt to phantasmagoria and its association with the supernatural:

> Depending on its placement, the vampire trap allowed the actor to be alternately body and spirit; the trap in the floor catapulted him back and forth, between hell and heaven, while the trap in the flats endowed him with the semblance of immateriality as he moved in and out of walls.[65]

Viewed in this way, the movements of the stage vampire are descended from Robertson's dancing demons and the old-style harlequinades. Interestingly, in 1818–19, a year before his vampire play launched, Planché wrote 'a speaking harlequinade', *Rodolph the Wolf*.[66] His *Recollections* revealed that he had a distaste for the extravagant Victorian pantomimes that superseded 'the bright and lively […] Harlequinades' of his earlier days'.[67] These were most certainly an influence on his stage vampire: the vampire trap itself was adapted from the harlequin's 'star trap'.

It is difficult to say with accuracy when the vampire trap is employed in Planché's play, but it is unlikely to have been saved for the finale. The first scene sees the fiend rising upwards from the sepulchre and then descending downwards through the floor. It is in the caverns of Staffa in the Inner Hebrides: the moon is shining through a chasm and several rude sepulchres are seen, on one of which Lady Margaret is sleeping:

> *Charm* – ARIEL *and* UNDA
> Phantom, from thy tomb so drear,
> At our bidding swift arise;
> Let thy Vampire-corpse appear,
> To this sleeping maiden's eyes.
> Come away! Come away!
> That the form she may know
> That would work her woe;
> And shun thee, till the setting ray
> Of the morn shall bid thy pow'r decay;
> Phantom, from thy tomb so drear,
> At our bidding rise! – appear!

(*Thunder*)
Chorus – ARIEL *and* UNDA

Appear! Appear! Appear!

(*A Vampire succeeds from the Tomb of Cromal and springs towards Margaret.*)

VAMPIRE:	Margaret!
ARIEL:	Foul spirit, retire!
VAMPIRE:	She is mine!
ARIEL:	The hour is not yet come.
UNDA:	Down, thou foul spirit; – extermination waits thee: Down, I say!

(*Music – The Vampire sinks again, shuddering, and the Scene closes.*)
End of the introductory vision[68]

This is the first ever use of the vampire trap, an essential part of the supernatural machinery of the production and a supreme moment in the history of the vampire.

The spirits and the cycle of the moon frame the action of the play, from the opening scene above, where it is rising, to the final scene in the chapel: '*a large gothic window, through which the moon is seen setting*' (II. 5). The moon aligns the vampire with phantoms and spectres, reminding the audience that it is a creature of enchantment. It was another of Polidori's innovations to have his vampire lord restored by moonbeams, his body 'exposed to the first cold ray of the moon that rose after his death'.[69] Twentieth-century vampires lose their affinity with the moon: following *Nosferatu* in 1922, it is the sun that takes priority.[70] Only James Rymer's Penny Dreadful vampire Varney continues the legacy, undergoing a ritual series of lunar resurrections in the course of the story.[71]

I will consider the question of vampire lore in relation to both Polidori and Planché, as it does throw up some anomalies. Lady Margaret, for example, will, in the morning, be claimed as the bride of Earl Marsden (Ruthven in disguise): she dreams that tomorrow will consign her to a vampire's power. The publicity material for Planché revealed the conceit that the vampire must marry his victims:

> THIS PIECE IS FOUNDED ON the various Traditions concerning THE VAMPIRES which assert that they are *Spirits* deprived of all *Hope of Futurity*, by the Crimes committed in their Mortal State – but, that they are permitted to roum [*sic*] the Earth, in whatever Forms they please, with *Supernatural Powers of Fascination* and, they cannot be destroyed, as long as they sustain their dreadful Existence, by imbibing the BLOOD of FEMALE VICTIMS, whom they are first compelled to marry.[72]

This added another strand to vampire lore, yet it is one that does not seem to have become part of the familiar conventions.

The vampire aristocrat: Nationality and naming

The figure of Earl Marsden and his relationship to the fictional Lord Ruthven is worth looking at in more detail. Lady Caroline Lamb (1785–1828) cast Byron as the dark and duplicitous Gothic seducer Lord Ruthven in her 1816 novel *Glenarvon*. In turn, Polidori took the name Lord Ruthven in order to create the first literary vampire. In Lamb, Clarence de Ruthven is Lord Glenarvon, a literary descendent of the historical Lord Ruthven, murderer and reputed warlock.[73] Planché's aristocrat Earl Marsden (Ruthven returned from the dead) is a reincarnation of Cromal 'the bloody', a Celt:

> Beneath this stone, the relics lie
> Of Cromal, called the bloody. Staffa still
> The reign of fear remembered. For his crimes
> His spirit roams, a Vampire, in the form
> Of Marsden's Earl; – to count his victims o'er
> Would be an endless task – suffice to say,
> His race of terror will to-morrow end,
> Unless he wins some virgin for his prey,
> Ere sets the full-orb'd moon
>
> (*The Vampire*, I.1, p. 48)

Planché's identification of Ruthven as the reincarnated Cromal may be a subtle appeal to notions of difference, and a manifestation of the interest in Celtic folklore at the time. He was unhappy with the setting in Scotland, rather than some Eastern European country where belief in vampires prevailed.[74] His *Recollections and Reflections* reveal that it was Samuel J. Arnold, manager of the English Opera House, who had insisted on him retaining the Scottish setting:

> The proprietor and manager had placed in my hands, for adaptation, a French melodrama, entitled 'Le Vampire', the scene of which was laid, with the usual recklessness of French Dramatists, in Scotland, where the superstition never existed. I vainly endeavoured to induce Mr Arnold to let me change it to some place in the east of Europe. He had set his heart on Scotch music and dresses – the latter, by the way, were in stock – laughed at my scruples, assured me that the public would neither know nor care – and in those days they certainly did not – and therefore there was nothing left for me but to do my best with it.[75]

Despite these later protestations, he used the Scottish elements to his advantage.[76] As he ascends from the tomb, Lord Ruthven's costume includes a plaid kilt and a grey cloak. Thus, the audience are treated to one of the most memorable moments in the vampire's history – the arrival of vampires in kilts (see Figure 2.3).[77]

Phantasmagoria 37

Figure 2.3 T. P. Cooke as the Vampire, Mrs Chatterley as Lady Margaret.

Planché took the audience (as Nodier had done) to the site of the bloody exploits sung by Macpherson's *Ossian* (1796). The name Cromal is reminiscent of names such as Cormal and Connal in Macpherson.[78] Planché's most significant change in the cast of characters was his addition of the Scottish drunkard McSwill (akin to the drunken porter in *Macbeth*). We see the heightening of supernatural effects through the folkloric beliefs of the common Scottish people, represented by the servants Bridget and McSwill; ironically, these superstitions prove more reliable than educated reason. The Scottish setting also brought Lord Ruthven closer to home and heightened the association with Lord Byron, born in London but reared in Aberdeen.

In the summer of 1829, Planché had the opportunity of treating the subject of the vampire in accordance with his own ideas. The melodrama had been converted into an opera for the German stage, with music composed by Marschner. Samuel Arnold was to produce the play at The Lyceum and Planché seized the chance to change the setting from Scotland to Hungary:

> I was engaged to write the libretto, and consequently laid the scene of action in Hungary, where the superstition exists to this day, substituted for a Scotch chieftain a Wallacian Boyard, and in many other respects improved upon my earlier version. The opera was extremely well sung, and the costumes novel, as well as correct, thanks to the kindness of Dr. Walsh, the traveller, who gave me some valuable information respecting the national dresses of the Magyars and the Wallachians.[79]

Planché, then, retained a long-held belief in the incongruity of the Scottish setting and its associated superstitions about vampires. Both the Hungarian and Scottish settings are notable for their deviation from Polidori's choice of Greece. The novel *Lord Ruthwen, ou Les Vampires* is set in Modena in northern Italy. Thus, any connection to the Greek vampire, the *vrykalokos*, or to the influence of de Tournefort (cited in the preliminaries to the publication of 'The Vampyre' in *The Monthly Museum* in 1819) are lost, along with the tragic ending.

The ending

Polidori's tale ends with Lord Ruthven disappearing, Aubrey's sister having 'glutted the thirst of a VAMPYRE'. The vampire is still at large, now moving among the drawing rooms of polite society in London. Planché avoids the tragedy of Polidori's tale. On stage, the vampire is destroyed, not by humans but by supernatural agency, in a nod to phantasmagoria shows, which delighted and horrified the public with disappearing demons and apparitions of angels:

> RUTHVEN: And I am lost
>
> (*A terrific peal of thunder is heard;* UNDA *and* ARIEL *appear; a thunderbolt strikes* RUTHVEN *to the ground, who immediately vanishes.*)
> (*The Vampire*, II. 5, p. 68)

This is the dramatic final use of the vampire trap. It was invented for this play; the concluding disappearance of the vampire was met with uproar and wonderment. Importantly, the humans have managed to resist the vampire, and the women have remained chaste. The *diabolus ex machina* that Planché employs, whereby Ruthven vanishes through the ground on his way to the annihilation the spirits describe earlier, erases human agency. The punitive stake through the heart, described in the anonymous introduction on human encounters with vampires published with Polidori's original tale, is noticeably avoided. Evil is eventually defeated – but not by the heroes of the play. In Polidori's version, Ruthven's Gothic excess triumphs over sentimental naivety. In Planché the exact reverse occurs; instead of the chaos of the vampire remaining at large, Planché allows happy domesticity to be restored. The emphasis is on the total destruction of the vampire and the audience's delight in it. Polidori's story works more subversively; his audience is exposed to a continuing threat, with an unsettling degree of moral uncertainty.

The Vampire was extraordinary successful at The Lyceum and the play was quickly taken up in provincial English theatres, opening in Hull in December and Bath in 1821.[80] The Scottish elements introduced by Nodier enabled the stage vampire to better resonate with English theatre-goers. The vampire in a kilt lived on in numerous English playhouses and rose again at The Lyceum's summer season in June. The actor-manager John Coleman saw a revival in Derby in his youth and shuddered at the 'gruesome Scottish horror feeding upon the blood of young maidens and throwing himself headlong through the solid stage, and vanishing into the regions below amidst flames of red fire'.[81] To the audience, the play insisted that the vampire lurked amid Britain's own shadow, determining the legacy of Polidori's vampire.

The importance of stage effects in the history of the literary vampire

In this final section, I elaborate on the importance of stage effects in mapping the afterlife of Polidori's vampire. I bring in the staging of Bram Stoker's *Dracula* briefly, by way of comparison. My aim is to emphasise that this theatrical phenomenon has been overlooked in wider histories of the vampire, where Lord Ruthven has been overshadowed by Count Dracula.[82] Both vampires are theatrical and connected to the stage, but it is Polidori, not Stoker, who has founded the entire modern tradition of vampire fiction. The vampire is not staked in the Polidori-inspired plays – he disappears into a vault and is subject to supernatural or divine interventions. Thus, the one stage prop that is missing from the Polidori adaptations is the vampire-slaying kit. These kits were as theatrical as the vampire trap itself, but they were sold to capitalise on the popularity of Count Dracula, not Lord Ruthven, and they date from the twentieth century, illustrating a similar but differently inflected taste for stage blood.

Stoker staged a reading of *Dracula-The-Undead* at London's Lyceum Theatre on 18 May 1897 to seal its copyright, but the first commercial dramatisation of *Dracula* (an adaptation by Hamilton Deane) was not until 1924, at the Grand Theatre in Derby.[83] Deane, who planned to play the vampire himself, eventually took on the role of the vampire hunter Van Helsing.[84] Dracula is staked in his coffin in the finale of this play.[85] This killing of the vampire was staged using a disappearing coffin: 'Dracula would drop through the box's false bottom, simultaneously pulling down two hinged wooden panels which gave the illusion of the empty box. The panels were generously packed with Fuller's earth, which created an impressive cloud of dust.'[86] Vampire slaying with a hammer and stake became a prominent part of these Dracula theatricals in the productions which followed.[87] The kits emerged to perform the staking of such vampires as entertainment in the theatre and yet the contents point to dark, unsettling undead issues. The boxes generally contained a crucifix, Bible, holy water, wooden stakes and a mallet, together with the *Book of Common Prayer* (1851 edition). Inside many there is an unnerving handwritten passage from Luke 19.27 which reads: 'but those mine enemies, [...] I should reign over them, bring hither and slay them before me'.

Over one hundred of these kits still exist, and many of them are quite professionally made and 'antiqued' in appearance. It is often claimed that vampire kits in general are late-Victorian novelties or were sold to tourists travelling to Eastern Europe in the wake of the publication of *Dracula* in 1897, but I would argue they are theatrical, inspired by Dracula's appearance on stage, not by the novel.[88] There are some 'Professor Blomberg' kits in circulation and these are conclusively recent creations, produced around the 1970s. Though constructed from antique boxes and contents, these modern vampire kits were most likely produced in the era of the classic Hammer vampire films.[89]

Vampire-slaying kits are not fakes per se, because there is no evidence of a Victorian original. They are not fake, and not reproductions; they are instead 'hyper-real', invented artefacts for stage and screen. They can also be regarded, and indeed have been sold, as pieces of art, the preserve of galleries and of course libraries. These enigmatic objects transcend questions of authenticity. They are part of the material culture of the Gothic, aspects of our shared literary and dramatic passions made physical. Most importantly, they are evidence of the lasting influence of the vampire theatre. Vampire-slaying kits date back to the writings on the stage vampire of the British vampirologist Montague Summers.

The theatre gave sustenance to Polidori's Romantic vampire, as I have shown; the character of Lord Ruthven flourished on the stage. He remained dominant as a vampire, despite the melodramatic works in which he was represented. Ruthven's creator Polidori died in London in August 1821, supposedly weighed down by illness, depression and gambling debts. It is said that he ended his life by means of Prussic acid (cyanide). Sadly, he was not to know the fame his creation would achieve as the star of hundreds of books, plays and films – and millions of phantasmagoria-inspired nightmares.

Notes

1 George, Lord Byron, 'A Fragment', Appendix 2 in this volume, p. 268. This incomplete tale, Byron's contribution to the ghost story competition in 1816, was first published at the end of *Mazeppa* (1819), where it was entitled 'A Fragment' and dated 7 June 1816. Byron sent the tale to his publisher, John Murray, shortly after Polidori's *The Vampyre* appeared.
2 Henry R. Viets, 'The London Editions of Polidori's *The Vampyre*', *The Papers of the Bibliographical Society of America*, 63:2 (1969), 83–103.
3 See Robert Morrison and Chris Baldick, 'Introduction', in *The Vampyre and Other Tales of the Macabre*, ed. by Robert Morrison and Chris Baldick (Oxford: Oxford University Press, 1998), pp. vii–xxii (p. x).
4 Byron and Mary Shelley's name for Polidori is well known and has shaped the title of the definitive biography of Polidori: D. L. Macdonald, *Poor Polidori: A Critical Biography of the Author of 'The Vampyre'* (Toronto, ON: University of Toronto Press, 1991).
5 Paul Barber, *Vampires, Burials and Death* (New Haven, CT and London: Yale University Press, 1988), p. 2.
6 Polidori, *The Vampyre*, Appendix 2, pp. 248–72 (p. 249).
7 Polidori, *The Vampyre*, Appendix 2, p. 261.
8 Polidori, *The Vampyre*, Appendix 2, p. 249.
9 Cullen is described as 'a perfect statue […] smooth like marble, glittering like crystal'; he is an expensive reproduction of an earlier model (Stephenie Meyer, *Twilight* (London: Atom Books, 2006), p. 228).
10 Catherine Spooner, 'Gothic Charm School; or, how Vampires Learned to Sparkle', in *Open Graves, Open Minds: Representations of Vampires and the Undead from the Enlightenment to the Present Day*, ed. by Sam George and Bill Hughes (Manchester: Manchester University Press, 2012), pp. 146–64 (p. 147).
11 E. T. A. Hoffmann, *Vampirismus* (1821); Dion Boucicault, *The Phantom* (1857); J. Sheridan Le Fanu, *Carmilla* (1872); Bram Stoker, *Dracula* (1897).
12 This is still manifested in Hollywood with Robert Pattison as Edward Cullen, continuing the tradition of British actors playing vampires, from Christopher Lee to Gary Oldman.
13 Cyprien Bérard, *Lord Ruthwen ou les vampires* (Paris: Ladvocat, 1820). There is a modern translation by Brian Stableford: *The Vampire Lord Ruthwen* (Encino, CA: Black Coat Press, 2011).

14 Richard Switzer, 'Lord Ruthwen and the Vampires', *The French Review*, 29:2 (December 1955), 107–11 (p. 110).
15 This work deviates from the usual sources on vampires and revenants at this time (i.e., Calmet and de Tournefort). I have not been able to trace the work cited by Nodier but it is most likely to be Jacques-Barthèlemy Salgues, *Des Erreurs et des préjugés répandus dans la société*, 3 vols (Paris: F. Buisson, 1810–13).
16 Augustine Calmet's treatise *Dissertations sur les apparitions des anges des démons et des esprits* was published in Paris in 1746 and London in 1759. It later appeared in a popular format as *The Phantom World*, translated into English by Rev. Henry Christmas in 1850. A discussion of these vampires can be found in Barber; for the Serbian vampire Arnod Paole, see pp. 15–16; for Peter Plogojowitz, a Hungarian, see pp. 4–9. In 1702, the French botanist Pitton de Tournefort recorded his observation of the Greek *vrykolakas* on the island of Mykonos. This was cited in the preliminaries to *The Vampyre*, when it appeared in *The Monthly Magazine* in 1819. It was widely read in translation (*A Voyage into the Levant* (London: D. Browne, 1718)).
17 Sources suggest the play may have been the work of three writers: Pierre Francois Adolphe Carmouche (1797–1868); Achille, Marquis de Jouffrey d'Abbans (1785–1859); and Charles Nodier (1780–1844). See Roxana Stuart, *Stage Blood: Vampires of the 19th-Century Stage* (Bowling Green, OH: Bowling Green State University Press, 1994), p. 41.
18 See Marvin Carlson, *The French Stage in the Nineteenth Century* (Metuchen, NJ: Scarecrow Press, 1972), p. 51.
19 A brief entry on Cicéri can be found in Stuart, *Stage Blood*, p. 307.
20 Monsieur Philippe (Emmanuel de la Villenie, d. 1824) was the actor who first played Nodier's Rutwen. His creation of the vampire gave him exceptional prestige. Marie Dorval (Marie Delaunay, 1798–1849) is best remembered for her role in *Le Vampire*. For brief biographies of these actors, see Stuart, *Stage Blood*, pp. 308, 309.
21 Nodier discussed the vampire myth in interviews in *Le Télégrafe Official*, 11 April 1813 and *Le Drapeau blanc*, 1 July 1819. After adapting Polidori successfully for the stage in France (*Le Vampire*, 1820), Nodier worked on further adaptations: *Bertram ou le Pirate* (1822), based on a play by Charles Maturin in England, and *Le Monstre et le Magicien* (1826), adapted from stage versions of Mary Shelley's novel *Frankenstein*. His novels, adult fairy tales, dictionaries, works of literary analysis (including *Du Fantastique en Littérature* (1830)) and commentaries on La Fontaine and Cyrano de Bergerac are listed in Matthew Loving, 'Charles Nodier: The Romantic Librarian', *Libraries & Culture*, 38:2 (2003) 166–68. For a brief summary of his output, see Stuart, *Stage Blood*, p. 307. His life is documented in Alfred Richard Oliver, *Charles Nodier: Pilot of Romanticism* (Syracuse, NY: Syracuse University Press, 1964)).
22 Nodier's biographer Oliver claims that 'he was at least a partner to the publishing artifice and had very likely written the novel in the first place' (Oliver, *Charles Nodier*, p. 90).

23 See Nick Groom, 'The Celtic Century and the Rise of Scottish Gothic', in *Scottish Gothic: An Edinburgh Companion*, ed. by Carl Margaret Davison and Monica Germana (Edinburgh: Edinburgh University Press, 2017), pp. 14–41.
24 Montague Summers, *The Vampire, His Kith and Kin* (London: E. P. Dutton, 1929; rpt. as *Vampires and Vampirism* (Mineola, NY: Dover, 2005)), pp. 306–07.
25 Roxana Stuart argues that 'The French, perhaps, with a fond nostalgia for the "Auld alliance" with Scotland of the sixteenth century, seem to have found Scotland an exotic locale and developed a romantic attachment to it which mystified and bemused the English' (*Stage Blood*, p. 47). For more recent discussions, see A. Owen Aldridge, 'The Vampire Theme, Dumas Père and the English Stage', *Revue des Langues Vivants*, 39 (1974), 312–24 (p. 315), and Frederick Burwick, who makes Scottishness a feature of his essay 'Vampires in Kilts', in *The Romantic Stage, A Many-Sided Mirror*, ed. by Lilla Maria Crisafulli and Fabio Libeto (Amsterdam: Rodopi, 2014), pp. 199–224 (Fingal's Cave and Nodier, p. 207; Planché and Scotland, p. 210).
26 First published as *Fingal, an Ancient Epic Poem in Six Books, together with Several Other Poems composed by Ossian, the Son of Fingal, translated from the Gaelic Language* (1761).
27 Charles Nodier, *The Vampire*, trans. by Frank J. Morlock, in *Lord Ruthven the Vampire*, ed. by Frank J. Morlock (Encino, CA: Black Coat Press, 2014), pp. 80–161 (Act 3, p. 161).
28 Alexandre Dumas, cited in Summers, *Vampires and Vampirism*, p. 294. *Mes Mémoires* was published in Paris in 1863.
29 This ending is attested to in Alexandre Dumas's eyewitness account in *Mes Mémoires* (Paris, 1863). An extract, 'A Visit to the Theatre', is in Christopher Frayling, ed., *Vampyres: Lord Byron to Count Dracula* (London: Faber & Faber, 1991), pp. 131–44.
30 A full account of Dumas's vampire play is given in Summers, *Vampires and Vampirism*, pp. 297–303. See also Roxana Stuart on the revenge motif in this play and comparisons to Nodier (pp. 136–69). The play appears in translation by Frank J. Morlock as *The Return of Lord Ruthven the Vampire* (Encino, CA: Black Coat Press, 2004).
31 Charles Nodier, *Mélanges de Littérature et de Critique*, vol 1. (1923), p. 417, cited in Summers, *Vampires and Vampirism*, p. 293.
32 Christopher Frayling's *Vampyres: Lord Byron to Count Dracula*, originally published by Gollancz in 1978, is the first academic study of the literary vampire. The stage vampire is only referred to critically on two of the pages, even in the revised editions (Frayling, *Vampyres*, pp. 37–38). Nick Groom's *The Vampire, A New History* (New Haven, CT and London: Yale University Press, 2018) allots less than one page to the stage vampire (p. 123).
33 Summers, 'The Vampire in Literature', in *Vampires and Vampirism*, pp. 271–340 (p. 303).
34 For a full account of France's vampire theatre at this time, see Stuart, *Stage Blood*, pp. 41–64; and Summers, *Vampires and Vampirism*, pp. 290–307.

Useful articles on the stage vampire include Katie Harse, 'Melodrama Hath Charms: Planché's Theatrical Domestication of Polidori's "The Vampyre"', *Journal of Dracula Studies*, 3:1 (2001) https://research.library.kutztown.edu/dracula-studies/vol3/iss1/1 [accessed 22 April 2023]; and Ronald E. McFarland, 'The Vampire on Stage: A Study in Adaptations', *Comparative Drama*, 21:1 (1987), 19–33.

35 'No evidence is lacking – depositions, certificates of notables, surgeons, priests and magistrates. The proof in law is utterly complete [...] yet with this [...] who actually believes in vampires?' (Jean Jacques Rousseau, 'Letter to Christophe de Beaumont, Archbishop of Paris', cited in Christopher Frayling and Robert Wokler, 'From the Orang-utan to the Vampire: Towards an Anthropology of Rousseau', in *Rousseau After 200 Years*, ed. by R. A. Leigh (Cambridge: Cambridge University Press, 1982), p. 116).

36 For a description of *Les Trois Vampires ou de la lune*, see Stuart, *Stage Blood*, pp. 273–74; Summers, *Vampires and Vampirism*, p. 304. *Le Vampire Amoureux* is described in Stuart, *Stage Blood*, pp. 55–56, and Summers, *Vampires and Vampirism*, p. 303.

37 Nicholas Brazier, Gabriel De Lurieu and Armand d'Artois, *Les Trois Vampires ou de la lune* (I. 3. 4), cited in Burwick, 'Vampires in Kilts', p. 206.

38 Planché was a formidable presence in the English theatre at this time, a specialist in historical costumes and fairy extravaganzas. According to Donald Roy, he wrote approximately 180 pieces for London's theatres, including Sadler's Wells, The Adelphi, The Haymarket and The Lyceum. He also stage-managed, designed and directed. He was the author of collections of verse and travel books and several volumes of French and German fairy tales in translation. A full record of his publications is given in Donald Roy, ed., *Plays by James Robinson Planché* (Cambridge: Cambridge University Press, 1986), pp. 36–41; a useful biographical note can be found in Stuart, *Stage Blood*, pp. 310–12. Planché's autobiographical writings were published in 1872 in J. R. Planché, *The Recollections and Reflections of J. R. Planché: A Professional Autobiography*, 2 vols (1872; Cambridge: Cambridge University Press, 2011). Useful general articles include P. T. Dirks, 'Planché and the English Burletta Tradition', *Theatre Survey*, 17 (1976), 68–81; Dougald Macmillan, 'Planché's Fairy Extravaganzas', *Studies in Philology*, 25 (1928), 790–98; 'Planché's Early Classical Burlesques', *Studies in Philology*, 25 (1928), 340–45; and Paul Reinhardt, 'The Costume Designs of James Robinson Planché (1796–1800)', *Educational Theatre Journal*, 20 (1968), 524–44.

39 Planché, *Recollections and Reflections*, I, p. 40.

40 W. T. Moncrieff's *Vampire* was performed at the Coburg in 1820. It is a crude copy of Planché and also draws on Nodier's play. It retains the Scottish setting and opens with singing vampires in the Cave of Fingal. It even contains traces of Walter Scott's *Bride of Lammermoor* (1819). For a full account, see Stuart, *Stage Blood*, pp. 95–97, pp. 278–79. A character named Ruthven appears in Charles Edward Walker's Gothic melodrama *Warlock of the Glen*, which was performed at Covent Garden in 1820 (see Stuart, *Stage Blood*, pp. 65, 97, 98).

41 See P. T. Dirks, 'Planché and the English Burletta Tradition', *Theatre Survey*, 17 (1976), 68–81. The vampire breeches role in Planché is discussed in Burwick,

'Vampires in Kilts', p. 218; Stuart, *Stage Blood*, pp. 99, 103. For the actress Mrs Waylett (1800–1841), see Stuart, *Stage Blood*, pp. 318–19.
42 Breeches roles were created by Planché for fairy tale productions from *Puss in Boots* (1837) to *The White Cat* (1842). See Roy, 'Introduction', *Plays*, pp. 1–35 (pp. 13, 31).
43 A full record of his adaptations is given in Roy, 'Introduction', *Plays*, pp. 36–41.
44 See Roy, 'Introduction', *Plays*, p. 17.
45 Michael R. Booth, *English Melodrama* (London: Herbert Jenkins, 1965), p. lv.
46 For nineteenth-century European phantasmagoria, see Terry Castle, 'Phantasmagoria: Spectral Technology', *Critical Enquiry* (Autumn 1988), 26–61 (p. 27); Marina Warner, 'Darkness Visible', in *Phantasmagoria: Spirit Visions, Metaphors, and Media into the Twenty-First Century* (Oxford: Oxford University Press, 2006), pp. 147–56; Laurent Mannoni, *The Great Art of Light and Shadow*, ed. and trans. by Richard Crangle (Exeter: University of Exeter Press, 2000); and Laurent Mannoni and Ben Brewster, 'The Phantasmagoria', *Film History*, 8:4 (1996), 390–415. The role of the magic lantern is explored in David J. Jones, *Gothic Machine: Textualities, Pre-Cinematic Media and Film in Popular Visual Culture, 1670–1910* (Cardiff: University of Wales Press, 2011). The figure of the vampire in phantasmagoria is briefly alluded to in Warner, *Phantasmagoria*, pp. 10, 147, 177, 357, 358, 366. For the influence of phantasmagoria on vampire film, see Stacey Abbott, 'The Cinematic Spectacle of Vampirism', in *Celluloid Vampires* (Austin: University of Texas Press, 2000), pp. 42–60.
47 Mannoni, *The Great Art*, p. 143.
48 The theatre, renamed The English Opera House (1816–17), burnt down in 1830. It resumed the name The Lyceum on its restoration, becoming a showcase for extravaganzas under the management team of Madame Vestris, Charles Matthews and Planché (c. 1847–55). See 'The Lyceum', in Stuart, *Stage Blood*, pp. 72–73; and Catherine Wynne, *Bram Stoker, Dracula and the Victorian Gothic Stage* (London: Palgrave, 2013), pp. 7–8, 78, 135–36, 143.
49 See Wynne, *Bram Stoker*, pp. 36–37.
50 See Mark Bartley, 'In Search of Robertson's Fantasmagorie', *The New Magic Lantern Journal*, 7:3 (November 1995), 1–5 (p. 5).
51 Etienne Gaspard Robertson, *Mémoires: récréatifs, scientifiques et anecdotiques* (Paris: Chez l'auteur et à la Librairie de Wurtz, 1831–33). Online at: Harry Houdini Collection, Library of Congress www.loc.gov/resource/rbc0001.2009houdini06148/ [accessed 29 November 2020].
52 Fabio Camilletti, 'On This Day in 1816: Polidori Finds a Book', BARS Blog, 12 June 2016 www.bars.ac.uk/blog/?p=1214 [accessed 24 May 2023].
53 *Fantasmagoriana* had been published in Paris by the bookseller Frédéric Schoell.
54 Camilletti, 'On This Day'.
55 For a contemporary translation of the original German tales, see *Fantasmagoriana: Tales of the Dead*, ed. by A. J. Day and C. Vorwerk (St Ives: Fantasmagoriana Press, 2005). The original French book was published as *Fantasmagoriana* (Paris: Frédéric Schoell, 1812). For a brief analysis of the stories, see Fabio Camilletti, 'Fantasmagoriana: The German Book of Ghost Stories that Inspired *Frankenstein*', *The Conversation*, 29 October 2018

https://theconversation.com/fantasmagoriana-the-german-book-of-ghost-stories-that-inspired-frankenstein-105236 [accessed 29 November 2020].

56 Fabio Camilletti, 'Phantasmagoria: Creating the Ghosts of the Enlightenment', *History Extra*, 17 August 2021 www.historyextra.com/period/stuart/phantasmagoria-creating-the-ghosts-of-the-enlightenment/ [accessed 24 May 2023].

57 Planché, *Recollections and Reflections*, II, p. 40.

58 Harlequin was a popular figure in English pantomime in the early nineteenth century. The harlequinade, a British comic genre, was popular in England up to the mid-nineteenth century. See David Meyer, *Harlequin in His Element: The English Pantomime, 1806–1836* (Cambridge, MA: Harvard University Press, 1969). Harlequin was the most widely known character of *Commedia dell'Arte*, which originated in Tuscany in around 1550. See also Allardyce Nicoll, *The World of Harlequin* (Cambridge: Cambridge University Press, 1963).

59 See Wynne, *Bram Stoker*, p. 162.

60 Bram Stoker, *The Primrose Path* (1875; Westcliff-on-Sea: Desert Island Books, 1999), p. 72. Jerry is badly injured in this incident and takes to drink; his unfortunate accident in the vampire trap triggers his eventual degradation.

61 'The Star Trap', in *The Bram Stoker Bedside Companion* (London: Victor Gollancz, 1973), pp. 102–14 (p. 108). The hinges of the star trap have in fact been tampered with by the master machinist at the theatre, Old Jack, who suspects the harlequin actor of having an affair with his young wife, who is a dancer in the play. Bram Stoker's 'A Star Trap' was first published in Stoker's second collection of short stories, *Snowbound: The Record of a Theatrical Touring Party* (London: Collier & Co, 1908).

62 Stoker, 'The Star Trap', p. 109.

63 Stoker, 'The Star Trap', p. 106.

64 Summers, *Vampires and Vampirism*, p. 306.

65 Nina Auerbach, *Our Vampires, Ourselves* (Chicago, IL: University of Chicago Press, 1995), pp. 6–7.

66 See Roy, 'Biographical Record', *Plays*, pp. 36–41 (p. 36).

67 *The Recollections and Reflections of J. R. Planché*, 2 vols (London: Tinsley Brothers, 1872; rpt. Cambridge: Cambridge University Press, 2011), II, p. 223. All further references are to this later edition.

68 J. R. Planché, *The Vampire; or, The Bride of the Isles* [1820], in *Plays by James Robinson Planché*, ed. by Donald Roy (Cambridge: Cambridge University Press, 1986), pp. 45–68 (I. 1, p. 47). All further references are to this edition.

69 Polidori, *The Vampyre*, p. n.

70 This film famously invented the trope that the vampire burns up in sunlight.

71 See James Rymer, *Varney the Vampire, or the Feast of Blood*, 2 vols (1845–47; London: Dover, 1972). 'Varney's Moon' is discussed in full in Auerbach, *Our Vampires, Ourselves*, pp. 27–40.

72 Stage bill for the ninth performance of 'The Vampire', 19 August 1820, reprinted in Stuart, *Stage Blood*, p. 75.

73 'At the beginning of the nineteenth century in England there was in fact a Lord Ruthven, the title dating from 1651. The bearer of the name was James, fifth Baron Ruthven', Switzer, 'Lord Ruthwen', p. 107.

74 The earliest published version of Planché's *The Vampire* is John Lowndes: London, 1820.
75 Planché, *Recollections and Reflections*, I, p. 40.
76 See Burwick, 'Vampires in Kilts', p. 206, note 22.
77 Lady Margaret also wore plaid trimming on her dress and a Scottish hat and feather (Stuart, *Stage Blood*, p. 81). The first printed version of the play lists all the original costumes.
78 *The Poems of Ossian* (London: A. Strahan and T. Cadell, 1796). Names in relation to Macpherson are discussed in McFarland, 'The Vampire on Stage', p. 31.
79 Planché, *Recollections and Reflections*, I, p. 151.
80 See Roy, 'Introduction', *Plays*, p. 4.
81 John Coleman, *Fifty Years of an Actor's Life*, 2 vols (London: Hutchinson, 1904), I, p. 30.
82 One of the perennial features of the theatrical vampire, the big stand-up collar on the cape, has almost become synonymous with the character of Dracula. Originally the collar had the distinct theatrical function of hiding the actor's head, thus allowing him to slip out of the cape and down a wall panel or trapdoor, effectively disappearing before the audience's eyes. Though it served no purpose in the film adaptations that followed, it has remained a signature feature of the vampire. See David J. Skal, *Hollywood Gothic: The Tangled Web of Dracula from Novel to Stage to Screen* (New York: Faber & Faber, 1990), p. 111.
83 See David J. Skal, '"His Hour Upon the Stage": Theatrical Adaptations of Dracula', in Bram Stoker, *Dracula*, ed. by Nina Auerbach and David J. Skal (New York and London: Norton, 1997), pp. 371–81; Wynne, *Bram Stoker*, pp. 186–89.
84 Skal, *Hollywood Gothic*, p. 109.
85 See Wynne, *Bram Stoker*, p. 169.
86 Skal, *Hollywood Gothic*, p. 108.
87 This is particularly true of the Fulton Theatre New York City production of Hamilton Deane and John L. Balderston's adaptation of *Dracula* (1927). The knife of the novel has been replaced with a hammer and stake and Mina too (not Lucy) is staked (though this is done offstage). See Hamilton Deane and John L. Balderston, *Dracula, The Vampire Play in Three Acts, Dramatized by Hamilton Deane and John L. Balderston, from the Novel by Bram Stoker* (New York: Samuel French, 1933), III. 2, p. 74.
88 A vampire-slaying kit went on display in the British Library's *Terror and Wonder: The Gothic Imagination* exhibition in 2014. It belonged to the Royal Armouries in Leeds. No mention of the theatre was made in the accompanying talks or in the exhibition catalogue edited by Dale Townsend. The date of the kit is unknown. The Open Graves, Open Minds project was gifted a vampire-slaying kit by a seller of rare books in Oxford. It has been traced to a travelling theatre company in the 1930s, seemingly confirming that they are theatrical in origin and inspired by the vampire theatricals that were Polidori's legacy.
89 See Peter Hutchings, *Hammer and Beyond* (Manchester: Manchester University Press, 1991).

3

A séance in Bristol Gardens: Reassessing *The Vampyre*

Fabio Camilletti

Prologue: The séance

On a November Saturday of 1865, William Michael Rossetti returned to visit Mary Marshall, a former laundress from Holborn who conjured the dead at 7 Bristol Gardens.[1] Rossetti's approach to Spiritualism, he would recall in 1903, was cautiously sceptical: 'I never paid much attention to what is called Spiritualism; and have a general impression that […] any great addiction to its phenomena tends to weaken […] the mind. Still I saw *something*.'[2] Dealing with the dead was a dangerous addiction, and by that date William Michael Rossetti knew it well. His brother Dante Gabriel had met the most eminent mediums of his age, from Mrs Guppy to Daniel Dunglas Home, and each time had asked to speak to his deceased wife, Elizabeth Siddal – who had poisoned herself, notwithstanding the verdict of accidental death returned by the coroner.[3] The first séance involving Siddal had taken place in November 1865, one day after William Michael's first visit to Marshall.[4] Over the years, Dante Gabriel had conjured his wife in more literal ways. Her tomb in Highgate had been opened in the night of 5 October 1869, apparently displaying an unnaturally incorrupt body.[5] In January 1882, three months before Rossetti's death, William Bell Scott had found 'him alone. Tells me all about the death of his wife. For 2 years after her death every night he saw her upon the bed as she died.'[6]

On that Saturday afternoon, the séance began at about 3 pm. Several people were present; they put questions, and 'spirits' answered by rapping on the table. One of them, running over the alphabet with a pencil, took note of letters every time a rap was heard, thereby forming more or less meaningful sentences. After a few unsuccessful attempts, an unannounced spirit stepped in:

> One of the gentlemen […] said: 'Is there a spirit who will communicate with me?' – Yes. – Who? – Uncle John. […] I […] said: 'Is it my Uncle John?' – Yes. I asked for the surname by the alphabet, but could not get it. Then: Is it an English surname? – No. – Foreign? – Yes. – Spanish, German, etc., etc.,

Italian? – Yes. – I then called over five or six Italian names, coming to Polidori. – Yes. – Will you tell me truly how you died? – Yes. – How? – Killed. – Who killed you? – I. – There was a celebrated poet with whom you were connected: what was his name? – Bro. This was twice repeated, or something close to it the second time. At a third attempt, 'Byron'. – There was a certain book you wrote, attributed to Byron: can you give me its title? – Yes. – I tried to get the title times, but wholly failed. – Are you happy? – Two raps, meaning not exactly.[7]

Precision of answers should not disconcert us. Marshall did not have the best of reputations, and as early as 1860 the *All the Year Round* had exposed her as a charlatan, only wondering whether to blame 'the unblushing impudence of the actors or the marvellous credulity of the spectators'.[8] Nobody had asked William Michael's name on his first visit: now, however, two weeks had elapsed, and Marshall could get all the information she needed.[9]

Questioning truth, however, is only one of the several ways we can react to an alleged supernatural phenomenon. As Andrew Lang admonished, '[e]ven ghost stories, as a rule, have some basis of fact, whether fact of hallucination, or illusion, or imposture. They are, at lowest, "human documents".'[10] As a document, therefore, we should read the laconic dialogue that occurred between John Polidori and his nephew, born eight years after his death – a dialogue in which questions are no less relevant than answers, and all revolve around a few crucial topics. A foreign name; the shadow of Byron and the elusive authorship of a certain book; and the joy or torment waiting for those who took their own lives.

These questions will provide the overall pattern for my essay, in which I will propose a general reassessment of Polidori's *The Vampyre* in relation to three aspects: the circumstances of the tale's composition; its troubled publication history; and the spectral legacy of Polidori within the Rossettis' family romance. My work has, consequently, a threefold aim. First, I will consider Polidori's perceived (and self-constructed) Italianness as a central element for evaluating his role in Byron's circle during the summer of 1816. Second, through the evidence provided by textual criticism, I will propose a new composition date for the tale, suggesting a more direct role of Polidori in the circumstances of its publication and a closer connection to Mary Shelley's *Frankenstein*. Third, I will show how Polidori acts as a veritable phantom – in the sense given to this term by psychoanalysts Nicolas Abraham and Maria Torok – within the mental topography of the Rossetti brothers, and particularly Dante Gabriel's. By so doing, I hope to shed some indirect light on the (doubtlessly curious) circumstance of the modern vampire – in both its male and female incarnations, later epitomised by Dracula and Lucy Westenra – being shaped, as an icon, within the unconscious of a single Anglo-Italian family.

'Is it an Italian surname?': Italianness and vampirism

Polidori's 'damned Italian polysyllabic name', to speak in John Hobhouse's terms, was deliberately misspelled by Byron and his acolytes as 'Pollydolly', an unfortunate yet revealing pun which, by assimilating its referent to a parrot, seemed to suggest a common propension to tiresomeness and obtuse imitation.[11] When editing Polidori's journal, in 1911, William Michael Rossetti utters a similar judgement: Polidori, he writes, often appears 'as overweening and petulant, too fond of putting himself forward face to face with those two heroes of our poetical literature' (that is, Byron and Percy Shelley).[12] The key point in this passage, however, is not so much Polidori's pitiless portrait – coming to Rossetti through the filter of biased sources such as Hobhouse, Leigh Hunt, or Thomas Medwin – but the expression '*our* poetry', while the list of Polidori's alleged faults – 'deficient in self-knowledge, lacking prudence and reserve, and ignoring the distinction between a dignified and a quarrelsome attitude of mind' – can be easily summarised as an irreparable lack of Britishness.[13]

In 1911, after all, William Michael Rossetti was a man who had buried all his illustrious siblings, whose memory he was administering: born in 1829, his life had crossed the whole of Victoria's reign, of which he is recalled as one of the acutest observers. He was, in other words, the ultimate outcome of a long process of integration, initiated by the emigration of his maternal grandfather, Gaetano Polidori, from revolutionary France (1790) and of his father, Gabriele Rossetti, from the Kingdom of Naples (1824). Such parabolas are rarely straightforward: in the case of the Polidori–Rossetti family, the victim was one, and his suicide the founding death that would shape their 'romance' for better or worse.

Polidori's biographer D. L. Macdonald stresses how, since his boyhood, Polidori nurtured a mythicised image of Italy, intermittently connected to Anglophobic tendencies: clearly a way to cope with his own Anglo-Italian heritage, but also an oblique answer to the contradictory expectations of his father, who encouraged the integration of his children while, at the same time, implicitly secluding the boys from public life by having them baptised as Catholic.[14] At the age of nine, John Polidori's written English was still wobbly, and the possibility of seeing this as a form of resistance is not only suggested by his fluency in other languages (he apparently read Dante in French), but also by the insistence of his father on correct orthography as the main gateway to integration: 'You make many faults in your english [*sic*]. I am afraid you neglect your language. [...] As you are born an englishman [*sic*], you must know english well [...].'[15] Years later, as a university student in Edinburgh, John Polidori defined his feelings in greater detail:

Italy is certainly my country. You have given me Italian blood: I feel that I am Italian. [...] I, although born in England, am not an Englishman – No. My disposition is not that of the English. They are automatons: they have no enthusiasm, nor other vivid passion. Moreover I feel that I can never be happy in this country. I am obliged to curb my tongue from saying things of which no one else here has any idea. They always think me mad; and so I have got to speak like them, and I can never say what I feel, for fear that they should treat me as crazy if I talk of liberty, war, literature.[16]

This concluding passage is particularly interesting. Certainly, the image of the Englishman as an 'automaton', compared to the passionate Italian, is a cliché: still, it is a cliché coming from the creator of Lord Ruthven, and therefore invites us to take a little bit more seriously this connection between the Anglo-Saxon and the inhuman.

Polidori's entire oeuvre, from his youthful dissertation on somnambulism to *The Vampyre* and *Ernestus Berchtold*, seems to be pervaded by an underlying reflection on the themes of free will and of the human being as the receptor and passive instrument of external forces: who – or *what* – performs the actions of somnambulists, while their consciousness remains dormant?[17] Who – or *what* – is actually Lord Ruthven, and what is the mysterious force driving Aubrey or Ernestus to their ruin? A similar question had animated the conversations at Villa Diodati in the summer of 1816: 'the principle of life', as per Mary Shelley's testimony of 1831, but also – following Polidori's journal note of 15 June – 'whether man was to be thought merely an instrument'.[18] Polidori's characters, just like somnambulists, are always represented as instruments controlled by a destructive, quasi-supernatural Id, which, in *The Vampyre*, takes the memorable looks of Lord Ruthven: modelled on Byron, certainly, but first of all an icon of both Britishness and aristocracy, two features that for Polidori always denounce an intimately inhuman, parasitic nature. After all, when living with automatons, Polidori had written, one ends up thinking and speaking like them; his juvenile refusal of English is, primarily, a strategy meant to avoid that 'newspeak' that vampirises all freedom of thought and independence of feeling.

'There was a certain book you wrote, attributed to Byron: can you give me its title?': Rethinking *The Vampyre*

Every obsession conceals an element of ambivalence. From this viewpoint, Polidori's choice of looking for literary fame in English does not only contradict but is also enlightened by his youthful resistance. The same can be said for his relationship with Byron and the Shelleys, veritable vampires and parasites – from Polidori's perspective – running across the routes of post-Waterloo Europe without the burden of any moral fetter (and of Gaetano Polidori's expectations). Both Polidori's heroes – Aubrey and Ernestus Berchtold – experience mixed feelings at the side of predatory masculine icons, be they Lord Ruthven or Olivieri: after all, as Abraham Van Helsing would put it, vampires never prey unbidden. They need someone to open the window for them, to invite them inside.

There is no need to discuss, here, how *The Vampyre* revolutionised the modern image of the vampire, the more so in a volume devoted to the tale's ramified legacy. It will be sufficient to remark how Polidori was not aware of it: in the several letters he wrote in 1819 in order to assert his authorship – to Henry Colburn (2 April), the publishers Sherwood & Neely (3 April), Hobhouse (30 April), or the director of the *Morning Chronicle* (24 September) – Polidori merely speaks of an occasional experiment and a variation on a Byronian theme.[19] Equally interesting is the fact that none of his correspondents – nor Byron himself – viewed it otherwise, perhaps distracted by the tale's patently autobiographic implications. In 1819, at any rate, the vampire was a much vaguer figure than today, which explains why the staff of *New Monthly Magazine* found it appropriate to specify the origins of the term in an editorial note.[20] The full appreciation of Polidori's work is the outcome of the popularity of Bram Stoker's *Dracula*, inviting scholars and readers to retrospectively read the literary history of the vampire in terms of continuity: in 1819, however, 'vampire' was essentially an old-fashioned term, vaguely exotic, which had enjoyed some ephemeral fame in eighteenth-century literary salons.[21] In this acceptation, Byron employed it in *The Giaour* and Mary Shelley used it in *Frankenstein*.[22]

In truth, we know very little about the gestation of *The Vampyre*, and all we know comes from Polidori himself, whose diary is tellingly silent in this respect. In September 1816, Polidori left Geneva, heading south. At some point – we do not know exactly when – he must have understood that Byron would never complete the Greek tale he told his guests; perhaps, as Hobhouse malignantly suggests, he stole or copied Byron's manuscript.[23] He might be mindful of several episodes of his father's life, when, as the secretary of dramatist Vittorio Alfieri, he had nonchalantly taken his revenge over his master's derogatory attitude:

> Alfieri several times asked me if I had read Dante's *Divine Comedy*, Petrarch's *Canzoniere*, the *Orlando furioso* and the *Gerusalemme liberata*, and every time when I would answer that I did, he would always impolitely reply: 'That's not true'. In 1787, it happened that the cultivated and kind abbot Tommaso di Caluso came to stay there for a while, and one day he chanced to see these poems on my desk. The abbot told Alfieri that he had heard my poems and had liked them. 'My secretary', he replied, 'writing poems! I don't believe so: he

must have plagiarised them from someone'. This insult, added to his 'That's not true', caused strong resentment in me: still, I kept it concealed, hoping to find some opportunity to take my revenge. On that very day, Alfieri called for my presence. 'It is quite an odd and bizarre thing', he said, 'that I have a secretary who writes poetry, and that I did not know anything about it. Have you read Horace's *The Art of Poetry*?' 'No, Sir', I replied. 'Pick the book'. I went to find it and, coming back with the book closed, I started to declaim *The Art of Poetry* by heart. He rose up full of rage and shouted: 'You are fooling me: you said you haven't read *The Art of Poetry*, and you know it by heart!' 'Yes, Sir', I answered, 'but every time you asked me whether I had read this or that book, and I answered that I did, you always replied, "That's not true": that's why, this time, I wanted to tell it myself, rather than hearing it from you'.[24]

Less than three years later, *The Vampyre* appeared in *The New Monthly Magazine*. The quarrel following the publication is well known.

As has been repeatedly remarked, Polidori's operation is intimately vampiric, beyond the merely thematic sphere: whereas Ruthven is explicitly modelled on Byron, Polidori's writing is in itself a cannibalistic act, possessing and inhabiting the textual body (*corpus*) of the Master. In the nineteenth century, after all, it was common to label as 'vampires' the plagiarists and authors of unauthorised sequels to the works of others: all those cultural operators – in other terms – who created and nourished the vast body of popular literature, slowly eroding the concept itself of authoriality (as well as of authority).[25] Hence the incapacity on the part of Hobhouse, Watts, or Byron (and even Polidori himself) to fully conceptualise what *The Vampyre* is. As individuals accustomed to think in terms of authorship, they all remain puzzled when confronting this tale, recurring to imperfect concepts such as 'idea', 'groundwork', '*ébauche*', or 'development' in order to account for a text resisting all stable attribution, as do the words written by a somnambulist or dictated to a Spiritualist medium. Which brings us to the most important question: when did Polidori write *The Vampyre*? And, first and foremost, why?

In *The New Monthly Magazine* and the London book editions, the tale was preceded by an accompanying letter, whose authorship has never been substantially questioned.[26] Whereas the editorial note was most likely the work of Alaric Watts, who 'virtually served as editor-in-chief', and the letter concerning Byron's life in Greece that was included in the book edition was certainly by John Mitford, the author of the 'Extract of a Letter from Geneva' has never been completely identified: attribution is the more important in that this text is actually the source through which *The Vampyre* was conveyed to the public.[27]

According to the letter, *The Vampyre* had been in the hands of a lady based in Genthod, a municipality near Geneva, and close to 'the Countess of Breuss, a Russian Lady'.[28] This narrative was substantially corroborated by Polidori in his letters: 'the tale of *The Vampyre* [...] was written *entirely* by me at the request of a lady, who [...] desired I would write it for her, which I did in two idle mornings by her side';[29] 'though *the groundwork* is certainly Lord Byron's, its development is mine, produced at the request of a lady':[30]

> [m]y development was written on the Continent, and left with a lady at whose request it was undertaken; in the course of three mornings by her side it was produced, and left with her. From her hands, by means of a correspondent, without my knowledge, it came into those of the Editor of *The New Monthly*, with a letter stating it to be an *ébauche* of Lord Byron's.[31]

Scholars have generally dismissed the question, uncritically relying on Polidori's version: Polidori, Christopher Frayling writes, 'left his manuscript behind in Geneva and thought no more of it. *Someone* then sent this to a publisher in London, without his consent, or so he subsequently claimed' (my emphasis).[32] Others have proposed more specific attributions. The first one, chronologically, was William Michael Rossetti, who supposed the author to be a lady, perhaps 'the Madame Gatelier who is named in the Journal'.[33] No trace of this lady, however, has ever been found, and the identification of 'Gatelier' with the informer seems inexplicable, given the numerous people Polidori mentions as members of the Genthod circle.[34] Henry Viets argued that the author might be the publisher/editor of the magazine, Henry Colburn, although there is no evidence to corroborate this attribution.[35] More reasonably, Macdonald proposed Mitford, who collaborated with the magazine and might 'have obtained the tale from Madame Brélaz' – a Portuguese woman with whom Polidori seemingly fell in love – 'or whoever the lady was at whose instigation Polidori had written it'.[36] It was unlikely, however, that Mitford could have been so precise about Byron's life in Geneva: in order to do so, he would have to have travelled to Switzerland and been admitted to the Countess's circle, which both his narrow means and unpresentable behaviour would certainly have prevented him from doing.[37]

In truth, there is no substantial reason to validate Polidori's version and localise the gestation of the tale within the Genthod environment in the late summer of 1816. Contemporaries, after all, had no doubts that Polidori himself had orchestrated the whole operation. Macdonald and Kathleen Scherf find it unlikely, given the disconcerted tone of Polidori's letters of 1819, but it remains a fact that Byron, Hobhouse, and John Murray never doubted that Polidori himself had proposed the story to the magazine, and that his later resentment was merely the result of his failure to be recognised as the author.[38] Watts, on his part, confirmed the assumption, suggesting that Polidori might be planning to publish a detailed memoir on Byron's life at Geneva: a strategy to lay the blame on Polidori, perhaps, and even to blackmail Byron, but perchance not without of a certain degree of truth.[39]

Although the 'Extract' is certainly not Polidori's – Watts confirmed the circumstance in a letter, and Polidori crossed it through on his own copy – it is evident that the person who wrote it must have relied on Polidori's diary, or a rough copy of it, which could only be provided by Polidori himself.[40] In describing the lake of Geneva and enumerating the illustrious personalities who lived there, the letter follows the same pattern as Polidori's entry for 25 May 1816; anecdotes concerning Byron, the Shelleys, or Claire Clairmont explicitly echo the diary's tone, and were virtually unknown to others than Polidori.[41] There is enough evidence, in sum, to abandon all hypotheses about any 'Madame Gatelier', 'Madame Brélaz', or 'Countess Breuss' whatsoever, whose names incidentally provide us with ultimate proof: the spelling adopted in the 'Extract' is the same used in Polidori's diary, but it is actually an inaccurate transcription, due to the fact that Polidori was writing down names heard orally and pronounced in the French way. As shown, for example, by the memoirs of Princess Natal'ja Ivanovna Kurakina, who lived in Geneva shortly after Polidori's departure, 'Breuss' was actually Catherine Bruce, a noblewoman raised in tsarist Russia, whose Scottish surname (originally pronounced /bɹuːs/) was pronounced according to the French rules (i.e., /bɹøs/, which could be perfectly transcribed as 'Breuss').[42] Equally, 'Gatelier' was actually 'Gastelier', and 'Madame Brélaz' was in truth a Portuguese lady, whose name was spelled 'Brelos'. It is impossible that the magazine's correspondent misspelled all these names in the same way as Polidori: a blatant case of 'conjunctive error', following the terminology of textual criticism, revealing the interdependence of two texts, in the impossibility that two copyists may independently make the same mistakes.

'Who killed you?': Polidori's Diodati tale

Once this connection has been ascertained, many of the assumptions related to the troubled editorial history of *The Vampyre* can be easily abandoned. If Polidori actually provided the magazine with his diary, there is no reason to assume that he wrote *The Vampyre* in 1816 and left it in Geneva, and it is far more probable that the idea of completing Byron's tale occurred to him in 1818, when the publication of *Frankenstein* created the veritable myth of the Diodati ghost-story-telling contest. In the brief introduction to the 1818 edition, Polidori was completely ignored (incidentally, he had no reason to suppose that Percy Shelley wrote it, and certainly believed it to be Mary Shelley's work). In the 'Extract', instead, Polidori regained a central role, becoming one of the protagonists of the 'haunted summer' of 1816.

It seems, therefore, that the publication of *The Vampyre* was not the main purpose of Polidori's broader plan, but rather a prelude: a way to gain the attention of the London cultural scene (and perhaps some money), even at the cost of bluffing about the tale's authorship, and to pave the way to some other work. Watts, in his bad faith, could well imagine it to be a gossiping memoir of Byron's life in Geneva, excerpted from Polidori's diary. Certainly, what Polidori had in mind was based on the diary, but Byron played no role in it; it is more plausible that his real purpose was to capitalise on the success of Shelley's *Frankenstein*.

Polidori's idea of drafting a diary of 1816 served a precise purpose: compiling a travel memoir, not different than the Shelleys' *History of a Six Weeks' Tour* (1817). As early as September 1816, his material was already unusable, but in the meantime Polidori crossed Switzerland, reached Lago Maggiore, went up the River Ticino, and headed to Milan.[43]

In January 1818, *Frankenstein* appeared: the preface was very short, but enough to transform the nights at Diodati into a veritable contemporary myth. Storms on the lake of Geneva, discussions on science and the supernatural, German ghost stories, Byron, and Godwin's daughter – there was even room for some gossip, and most of all for the suggestive power of the *other* stories, the unwritten ones, which were enough to tempt English publishers. In the 1810s, these were resorting to the dullest imitators of Ann Radcliffe: how successful might, therefore, be a fresh Gothic tale, and furthermore by Byron?[44] It was just a draft, but Polidori might approximately remember its plot. And, of course, there was his own ghost story, the one the Shelleys forgot to mention. Thanks to *The Vampyre*, Polidori might finally access the editorial scene through the main door; the idea would result in a failure, but we can appreciate the strategy.

Polidori's insistence in reasserting that his own Diodati story was *Ernestus Berchtold* – and not *The Vampyre*, which he always regarded as a personal variation on a Byronian idea – can be only compared to the insistent indifference of scholarship towards this novel. Certainly, in the summer of 1816, *Ernestus Berchtold* was nothing but a narrative germ, the image of a girl peeping through a keyhole and seeing something, that is, Julia's story as narrated in the ending of the second part: this is what Mary Shelley would remember in 1831, recalling it in the usual parodic tones that seemed to be inevitable when talking of Polidori.[45] Even *Frankenstein*, however, in the summer of 1816, was nothing but an image – that of a monstrous, nameless creature at the bolster of its maker's bed. In truth, exactly like *Frankenstein*, *Ernestus Berchtold* was an attempt to transfigure the experience of that summer by novelising it, and, indirectly, of the new world opened by the French Revolution and the Napoleonic wars, a world that we have learned to call 'Romantic'. Differences in outcome are merely incidental.

In *Ernestus Berchtold* – a novel that tries to capitalise on *Frankenstein* even from its title, a German name followed by a Classical reference in the subtitle (Prometheus or Oedipus) – everything Polidori recorded in his diary finds its place: Switzerland and the war against the French; Milan and the *demi-monde* of Classicism; Byron, under the guises of Olivieri and Count Wilhelm; a duel fought for futile reasons; and the memories of the devils and saints, of the sickened bodies of the plague-stricken and the enticing eyes of prostitutes that Polidori had seen in Rubens's and Van Dyck's paintings in the galleries of Flanders. The result is a confused, dream-like novel, pervaded by images of death: the pale figure of old Doni in his somnambulist trance, or the marmoreal paleness of Louisa in death, creating the impression that she is still alive. In both cases, the author of *The Vampyre* seems to be attracted to dead or sick bodies. This is perhaps understandable, coming from one who had always fought with his own death drive, and who – when confronting Flemish art – had systematically noticed the way painters portrayed dead bodies, the ecstatic expression of a woman beholding the True Cross, or the 'most hellish' breasts of another woman, which a child refuses with a horrified expression.[46]

'Are you happy?': Conclusion

'Who killed you? – I'. As usual, spirits were not revealing anything new: the coroner had employed a standard formulation, but it was well known in the family that John Polidori had killed himself.[47] The same could be said for the laudanum overdose which killed Elizabeth Siddal on the night of 10 February 1826. On that occasion, authorities had been less accommodating, and William Michael's notes of those days are tellingly cautious: '[t]he poor thing looks wonderfully calm now and beautiful', he wrote, adding two lines in Italian from Dante's *Vita Nova*.[48] Following Siddal's death, the Rossetti brothers began to experiment with Spiritualism: they expected to contact Siddal, but on a November afternoon it was 'uncle John' who answered the call. William Michael asked him if he was happy; a few years later, he would pose Elizabeth Siddal the same question.[49]

Two suicides, two investigations, two family secrets, and, behind both suicides, an unresolved relationship with authorship and imitation, within the context of an agonic relationship with a male, dominating figure, be it Byron or Dante Gabriel Rossetti. In a Gothic novel such as *Ernestus Berchtold*, one would speak of a family curse, and so does Nicolas Abraham's and Maria Torok's psychoanalysis, introducing the idea that family secrets are in all respects phantoms and curses haunting family descendants and their loved ones, especially those who – like Siddal – are unaware of them.

All the dead, Abraham writes, can return; only a few, however, are doomed to haunt the living, that is, 'those who were shamed during their lifetime or those who took unspeakable secrets to the grave' (Polidori, interestingly, matches both categories).[50] Abraham cites an old clinical case in which a butcher abuses his daughter and then hangs himself from a window; the family tries to forget, to the point of banishing the man's name from every conversation.[51] Years later, one of his daughters gives birth to a baby girl. The latter ignores everything about her grandfather, and yet she develops symptoms that constantly revolve around meat, incest, and hanging; in her dreams, as a veritable 'butcher of words', she creates puzzles and anagrams, such as a coleopteron (*bogar*) whose name conceals, encrypted, that of her grandfather (*Gabor*). Nobody ever told her about him, not even her mother, who was a child at the time of the events, and yet she ended her own life in the same way as her father, by hanging herself from a window. Grandfather Gabor, Abraham concludes, is fully a family ghost, in no way different from the ones featured in Gothic novels: a phantom who inhabits the lacunae and the omissions of family memories, remaining undecipherable to his descendants.

The Rossetti brothers had grown up amid more or less tangible memories of 'uncle John'. The diary was in the hands of their Aunt Charlotte, who would later expurgate it and burn the original copy; their mother, Frances, had carefully kept the newspaper articles concerning his death, as well as the eulogy she had composed back then and a quotation on suicide she had copied from a seventeenth-century religious treatise.[52] Furthermore, there were her inexplicable repugnance for gambling and the ban on naming John in the presence of their grandfather, Gaetano:[53] the kind of implicit taboos, in sum, through which children, according to psychoanalysis, eavesdrop the secrets predating their birth.[54]

Consequently, for the Rossetti children, the memory of John Polidori – as a paradigm of failed integration, and the victim of a literary *damnatio memoriae* – cannot be fully laboured, appearing more as a presence buried in family discourses (and silences). To speak in Abraham's and Torok's terms, the ghosts who really haunt are the inexplicable phantoms of others: in their formulation, the phantom is primarily the afterimage of an unresolved trauma passing from the unconscious of parents and grandparents to that of their children, which operates in their mental topography with the voracity of a vampire and the mechanical nature of an automaton. Doni's demonic attendant in *Ernestus Berchtold* acts similarly, spreading death and misfortune among his fully unaware children.

William Michael's way of coping with the phantom was a fully Victorian one: the Spiritualist medium's table or the archive are both ways of negotiating the past precisely by leaving it past, thereby reinserting it within the continuum of history.⁵⁵ Dante Gabriel reacted in a completely different way – a reaction that, in the long run, would also kill him, if the prolonged ingestion of opioids can be considered as a long-term suicide by means of poison, but which, since Siddal's death, would enable him to create a deadly, pale feminine type combining the angelic appearance of Luisa Doni and the unnatural coldness of Lord Ruthven. In his late years he counted among his neighbours a young Irish writer named Bram Stoker: in 1892, Stoker would write a tale inspired by the legend of Siddal's hair, heralding a later novel and a lady in white walking amid the tombs of a London cemetery, the corpse bride of a much more powerful Master than Lord Ruthven.⁵⁶ But this is another, still unfinished, story.

Notes

1 The séance is related in William Michael Rossetti, *Rossetti Papers 1862 to 1870* (London: Sands & Co, 1903), pp. 157–61. Rossetti relied on a séance diary he kept at the time: see Andrew Stauffer, 'Speaking with the Dead: The Séance Diary of William Michael Rossetti, 1865–68', *The Journal of Pre-Raphaelite Studies*, 24 (Spring 2015), 35–43.
2 Rossetti, *Rossetti Papers*, p. 153.
3 I rely here on chapters 17 and 18 of Lucinda Hawksley, *Lizzie Siddal: The Tragedy of a Pre-Raphaelite Supermodel* (London: André Deutsch, 2004).
4 Anna Francesca Maddison, 'Conjugal Love and the Afterlife: New Readings of Selected Works by Dante Gabriel Rossetti in the Context of Swedenborgian-Spiritualism' (unpublished doctoral thesis, Edge Hill University, 2013), p. 72.
5 T. Hall Caine, *Recollections of Dante Gabriel Rossetti* (London: Elliot Stock, 1882), p. 59.
6 Quoted in William E. Fredeman, 'The Letters of Pictor Ignotus: William Bell Scott's Correspondence with Alice Boyd, 1859–1884. Part II', *Bulletin of the John Rylands Library*, 58:2 (1976), 306–52 (p. 339, n. 2).
7 Rossetti, *Rossetti Papers*, p. 159.
8 Quoted in Frank Podmore, *Modern Spiritualism: A History and a Criticism*, 2 vols (London: Methuen & Co., 1902), II, p. 48.
9 Rossetti, *Rossetti Papers*, p. 154.
10 Andrew Lang, *The Book of Dreams and Ghosts* (London: Longman, Green, and Co., 1897), p. viii.
11 Letter to Lord Byron, 3 May 1819, quoted in D. L. Macdonald, *Poor Polidori: A Critical Biography of the Author of 'The Vampyre'* (Toronto, ON: Toronto University Press, 1991), p. 182.
12 John William Polidori, *The Diary 1816: Relating to Byron, Shelley, etc.*, ed. by William Michael Rossetti (London: Elkin Mathews, 1911), p. 1.
13 Polidori, *The Diary*, p. 2. The memorials in questions are: Lord Broughton [John Hobhouse], *Recollections of a Long Life*, ed. by Lady Dorchester, 2 vols

(New York: Scribner's Sons, 1909); J. H. Leigh Hunt, *Lord Byron and Some of His Contemporaries; with Recollections of the Author's Life, and of His Visit to Italy* (London: Colburn, 1828); Thomas Medwin, *The Life of Percy Bysshe Shelley*, ed. by Harry Buxton Forman (London: Oxford University Press, 1913.

14 Macdonald, *Poor Polidori*, p. 5. The girls received instead an Anglican baptism.
15 Letter of Gaetano Polidori to John Polidori, November 1804, quoted in Macdonald, *Poor Polidori*, p. 9. For the anecdote of Dante in French, see Macdonald, *Poor Polidori*, p. 5.
16 Letter of John Polidori to Gaetano Polidori, December 1813, quoted in Macdonald, *Poor Polidori*, pp. 19–20.
17 See Anne Stiles, Stanley Finger, and John B. Bulevich, 'Somnambulism and Trance States in the Works of John William Polidori, Author of *The Vampyre*', *European Romantic Review*, 21:6 (2010), 789–807. This article is preceded by an English translation of Polidori's university dissertation by David E. Petrain: 'An English Translation of John William Polidori's (1815) Medical Dissertation on Oneirodynia (Somnambulism)', *European Romantic Review*, 21:6 (2010), 775–88.
18 Mary Shelley, 'Introduction', *Frankenstein; or, The Modern Prometheus*, ed. by M. K. Joseph (1831; Oxford: Oxford University Press, 1998), pp. 5–11 (p. 8); Polidori, *The Diary*, p. 123.
19 For the first two letters, see Macdonald, *Poor Polidori*, pp. 179–80. The letter to Hobhouse is, as far as I know, unpublished; I accessed it at the National Library of Scotland in Edinburgh (MS.42290). The last one was published in the issue of 24 September 1819 of the *Morning Chronicle*, p. 4.
20 [Alaric Watts], editorial note to 'The Vampyre', *The New Monthly Magazine*, 11:63 (1 April 1819), 195–96.
21 See Paul Barber, *Vampires, Burial, and Death* (London: Yale University Press, 1988) and Tommaso Braccini, *Prima di Dracula. Archeologia del vampiro* (Bologna: Il Mulino, 2011).
22 Lord George Gordon Byron, *The Giaour, Fragment of a Turkish Tale* (London: John Murray, 1813), pp. 37–38 (lines 747–70); p. 72; Shelley, *Frankenstein*, p. 77.
23 Letter of John Hobhouse to John Polidori, 29 April 1819, now at the National Library of Scotland (MS.42290).
24 '[Alfieri] mi aveva dimandato in diversi tempi s'io aveva letto la Divina Commedia di Dante, il Canzoniere del Petrarca, l'Orlando furioso e la Gerusalemme liberata, ed ogni volta ch'io gli aveva detto di sì, egli mi aveva sempre risposto sgarbatamente: 'Non è vero'. Nel 1787, accadde che il dotto e cortese abate Tommaso di Caluso venisse là a far dimora per qualche tempo, e [...] accadde che vedesse un giorno questi versi sul mio tavolino [...]. [...] L'Abate [...] disse [ad Alfieri] che aveva udito i miei versi e che gli eran piaciuti. 'Il mio segretario, rispos'egli, far versi! non lo credo: gli avrà rubati a qualcuno'. Questo insulto aggiunto al 'non è vero', destò in me ardente risentimento, ma lo tenni celato sperando che l'occasione mi si presentasse di farne vendetta. Quel medesimo giorno, [Alfieri] mi mandò a chiamare. [...] 'È cosa

curiosa e strana, mi disse, ch'io abbia un segretario che fa versi, e che non ne abbia prima saputo nulla. [...] Ha ella letto la Poetica d'Orazio? [...] 'No signore', gli risposi. 'Prenda Orazio'. Andai a prenderlo, e tornando col libro chiuso, cominciai a recitar la Poetica a mente. Egli allora si alzò incollerito e gridò ad alta voce. 'Ella si burla di me: mi dice che non ha letto la Poetica e la sa a mente!' 'Sì Signore, gli risposi, ma ogni volta ch'ella mi ha dimandato s'io aveva letto il tal libro e il tal altro, e che io le ho detto di sì, ella mi ha sempre risposto "non è vero": questa volta ho voluto dirlo io per non sentirmelo dire da lei'. (Gaetano Polidori, *La Magion del Terrore con note che contengono le memorie di quattro anni nei quali l'autore fu segretario del Conte Alfieri*, ed. by Roberto Fedi (Palermo: Sellerio, 1997), pp. 79–81, my translation. The book was originally published in 1843, but anecdotes about Alfieri must have been recurrent in the Polidori household.)

25 See Sotirios Paraschas, 'The Vampire as a Metaphor for Authorship from Polidori to Charles Nodier', *Compar(a)ison*, 1–2 (2015), 83–97.
26 'Extract of a Letter from Geneva, with Anecdotes of Lord Byron, &c', *The New Monthly Magazine*, 11:63 (1 April 1819), 193–95.
27 Henry R. Viets, 'The London Editions of Polidori's *The Vampyre*', *The Papers of the Bibliographical Society of America*, 63:2 (1969), 83–103 (p. 84). The 'Account of Lord Byron's Residence in the Island of Mitylene' had already been published by the magazine a year before and was signed by John Mitford, an occasional writer who was active in the low life of London periodicals (*The New Monthly Magazine*, 10:58 (1 November 1818), 309–11).
28 'Extract of a Letter from Geneva', pp. 194–95.
29 To Henry Colburn, 2 April 1819. Quoted in Polidori, *The Diary*, p. 15.
30 To the editors of *The New Monthly Magazine*, April 1819. *The New Monthly Magazine*, 11:64 (1 May 1819), 332.
31 Letter to the editor of the *Morning Chronicle*, 24 September 1819. Quoted in Polidori, *The Diary*, pp. 17–18.
32 Christopher Frayling, *Vampyres: Genesis and Resurrection from Count Dracula to Vampirella* (London: Thames & Hudson, 2016).
33 Polidori, *The Diary*, p. 13.
34 In the identification of 'Madame Gatelier' with the 'lady', however, Rossetti was followed by James Rieger, 'Dr. Polidori and the Genesis of *Frankenstein*', *Studies in English Literature 1500–1900*, 3:4 (Winter 1963), 461–72.
35 Viets, 'The London Editions', p. 96.
36 Macdonald, *Poor Polidori*, p. 178.
37 Andrew McConnell Stott, *The Poet and the Vampyre: The Curse of Byron and the Birth of Literature's Greatest Monster* (New York: Pegasus Books, 2014), p. 243.
38 D. L. Macdonald and Kathleen Scherf, 'A Note on the Texts', in John Polidori, *The Vampyre and Ernestus Berchtold; or, The Modern Oedipus: Collected Fiction of John William Polidori*, ed. by D. L. Macdonald and Kathleen Scherf (Peterborough, ON: Broadview, 2008), pp. 36–37 (p. 36). See Hobhouse's letter to Byron of 3 May 1819, quoted in Macdonald, *Poor Polidori*, p. 182.

39 Quoted in Macdonald, *Poor Polidori*, pp. 183–84.
40 Watts's letter, unpublished, is held at the National Library of Scotland. The date is missing, but internal references suggest it was written on 27 April 1819. For the detail of Polidori's copy, see 'Preliminaries for *The Vampyre*', in *The Vampyre and Other Tales of the Macabre*, ed. by Robert Morrison and Chris Baldick (Oxford: Oxford University Press, 1997), pp. 235–43 (p. 235).
41 For a detailed comparison of the two texts, see my 'A Note on the Publication History of John Polidori's *The Vampyre*', *Gothic Studies*, 22:3 (November 2020), 330–43.
42 Viets, 'The London Editions', p. 88 correctly identifies 'Breuss' as 'Bruce', without noticing the philological implications of the circumstance (Théodore Kourakine, ed., *Souvenirs des voyages de la princesse Natalie Kourakine 1816–1830* (Moscow: Grosman, 1903), pp. 82 and 129).
43 On the literary quarrel enflaming Italy in 1816, see my *Classicism and Romanticism in Italian Literature* (London: Pickering and Chatto, 2013).
44 In 1813, the English translator of *Fantasmagoriana*, Sarah Elizabeth Utterson, remarked that '[f]rom the period when the late Lord Orford first published The Castle of Otranto, till the production of Mrs. Ratcliffe's [*sic*] romances, the appetite for the species of reading in question gradually increased; and perhaps it would not have been now surfeited, but for the multitude of contemptible imitations which the popularity of the latter writer called forth, and which continually issued from the press, until the want of readers at length checked the inundation' (*Advertisement to Tales of the Dead* (London: White, Cochrane, and Co., 1813), pp. i–ii (p. i)).
45 Shelley, 'Introduction', *Frankenstein*, p. 7.
46 Polidori, *The Diary*, pp. 41 and 52.
47 William Michael Rossetti, 'Introduction', *The Diary of Dr. John William Polidori, 1816: Relating to Byron, Shelley, etc.*, ed. by William Michael Rossetti (London: Elkin Mathews, 1911), p. 4.
48 Dante Gabriel Rossetti, *His Family-Letters with a Memoir by William Michael Rossetti*, ed. by William Michael Rossetti, 2 vols (Boston, MA: Roberts Brothers, 1895), vol. I, pp. 221–22.
49 'Are you now happy?', quoted in Maddison, *Conjugal Love and the Afterlife*, pp. 147–48.
50 Nicolas Abraham, 'Notes on the Phantom: A Complement to Freud's Metapsychology', in Nicolas Abraham and Maria Torok, *The Shell and the Kernel: Renewals of Psychoanalysis*, ed. by Nicholas T. Rand (Chicago, IL: University of Chicago Press, 1994), pp. 171–76 (p. 171).
51 The text discussing this case is absent from the American edition: Nicolas Abraham, 'Notes du séminaire sur l'unité duelle et le fantôme', in Nicolas Abraham and Maria Torok, *L'Écorce et le noyau* (Paris: Flammarion, 1987), pp. 393–425 (pp. 408–11).
52 Macdonald, *Poor Polidori*, pp. 238–39.
53 Rossetti, *His Family-Letters*, I, p. 33.
54 See Serge Tisseron, *Secrets de famille, mode d'emploi* (Paris: Ramsay, 1996).

55 Jacques Derrida, *Mal d'archive: Une impression freudienne* (Paris: Galilée, 1995).
56 Stoker's 'The Secret of the Growing Gold' was originally published in the magazine *Black and White* on 23 January 1892. *Dracula* (1897) is dedicated to Rossetti's friend, Hall Caine, one of the first to disseminate the legend of Siddal's hair grown unnaturally in death.

4

Byromania: Polidori, fandom and the Romantic vampire's celebrity origins

Harriet Fletcher

From canonical Gothic texts to popular literature and media, there is a long-standing tradition of associations between vampirism and celebrity that can be traced back to the barely disguised representation of Lord Byron in John Polidori's *The Vampyre* (1819) – the first Gothic prose text to consciously engage with modern conceptions of fame. This essay maps the text's preoccupation with Byron's literary celebrity and Byronic fan culture primarily through the parasocial relationship: a perceived sense of intimacy between the fan and the celebrity catalysed by Byron's authorial personality. In Polidori's vampire tale, this manifests with Aubrey as a Gothicised model of the Byron fan or 'Byromaniac' who indulges in excessive reading and constructs fan fiction. This essay argues that Polidori uses vampirism to interrogate the workings of Byronic fan culture, particularly the mutual relationship of consumption between Byron and his readers. As I will show, the Byronic personality is the product of a thriving literary consumer culture and would not exist without an active and voracious readership that played a fundamental role in shaping, perpetuating and eventually immortalising this aspect of Byron's celebrity. Imagery of vampirism often appears in writing about Byron and his fans: for example, Frances Wilson argues that by seducing his readers, he made 'vampires' of them.[1] By making Gothic studies more central in this existing narrative surrounding Byron's literary celebrity, it can be said that Polidori not only constructs Byron's fame as a form of vampiric monstrosity, and in turn his fans as vampiric consumers, but illuminates the Gothic sensibilities of this parasocial relationship.

In Gothic studies, existing readings of Lord Ruthven have focused on Byronic attributes including aristocracy, sexuality and dandyism. David Punter acknowledges the character's connection to Byron as a representation of a wider mythologised class, arguing that Polidori's vampire 'requires blood because it is the business of aristocracy'.[2] Robert Morrison and Chris Baldick's introduction to *The Vampyre and Other Tales of the Macabre* (2008) emphasises the Byronic rakery of Lord Ruthven by arguing that Polidori's vampire story is 'a tale designed as a warning against the fascinating power of libertinism represented by Byron'.³ Catherine Spooner's *Fashioning Gothic Bodies* (2004) uses Lord Ruthven's Byronic dandyism to argue that this character is the template for a new kind of stylish Gothic villain, which developed from the Byronic hero.⁴

The Vampyre is clearly fertile ground for Byronic readings, but no one has drawn out the text's obvious preoccupation with Byron's celebrity. For Nick Groom in *The Vampire: A New History* (2018), 'Our age has reworked the vampire into an all-embracing cipher, a cosmic vessel to be filled and refilled with endless readings and re-readings – a veritable multiplicity.'⁵ While this may be true of many readings, acknowledging the preoccupation with celebrity in *The Vampyre* is an exception. This is not simply a case of projecting new meaning onto the vampire, but uncovering an integral facet of Polidori's text that has been present since its creation and inspired the image of the modern vampire as we know it. The desire elicited by the Romantic vampire fundamentally works on the level of celebrity and this elicited desire can be experienced on the level of fandom.

The Vampyre is inseparable from discourses of fandom because the sensational appeal of Byron's celebrity enabled the story to be published. When the original manuscript arrived at the office of *The New Monthly Magazine* in autumn of 1818 – ostensibly written by Byron but not authenticated with a signature – it was accompanied by a letter detailing his supposed adventures in Lake Geneva during the summer of 1816.⁶ Notably, the author of the letter recalls a moment when a woman was so overwhelmed by meeting the famous poet that she fainted: 'It is said, indeed, that upon paying his first visit at Coppet, following the servant who had announced his name, he was surprised to meet a lady carried out fainting.'⁷ After experiencing a decline in sales, the publisher Henry Colburn's decision to print the vampire story as 'A Tale by Lord Byron' alongside the accompanying letter demonstrates the growing commercial value of celebrity in the Regency literary marketplace.⁸ *The New Monthly Magazine* vampirically fed from Byron's celebrity to create a more enticing narrative for an increasingly active readership driven by a desire for the author's personality.

Lord Byron's rise to fame and the Romantic cult of personality

While Byron's Romantic and posthumous celebrity image is multifaceted, encompassing qualities such as his status as a sex symbol, a fashion icon and a figure of notoriety, the many facets of this image were chiefly enabled by his status as a poet. This essay therefore regards Byron as first and foremost a literary celebrity. For Tom Mole, celebrity became a modern cultural phenomenon 'because it answered an "urgent need" created by the industrialised print culture of the Romantic period'.[9] This encapsulates Byron's rise to fame, which is characterised by an instant form of celebrity-making that is facilitated by mass print culture and its rapid circulation of material. Significant technological developments at the turn of the century in papermaking, printing and engraving, along with improvements in infrastructure and new promotional opportunities afforded by an enlarged market for newspapers, magazines and literacy journals, led to the mass production of literary works in record numbers that were then distributed nationally and later internationally.[10] By the turn of the century, literacy rates had also increased, meaning that the demand for reading material was greater than ever and there was now a technologically advanced literary industry prepared to cater for this demand.[11]

Byron was propelled into this new culture of literary celebrity following the publication of the first two cantos of *Childe Harold's Pilgrimage* (1812–18), which he wrote during his Grand Tour through the Mediterranean (1809–11). The poem contained a fictional account of this journey and was published by John Murray in March 1812, after Byron had returned to England.[12] Initially targeted towards an exclusive group of affluent upper-class readers, the poem sold out in three days and Byron became an overnight sensation.[13] This triumph prompted his renowned statement, 'I awoke one morning and found myself famous'.[14] In 1812, after the publication of *Childe Harold's Pilgrimage*, the Duchess of Devonshire (herself no stranger to the world of celebrity) remarked that Byron 'is really the only topic of almost every conversation – the men jealous of him, the women of each other'.[15] Murray's plan for the poem was to establish it among this elite group of readers, then branch out to wider audiences with cheaper editions, which is when Byron would achieve fame among the masses.[16] The publication of *Childe Harold's Pilgrimage* reveals the emergence of a new form of celebrity that is emblematic of modernity – one that is constantly in motion, evolving and diversifying with new audiences and trends, much like the industry that manufactured it.

From these events, it is possible to map the evolution of Byron's fame from poet to personality, the latter being an essential component for the formation of modern literary celebrity, and in turn Byronic fan culture. David Higgins notes that the growth of the periodical was the most crucial development for the emergence of a literary celebrity culture because certain writers, like Byron, became of interest to the public as much for their personal appearance and private lives as for their literary works.[17] This interest in the author as a personality is in dialogue with an increasing number of literary works being published with the author's name as opposed to anonymously.[18] As authors become recognisable to audiences, literary celebrity becomes closely tied to the consumerism at the heart of print culture because popular known authors effectively become unique brands that can be marketed as commodities by publishers – *The New Monthly Magazine* publishing Polidori's *The Vampyre* as 'A Tale By Lord Byron' being a prime example. This suggests that personality – encompassing a persona, an image and a set of signifiers that correspond to this personality – is taking precedence over the author's status as a producer of literature. In this modern literary celebrity culture, the author and the personality are inseparable, and the latter is key to the former's ability to achieve celebrity status among a mainstream readership.

Byromania and the desire for intimacy

After the success of *Childe Harold's Pilgrimage*, Byron's celebrity status gained an important dimension through a new culture of literary fandom, which was enabled by the accessibility of print and visual material. While fandom is a modern concept that is usually explored in media and cultural studies using twentieth- and twenty-first-century case studies, I will be using this term to describe Byron's readership because it exhibits many similarities to our understanding of fan culture in the present day. As Henry Jenkins argues, 'fandom originates in response to specific historical conditions', citing the development of new technologies as a key factor.[19] Byron's fandom, or 'Byromania', as it was dubbed by the poet's wife Annabella Milbanke, is born out of the industrialisation of print culture and rise of modern celebrity culture in the early nineteenth century.[20] For Corin Throsby, the genesis of modern fan culture can be traced back to the Romantic period, when the largest and most collective group of readers were of Byron's poetry.[21] Byron was one of the first writers to receive fan mail in the form of unsolicited letters from his readership, which he received on a mass scale.[22] Additionally, fans would gather outside his publisher's office on Albemarle Street, hoping to see Byron in the flesh or receive a copy of his latest work.[23] Readers would also engage in creative activities such as writing fan fiction, which involves creating a new narrative based on the original work. Legitimate excerpts of Byron's work were published alongside various recreations of poems attributed to Byron, poems written in his authorial voice, responses to his poetry and continuations of his printed work.[24] Byron himself also became the subject of fan fiction, in which mock-Byronic narratives were written with the poet as the central character.[25]

If personality is the driving force behind Byron's literary celebrity, then exclusive access to this personality becomes a central concern for his fans. This can be seen in the semi-autobiographical elements of *Childe Harold's Pilgrimage*, which played a significant role in exposing Byron's private life to readers. One of Mole's most compelling arguments deals with the historical context of industrial growth and claims that celebrity culture constructed a sense of intimacy with audiences to relieve feelings of alienation. This is particularly present in Byron's work: 'Instead of appearing as industrial productions competing for attention in a crowded market made up of increasingly estranged readers and writers, the poems fostered a hermeneutic of intimacy.'[26] In a fan studies and celebrity studies context, this intimacy is known as a parasocial relationship. The term was coined by psychologists Donald Horton and Richard Wohl in their 1956 study of television and refers to the illusion of intimacy between audiences and performers.[27] While parasocial relationships were originally explored in the context of television audiences, they are equally applicable to readers of literary texts. This is corroborated by Chris Rojek, who explains that in early print culture, celebrity authors found that they were 'plagued by adoring fans who supposed that, by virtue of being familiar with their words in print, they were on intimate terms with them'.[28] In the case of Byron, Mole notes that his poems fostered intimacy with readers due to the suggestion that they 'could only be understood fully by referring to their author's personality, that reading them was entering a kind of relationship with the author and that that relationship resembled an intimate connection between individuals'.[29] The instant success of *Childe Harold's Pilgrimage* indicates that Byron was able to capitalise on this relationship of intimacy by placing himself in his work, and in doing so constructing a provocative celebrity persona centred on the pleasure of scandal for public consumption.

This desire for intimacy is also reinforced by the volume of visual material that accompanied the author's works. For Ghislaine McDayter, the phenomenon of Byromania was not simply born out of the production and consumption of literature, but the proliferation of new media forms.[30] These include prints and engravings that contributed to Byron's visual celebrity, many of which were based on his official portraits and were reproduced in editions of his poetry and in separate engravings for individual purchase.[31] The mass circulation of these visual materials creates another layer to the personality of the author by allowing them to be seen, and therefore desired. Visual celebrity is key to constructing this desire that is central to Byronic fan culture. A named author creates a certain level of intimacy for fans by allowing the author to be known, but the physical image of the author takes this one step further by allowing the author to be seen. The physical image of Byron in the form of a print or engraving is effectively a canvas onto which fantasy narratives can be projected by fans, a practice already encouraged by his poetry through the suggestion that the Byronic heroes are models of him. The accessibility of Byron-related material, both print and visual, enables readers to develop an attachment to the author and therefore gives them permission to become fans and affords them agency to engage in fan activity.

Celebrity vampires: Lord Ruthven and beyond

Polidori redefines the Gothic, not only by orchestrating the birth of the modern, Romantic vampire in the form of the Byronic Lord Ruthven, but by inaugurated an extensive tradition of vampires modelling celebrity that continued throughout the nineteenth century and flourished in twentieth- and twenty-first-century popular culture. The extent of this tradition is unsurprising when considering the historical affinity between the Gothic and celebrity. The term 'celebrity', referring to the state of being well known, was used by Samuel Johnson in a 1751 article for *The Rambler* to describe his personal attribute, while the term 'star' emerged in Romantic writing in 1824 to mean 'a person of brilliant reputation or talents', which is also the year of Byron's death.[32] These emerging discourses of celebrity are contemporaneous with the rise of the Gothic novel in the eighteenth century through Horace Walpole's 'Gothic Story' *The Castle of Otranto* (1764). From Polidori and beyond, the Gothic mode perpetually demonstrates its suitability for representing and interrogating celebrity because, as Mark Edmundson puts it, celebrity itself 'has a streak of Gothic running through it'.[33]

A key facet of Polidori's legacy, 'the celebrity vampire tradition', as I call it, is a body of vampire texts that fictionalise real-life celebrities or portray vampires as famous individuals. Fictional vampires are afforded celebrity status, such as in Anne Rice's novels *Interview with the Vampire* (1976), where the vampire is celebrified through the interview, and *The Vampire Lestat* (1985) and *Queen of the Damned* (1988), which detail the life of the vampire-turned-rock star Lestat de Lioncourt. Real-life celebrities are also fictionalised as vampiric versions of themselves, or, in the case of visual media, a high-profile celebrity is cast in the role of a fictional vampire that often resonates with their own celebrity image. In literature, examples include the fictionalisation of the Victorian actor-manager Sir Henry Irving in Bram Stoker's *Dracula* (1897) and the Victorian theatre star Mrs Patrick Campbell in Rudyard Kipling's poem 'The Vampire' (1898). In film and television, David Bowie is cast as the rapidly ageing vampire John Blaylock in *The Hunger* (1983), Aaliyah as the Queen of Vampires Akasha in *Queen of the Damned* (2002) and Lady Gaga as the Countess in *American Horror Story: Hotel* (2015). The fan is never far from the object of their adoration in celebrity vampire texts and often demonstrates their own vampiric characteristics, which is best demonstrated in *Interview with the Vampire* when the interviewer is so captivated by Louis's story that he desires the vampire lifestyle for himself. Polidori assembles the blueprint for this vampiric relationship between celebrities and fans in Gothic texts through his depiction of Lord Ruthven as a model of Byron and Aubrey as a model of the Byron fan.

The fascination with vampires in Western culture is undoubtedly concerned with the Romantic vampire more than any of this Gothic figure's other manifestations, which is epitomised by beautiful, stylish and sophisticated characters like Lord Ruthven and Anne Rice's Lestat de Lioncourt, both of whom are 'enchanting companions' and 'media stars', according to Nina Auerbach.[34] As Spooner rightly points out, this type of vampire is 'more likely to be regarded as a desirable romantic partner than a bloodthirsty killer'.[35] The Romantic vampire's celebrity origins have been touched upon by a small number of critics but have not formed the basis of an in-depth study. Sorcha Ní Fhlainn draws out the celebrity elements of late-twentieth-century novels such as Michael Romkey's *I, Vampire* (1990) and Kim Newman's *Anno Dracula* (1992) due to their vampiric depictions of real-life historical figures.[36] Fred Botting takes this further by observing that Rice's postmodern vampire 'signifies a creature at the heart of the lifestyles and identities of consumer culture'.[37] Cinematic adaptations starring A-list Hollywood actors such as Neil Jordan's *Interview with the Vampire* (1994) then augment the desirability of Rice's vampires by enabling them to 'assume the glitzy celebrity glossing consumer culture and orientating its desires'.[38] Tracing this figure back to Polidori's *The Vampyre*, Spooner argues: 'Byron, widely described as the first celebrity in the modern sense of the word, provides a model that informs the development of the vampire myth in the succeeding two centuries: witty, aristocratic, intelligent, tormented and wildly sexually attractive to both sexes.'[39]

While acknowledging the importance of Rice and other notable late-twentieth-century authors, it is possible to uncover a longer history of the celebrity vampire. The modern vampire in Polidori's prose fiction was Romantic, glamorous and desirable because it was an embodiment of a new brand of literary celebrity in the early nineteenth century whereby the author was no longer an anonymous remote figure but a commercial personality who can be known, seen and, most importantly, desired by fans. While Spooner acknowledges the influence of Byron through various traits that inform later vampire narratives, her observation underestimates the complexity of his celebrity because his poetic personality must be examined in relation to his readers, whose fan activities are vital for developing and consolidating this quintessential Byronic image. Byron's named literary work alone constructed a desire for the poet, but the addition of his personality catered for this desire by sparking the imagination of his fans. *The Vampyre* gothicises these attributes of Byron's celebrity through Aubrey's obsessive reading and the creation of fan fiction narratives.

Byromaniacs: Readers as fans

In Polidori's *The Vampyre*, Aubrey's fan behaviour manifests in two distinct ways: reading Romance texts, and as a result constructing a parasocial relationship with the author. Aubrey's reading can be explored from a fan studies perspective because the character more widely engages in activities and behaviours that are central concerns in this field of criticism, including producing fan fiction and desiring intimacy with the object of his attachment. Fan studies is historically situated in the late twentieth century and tends to explore specific media texts, such as popular television series.[40] However, this chapter focuses on early-nineteenth-century Gothic literature and depictions of the reader as a fan to develop a celebrity-focused reading of Polidori's *The Vampyre* through the discourse of fan studies. If fandom, according to Cornel Sandvoss, can be defined as the 'regular, emotionally involved consumption of a given popular narrative or text', then Aubrey's reading can certainly be regarded as a mode of fandom.[41]

The term 'romance' is used several times in *The Vampyre* to describe Aubrey's reading habits, which is particularly revealing when considering that Byron's poetry draws on this literary tradition. Defined as 'a fictional story in verse or prose that relates improbable adventures of idealised characters in some remote or enchanted setting', Romance is a suitable term to describe Byron's early poetic work.[42] For example, the advertisement that appears in the 1813 printed edition of *The Giaour* describes the poem as the 'adventures of a female slave, who was thrown, in the Mussulman manner, into the sea for infidelity, and avenged by a young Venetian, her lover, at the time the Seven Islands were possessed by the Republic of Venice'.[43] McDayter makes a connection between Byron's Romance poems and Byromania by noting the belief that they 'fed the frenzy of the poet's fan base, and ultimately created the monster of Byromania since these poems were read as erotic fantasies'.[44] Taking this into account, it is highly likely that 'romance' in *The Vampyre* is in part referring to Byron's early verse tales, such as *Childe Harold's Pilgrimage* and the Turkish Tales, which also happen to be recognisable intertexts in Polidori's tale.[45]

Aubrey is described as a keen reader of poetry: 'He thought, in fine, that the dreams of poets were the realities of life.'[46] He also indulges in 'solitary hours' reading 'volumes' of 'romance' containing 'pleasing pictures and descriptions'.[47] In 1816, when Polidori was writing *The Vampyre*, Byron was internationally famous; his poetry was widely published and read among both fashionable audiences and the wider reading public. Byron's work would certainly be known to a reader like Aubrey, who socio-economically fits the image of the implied reader that Byron became associated with following his rise to fame. Aubrey is a 'young gentleman' who is in 'possession of great wealth' and evidently well read with a passion for Romance literature.[48] Mole notes that the first edition of *Childe Harold's Pilgrimage* was initially sold to Regency fashionable society as an 'elite group of trendsetters' in order to generate interest.[49] Equally, many of the early readers of *The Giaour* belonged to the upper levels of this society.[50] Aubrey too belongs to Regency fashionable society and can be regarded as part of this elite class that had privileged access to Byron's newly published work.

Through Aubrey's obsessive Romance reading, with implied connections to Byronic Romance, Polidori creates a monstrous image of fan behaviour that gothicises Byron's relationship with his readers. First, Aubrey's fan activity is portrayed as a clandestine solitary practice, which stands in opposition to common fan activities practiced by readers of Byron in Regency fashionable society:

> Attached as he was to the romance of his solitary hours, he was startled at finding, that, except in the tallow and wax candles that flickered, not from the presence of a ghost, but from want of snuffing, there was no foundation in real life for any of that congeries of pleasing pictures and descriptions contained in those volumes, from which he had formed his study.[51]

Throsby notes that commonplacing (a form of scrapbooking) was a popular activity for readers, who would collect Byron-related writings and images and compile them in books.[52] Most importantly, commonplace books were often shared among multiple readers, displayed in homes and circulated among friends and visitors.[53] This particular fan activity is remarkably social: there is a clear sense of community and shared pleasure in reading and discussing Byron with like-minded others. From Throsby's descriptions, there is scope to argue for the commonplacing book as an early example of the fanzine – a niche publication that similarly offers a place for fans to socialise and express their creativity.[54] In contrast, the solitary nature of Aubrey's reading appears obsessive, creating a more psychologically disturbing image of fandom compared to the commonplacing activities of society drawing rooms. For Mark Duffett, collecting is an important fan activity and the placement of the fan's collection in a domestic space can 'manifest the individual self in a way that is a potential focus for either shared pleasures or anxieties and conflicts'.[55] Unlike the society drawing room, the setting of a darkened room with 'wax candles that flickered' is not a social space that others can be invited into. Aubrey's collection of Romance literature is certainly not designed for shared pleasure like the commonplacing book, which suggests that his engagement with it is unhealthy and potentially sinister. This image of Aubrey's reading space suggests that there is something ritualistic and pseudo-religious about this activity. Aubrey's reading appears less like a social activity and more like a form of worship. This image of toxic fandom is often reproduced in contemporary culture, a key example being Eminem's music video for 'Stan' (2000), in which an obsessive fan writes letters to the rapper in a secret darkened basement decorated with posters of his idol.[56]

For Jenkins, fandom is a social experience. He stresses that the 'ability to transform personal reaction into social interaction, spectatorial culture into participatory culture, is one of the central characteristics of fandom'.[57] However, Aubrey's fan behaviour is distinctly antisocial. This does not erase Aubrey's status as a fan, but instead suggests that his fandom operates inversely to social norms within Byronic fan culture. In the eyes of Regency society, a fan activity like commonplacing can be regarded as a healthy way of channelling fandom and therefore containing the perceived threat of obsessive behaviour that notoriously surrounds the fan in modern culture. Yet Aubrey's solitary fan activity refuses to be contained in such a way and creates a significant slippage between fandom and obsession. It is Aubrey's disruption of the norm that gothicises his fandom.

Echoes of Aubrey's Gothic fandom can be found in sensationalised accounts of Lady Caroline Lamb, the author of *Glenarvon* (1816) – a key source of inspiration for Polidori's Lord Ruthven – and Byron's most notorious former lover. Lamb is often figured as both an obsessive Byromaniac and a hysterical lover who is reported to have done some outrageous deeds during her affair with Byron, including sending him cuttings of her pubic hair, cutting her wrist at Lady Heathcote's ball, breaking into his rooms to inscribe 'Remember me' in his copy of *Vathek* (1786) and performing a ritual that involved burning his effigy on a pyre at Brocket Hall while village girls wearing livery inscribed with *Ne Crede Byron* (don't trust Byron) danced chanting round the flames.[58] These exploits create a gothicised narrative around Lamb as a fan figure that parallels the excessive image of fandom that Polidori constructs. Lamb's style of fandom resonates with later Gothic texts that portray the fan as a fanatic, a prime example being Stephen King's novel *Misery* (1987) and Kathy Bates's chilling performance in the 1990 film version.[59] This is a distinctly Gothic rendering of the fan that has possible roots in Byromania. Lamb's obsessive behaviour as a reader of Byron has become a representation of Byron's wider fan culture; as McDayter notes, 'references to Byron's readers as "squealing females" and neurotics have become commonplace and largely unquestioned in Romantic criticism'.[60] Through Aubrey's obsessive reading of Romance, with the implication that this literature may well be Byronic, and his subsequent obsession with

Romantic heroes that drives him to fixate on Lord Ruthven, the character exhibits fanatical sensibilities and is figured as the kind of Byron reader that Lamb typifies: infatuated, excessive, melodramatic and desiring. By constructing Aubrey as a double of Lamb, Polidori further critiques Byron's fan culture by emphasising its Gothic aspects as something that is uncontrollable and addictive but potentially dangerous and unsettling.

Fan fiction and fantasies of intimacy

Reading Romance grants Aubrey an intimate connection with the author that makes him feel entirely unique – a dynamic that typifies Byron's work and the fan culture that it created. For Mole, this intimacy is maintained by the belief that Byron reveals himself in his poetry and that his poetry offers readers a form of access to him.[61] This is perfectly exemplified by the interplay between fiction and reality in *Childe Harold's Pilgrimage*. The poem contains many semi-autobiographical narrative events that mirror Byron's experiences during his Grand Tour through the Mediterranean. Most importantly, though, a rather perverse dedication to 'Ianthe' (an alias for the adolescent daughter of his lover Lady Oxford) creates a Romance narrative between the poet and Ianthe that emphasises her uniqueness and resonates with readers who wish to experience this themselves:

> Such is thy name with this my verse entwined;
> And long as kinder eyes a look shall cast
> On Harold's page, Ianthe's here enshrined
> Shall thus be first beheld, forgotten last.[62]

Mole argues that this dedication 'fantasises that although *Childe Harold's Pilgrimage* is sold to a faceless commercial audience, it is received by a single special reader, who accepts it as a billet-doux inviting her to a reading which is a kind of tryst'.[63]

For Romance readers such as Aubrey, the thrill of reading Byron's poetry is not only gaining intimate access to him but acquiring hidden knowledge about him and attempting to pin down his elusive personality. Mole draws attention to a similar phenomenon in *The Giaour*, noting that 'Byron used the fragmentary form and multiple editions of *The Giaour* to arouse his readers' desire to possess the story completely'.[64] As a result, this desire 'overflowed the poem and fixed on the poet as its object'.[65] Aubrey's belief that 'the dreams of poets were the realities of life' suggests a blurring of fiction and reality in the mind of the reader that speaks to the parasocial relationship enabled by Byron's poetry and personality. As a reader of Romance and a likely reader of Byronic Romance due to the established connections between Byron's poetry and the Romance tradition, Aubrey behaves as though he is seduced by the kind of authorial personality that Byron cultivated. His parasocial relationship collapses the distinction between the fictional world of Romantic heroes and the author who creates them, meaning that the celebrity can be known and accessed on intimate terms that are not available to him in real life.

Aubrey's parasocial relationship evolves from reading Romance to constructing his own narratives, which draws on the popular trend of Byronic fan fiction. Aubrey imagines Lord Ruthven as a real-life manifestation of his literary fantasies. He is described as lamenting the dullness of real life and longing for the kind of excitement that Romance literature gives him. Lord Ruthven soon fulfils this desire for Aubrey when the two cross paths in Regency fashionable society: 'he was about to relinquish his dreams, when the extraordinary being we have above described, crossed him in his career'.[66] Aubrey's fan behaviour towards Lord Ruthven manifests by regarding him as a work of fiction: 'allowing his imagination to picture every thing that flattered its propensity to extravagant ideas, he soon formed this object into the hero of a romance, and determined to observe the offspring of his fancy, rather than the person before him'.[67] Aubrey's image of Lord Ruthven as 'the hero of a romance' may well refer to the Byronic hero because, in Aubrey's mind, Lord Ruthven takes on the role of the lead character from the kind of Romance literature he has been reading.

Aubrey's pleasure in constructing these narratives echoes that of amateur writers who would send Byron poems written in the latter's own style, as well as alternative cantos and endings to his work, some of which were actually published.[68] For Jenkins, fan fiction is a way for individuals to 'actively assert their mastery over the mass-produced texts which provide the raw materials for their own cultural productions'.[69] In the process of creating fan fiction, fans become 'active participants in the construction and circulation of textual meaning'.[70] Jenkins draws on the work of Michel de Certeau to characterise this practice as textual poaching, whereby fans 'salvage texts for their interests rather than dismiss them altogether'.[71] Aubrey effectively creates a fan fiction narrative that casts Lord Ruthven as a Romantic, perhaps even Byronic, hero. Due to the widely held belief that Byron's heroes are models of himself, fan fiction affords a reader like Aubrey access to Byron through the construction of a fictional world in which a personal encounter with Lord Ruthven becomes equivalent to an encounter with Byron. The motivation for this narrative is intimacy with the author on the level of fandom, with the potential for eroticism. Throsby explains that works of Byronic fan fiction made the usually clear-cut boundary between author and reader difficult to define.[72] In the practice of fan fiction, the reader also becomes the author, and the fan becomes the author-fan. If there are no clear boundaries to separate the roles of author and reader, then fan fiction creates a significant level of intimacy that allows readers to step into the author's world and create narratives that are special to them as individuals. As Duffett explains, writing fan fiction allows fans to feel more invested in characters and explore them in richer narrative worlds.[73]

The Gothic literary model for Aubrey and Lord Ruthven's parasocial relationship can be located in Byron's unfinished vampire tale 'A Fragment' (1819). Like Aubrey, the unnamed narrator of Byron's narrative is in awe of the Lord Ruthven-esque character Augustus Darvell and takes on the role of the fan. In fact, the term 'intimacy' is used several times throughout the text to describe the relationship between the two characters from the perspective of the narrator:

> My advances were received with sufficient coldness; but I was young, and not easily discouraged, and at length succeeded in obtaining, to a certain degree, that common-place intercourse and moderate confidence of common and every day concerns, created and cemented by similarity of pursuit and frequency of meeting, which is called intimacy.[74]

For Auerbach, this emphasis on intimacy refers to homosocial friendship, but a celebrity-focused reading reveals that it sets up the narrator's desire for access and knowledge of Darvell on the level of fandom.[75] This passage adds a sinister edge to the narrator, whose efforts to gain access to Darvell are comparable to stalking. He endeavours to achieve access by relentlessly watching and following the object of his fandom until, in keeping with vampire lore, he can gain their trust and be invited in, allowing him to become the vampiric fan to Darvell's vampiric celebrity. Traces of the Gothic fan in Byron's unfinished celebrity vampire narrative reinforce the vampiric nature of the celebrity–fan relationship in Polidori's tale, which itself is a work of fan fiction as a rewriting of Byron's 'A Fragment'. Aubrey echoes the image of the Byron fan who desires intimacy with the author after reading Romance, and Lord Ruthven is a vehicle for simulating this intimacy because he is a real-life Byronic individual that Aubrey can access and form an attachment to.

Conclusion

Forming the blueprint for a rich tradition of celebrity vampire texts, the defining legacy of Polidori's *The Vampyre* is the synthesis of vampirism and celebrity that was first inspired by Byron's unprecedented level of fame in Regency print culture. Fandom and celebrity are intrinsically woven into the Romantic vampire and its progeny. Aubrey's obsession with Romance fiction and subsequently the Byronic Lord Ruthven brings to the surface the vampiric qualities of the Byromaniac who feeds from the poet and reproduces his work through fan fiction fantasies. However, this vampiric relationship between Byron and his readers must be understood as mutually beneficial because the labour of fans enables the Byronic personality to exist, evolve and eventually transcend his poetry. If Byron is always bound up with his Byronic heroes, then he is immortalised through such characters and lives on through every new poem and newly published edition, whether authorised or fan constructed. As a work of fan fiction, Polidori's *The Vampyre* plays a significant role in this preservation of Byron's image. By remaking the vampire in the sophisticated and desirable image of Byron's Romantic celebrity, Polidori has immortalised the poet through this Gothic trope. From Lord Ruthven to Lestat de Lioncourt and beyond, the Byronic personality, and in turn discourses of celebrity, are inseparable from the Romantic vampire.

Notes

1. Frances Wilson, 'Byron, Byronism and Byromaniacs', in *Byromania: Portraits of the Artist in Nineteenth- and Twentieth-Century Culture*, ed. by Francis Wilson (Basingstoke: Palgrave Macmillan, 1999), pp. 1–24 (p. 15).
2. David Punter, *The Literature of Terror: A History of Gothic Fictions From 1765 to the Present Day*, 2 vols (New York: Longmans, 1996), i: *The Gothic Tradition*, p. 104.
3. Robert Morrison and Chris Baldick, 'Introduction', *The Vampyre and Other Tales of the Macabre*, ed. by Robert Morrison and Chris Baldick (Oxford: Oxford University Press, 2008), pp. vii–xxiii (p. xix).
4. Catherine Spooner, *Fashioning Gothic Bodies* (Manchester: Manchester University Press, 2004), p. 96.
5. Nick Groom, *The Vampire: A New History* (New Haven, CT: Yale University Press, 2018), p. 201.
6. D. L. Macdonald, *Poor Polidori: A Critical Biography of the Author of 'The Vampyre'* (Toronto, ON: University of Toronto Press, 1991), pp. 177–84; p. 276, n. 3.
7. 'Preliminaries for *The Vampyre*', in *The Vampyre and Other Tales of the Macabre*, ed. by Robert Morrison and Chris Baldick (Oxford: Oxford University Press, 2008), pp. 235–43 (p. 238).
8. Morrison and Baldick, 'Introduction', *The Vampyre and Other Tales*, pp. vii–viii.
9. Tom Mole, *Byron's Romantic Celebrity: Industrial Culture and the Hermeneutic of Intimacy* (London: Palgrave Macmillan, 2007), p. 10.
10. Mole, *Byron's Romantic Celebrity*, p. 2.
11. Mole, *Byron's Romantic Celebrity*, p. 10.

12 Jerome McGann, 'Byron, George Gordon Noel, Sixth Baron Byron (1788–1824), Poet', in *Oxford Dictionary of National Biography*, ed. by H. C. G. Matthew and Brian Howard Harrison (Oxford: Oxford University Press, 2004), pp. 1–32 (p. 15).
13 McGann, 'Byron', p. 15.
14 Lord Byron, *Letters and Journals of Lord Byron: With Notices of His Life*, ed. by Thomas Moore, 2 vols (New York: Harper & Brothers, 1855), I, p. 255.
15 The Duchess of Devonshire, quoted in Samuel Rogers, *Table Talk* (New York: Appleton, 1856), p. 229.
16 Mole, *Byron's Romantic Celebrity*, p. 55.
17 David Higgins, 'Celebrity, Politics and the Rhetoric of Genius', in *Romanticism and Celebrity Culture 1750–1850*, ed. by Tom Mole (Cambridge: Cambridge University Press, 2009), pp. 41–60 (p. 42).
18 Mole, *Byron's Romantic Celebrity*, pp. 11–12.
19 Henry Jenkins, *Textual Poachers: Television Fans and Participatory Culture* (London: Routledge, 2013), p. 3.
20 Wilson, 'Byron', p. 3.
21 Corin Throsby, 'Byron, Commonplacing and Early Fan Culture', in *Romanticism and Celebrity Culture 1750–1850*, ed. by Tom Mole (Cambridge: Cambridge University Press, 2009), pp. 227–45 (p. 227).
22 Throsby, 'Byron', p. 228.
23 Ghislaine McDayter, *Byromania and the Birth of Celebrity Culture* (Albany, NY: SUNY Press, 2009), p. 3.
24 McDayter, *Byromania*, p. 115.
25 Throsby, 'Byron', p. 228.
26 Mole, *Byron's Romantic Celebrity*, pp. 22–23.
27 Chris Rojek, *Fame Attack: The Inflation of Celebrity and Its Consequences* (London: Bloomsbury Academic, 2012), p. 124.
28 Rojek, *Fame Attack*, p. 124.
29 Mole, *Byron's Romantic Celebrity*, p. 23.
30 McDayter, *Byromania*, p. 108.
31 McDayter, *Byromania*, p. 106.
32 Samuel Johnson, *The Rambler*, ed. by Alex Chalmers, 4 vols (Philadelphia, PA: E. Earle, 1812), IV, p. 42; Mole, *Byron's Romantic Celebrity*, p. xii.
33 Mark Edmundson, *Nightmare on Main Street: Angels, Sadomasochism, and the Culture of Gothic* (Cambridge, MA: Harvard University Press, 1997), pp. 88–89.
34 Nina Auerbach, *Our Vampires, Ourselves* (Chicago, IL: University of Chicago Press, 1995), p. 1.
35 Catherine Spooner, *Post-Millennial Gothic: Comedy, Romance and the Rise of Happy Gothic* (London: Bloomsbury Academic, 2017), p. 83.
36 Sorcha Ní Fhlainn, *Postmodern Vampires: Film, Fiction, and Popular Culture* (London: Palgrave Macmillan, 2019), pp. 98–100.
37 Fred Botting, *Gothic*, 2nd edn (New York: Routledge, 2014), p. 188.
38 Fred Botting, *Limits of Horror: Technology, Bodies, Gothic* (Manchester: Manchester University Press, 2013), p. 41.

39 Spooner, *Post-Millennial Gothic*, p. 85.
40 Karen Hellekson and Kristina Busse, 'Introduction: Why a Fan Fiction Studies Reader Now?', in *The Fan Fiction Studies Reader*, ed. by Karen Hellekson and Kristina Busse (Iowa City: University of Iowa Press, 2014), pp. 1–19 (p. 7).
41 Cornel Sandvoss, *Fans: The Mirror of Consumption* (Cambridge: Polity Press, 2005), p. 8.
42 'Romance', *The Oxford Dictionary of Literary Terms* www.oxfordreference.com/view/10.1093/acref/9780198715443.001.0001/acref-9780198715443-e-997 [accessed 4 February 2022].
43 Lord Byron, *The Giaour*, in *Lord Byron: The Major Works*, ed. by Jerome J. McGann (Oxford: Oxford University Press, 2008), pp. 207–47 (p. 207).
44 McDayter, *Byromania*, p. 33.
45 The Turkish Tales include *The Giaour* (1813), *The Bride of Abydos* (1813), *The Corsair* (1814), *Lara, A Tale* (1814) and *The Siege of Corinth* (1816).
46 John Polidori, *The Vampyre*, Appendix 1 in this volume, pp. 240–67 (p. 247).
47 Polidori, *The Vampyre*, p. 247.
48 Polidori, *The Vampyre*, p. 247.
49 Mole, *Byron's Romantic Celebrity*, p. 55.
50 Mole, *Byron's Romantic Celebrity*, p. 72.
51 Polidori, *The Vampyre*, p. 247.
52 Throsby, 'Byron', p. 236.
53 Throsby, 'Byron', p. 230.
54 Mark Duffett, *Understanding Fandom: An Introduction to the Study of Media Fan Culture* (New York: Bloomsbury, 2013), p. 185.
55 Duffett, *Understanding Fandom*, p. 182.
56 Eminem, 'Stan (Long Version) ft. Dido', YouTube www.youtube.com/watch?v=gOMhN-hfMtY&ab_channel=EminemVEVO [accessed 28 February 2022].
57 Henry Jenkins, *Fans, Bloggers, and Gamers: Exploring Participatory Culture* (New York: New York University Press, 2006), p. 41.
58 Frances Wilson, '"An Exaggerated Woman": The Melodrama of Lady Caroline Lamb', in *Byromania: Portraits of the Artist in Nineteenth-and Twentieth-Century Culture*, ed. by Frances Wilson (Basingstoke: Palgrave Macmillan, 1998), pp. 195–220 (p. 199).
59 Duffett, *Understanding Fandom*, p. 5. The term 'fan' first appeared in late-seventeenth-century England, where it was a common abbreviation for 'fanatic' (a religious zealot); Stephen King, *Misery* (New York: Signet, 1988); *Misery*, dir. by Rob Reiner (Columbia Pictures, 1990).
60 McDayter, *Byromania*, p. 31.
61 Mole, *Byron's Romantic Celebrity*, p. 24.
62 Lord Byron, *Childe Harold's Pilgrimage*, in *Lord Byron: The Major Works*, ed. by Jerome J. McGann (Oxford: Oxford University Press, 2008), pp. 19–207 (p. 22).
63 Mole, *Byron's Romantic Celebrity*, p. 58.
64 Mole, *Byron's Romantic Celebrity*, p. 64.
65 Mole, *Byron's Romantic Celebrity*, p. 64.
66 Polidori, *The Vampyre*, p. 247.

67 Polidori, *The Vampyre*, p. 247.
68 Throsby, 'Byron', p. 228.
69 Jenkins, *Textual Poachers*, p. 23.
70 Jenkins, *Textual Poachers*, p. 24.
71 Jenkins, *Textual Poachers*, p. 23.
72 Throsby, 'Byron', p. 228.
73 Duffett, *Understanding Fandom*, p. 171.
74 Lord Byron, 'Augustus Darvell', in *The Vampyre and Other Tales of the Macabre*, ed. by Robert Morrison and Chris Baldick (Oxford: Oxford University Press, 1997), pp. 246–51 (p. 247).
75 Auerbach, *Our Vampires, Ourselves*, p. 14.

5

Rebellion, treachery, and glamour: Lady Caroline Lamb's *Glenarvon*, Polidori, and the progress of the Romantic vampire

Bill Hughes

Polidori's vampire, Lord Ruthven, is distinguished by 'the deadly hue of his face, which never gave a warmer tint, either from the blush of modesty, or from the strong emotion of passion'.[1] Ruthven, then, certainly does not have the ruddiness of the blood-bloated vampire of folklore described in the prefatory material to his tale when it was first published.[2] This pallor instead recalls another important predecessor. Lady Caroline Lamb wrote in her commonplace book on seeing the poet Byron for the first time: 'That beautiful pale face is my fate' (see Byron's portrait, Figure 5.1).[3] That facial pallor and that idea of fatalistic passion will reappear throughout this essay. Lamb's novel *Glenarvon*, first published in 1816, is usually seen in terms of her revenge for Byron's ill treatment of her after their brief but fiery love affair. Lamb met Byron in March 1812; she was twenty-seven, he was twenty-four. The affair was over by November.

It is a mistake, I think, to stress the novel's autobiographical elements, as many people have done.[4] For example, Paul Douglass claims that Lamb's 'undiagnosed mental problems are crucial to understanding her literary efforts', while Peter Graham thinks Lamb 'unwilling or unable to get beyond her own story'.[5] John Chubbe takes a similar stance, though he does acknowledge Lamb's accurate pictures of social life.[6] The lack of attention to *Glenarvon* as a literary fiction is owing, in part, 'to its status as a roman à clef', as Barbara Judson says.[7] (Judson goes on to argue for the particular pleasures and powers of this form.)[8] I want to take this further and challenge the consensus: *Glenarvon* stands on its own as a novel and has as much merit as many Gothic/sentimental fictions of the period, if not more – it is quite a dazzling achievement. Yet as Nicola Watson has shown, there is a strong intertextual relationship with Byron's poems, the letters between the two, and other works by Lamb.[9] And one aspect of their lives is important – that is, the way their public personas were invented and manipulated. That was part of the celebrity status that hung around Byron.[10] It has been argued that Byron was the first celebrity in the modern sense.[11] Byron himself talked of his celebrity as 'the contagion of Byronism' spreading across Europe;

Figure 5.1 *Lord Byron*, by Richard Westall (1813). NPG 4243.
© National Portrait Gallery, London.

this idea of contagion is another theme I will be tracking.[12] Then there is the further intertextuality of Byron's fragmentary vampire tale, upon which Polidori drew for his 1819 novella *The Vampyre*, fusing this with his personal acquaintance with Byron and elements from *Glenarvon*. Thus there is a complex criss-crossing between lives, life-writing, and fiction.

This chapter will show how the Romantic vampirism that became concentrated in *The Vampyre* is already latent in *Glenarvon*. There, through its interaction with and mediation of the Byron phenomenon in real life, it becomes a complex exploration of a politics that embraces both the sexual, domestic sphere and public life, notably in the arena of national liberation. *Glenarvon* is a particularly powerful exposure of the contradictions, hypocrisies, and limits of reformist Whig politics. Lamb herself is ambivalent but there is a strain of radicalism in tension with her fears over the dangers of rebellion.[13] Ghislaine McDayter argues that, against those that see *Glenarvon* as the product of hysteria, Lamb was 'thoroughly conscious of the political ramifications within her text'.[14] She reads the novel's political force through an analysis that focuses on hysteria itself and which draws on Mary Wollstonecraft's theorising of the distortion of the intellect in the education of women (Lamb knew Wollstonecraft well). In addition to its political content, I explore how the novel also sows the seeds for future generic incarnations of Romantic vampirism both through Polidori's vampire and through a parallel development of demonic lovers. This is enabled in part by its generic hybridity.

A strange farrago

Glenarvon was seen by critics as transgressing gender norms by its clashing of genres. The *Monthly Review* 'could not decide whether [it] was romance or biography', calling it 'of the *doubtful gender*, though a feminine production'; genre and gender become confused – like 'the doubtful gender' of Lamb herself, with her notorious cross-dressing (see Figure 5.2).[15] Lady Holland thought it a 'strange farrago'.[16] Gary Kelly classifies it as a 'novel of passion' and as 'quasi-Gothic'.[17] Clara Tuite says the novel also initiates the genre of 'Byronic silverfork', a subdivision of silverfork novels.[18] (The silverfork novel, for Tuite, is 'a critical genre of celebrity culture' (of which Byromania is a founding moment) and 'the commodification of scandal'.)[19] Barbara Judson describes it as 'historical romance' while detailing the consequences of its status as *roman à clef*.[20] With regard to this latter, McDayter argues that Lamb's concerns with the source figure Byron (and, I would add, the other characters) are more political than personal: this aspect of *Glenarvon* as a political novel is important for my argument.[21] With its Irish setting and concerns, *Glenarvon* is also related to the national tale as exemplified by Edgeworth and Owenson, aligning itself in addition with the 'convention of a Gothic Ireland' that Joseph Garver talks about.[22] For Frances Wilson, *Glenarvon* is both 'a comedy of social realism' and a 'wild, gothic tale of desire'.[23]

This clashing of genres – of autobiography, political adventure, high-society satire, love story, and Gothic novel – accounts for much of *Glenarvon*'s interest and value. It is not the flawed outburst of a hysterical and undisciplined woman: this heterogeneity allows multiple perspectives to

Figure 5.2 Lady Caroline Lamb in her page's costume, by Thomas Phillips. CTS336396. The Devonshire Collections, Chatsworth. Reproduced by permission of Chatsworth Settlement Trustees/Bridgeman Images.

coexist in that dialogic manner lauded by Mikhail Bakhtin.[24] Both the contradictory nature of female desire and the tension between political anxieties and aspirations can be expressed and examined. It reveals the dialectical interplay of the personal and the political. One of Caroline Lamb's distant heirs may be the paranormal romance of our times, which involves a similar hybridity.

Glenarvon, the Gothic hero

Glenarvon inaugurates a fictional motif that is now very familiar, with a vampiric figure that is hypnotic and sexually seductive. Lamb turned her own attraction–repulsion to Byron into a Gothic and sentimental fiction where amatory seduction and betrayal are aligned with the political upheaval of the Irish Rebellion of 1798.[25] Here, the eponymous Lord Glenarvon, or Clarence de Ruthven (the name appropriated by Polidori), is notably Byronic, feeding off Byron's own self-creation and Lamb's mimicry of him, while drawing on Milton and Richardson. Stressing the artifice and self-fashioning of his persona, Lamb writes that Glenarvon 'had a mask for every distinct character he wished to play'.[26]

Glenarvon is characterised with the melancholy nobility and satanic allure that inaugurates a series of demonic lovers through the Brontës, the Gothic Romance of du Maurier and others, to the sympathetic vampires of paranormal romance.[27] Lamb had already set up themes that allude to vampirism in her real-life encounters with Byron and she creatively infused these associations into the novel. She referred to Byron as 'the Giaour' (the doomed vampire in Byron's poem of the same name).[28] She mirrored Byron's vampirism in a startling letter to him which refers to an exchange of blood and the gift of her pubic hair:

> I askd you not to send blood but Yet do – because if it means love I like to have it. I cut the hair too close & bled too much more than you need – do not do the same & pray put not scizzors points near where quei capelli grow – sooner take it from the arm or wrist.[29]

For Tuite, the story of this exchange is involved in 'the interrelations between Romantic literature, romantic love, Romantic-period scandal, and the emergence of celebrity culture'.[30]

Glenarvon is frequently characterised by diabolical epithets such as 'arch fiend' (111) and 'fallen angel' (121). (Annabella Milbanke also called Byron a 'fallen angel'; she would later become his wife.)[31] The heroine Calantha observes Glenarvon's 'almost demoniac smile' as 'his livid cheeks became pale' (204), associating Byronic pallor with the supernatural. He howls at the moon and his ancestor is said to have drunk blood from a skull (as was Byron's). Similar imagery occurs in the Brontës' novels and is a stylistic marker of the genre known as Gothic Romance which developed out of the Brontës and Daphne du Maurier and flourished from the 1950s to the 1980s.

Lamb describes Glenarvon's 'splendid genius and uncommon faculties' (139) as developing 'amidst the ruins of ancient architecture, and the wild beauties of Italian scenery' (138–39) – a backdrop of sublime architecture and landscape, hinting at the infectious dangers of a peculiarly Gothic aesthetic. He is 'melancholy, unsocial [and] had centred upon himself every strong interest' (139). Thus his poetic imagination, his '[d]welling everywhere in the brilliant regions of fancy', has rendered him asocial and estranged from 'the ordinary cares of life' (139). The aimlessly hedonistic Byronic persona is elaborated further, emphasising an unhealthy complexion that vacillates between that pallor Lamb fixated on in Byron and a pathological ruddiness: 'Flushed with the glow of intemperate heat, or pale with the weariness of secret woe, he vainly sought in a career of pleasure, for that happiness which his restless soul prevented him from enjoying' (139).

Glenarvon becomes involved in the 1798 anticolonial rebellion of the United Irishmen against the British rulers, inciting the people with his rhetoric and personal charm. Political subversion in the domestic sphere and at the level of the nation is equated with madness and yet with glory. Glenarvon's political persuasiveness is linked to his sexual glamour. Leigh Wetherall Dickson stresses Lamb's 'concern with the deceptive and persuasive nature of social signifiers and rhetoric', and the infectious, hypnotic power of the aesthetic is crucial to the novel.[32] All this resembles the satanic revolt of the Byron figure. Foreshadowing Glenarvon, in Byron's *Lara* (1814) the Byronic hero does actually lead a revolution, though his motives (as are Glenarvon's) are mixed. (Kaled, Lara's lover, even disguises herself as a pageboy, as will Lamb and one of her fictional incarnations, Elinor St Clare).[33] Glenarvon's women themselves become Byronic, denouncing God, family, and society, and swearing satanic vows of abjuration; Byronism is an infection, like vampirism.

At the novel's centre is the heroine, Calantha. She is an intelligent, passionate young woman, somewhat untamed, whose education has been indulgent. She has married Lord Avondale but has become discontented by his absences on business. In the amoral society life of London, she meets the charismatic Glenarvon and is fascinated by him. She eventually becomes his lover and, in her resemblance to and derivation from Lamb herself, is one of those female incarnations of Byronism.[34]

It is impossible to read the novel without being reminded of the flamboyant life of its author, whom Calantha strongly resembles, and one senses Lamb judging herself in the novel. Calantha dresses as a pageboy for her first secret assignation with Glenarvon (219). Lamb notoriously cross-dressed: as a pageboy on numerous occasions, to get admittance to Byron, even to dictate her novel. And yet we must still be careful to separate life from fiction; Lamb is refashioning moments from her own life for aesthetic ends.

Byron and his avatars

Byron saw Lamb as his 'evil genius'.[35] Frances Wilson says, 'Lamb struggled not to regain him but to become him'.[36] Byron's persona in some ways was also Lamb's creation; they invent and reflect each other. As James Soderholm says, 'Both conjured up images, deceits, and forgeries in order to rival each other's most potent fantasies.'[37] She would return to Byron and his persona as a focal point of her writing. In her last novel, *Ada Reis*, of 1823, the hero is 'the Don Juan of his day'.[38] And at a ball in 1820, Lamb appeared dressed as Don Juan.[39] Mimicry abounds as her novelistic practices invade her actual life; she forges letters from Byron and imitates his style with great accuracy in *The New Canto* (1819), an apocalyptic political satire which also takes aim at Byron while mimicking his poetic style to perfection and which she tried to pass as a continuation of *Don Juan*.[40] Frances Wilson argues that the nature of Byronism itself inspired mimicry.[41] One sceptical observer of this feverish imitation was Annabella Milbanke, who, before she became his wife, coined the word 'Byromania' for the infectious glamour the poet dispersed:

> See Caro, smiling, sighing o'er his face
> In hopes to imitate his strange grimace
> [...]
> Is human nature to be cast anew,
> And modelled to your Idol's Image true?[42]

Thus Milbanke resisted the infectious force of Byronism which reshaped the self into the form of the poet. This parasitical mimicry – which might be called vampiric – lies behind the character of Glenarvon, who is, as I have noted, recognisably Byronic. And of course this mimicry is inherited with Polidori's creative reappropriation.[43]

Glenarvon is not the only Byronic figure; the novel is like a hall of mirrors, where facets of the diabolic poet-hero can be found anywhere. The mysterious and sinister Viviani is one such figure: 'A deep melancholy played upon his spirits; a dark mystery enveloped his fate' (13). He is – apparently – a scheming Italian, often appearing as a monk, who owes much to Ann Radcliffe and Matthew Lewis's versions of Gothic. Who is Viviani?, asks the Duke; Glenarvon says:

> [a]n idol [...] whom the multitude have set up for themselves, and worshipped, forsaking their true faith [...] a man who is in love with crime and baseness –
>
> [...] he hath an imagination of fire playing round a heart of ice – one whom the never-dying worm feeds on by night and day.
>
> (335)

Glenarvon, in deprecating Viviani, is bitterly self-lacerating about the infectious charm of celebrity, especially its effect on women: 'He is [...] the idol of the fair, and the great. Is it virtue that women prize? [...] Throw but the dazzling light of genius upon baseness, and corruption, and every crime will be to them but an additional charm' (335). But this is Glenarvon's confession, too: 'Viviani' is an identity he has assumed, revealing the propensity for masquerade Lamb has announced.

Other figures are cast in the Byronic mould; the Byrons proliferate like a virus. Viviani, with little justice, blames Calantha's scheming aunt, Lady Margaret, for her own malignant influence over himself: he calls her 'something even more treacherous and perverted than myself' (345). Lady Margaret 'concealed a dark intriguing spirit' (10) and has a 'face of an Angel, distorted by the passions of a Dæmon' (14).

Lady Margaret is similarly blamed for her influence on Calantha through an over-liberal education. But this corrupting power is itself a form of the Byronic. Lady Margaret wants to educate Calantha to submit to nature rather than convention and 'the absurd opinions of others'. This educational system, which 'nature dictates and which every feeling of the heart willingly accedes to' (29), will aggravate her future ruin.[44] And the indulged childhood is, in part, Lamb's self-justification of her own deviant conduct. Calantha becomes a creature of spontaneity and impulse, inspired by 'projects, seducing, but visionary' (30). She is 'without a curb', untamed by the forces of social intercourse. Yet Lamb describes these in ambivalent terms: 'Early and constant intercourse with the world [...] smooths away all peculiarities; and whilst it assimilates individuals to each other, corrects many faults, and represses many virtues' (30). Calantha is disgusted by 'slavish followers of prejudice' (30), and one senses Lamb's sympathy here. However, 'a fearless spirit raised her, as she fondly imagined, above the vulgar herd; self-confident, she scarcely deigned to bow the knee before God' (31). That 'fondly imagined' betrays the delusional aspect of her rebelliousness individualism and there is a suggestion of Miltonic revolt in her pride before God. There is a critique of Byronism here, but perhaps aimed more at those infected by it, or who imitate celebrity, rather than the source itself.

Thus, Calantha has herself become Byronic through contagion. She later swears an 'impious oath' to Glenarvon: 'I will leave all for you: – I love but you: be you my master'; she 'considers herself as no longer under the protection of God' (221). Comparing herself to another of Glenarvon's victims, Elinor St Clare, she fatalistically prophecies her own doom:

> her uncontrolled passions must have depraved her heart. [...] I think I understand the feelings which impelled her to evil. [...] Something seems to warn me [...] that, if I wander from virtue like her, nothing will check my course – all the barriers, that others fear to overstep, are nothing before me.
>
> (119)

She calls to her husband: 'Save me. [...] who knows whither the path I follow leads? My will – my ungoverned will, has hitherto, been my only law' (119).

There is a significant moment in one of Calantha's complaints about marriage where the resentment at women's subordination takes on a Byronic hue, redeploying what may be a typically masculine irresponsibility for feminist ends. Lamb sees domesticity as exile from the public sphere and married women become outcast from society simply by their choice of 'one strong engagement'. If marriage fails, they become 'beings without hope [...] solitary wanderers in search of false pleasures – or lonely recluses' (102). They thus parallel the exiled nomads of Byron's poems. This is prophetic, too, of her own fall.

Calantha torments herself with deep Byronic introspection:

> Oh I am changed, she continually thought; I have repressed and conquered every warm and eager feeling; I love and admire nothing yet am I not heartless and cold enough for the world in which I live. What is it that makes me miserable? There is a fire burns within my soul; and all those whom I see and hear are insensible.
>
> (105)

This, too, is Byronic in its doubt, its solitariness, its sense of a passion which is at odds with the world. However, part of her yearning is for mutual companionship with Avondale (who is now away from home a lot): 'I am as a child, as a mistress [...] but never his friend, his companion' (106). Here, Lamb sets up a causal justification for her heroine's later progress. Urban life and the idleness from childhood both weaken her and she plunges into 'useless and visionary' (106) pondering, alienating her further from society.

Elinor St Clare, the daughter of a nomadic and somewhat feckless poet, raised in a convent by her aunt, is another female Byron. She is seduced and abandoned by Glenarvon but will take on a prominent political role. The fallen Elinor has succumbed to the ultimate Byronic scepticism: 'It were presumption to believe: I doubt all things' (319). Elinor is another avatar of Lamb, or of the female equivalent of the Byronic persona; she 'unblushingly' follows Glenarvon in 'the attire of a boy' (142) on becoming his mistress. When Elinor's uncle is injured, his outcast niece seeks a reconciliation, dressing as a pageboy to effect an entrance (194), taking the name 'Clarence', thus repeating Lamb's cross-dressing and impersonations of Byron. These Byronic women form a species of their own and may be redeemed from the curse of duplicity that haunts both Byron and Glenarvon; they have a certain authenticity, though they are still fatally attracted to the visual glamour of the latter. (There is a notable contrast with the female victims of Polidori's Ruthven who are either virtuous and are fed on or, it is hinted, are already corrupt, then ruined. Neither gain much agency.)

Pallor and infection

I have mentioned the significance of Byron's pale, beautiful features. Polidori's Lord Ruthven is attractive to women 'In spite of the deadly hue of his face' (246), from which passion is absent though the features are beautiful. Lamb wrote to Byron: 'How very pale you are [...] a statue of white marble, so colourless, and the dark brown hair such a contrast. I can never see you without wishing to cry.'[45] When Calantha first encounters Glenarvon in society, she observes with sympathy that his 'pale cheek and brow expressed much of disappointed hope' (147). Thus, the pallor is bound up with the characteristically Byronic inner torment. We can already see prefigured here Anne Rice's marble-like Lestat in *Interview with the Vampire* and *Twilight*'s glittering Edward Cullen.[46] Octavio Paz describes the 'sombre portrait of the idealised [Byronic] self' thus: 'The pale face furrowed by an ancient grief, the rare satanic smile, the traces of obscured nobility [...] worthy of a better fate.'[47]

Such pallor is associated with ill health.[48] This makes Glenarvon a Gothic figure, more living dead than truly alive and clearly laying the ground for his literary metamorphosis into vampire. In the fragment by Byron that was the basis of Polidori's tale, we read that Darvell is 'a prey to some cureless disquiet'.[49] 'Cureless' suggests both psychic homelessness and illness. The incurable malady here may, says the narrator, have arisen from 'ambition, love, remorse, grief [...] or a morbid temperament'.[50] This combination of qualities is again typically Byronic. Polidori's Ruthven is a similar outcast; immune to 'the mirth around him', it is 'as if he could not participate therein' (246).

Annabella Milbanke compared Lamb at the time of her infatuation to a rabid dog and 'thought that [she] had bit half the company and communicated the *Nonsense-mania*'.[51] Thus, the Byronic vampire is diseased, and Byronism is a contagious disorder; Byron himself wrote of the 'contagion of Byronism'.[52] Tuite suggests that this contagion yet has an ambivalently emancipatory force, being 'a new mode of enchantment that not only solicits people to resist divine majesty [...], but displaces divine majesty with [...] Byron's "Satanic Majesty" '.[53] Lamb echoes this ambivalence, confounding the dangers of charismatic enchantment for women with her own political hesitancy over revolt. Byromania was certainly seen at the time as dangerously subversive, even when not harnessed to an object as in Glenarvon's revolt. As McDayter says, drawing on Jon Mee's work on enthusiasm, it evoked the spectre of 'mass insurrection' from 'republican contagion'.[54] Again, Byromania was 'repeatedly discussed' in terms of 'contagion'.[55] Polidori's Aubrey, already deluded by 'romances' (247), is infected into seeing Ruthven as 'the hero of a romance' (247), possibly the sort of fashionable romances Byron himself wrote.

Byronism is contagious; as has Calantha, so Elinor St Clare has become an image of Glenarvon. This Byronism dissolves gender boundaries, as Lamb herself did. Elinor displays a femininity modulated by a masculine, soldierly identity, one which is now affiliated with revolution: 'The soft smile of enchantment blended with the assumed fierceness of a military air, the deep expressive glance of passion and sensibility, the youthful air of boyish playfulness' (321).

Her aunt, the abbess, sees the Byronic influence in terms of her being 'decoyed' by 'fiends' and 'daemons' (321), but Elinor attributes this to forces within herself, wild, animalistic forces of nature: God has 'implanted in my breast [...] passions fiercer that I had power to curb' (321). She likens herself to a 'wild tygress', a 'young lion', a 'fierce eagle'; 'Nature formed me fierce', she declares (321–22). However, this innate wildness has also been cultivated by an indulgent education (322) (just as Calantha's has). Now she is a social outcast: 'I am deserted, it is true; but my mind is a world in itself, which I have people with my own creatures' (322). This again is an avatar of the solipsistic Byronic persona, who can exclaim, 'let us doubt all things' (322). But belying the narrative of infection, Elinor can only 'with justice accuse but myself'. She insists that she was born with 'a perversion of intellect, a depravity of feeling, nothing can cure' (323) – a congenital pathology, then, but this raises questions about the innateness of character and undermines the infection trope. Thus there is a dialectic between a deterministic account of human existence and one that rests on self-invention. This fatalism resonates with Lamb's response to being struck by Byron's pale beauty.

Revolt and betrayal

In Ireland, Calantha reads Glenarvon's 'address to the United Irishmen' that has been circulating to much effect. This is her first awareness of Glenarvon. It is 'so eloquent, so animated', that she fears its infectious potential. The worldly Mrs Seymour, on the other hand, denounces it as an 'absurd rhapsody' (108) that aims to 'spread the flames of rebellion' (109) among 'an innocent but weak people' (109). Then Sir Everard appears, raging about the 'licentious democrats' and 'rebellious libertines' that have infected his wife and daughters and, in particular, his niece, Elinor, who lives with them. They have been 'struck mad, like Agave in the mysteries of Bacchus', he says.[56] They are 'running wild [...] hair dishevelled [...] ornamented with green cockades' (111) – the Irish nationalist symbol. This rabid ecstasy has been stirred up by the 'arch fiend' Glenarvon (111). The women follow Glenarvon 'as if he were some god' (111); this is the same celebrity fervour that surrounded Byron.[57] The castle retainer MacAllain says, 'The whole country are after him [...] it's a rage, a fashion' (111), accurately describing the Byron phenomenon. The doctor retorts that it is pathological: 'a frenzy' (111) and 'a pestilence' (112). The Duke, Calantha's father, thinks Glenarvon himself is diseased and 'acting under the influence of a mad infatuation' (112). Thus the unhealthy plague of Byronism becomes overtly political, including the Bacchanalian sexual politics of the women.[58]

Glenarvon has been holding secret nocturnal meetings in his ruined ancestral property. He has even dared to build a library, says the outraged Sir Everard – a very subversive act. And in a portentous vision of misogynistic comic Gothic, Glenarvon takes on supernatural powers: 'strange things have occurred [...] Captain Kennedy, commander of the district, can't keep his men. Cattle walk out of the paddock of themselves: women, children, pigs wander after' him (113). Glenarvon's glamour works on soldiers, women, and animals alike. Likewise, Polidori's Ruthven has, for women, a 'winning tongue' (246) and Aubrey is fascinated by him. This, too, is much like Dracula's hypnotic powers over female victims and rats, though I am not suggesting a direct influence; however, infection as a mesmeric quality is one well-known motif in later vampire fictions.[59] Yet something is transmuted in the course of infection from Glenarvon to the mesmerised women: their fervour has an authenticity that he does not possess. As Judson says, 'Lamb effectively distinguishes between Byron's revolutionary charade, which, she implies, is motivated by self-seeking, and the women's revolt, which, however marred by histrionics, is redeemed by a desire for equality and freedom.'[60]

Glenarvon's influence is characterised by Sir Everard as 'the infection, the poison in the fountain of life' (119). 'The whole kingdom' is in 'a state of ferment and disorder' (137), with many grievances over absentee landlords and intensive exploitation (echoing themes in the national novels of Edgeworth and Owenson). Though some rebels are more moderate, 'the more violent', free from 'every restraint of prejudice or principle', wanted 'the equalisation of property, and the destruction of rank and titles' (138).

All this 'revolutionary spirit' (138) has been roused by the presence of Glenarvon.

Calantha's domestic rebellion against her husband as her passion for Glenarvon develops mirrors the unrest in Ireland, and Lamb diagnoses this too as diseased fantasy: 'like madness, these disturbed characters see things not as they are' (161). This mental disturbance is analogous to the heroic glamour of political revolt in the way it finds 'a degree of glory to every degree of privation and punishment in the noble cause of opposition to what they conceive is unjust authority' (161).

Glenarvon makes the descent from Richardson's Lovelace to the Romantic vampire explicit. The seduction narrative established in *Clarissa* had been frequently employed by anti-Jacobin writers to show young women led astray by immoral radicals, conflating sexual and political rebellion.[61] Glenarvon presents Calantha with an emerald ring engraved with the harp of Ireland and the motto 'let us be firm and united': ' "I mean it merely politically," he said, smiling. "Even were you a Clarissa, you need not be alarmed: I am no Lovelace, I promise you" ' (166).

However, for all his avowed anti-imperialism at the level of the state, Glenarvon sees Calantha in the light of imperial conquest. In her face he reads 'his empire and her own weakness' (177). In the manner of the demonic lover of many a romance, he asserts his dominance: 'I must be obeyed: – you will find me a master – a tyrant perhaps; not a slave. If I once love, it is with fervour – with madness' (182). But, in the context, this has wider political overtones. He tells her, ' "I know my empire. Take off those ornaments: replace what I have given you" […], throwing a chain around her' (192). There is a hint that she is bound by him with jewellery that is imperial plunder: 'richest jewels brought by him from distant countries' (194). So Glenarvon's political radicalism is shown to be suspect. Glenarvon's politics can already be seen as superficial and tied up with his egotism, as he declares his abandonment of Ireland: 'What are the wrongs of my country to me? […] I now abandon [these shores]' (243).[62]

Glenarvon ultimately betrays Calantha and this is connected to his apostasy over revolution; it is not made explicit, but both coincide with the restoration of his property and granting of a ship by the English court and with the prospects of his marriage to the eligible society woman Miss Monmouth. Calantha has died of grief. At this point, Elinor declaims, 'I forgive you my own injuries, but not Calantha's and my country's' (315). The betrayals are twinned, casting doubt on his love and patriotism both, which appear now to be motivated by self-interest and self-love. Yet the infected Elinor *is* authentic and she dies for the cause. This cause is justified: the inhabitants of one region, though 'uncivilised and ferocious', show, to the apparently impartial narrator, signs of 'oppression, poverty, and neglect' (316).

The abandoned Elinor, who has gone further in depravity than Calantha, spurns religion and turns instead to revolution: 'It is a bloody war we are going to: this is the year of horror!!!' (291). It is Elinor who, after Glenarvon's betrayal, continues the authentic rebellion for Ireland, which is represented as an injured mother. 'Have I lived to see my country bleeding', she declaims, 'and is there not one of her children firm by her to the last?' (351). The image of Ireland as wronged woman is frequent in nationalist iconography – even, on occasion, as victim of vampirism (see Figure 5.3). Elinor St Clair redeems Byronism by embodying something authentic drawn from its contradictory impulses of rebellion and individualistic self-creation, though it will doom her. As Judson says:

> At first, St. Clare seems to illustrate Lady Caroline's penchant for playing Byron, because she, too, is a darkly alienated poet [...] set apart by obligatory crime and guilt. But [...] in the end she stands for the authenticity of Gaelic culture in stark opposition to the mummery of the Byronic hero.[63]

Figure 5.3 'The English Vampire', in *The Irish Post* [Dublin]: [Richard Barratt], 7 November 1885. A response to John Tenniel's 'The Irish Vampire' in *Punch*, 24 October 1885, which denigrated Charles Stewart Parnell and his National League. Reproduced courtesy of the National Library of Ireland.

She remains true to the radical cause and untainted by manipulation, vampiric parasitism, or betrayal, though she dies for it and is 'branded with infamy' (352) for her sexual transgression. Elinor denounces the betrayal of Ireland, an 'injured friend', by the 'kings and oppressors' of the earth (351). England's treachery and that of Glenarvon towards both his lovers and the rebellion are metonymous.

Elinor takes up her harp and adopts the role of 'prophetess' (352). In rhyming tetrameters, she curses 'the fiend's detested arts / Impress'd upon this breaking heart' (352); this is most likely aimed at Glenarvon. His 'art' had inspired her own art of 'sweetest notes' but now 'The spell that gave them power is o'er' (352). She has cast off Glenarvon's malignantly infectious glamour and yet still prophesies on and does not abandon the fight. She foretells 'pain and sickness' and the doom of 'Glenarvon's hall' and its master (353), but also the defeat of the rebellion:

> The star of freedom sets, to rise no more.
> Quench'd is the immortal spark in endless night;
> Never again shall ray so fair, so bright,
> Arise o'er Erin's desolated shore.
>
> (353)

Yet again, she rebukes England: 'You have destroyed thy sister country' (354). This betrayal of kinship is itself a characteristic of vampires, in Greek folklore and with Byron's version in *The Giaour*.[64]

Elinor now appears to have persuaded herself that 'The hour of retribution is at hand', calling on England to 'give back the properties that thy nation has wrested from a suffering people' (354). It is hard to doubt the sincerity of the lyrical voice here, adding to the novel's polyphonic ambivalence where voices of loyalism and revolution are represented side by side. The narrator talks of her 'deluded followers' and yet Elinor's speech is rational and persuasive in ways that work against this characterisation, moving the reader to question on whom precisely the glamour of delusion has fallen. 'The splendid hope was conceived – the daring effort was made' (354), she proclaims. The utopian dream that lies concealed in the contradictions of heroic Byronism will be remembered in 'eternal splendour' (355) as 'the spirit of liberty flourished at least' (354). Wounded, about to plunge on horseback over a cliff, she cries out: 'The dream of life is past; the song of the wild harper has ceased; famine, war, and slavery, shall encompass my country' (356). The 'splendid hope' of liberty and its wild music have been noble but futile.

Meanwhile, Glenarvon has joined the British Navy, in preparation for an attack on the Dutch, but his Gothic fate is upon him. He has a brief vision of the 'fearful spectre' of Lord Avondale (who has died) reproaching him

(361). His sleep disturbed, he broods on 'broken vows, of hearts betrayed, and of all the perjuries and treacheries of a life given up to love' (362). He has a vision of Calantha who, too late, tries to warn him to save himself. Then he dreams of his betrayed lover, Alice McAllain, and his dead child. He fights courageously in a naval battle. 'Visions of death and horror persecute' him (365) as he sees a ghost ship with black sails and a sinister friar at whose feet kneels Glenarvon's first love, Fiorabella. He wonders in terror if this is 'that famed Dutch merchantman, condemned through all eternity to sail before the wind' (365). (The Flying Dutchman resembles the Byronic hero in some respects.)[65] He wonders if all this is real or whether his eyes are 'distempered by some strange malady' (365–66). But a diseased and distorted vision has ruled his whole life and infected others too. In a frenzy, he flings himself into the sea and amid 'visions of punishment and hell' hears a 'loud and terrible' voice announce his eternal damnation (366).

Glenarvon ultimately betrays both his women lovers and Ireland.[66] Yet he remains Elinor's muse, of lyrical poetry and revolt, though for rebellions doomed to tragedy, both for the transgressive women and for the nation. With all these conflicting forces, Lamb's novel shifts between an anti-Jacobin stance and radicalism.

Glenarvon's heirs

As I have said, Clara Tuite characterises the novel as inaugurating the genre of Byronic silverfork, which involves the 'magic conjunction of lordliness and literary authority' of Byron.[67] This 'magic' appears as the fantastic, Gothic strand in the novel, with the hypnotic power that gives Glenarvon his 'lordliness' and political force. This is inseparable from the rhetorical magnetism of his 'literary authority'. Lamb's generic innovations also seed further texts, most famously John Polidori's *The Vampyre*, with whose legacy this collection is concerned.

David Punter downplays the importance of Byron as the model for Polidori's Lord Ruthven: 'Ruthven is the representation not of a mythological individual but of a mythologised class. He is dead yet not dead, as the power of the aristocracy in the early nineteenth century was dead and not dead' (104). Yet the direct link via *Glenarvon*, taking the name 'Ruthven' and the vampiric characteristics must surely be significant.[68] Polidori's target may be seen more fruitfully as a particular fraction of the aristocracy rather than the class as a whole – one which is peculiarly contemporary and aligned with the bourgeoisie rather than a decaying power; this contradictory position is embodied in Byron.[69] In *Glenarvon*, too, Glenarvon is aligned with the progressive classes in siding with radical reform, though insincerely. The milieu which Lamb describes and which Polidori will satirise is precisely that Whiggish strand of the aristocracy rather than its reactionary counterpart.

As Punter notes, in *Prometheus Unbound*, Shelley figures the vampire's danger as being infectious.[70] Shelley's vampire, in that tradition of political metaphor, represents tyrannical powers. He identifies the same diseased psychology as Lamb and Polidori – an excessive inwardness and distorted individualism. Shelley's vampire is 'a soul self-consumed, / [...] a vampire among men, / Infecting all with his own hideous ill'. Polidori's Ruthven is 'a man entirely absorbed within himself' (247); these echo Lamb's characterisation and, of course, the persona of Byron's poems.[71] Skarda says *The Vampyre* 'unquestionably draws on Byron's characterisation of Childe Harold, the self-exile set apart from cultural and personal community' (250). As we have seen, these traits are to be found in Lamb's Ruthven too.

Simon Bainbridge notes the parallels between *Glenarvon* and *The Vampyre*, but claims that Polidori, unlike Lamb (and the folkloric sources), does not make use of the trope of vampirism as infection.[72] Yet, as I have argued, the hypnotic powers of the vampiric Byron figure operate themselves as a kind of contagion. Polidori's Ruthven, too, has 'irresistible powers of seduction' (249). Aubrey succumbs to this seduction but the victims are mainly women. Bainbridge argues that Polidori sees Byronism as 'a phenomenon that was perceived to feed off [Byron's] female readers', implicating the commercial literary system itself (which Polidori was to fall foul of).[73]

We can see that the depiction of the mesmeric powers to stir up women's desire is strong in *Glenarvon* but becomes attenuated in Polidori – necessarily, I think, to keep the satiric force by downplaying any sympathy for the victims as much as the vampire. Apart from Aubrey's sister and the innocent Greek peasant girl Ianthe, Ruthven's prey are already corrupt. (Aubrey himself is, of course, among the mesmerised innocents.) Polidori is satirising the aristocratic women of Whiggish high society. The sympathies aroused in *Glenarvon* are erased in Polidori; he casts Lady Caroline Lamb as Lady Mercer, 'the common adulteress' who 'dressed as a mountebank' (246).[74]

Thus Polidori, seizing on elements of Byron's life in the flesh and within literature, particularly Lamb's novel, transformed the blood-bloated vampire of the Eastern European peasantry into a pale, cold aristocrat. This also continued a tradition in ethnographic accounts of Enlightenment satire against *ancien régime* tyranny but, in addition, spawned a long-lasting archetype of Gothic horror.[75]

However, there is a parallel strand of the Byronic figure as demonic lover and betrayer, initiated by Lady Caroline Lamb and enduring through Gothic romance. Demon lovers appear in this genre but not in supernatural form. They do, however, get labelled with supernatural epithets; they are 'satanic', 'demonic', 'Luciferean', and so on, just as Heathcliff in *Wuthering Heights* is repeatedly described as 'Devil' or 'demon'.[76] The housekeeper, Nelly Dean, says, ' "Is he a ghoul or a vampire?" I mused. I had read of such hideous incarnate demons.'[77]

The demon lovers of the Gothic romances that follow the Brontës via Daphne du Maurier repeat this imagery. In this genre the hero will be brooding and have dark secrets. Often an antiquated family home is central; abbeys or castles may appear. The book covers for this genre notoriously feature women with great hair and flowing dresses fleeing a sinister mansion or castle by moonlight. At the height of this trend, *Glenarvon* itself was published in a Gothic romance series, with all the typical hallmarks on the cover (Figure 5.4). This cover is amusingly kitsch and does not really illustrate the plot well, yet it does alert us to one of the formal templates of *Glenarvon* – the original Gothic novel – and establishes a generic lineage from that through Lamb to its twentieth- and twenty-first-century heirs.

Polidori made the monster explicitly a vampire; Lamb's Glenarvon is only implicitly so. Polidori's Ruthven is somewhat reified, made thing-like rather than humanised, whereas the demon lovers that follow Lamb are sympathetic despite their treachery. The two strands – Polidori's vampire aristocrat and Lamb's destructive, Byronic lover – reunite in the paranormal romances of the present day. Frances Ford Coppola's incarnation of Dracula and Anne Rice's Lestat are sympathetic lovers.[78] Joss Whedon's broody, tormented Angel is in the same vein, and then followed that explosion of vampire lovers of whom *Twilight*'s Edward Cullen is the most famous. This has enabled a whole brood of charismatic, mesmeric monsters as lovers – werewolves and fairies, and even gargoyles, mermen, and zombies.

Polidori's revision of Ruthven stripped away Lamb's ambivalence, but by clearly marking the aristocratic demon lover as both Byronic and a vampire, inaugurated a literary archetype. Polidori also undermines the glamour of romantic villainy – his naïve protagonist, Aubrey has cast Ruthven 'into the hero of a romance' (247) just as, in effect, Lamb had done, but Ruthven is quickly exposed as repulsive. Yet many of the descendants, both those that are only metaphorically vampiric and the more explicit incarnations in paranormal romance, resurrect the alluring mix of rebellion and faithlessness that Lamb depicted. Among the later vampiric progeny of Polidori, such as in *Dracula*, the hypnotic act is seen as repellent because observed by men unsympathetic to the monster who see 'their' women alienated from them. But in woman-centred fictions such as Gothic romance and paranormal romance, this aspect becomes alive again, and the hypnotic power of the vampire lover is a metaphor for a sexual glamour that is intense but often dangerous.

Figure 5.4 Cover of Lady Caroline Lamb, *Glenarvon* [1816], Empress Gothic (New York: Curtis Books, 1973).

As I have shown, Lamb's vampiric love story also performs political commentary; Polidori likewise engages in political satire. But what has happened to this political critique? Heathcliff has buried energies of class revolt; Anne Rice's Lestat and others are perhaps sexual revolutionaries. Often, like Whedon's Angel, romantic vampires may act as conservative guardians of order. Paranormal romances conjoin Gothic and romance fiction, inheriting the figure of the demon lover. One recent and very sophisticated example, Holly Black's *The Coldest Girl in Coldtown*, echoes the generic hybridity of *Glenarvon*, incorporating the additional genre of post-apocalyptic dystopia.[79] In this novel the vampire Gavriel does appear pitted against oppressive systems, both the feudalism of the old order of vampires and the neoliberalism of the dystopian present; the novel has a biting political edge.[80] But perhaps the novel of the radical vampire lover as an agent of emancipation – a sort of Bolshevik *Twilight* – has yet to be written, revivifying the legacy of Lamb and Polidori. We await the resurrection of a contemporary Ruthven, a pale-faced demon lover and vampiric social justice warrior.

Notes

1 John Polidori, *The Vampyre*, Appendix 1 in this volume, pp. 240–67 (p. 246). All further references are from this edition and are given as page numbers in parentheses.
2 See 'Preliminaries for *The Vampyre*', in *The Vampyre and Other Tales of the Macabre*, ed. by Robert Morrison and Chris Baldick (Oxford: Oxford University Press, 1997), pp. 235–43 (pp. 240, 241); and Paul Barber, *Vampires, Burials and Death* (New Haven, CT and London: Yale University Press, 1988), p. 2.
3 Lamb, in her commonplace book, 24 March 1812 (cited in Paul Douglass, *Lady Caroline Lamb: A Biography* (New York: Palgrave Macmillan, 2004), p. 104).
4 Though Lamb's life was certainly fascinating; standard biographies are: Henry Blyth, *Caro the Fatal Passion: The Life of Lady Caroline Lamb*, ed. by Frances Wilson (New York: Coward, McCann & Geoghegan, 1973); Elizabeth Jenkins, *Lady Caroline Lamb* (London: Cardinal Books, 1974); Susan Normington, *Lady Caroline Lamb, That Infernal Woman* (London: House of Stratus, 2001); Douglass, *Lady Caroline Lamb*; and Lady Antonia Fraser, *Lady Caroline Lamb: A Free Spirit* (London: Weidenfeld & Nicolson, 2023). Frances Wilson provides an incisive analysis of how Lamb has been represented in '"An Exaggerated Woman": The Melodramas of Lady Caroline Lamb', in *Byromania: Portraits of the Artist in Nineteenth- and Twentieth-Century Culture*, ed. by Frances Wilson (London: Palgrave Macmillan, 1998), pp. 195–220.
5 Paul Douglass, 'The Madness of Writing: Lady Caroline Lamb's Byronic Identity', *Pacific Coast Philology*, 341 (1999), 53–71 (p. 53); Peter Graham,

'Fictive Biography in 1816: The Case of Glenarvon', *The Byron Journal* (1991), 53–68 (p. 57).
6. John Chubbe, 'Glenarvon Revised – and Revisited', *The Wordsworth Circle*, 10:2 (1979), 205–17.
7. Barbara Judson, 'Roman à Clef and the Dynamics of Betrayal: The Case of *Glenarvon*', *Genre*, 33:2 (2000), 151–69 (p. 151).
8. As does Lauren McCoy in 'Literary Gossip: Caroline Lamb's *Glenarvon* and the Roman à Clef', *Eighteenth-Century Fiction*, 27:1 (2014), 127–50.
9. Nicola J. Watson, 'Trans-Figuring Byronic Identity', in *At the Limits of Romanticism: Essays in Cultural, Feminist, and Materialist Criticism*, ed. by Mary A. Favret and Nicola J. Watson (Bloomington: Indiana University Press, 1994), pp. 185–206.
10. For Byromania and celebrity culture, see Frances Wilson, ed., *Byromania: Portraits of the Artist in Nineteenth- and Twentieth-Century Culture* (Basingstoke: Palgrave Macmillan, 1998); Tom Mole, *Byron's Romantic Celebrity: Industrial Culture and the Hermeneutic of Intimacy* (New York: Palgrave Macmillan, 2007); Ghislaine McDayter, *Byromania and the Birth of Celebrity Culture* (Albany, NY: SUNY Press, 2010); and Clara Tuite, *Lord Byron and Scandalous Celebrity* (Cambridge: Cambridge University Press, 2015). See also Harriet Fletcher's Chapter 4 in this volume.
11. On the publication of *Childe Harold's Pilgrimage*, 'he had become the first living literary "celebrity"' (Ghislaine McDayter, 'Conjuring Byron: Byromania, Literary Commodification and the Birth of Celebrity', in Wilson, *Byromania*, pp. 43–62 (p. 46)). McDayter articulates Byron's celebrity status in terms of 'the nineteenth-century explosion of literary commodification' (p. 44).
12. Tuite, *Lord Byron*, p. xx.
13. Discussions of Lamb's politics in the novel can be found in Judson, 'Roman à Clef'; Malcolm Kelsall, 'The Byronic Hero and Revolution in Ireland: The Politics of Glenarvon', *The Byron Journal*, 9 (1981), 4–19; and Watson, 'Trans-Figuring Byronic Identity'. Judson disagrees (as do I) with Kelsall and Watson that Lamb's political allegiance lies with the English against the rebellious Irish (pp. 168–69).
14. Ghislaine McDayter, 'Hysterically Speaking: Lady Caroline Lamb's *Glenarvon* and the Revolutionary Voice', in *Romantic Generations: Essays in Honor of Robert F. Gleckner*, ed. by Barry Milligan and Ghislaine McDayter (Lewisburg, PA: Bucknell University Press, 2001), pp. 155–77 (p. 161).
15. Douglass, *Lady Caroline Lamb*, p. 198.
16. Tuite, *Lord Byron*, p. 34.
17. Gary Kelly, *English Fiction of the Romantic Period 1789–1830*, Longman Literature In English Series (London and New York: Routledge, 1989), pp. 59, 189. Kelly discusses *Glenarvon* further in this book (pp. 185–87) and in 'Amelia Opie, Lady Caroline Lamb, and Maria Edgeworth: Official and Unofficial Ideology', *Ariel: A Review of International English Literature*, 12:4 (1981), 3–24.
18. Clara Tuite, 'Tainted Love and Romantic Literary Celebrity', *ELH*, 74:1 (2007), 59–88 (p. 73).
19. Tuite, 'Tainted Love', pp. 71, 72.

20 Judson, 'Roman à Clef', p. 153.
21 McDayter, *Byromania*, p. 127.
22 Joseph Garver, 'Gothic Ireland: Lady Caroline Lamb's "Glenarvon"', *Irish University Review*, 10:2 (1980), 213–28. See also Christina Morin, *The Gothic Novel in Ireland, c. 1760–1829* (Manchester: Manchester University Press, 2021). Garver calls it a 'bad novel' (p. 223) and misses, I think, the dialectical treatment of politics in the novel, seeing it as merely a projection of Lamb's 'hysteria' and 'a Whig reaction against "liberty"' (p. 227).
23 Wilson, '"An Exaggerated Woman"' p. 215.
24 See Mikhail Bakhtin, 'Discourse in the Novel', in *The Dialogic Imagination: Four Essays*, ed. by Michael Holquist, trans. by Caryl Emerson and Michael Holquist (Austin: University of Texas Press, 1981), pp. 259–422.
25 *The Cambridge History of Ireland: Volume 3, 1730–1880*, ed. by James Kelly and Thomas Bartlett (Cambridge: Cambridge University Press, 2020), pp. 83–92.
26 Lady Caroline Lamb, *Glenarvon*, intr. by Frances Wilson (1818; London: Everyman, 1995), p. 288. All further references are from this edition and are given as page numbers in parentheses.
27 See Deborah Lutz, *The Dangerous Lover: Gothic Villains, Byronism, and the Nineteenth-Century Seduction Narrative* (Columbus, OH: Ohio State University Press, 2006).
28 Tuite, *Lord Byron*, p. 39. In Lamb's casting of Byron as vampiric, she 'compounded the model of vampiric desire with that of the Romantic sublime', says Frances Wilson, so that the vampire's victim also becomes a vampire, just as Elinor St Clair will become 'more Byronic than the hero himself' (Wilson, 'Introduction', in Caroline Lamb, *Glenarvon* (1818; London: Everyman, 1995), pp. xx–xxi). McDayter talks of Byron and vampirism in terms of the growing alienation of the producer (here, the poet) from their product, a metaphor that Marx would later take up (McDayter, 'Conjuring Byron', p. 44).
29 Letter, quoted in Tuite, *Lord Byron*, p. 20.
30 Tuite, *Lord Byron*, p. 20.
31 Wilson, *Byromania*, p. 163.
32 Leigh Wetherall Dickson, 'Authority and Legitimacy: The Cultural Context of Lady Caroline Lamb's Novels', *Women's Writing*, 133 (2006), 369–91 (p. 384). Wetherall Dickson defends Lamb's novelistic skills and the sharpness of her critique of Whig politics.
33 For McDayter, this episode suggests a view of Byromania as desire not for the poet but for freedom itself (*Byromania*, p. 102).
34 There are precedents for the female Byronic hero in Byron's own poems, such as Gulnare in *The Corsair* (1814); see Gregory Olsen, 'Rewriting the Byronic Hero: "I'll Try the Firmness of a Female Hand"', *European Romantic Review*, 25:4 (2014), 463–77.
35 Douglas, *Lady Caroline Lamb*, p. 205.
36 Frances Wilson, 'Introduction', *Glenarvon*, p. xxxii.
37 James Soderholm, *Fantasy, Forgery, and the Byron Legend* (Lexington: University Press of Kentucky, 1995), p. 11.

38 Lady Caroline Lamb, *Ada Reis: A Tale*, 3 vols (London: John Murray, 1823), I, p. xi.
39 Duncan Wu, 'Appropriating Byron: Lady Caroline Lamb's "A New Canto"', *The Wordsworth Circle*, 26 (1995), 140–46 (p. 46).
40 [Lady Caroline Lamb], *A New Canto* (London: William Wright, 1819).
41 Frances Wilson, 'Introduction: Byron, Byronism and Byromaniacs', in Wilson, *Byromania*, pp. 1–23 (pp. 5–7).
42 Annabella Milbanke, 'The Byromania' [1812], lines 13–14, 17–18, in Wilson, 'Introduction', *Byromania*, p. xii. 'Caro' is Lady Caroline Lamb.
43 See our Introduction to this volume for the debates about Polidori's intertextuality and alleged plagiarism.
44 McDayter argues that Lamb, through her acquaintance with Wollstonecraft's ideas, elucidates the disastrous effect on both personal and national politics of an education that fails to cultivate women's intellectual faculties (McDayter, 'Hysterically Speaking', pp. 163–65).
45 Lamb to Byron, in Blyth, *Caro*, p. 120.
46 Anne Rice, *Interview with the Vampire*, The Vampire Chronicles, 1 (1976; London: Sphere, 2008); Stephenie Meyer, *Twilight*, Twilight, 1 (2005; Atom, 2006). Kaja Franck develops this idea in her Chapter 11 in this volume.
47 Mario Praz, *The Romantic Agony*, trans. by A. Davidson, rev. edn (Oxford: Oxford University Press, 1970), pp. 64, 68. These characteristics, claims Praz, are derived from the novels of Ann Radcliffe.
48 As a medical symptom that connotes glamour, this is linked to tuberculosis; Marcus Sedgwick discusses this in his Chapter 6 in this volume.
49 Lord Byron, 'A Fragment', Appendix 2 in this volume, pp. 268–72 (p. 268).
50 Lord Byron, 'A Fragment', p. 268.
51 Andrew McConnell Stott, *Summer in the Shadow of Byron* (Edinburgh: Canongate Books, 2015), p. 153.
52 Tuite, *Lord Byron*, p. xx.
53 Tuite, *Lord Byron*, pp. xx–xxi.
54 McDayter, *Byromania*, p. 20. See also Jon Mee, *Romanticism, Enthusiasm, and Regulation: Poetics and the Policing of Culture in the Romantic Period* (Oxford: Oxford University Press, 2003).
55 McDayter, *Byromania*, p. 22.
56 Agave is the princess and Maenad who tears apart her own son Pentheus in Euripides' *The Bacchae*.
57 In McDayter's words, 'with Byron playing the role of lustful magus in a sexual debauch with a crowd of innocent victims' ('Conjuring Byron', p. 47). Even more explicitly, 'Byron's following' might be seen as 'an undiscriminating and addicted mob of Bacchantes' (p. 50).
58 Glenarvon's 'cult against authority', says Judson, 'combines carnivalesque license with feminist rebellion' (p. 161).
59 Anne Stiles, Stanley Finger and John Bulevich argue that Polidori's Ruthven draws on his medical dissertation, his 'thesis on somnambulism [which] responds to the influences of mesmerism and phrenology', and that vampirism in this text expresses anxieties about human beings becoming automata

('Somnambulism and Trance States in the Works of John William Polidori, Author of The Vampyre', *European Romantic Review*, 21:6 (2010), 789–807 (p. 790). For further details of mesmerism in this period, see William Hughes, *That Devil's Trick: Hypnotism and the Victorian Popular Imagination* (Manchester: Manchester University Press, 2018).

60 Judson, 'Roman à Clef', p. 162.
61 See, for example, the Jacobin seducer in Vallaton in Elizabeth Hamilton's *Memoirs of Young Philosophers* (1800). The radical Thomas Holcroft neatly reverses the motif by having a Lovelace figure repent and redeem himself through the rational persuasiveness of his would-be victim in *Anna St Ives* (1792).
62 For the egotism and self-interested individualism of Glenarvon's politics, see Kelsall, 'The Byronic Hero'. Peter Graham praises Lamb's depiction of Byron's special blend of liberal politics and conservative social values' (Graham, 'Fictive Biography', p. 65).

For Byron's politics, see also Malcolm Kelsall, 'Byron's Politics', in *The Cambridge Companion to Byron*, ed. by Drummond Bone, Cambridge Companions to Literature (Cambridge and New York: Cambridge University Press, 2004), pp. 44–55; and Malcolm Kelsall, *Byron's Politics* (Brighton and Totowa, NJ: Prentice Hall / Harvester Wheatsheaf, 1987).
63 Judson, 'Roman à Clef', p. 166.
64 These beliefs and the vampire's curse against kin in *The Giaour* appear in the prefatory material to the first edition of *The Vampyre*: 'Preliminaries', p. 242.
65 Glenarvon's end recalls the Flying Dutchman or the Wandering Jew – both components of the Byronic hero as discussed by Thorslev (P. L. Thorslev, *The Byronic Hero: Types and Prototypes* (Minneapolis: University of Minnesota Press, 1962), p. 162). This figure is also incarnated in *Childe Harold*: 'But there are wanderers o'er Eternity / Whose bark drives on and on, and anchored ne'er shall be' (Lord Byron, *Childe Harold's Pilgrimage*, in *Lord Byron: The Major Works*, ed. by Jerome J. McGann (Oxford and New York: Oxford University Press, 2008), III. 70, lines 669–70, p. 125).
66 Though Lamb's revisions for the second edition 'blunt slightly the criticism of Glenarvon's political hypocrisy' (Paul Douglass, 'Twisty Little Passages: The Several Editions of Lady Caroline Lamb's "Glenarvon"', *The Wordsworth Circle*, 40:2/3 (2009), 77–82 (p. 82)).
67 Tuite, 'Tainted Love', p. 73.
68 Though Polidori, perhaps weary of the problems over the past association of the text with Byron, changed the protagonist's name to 'Strongmore' for an intended second edition. See John William Polidori, *The Vampyre and Ernestus Berchtold; or, the Modern Oedipus*, ed. by D. L. Macdonald and Kathleen Scherf (Peterborough, ON: Broadview Press, 2007). This edition is constructed from Polidori's notes towards a second edition and uses the substituted name.
69 See our Introduction to this volume for the debates over Ruthven's class status.

70 David Punter, *The Literature of Terror: A History of Gothic Fictions from 1765 to the Present Day*, 2 vols (London and New York: Longman, 1980), I: *The Gothic Tradition*, pp. 103–04.
71 Percy Bysshe Shelley, *Prometheus Unbound*, III, 4, lines 146–48, in Percy Bysshe Shelley, *The Major Works*, ed. by Zachary Leader and Michael O'Neill (Oxford and New York: Oxford University Press, 2009), pp. 227–313 (p. 292).
72 Simon Bainbridge, 'Lord Ruthven's Power: Polidori's "The Vampyre", Doubles, and the Byronic Imagination', *The Byron Journal*, 34:1 (2006), 21–34 (p. 26).
73 Bainbridge, 'Lord Ruthven's Power', pp. 23–24.
74 Lady Mercer is 'a fictionalized Lady Caroline Lamb' (Patricia L. Skarda, 'Vampirism and Plagiarism: Byron's Influence and Polidori's Practice', *Studies in Romanticism*, 28 (1989), 249–69 (p. 250).
75 See Sam George and Bill Hughes, 'Introduction', *Open Graves, Open Minds: Representations of Vampires and the Undead from the Enlightenment to the Present Day*, ed. by Sam George and Bill Hughes (Manchester: Manchester University Press, 2013), pp. 1–23 (pp. 7–15).
76 See Joseph Crawford, *The Twilight of the Gothic: Vampire Fiction and the Rise of the Paranormal Romance*, Gothic Literary Studies (Cardiff: University of Wales Press, 2014), p. 34.
77 Emily Brontë, *Wuthering Heights*, ed. by Pauline Nestor (1847; London: Penguin, 1995), p. 330.
78 *Bram Stoker's Dracula*, dir. by Frances Ford Coppola (Zoetrope, 1992) and Rice, *Interview*.
79 Holly Black, *The Coldest Girl in Coldtown* (London: Indigo, 2013).
80 See my analysis, 'Genre Mutation in YA Gothic: The Dialectics of Dystopia and Romance in Holly Black's *The Coldest Girl in Coldtown*', in *Young Adult Gothic Fiction: Monstrous Selves/Monstrous Others*, ed. by Michelle J. Smith and Kristine Moruzi, Gothic Literary Studies (Cardiff: University of Wales Press, 2021), pp. 37–59.

6

Sexual contagions: Romantic vampirism and tuberculosis; or, 'I should like to die of a consumption'

Marcus Sedgwick

The modern notion of a vampire presents a conundrum. The creature found in the original folklore of Eastern Europe and the Near East is closer to our idea of a zombie – a repulsive, swollen figure, often a peasant, farmer or labourer, freshly returned from the grave. Apart from their revenant nature, almost nothing links this beast to our prevailing conception of a vampire as a thin, pale, sexually attractive supernatural being. This essay argues for a pivotal role in this transformation for Dr John Polidori, his presentation of the creature in *The Vampyre* and nineteenth-century beliefs about one particular disease: tuberculosis (TB). Let me begin with an often-repeated quote:

> [T]he emaciated figure strikes one with horror; the forehead covered with drops of sweat; the cheeks painted with livid crimson; the eyes sunk; the little fat that raised them in their orbits, entirely wasted; the pulse quick and tremulous; the nails long, dry, and bending over the end of the fingers; [...] the breath offensive.[1]

This gives a vivid depiction of the appearance of a victim of late-stage TB, but it has been noted by various commentators that it might as well be portraying one particular form of the vampire[2] – that is to say, the monstrous form of the vampire, as found originally in folklore and in some later depictions such as that of Count Orlok in 1922's *Nosferatu*, and certainly not as found in nineteenth-, twentieth- and twenty-first-century fiction, for example, the vampires Dracula, Lestat and Edward Cullen, to name one from each century. This quote does, however, form a good starting point for the investigation of the marriage between TB and the vampire.

The passage is cited in numerous works and on various websites as being by a notable physician of the late eighteenth century, Dr Thomas Beddoes, who, because he wrote in English rather than Latin, was read by a much broader section of society than were many of his peers in the scientific community of the age.[3] Page 8 of Beddoes's 1799 *Essay on the Causes, Early Signs, and Prevention of Pulmonary Consumption for the use of Parents and Preceptors* is the source usually given, but, unfortunately, it is an error.

This page does have an unpleasant description of the appearance of the consumptive, but it is not nearly as brutal as the above. The error originates in what is a classic lay work of the twentieth century on tuberculosis: *The White Plague*, by René and Jean Dubos, where Beddoes is given as the source of the 'emaciated figure' quote.[4] In fact, this emaciated figure comes from a slightly earlier work of 1795 by William Nesbit. However, this is not the end for Dr Thomas Beddoes in this story; he will yet return, as all good revenants should.

Such depictions of the classic, late-stage tubercular appearance have a long history. Aretaeus of Cappadocia, writing in the first century CE, told us that the appearance of the victim was:

> slender, but joints thick; of the bones alone the figure remains, for the fleshy parts are wasted; the nails of the fingers crooked, their pulps are shriveled and flat [...] Nose sharp, slender; cheeks prominent and red; eyes hollow, brilliant and glittering; swollen, pale or livid in countenance; the slender parts of the jaws rest on the teeth as, as if smiling; otherwise of cadaverous aspect.[5]

The stark image given here in *De causis et signis diuturnorum morborum* is remarkably similar in tone to Nesbit's over 1,700 years later, and again, Aretaeus might have been giving a good description of some gaunt vampiric creature in the Orlok mode, or the 'monstrous strain', as Stacey Abbot terms it.[6] This may not seem noteworthy, given that a disease ought to just be a disease, but diseases are never just diseases: as Susan Sontag in her seminal *Illness as Metaphor* noted, each has its plethora of cultural attachments and superstitions; those of tuberculosis are highly relevant here.[7]

Part of the mystery of tuberculosis arises from its variable nature; the bacillus responsible, *Mycobacterium tuberculosis*, can infect almost any bodily tissue, from the central nervous system to the lymphatic system to the urogenital system, to bones and joints. However, these extra-pulmonary varieties only account for a total of about 15–20 per cent of cases, and it is pulmonary tuberculosis, with its characteristic symptoms, that is the best-known form.

In 1689, Richard Morton identified the tubercle, the classic lesion caused by the bacterium, as being at the root of the disease, though the concept of bacteria was still centuries off. In 1720, Benjamin Marten proposed that some kind of 'animacula' or microscopic organism was present in victims and was the cause of consumption, but his idea was utterly scorned. Although, in the intervening period, in 1839, Johann Lukas Schönlein coined the term 'tuberculosis', it took 162 years from Marten's proposal of his 'animacula' concept for it to be proved by Robert Koch, who, in 1882, isolated the bacteria and, critically, also proved that infection was the route of transmission.

But we have had a much longer relationship with tuberculosis than this – the disease was present in humans in the Neolithic period – and only very recently has it been understood.[8] In this vacuum of knowledge, strange beliefs about the disease were able to proliferate.

Diseases were, of course, plentiful in the nineteenth century as during all periods of history, yet there was something different about TB. It was not just that it was prevalent, because other diseases periodically came in just as terrible numbers, as epidemics of cholera or typhus, for example, might strike.[9] It was not just that it was on the rise, as appeared to be the case; figures from Thomas Beddoes showed an increase of deaths from consumption of 18 per cent between 1790 and 1799.[10] What really made consumption different was the mysterious way that it struck. It did not take out everyone and anyone, indiscriminately, as other diseases could; it would affect some in a household yet leave others untouched. Susan Sontag argues that TB was not perceived as a disease of society as a whole, but of individuals:

> In contrast to the great epidemic diseases of the past, which strike each person as a member of an afflicted community, TB was understood as a disease that isolates one from the community. However steep its incidence in a population, TB – like cancer today – always seemed to be a mysterious disease of individuals, a deadly arrow that could strike anyone, that singled out its victims one by one.[11]

Ignorance is a great breeding ground for superstition, and while we now know how tuberculosis operates, we must look at it through the lens of the time during which it managed to achieve an extraordinary thing for any disease – it succeeded in becoming fashionable. The period in question is the end of the eighteenth century and the beginning of the nineteenth, the period of the brief life of John William Polidori.

According to William Michael Rossetti, Polidori's nephew and first biographer, John took his degree in medicine at 'a singularly early age – I believe almost unexampled'.[12] According to the registers of the University of Edinburgh, he went up in October 1811, when aged barely sixteen, and graduated on 1 August 1815, five weeks short of his twentieth birthday, with the publication of his inaugural dissertation, 'De Oneirodynia' ['On Sleepwalking']. Eighty-two other men from Scotland, England and sundry other lands including Jamaica, Trinidad and 'the Brazils' graduated along with the young Polidori, publishing theses on a range of medical matters. Each year, alongside treatments of various other maladies, there would typically be one or two theses on *Phthisi Pulmonali*, that is to say, pulmonary tuberculosis. In John's 'class of 1815', there were three.

Despite Edinburgh's reputation, learning was rather hit-and-miss during John's time there. Lecturers were not paid by the university directly, but rather received fees individually from each student. While a classical economist might expect this competitive system to reward and therefore deliver only the best lecturers, the result in practice was anything but, and nepotism was rife; eight of the ten professors hired in the two decades prior to John's arrival were sons of incumbents.[13]

What would John have learned of consumption itself? Beddoes's popular book of 1799 is as good as any for a typical contemporary overview of the disease and its modus operandi. Certain types of person, he explains, were exempt from the ravages of the disease. Consumption, it was thought, did not affect butchers, makers of catgut, fishwives, sailors and other watermen, stable boys and grooms, among various other occupations. There were other professions, however, that were more liable to attack. Stone cutters, needle grinders and miners, for example, as well as tailors, glovers, shoemakers, weavers, spinners and carpet makers – 'all in short, who follow sedentary occupations in confined rooms, whatever their habitual posture – are extremely liable to this fatal disease'.[14]

As mentioned above, Dr Beddoes, though not responsible for the 'emaciated figure' quote, did include a similarly harrowing passage in his 1799 work, detailing the appalling end for a victim of consumption.[15] He argued that the reality of this disease was very different from popular, romanticised notions about the disease:

> The fatality and frequency of consumption are better understood than its severity. Writers of romance (whether from ignorance or because it suits the tone of their narrative) exhibit the slow decline of the consumptive, as a state on which the fancy may agreeably repose, and in which not more misery is felt, than is expressed by a blossom, nipped by untimely frosts.[16]

Beddoes argues that unfamiliarity with consumption's true nature allowed those who had not been literally face-to-face with its end stages, 'writers of romance' and others, to make it seem less awful than it truly was. Instead, there was the opportunity for a tragic-romantic image of chronic illness (albeit fatal at some distant, unspecified time) to flourish, which is indeed what happened.

As Katherine Byrne has noted, and Sontag before her, the fact that certain people were struck by consumption while others in close proximity were not seemed to imply that there must be something about the *individual* that was responsible.[17] Today, we know that many people are infected with the bacillus without effect, and even this knowledge seems to imply that the individual host is what makes the difference; without this knowledge, it seemed only the more to be the case that it was the individual who was to blame. Doctors of the eighteenth and nineteenth centuries had a word for the predisposition of an individual to succumb to a particular illness – diathesis. So what was the consumptive diathetic type?

First, there were physical characteristics. On his voyage with Byron through Flanders, Polidori noted in his diary entry for 26 April 1816 that they had come across a group of musicians, one of whom, the trombonist, was 'manifestly consumptive'.[18] It was well known what comprised the look that made it so easy to spot the victim of TB. Writing in 1814, Dr Henry Herbert Southey wrote of pulmonary consumption that:

> The individuals most liable to be attacked by this form of the disease are distinguished by a combination of many of the following marks, sometimes by all of them; Fair thin smooth skin, through which the blood vessels may be seen – blooming cheeks – light soft hair – light eyes with dilated pupils – thick nose and upper lip – white teeth – head rather large – narrow chest – flaccid muscles, and long weak fingers, of which the last joint is large.[19]

The narrow chest is frequently mentioned in such accounts, and medical writers attributed the susceptibility to consumption to be likely both in the case of those born with a naturally compressed chest, or one that had been compressed through the wearing of corsets. The supposed evils of the corset in causing consumption is an old story; the medical literature of the early eighteenth century already abounds in doctors railing against this fashion.[20] Witness Edward Delafield in his doctoral thesis of 1816:

> The thorax may become accidentally deformed form any violence done to it [...] The corset, to which I allude, when worn only with moderate firmness, and by those not otherwise predisposed to Phthisis, serves but to add elegance and beauty to the female figure: but when applied with the object of converting it into a delicate and slender waist, one naturally otherwise, it cannot but do injury.[21]

Likewise, Alire Raffeneau Delile wrote, in 1807: 'Tight lacing the chest, and the use of corsets, by impeding respiration and confinement of the motion of the ribs, of themselves become, in some instances, exciting causes of phthisis.'[22] Or, here is an epigram found in another work of Thomas Beddoes: 'On verra toujours beaucoup de pulmoniques parmi nous, tant que nos modes tendront à l'affaiblissement de la poitrine et que peu de personnes auront l'esprit assez fort pour se mettre au dessus de l'usage' ('We will continue to see lots of consumptives among us, as long as our fashions tend towards the enfeeblement of the chest and while few people have sufficient strength of mind to put them out of use').[23]

Narrow chests were seen as a big problem. And if you didn't have one to start with, you soon would – recording the progression of the disease, William Turton of Oriel College, Oxford wrote in 1813 of: 'that appearance of high cheek and shoulder bones, long neck, and narrow confined chest: the angles of the jaw bones seem prominent and sharp-edged, and the nose thin and pointed: the fingers when held before a candle are transparent at the edges.'[24]

But the diathesis of consumption also included psychical factors. Here is William Turton again: 'the faculties of the mind seem to develope [sic] themselves with unusual facility and precocity; and the senses of hearing, taste, and smell to be singularly acute'.[25] This aspect of the tubercular is noteworthy, being highly reminiscent of Bram Stoker's *Dracula* (1897), where Lucy Westenra's faculties sharpen as she is slowly consumed by Dracula over a period of days. Though it is never specified, Stoker plays with the reader's knowledge of consumptive tropes in Lucy's last days – in addition to the blood loss, which we might expect in a case of vampire attack, there are frequent references to her struggling for breath, which we might not, in addition of course to the general pallor and thinness which has overcome her. During a period of remission, Mina writes, 'she is a trifle stouter, and her cheeks are a lovely rose pink. She has lost that anaemic look which she had.'[26] And by the end, we are told, Lucy made 'a very beautiful corpse', according at least to the woman who has laid her body out.[27]

But this is at the far end of the century. Back in 1808, James Sanders, 'one of the Presidents of the Royal Medical and Royal Physical Societies of Edinburgh' and indeed writing in Edinburgh, just three years before Polidori came up, records the nature of the typical consumptive:

> To them, frightful dreams with muttering or even walking in sleep, and incubus, are not unusual. They are whimsical, naturally generous, sometimes prodigal; they are often remarkable for the finer sympathies, are sometimes adorned by nature with personal grace and intellectual superiority; they are generally addicted to the pleasures of love, are of acute sensibility and irascible, they often abound in mirth and fancy, but are more often affected with melancholy.[28]

Such assumptions were more or less the norm both inside and outside of the medical sphere, but not everyone was convinced. Despite his status in the medical circle of the city, an unnamed critic in the *Edinburgh Medical and Surgical Journal* roundly lambasted Sanders's book. In a seven-page assault that would make anyone weep, not only the president's work, but the president himself, are torn apart; even the title page does not escape mockery. Aside from the excoriation, one passage should be halted at: 'The author, being strongly impressed with the doctrines of the Brunonian school, seems to consider increased or diminished action of the circulating system, as constituting the sum total of disease.'[29]

'Brunonian' is a reference to a new theory of medicine by John Brown, a major figure of the medical scene in Edinburgh in the eighteenth century, a theory that had some few but devoted followers during the period. One of them was none other than Dr Thomas Beddoes, who in 1795 translated John Brown's major work of 1780, *Elementa Medicinae*, into English and thus popularised his theory that all disease was due to 'under-' or 'over-excitability' of the human organism; diseases were either 'asthenic' (the body doing too little) or sthenic (the body doing too much). Under this theory, consumption was a case of over-excitation of the individual. At first sight there seems to be a contradiction here – one might assume that the archetypal 'wasting' disease would be an asthenic condition – but Clark Lawlor explains that although Brown considered consumption to be a general wasting of the body, and therefore to be an asthenic disease,

> this was only part of a more complex disease process. Consumption could be the result of a chronic *sthenic* condition: if a poet [...] worked too hard and too quickly, his genius at full stretch, mental and physical over-stimulation would eventually result in languorous exhaustion and disease.[30]
>
> [my italics]

One of Brown's other admirers, and a close friend of Beddoes himself, was a man who did no small work in promoting his ideas in Germany, namely Samuel Taylor Coleridge. In his letters, Coleridge several times refers to Brown as a genius.[31] Coleridge was a close acquaintance of one of the few friends John Polidori made through his time at Edinburgh, Robert Gooch. Gooch was not a strict contemporary of Polidori, but a thirty-year-old alumnus of the medical school at which John still had a year to go before graduation. John met Gooch while back in London in 1814, around the time that the former wrote the first of his tragedies, *Count Orlando* (later called *Ximenes*), which borrowed heavily from Coleridge's play *Remorse*. With Coleridge, the Romanic poets enter the picture.

The Brunonian theory of disease is typified by a consumptive poet like John Keats, 'half in love with easeful Death' – that merciful release from this real world 'where youth grows pale, and spectre thin, and dies'.[32] The latter line from 'Ode to a Nightingale' is commonly held to refer to John's brother's death from consumption in late 1818, just twenty-seven months before his own. Or a poet like Percy Shelley, of whom Henry Southey's description above of 'Fair thin smooth skin – blooming cheeks – light soft hair' could be of the man himself. Shelley's first wife, Harriet Westbrook, had called him a vampire when he abandoned her for Mary Wollstonecraft Godwin. Shelley was a man who believed he was dying of consumption, having been told so by his doctor. His and Mary's doctor was William Lawrence, the scientist locked in a battle with John Abernethy over the 'vital spark' versus 'instrument' debate about the wherefore of mankind, which found its way into the debates at the Villa Diodati and from there into Mary's *Frankenstein*; these are the 'philosophical doctrines' about the 'principle of life' that she refers to in her 1831 introduction to the book.[33] Whether Percy was actually consumptive or not is beside the point: his was the classic appearance of the consumptive. Shelley in turn sympathised with his friend Keats over his illness, and tried to console him by pointing out that 'this consumption is a disease particularly fond of people who write such good verses as you have done' – that is, it takes a certain sensitive kind of soul to succumb to TB.[34] Mario Praz argues: 'There is no end to the examples which might be quoted from the Romantic and Decadent writers on the subject of the indissoluble union of the beautiful and the sad, on the supreme beauty of that which is accursed.'[35] It is around this time that tuberculosis starts to become fashionable – a disease that people *thought* they wanted (even if the reality would have been very different); by 1810, it was already a sufficiently well-established notion for Lord Byron to declare to Lord Sligo, 'How pale I look! I should like, I think, to die of a consumption.' Upon being asked why, Byron's famous reply was, 'Because then the women would all say "See that poor Byron – how interesting he looks in dying".'[36]

Here we approach perhaps the most important, if paradoxical, key to the understanding of how tuberculosis and the vampire became intertwined. To summarise, the consumptive was intelligent, of quick wit and nervous sensibility, of narrow chest and flaccid musculature. They were beautiful and tragic. But in addition, at first sight seemingly incongruously, they were innocent and pure of heart and yet, as the same time, deeply sexy. Not only were consumptives thought to be highly attractive, but it was also believed that they had heightened sexual appetites, something I will turn to now, for how this apparent contradiction of sexuality and innocence came to be takes some unpicking.

There were an increasing number of medical men who held that a great part of the cause of consumption was, in short, licentious behaviour. For example, Charles Pears, MD, FLS, wrote (in handsome capital letters) in 1814 that there were four main causes of consumption:

THE INCREASED VARIABLITY OF OUR ATMOSPHERE
THE PREVAILING FASHIONS
THE INCREASED MERCANTILE INTERESTS, and
GENERAL INTEMPERANCE, EXCESS and DEBAUCHERY.[37]

It was never quite specified precisely what that debauchery entailed, but Pears assigned 'more than one fourth of the whole number' of deaths from consumption to these factors.[38] While the cause behind syphilis was all too well known, and its horrible effects too ghastly to be ignored, unknown, downplayed or turned into a thing of agreeable fancy, consumption was, as always, more mysterious. These doctors did not spell it out, but they knew the consumptive was indulging in something scandalous. This association with heightened sexual appetites has distant roots. At least as far back as Shakespeare, consumption was a metaphor for thwarted love: *Much ado About Nothing* contains a joke about the illness, as Beatrice tells Benedick that she might yield to him, 'partly to save your life, for I was / told you were in a consumption' – the idea being that his lovesickness is the root of the disease, that his unsatisfied sexual desires are what lie behind his illness.[39]

As I return to the late eighteenth century, to Thomas Beddoes, the question of gender arises. Doctors of the period had a lot to say about women and TB. Having duly noted certain women's narrow chests, Beddoes moves on to discuss the daily habits of those females 'not being obliged to work hard for their subsistence', and then, with a notable use of vampiric metaphor, argues that:

> Our ladies, unable to receive and digest a proper quantity of aliment, are apt to fall farther short of immortality than their equals in society. They are scarce alive, while they continue to breathe; and, in numberless instances, *a fiend, infinitely more cruel than the nightmare*, makes a lodgement in the bosom; and finishes by strangling them, after he has oppressed them long.[40]
>
> [my italics]

The 'nightmare' here is possibly a reference to Fuseli's scandalously sexual painting of 1781, which had become a worldwide sensation, and in this passage Beddoes shows he may have been even better suited to the role of writer of Gothic Romance than Polidori himself. If we were in doubt of the supernatural reference, Beddoes continues:

> Effeminate men, of course, become the prey of the same malignant imp. But *men*, at least *young men*, cannot easily devote themselves so entirely to indolence, as women have the misfortune to be devoted by our usages. They indeed make it up in a degree, but not completely, by wantonly braving the agents of destruction.[41]

So here we have it – women, being indolent, open themselves to the 'malignant imp' of consumption through their wanton behaviour, something that young men, being unable to devote themselves to indulgence and idleness, cannot do. Unless they happen to be poets, no doubt. Note that Beddoes excuses the women from total blame; being the subject of 'our usages', they have little choice in the matter. Presumably those sensitive poets are likewise excused, and this idea that consumptives had a pure, innocent, almost child-like naivety was also frequently touted. As noted, not only were consumptives thought to look more attractive that the average mortal, but they were also thought to have greater sexual appetites. Part of this latter myth may have been connected with the notion of *spes phthisica* – an aspect of the very final stages of the disease, the consumptive would suddenly be blessed with a state of euphoria, and energy, in which at times the patient might well indulge in some sexual activity, something that could be perceived to be bizarre behaviour for someone who is dying. The sage doctor, however, knew this to be a very bad sign, for it meant that the end was imminent, while for the patient it provided welcome, if ultimately illusory, relief. Thus, the consumptive, at different times and to different people, is able to be pure and virtuous, but yet also is believed to indulge in the licentious behaviour that is causing their own destruction.

For poets such as Shelley, then, consumption provided the perfect vehicle upon which to lay their melancholy. The victim (Keats, for example) was held to be more sensitive, more refined. The disease often moved slowly, leaving the sufferer well enough able to function for months, if not years, before the end. It rendered the victim thinner, and more attractive, with cheek bones becoming prominent, above perhaps just a periodic touch of the characteristic rose-pink blush on paling skin – disease as cosmetics.

Finally, apply the notion that tragedy renders the beauty that it strikes yet more beautiful, and the picture is complete. In consumption were two powerful poetic forces inextricably linked: Beauty and Death. All that was needed now was a monster to take advantage of this conjunction.

In *Vampires, Burial and Death*, his otherwise excellent examination of how the decomposition of the human corpse may have given rise to the vampire legend, Paul Barber makes one notable omission, in that there is almost no discussion of disease.[42] While noting that it may have been supposed that the first to die of an epidemic has become a vampire and is causing all the subsequent deaths, there is no discussion of individual candidates, of which diseases may have best leant themselves to giving birth to vampire lore.

Some have tried to apply the characteristics of certain diseases to the vampire legend, for example, Dr David Dolphin's suggestion that porphyria is the origin of the vampire myth.[43] As I have argued elsewhere, the vast majority of supposedly classic vampiric characteristics do not feature in the original folklore of Eastern Europe and are instead of relatively modern origin, one main exception to this being garlic aversion.[44] Such explanations tend to tie themselves in knots for the simple reason that they are trying to explain the wrong thing, that is, the modern, Byronic vampire, not the original folkloric one.

Nevertheless, as Stoker would make much play of in *Dracula*, vampirism is well-thought-of as disease. Never mind 'Illness as Metaphor'; this is vampirism as metaphor, metaphor for disease, and while over the centuries all diseases may have contributed something to the vampire lore in general, consumption added some very specific aspects during a very specific period, namely the late eighteenth and early nineteenth century.

Folk remedies for consumption were, inevitably, ineffective. They included such things as ingesting spoonsful of ashes from Midsummer fires in Belgium or being passed through a certain cleft in the rocks on the Isle of Mull.[45] Since these cures were doomed to failure, it is no surprise that occasionally, stronger measures were taken. In his book *Food for the Dead*, Michael E. Bell catalogues the cases of outbreaks of consumption in New England between 1793 and the end of the following century, in which it was not only believed that the sickness was the result of revenant activity, but in which bodies were exhumed and burnt, or the hearts burnt, and sometimes the ashes consumed as a remedy for the problem. Although the desperate practitioners of these acts themselves never used the word 'vampire', they truly believed their relatives were returning from the grave to drain the life from the living but slowly wasting members of the family – just the way that consumption would have appeared to them.

These accounts, the most famous of which is the Mercy Brown case of Exeter, Rhode Island, immediately recall exactly the same practice from Transylvanian and other Eastern European countries of exhuming supposed vampires and burning and eating the heart in the form of ashes, right into the twentieth century, as with the case of Petre Toma in 2003/04.[46] Indeed, though writing about New World events, Bell argues that this practice was an Old World custom being enacted by relatively recent immigrants. He cites one reference of consumption-as-vampire from the Old World from an 1893 essay by C. A. Fraser on Scottish legends from Ontario which, at one point, breaks off to recount the following story:

> I was a little shocked to hear of a repulsive superstition which I have read of as being peculiar to certain parts of England, – I mean a horrible vampire story given in explanation of the ravages often made in a family by consumption. I did not meet this superstition myself, but was told that it was among them. Consumption was rife among them; it seemed to be hereditary. They looked so remarkably robust, and yet fell so easily a prey to this disease, and it seldom lingered! It was nearly always a very rapid illness.[47]

This is a tantalising reference that seems to imply the existence of an established folk legend connecting vampirism and tuberculosis found in Europe, but sadly further evidence of this has not yet been found. Yet this one reference alone shows that, just as our relationship with disease in general and tuberculosis in particular has not stayed the same throughout time, neither have our relationships with the monsters of myth and legend, nor our innate desire to explain the real world through storytelling. Perhaps one monster more than any other seems adept at changing its face when needed, just as consumption has been able to. That monster is, of course, the vampire. In 1816, John Polidori was surrounded by them, figuratively. At twenty, he was not the youngest of the parties that travelled to Cologny that ungenial summer, but he was the most inexperienced in the ways of the world. Having spent his adolescent years at a remote and strict Catholic boarding school in Yorkshire, he found he did not really understand or mix with his contemporaries at Edinburgh. He showed the classic syndrome of the prodigy who attends university at a precocious age: mature in his interests and studies, yet immature in nature; hot-headed, naïve and guileless. Before Byron and he had even left England, his employer and two old friends had humiliated John by sniggering and buffooning as they read one of his pieces of writing out loud in the Ship Inn at Dover.[48] By the time they reached Switzerland the relationship between Byron and a man whom Byron always saw as an employee, one who had initially written to his sister saying he felt on 'an equal footing' with his master, was already stretched.

Yet domineering as he was, Polidori still idolised Byron at this time, as he did Percy Shelley, whose work he also greatly admired. Though he had not managed to become friends with Coleridge, he was now spending the time in the company of a couple who were, like him, ardent admirers of the great poet. Shelley had pursued Coleridge halfway across England and back trying to meet his hero, while Mary Godwin had heard Coleridge recite his *Rime of the Ancient Mariner*, with its Gothic imagery, in her own home while she sat on the stairs, aged just eight years old.[49]

On to Cologny in 1816, where the idea of vampires was prevalent. Polidori was present on the evening of 18 June when Byron recited Coleridge's *Christabel* – a poem which arguably features a vampiric element. The reading caused Shelley to dash from the room at the horror of his eyes-for-nipples hallucination.[50] Byron had included a vampire in his poem *The Giaour*, of 1813, in which the narrator prophesies how the title character will be cursed to return from the grave and prey upon his own family. And the very title page of *Fantasmagoriana*, the book of German ghost stories (read in French translation by the party) that prompted the story-writing competition in the first place, mentions 'revenans'.[51]

Later that year, Polidori picked up the 'Fragment' that Byron had begun during the well-documented lakeside ghost-story-writing competition that led to *Frankenstein*, and he chose to borrow freely from and complete a tale of terror using vampires as the operant of that fear. The precise nature of this vampire, however, is down to three things: Lord Byron; the 'Fragment' of a story he left as a starting point; and the contemporary conception of tuberculosis.

All the ingredients were there. There was Byron, mysterious and handsome, with a consumptive's pale skin and poetic sensitivities. There was the fact that consumption, like the vampire, sometimes seemed to return to prey upon members of a family, one by one, each one wasting away to death from seemingly unknowable causes. There was the fact that his love–hate relationship with his employer presented him with a tailor-made candidate for a monster, especially one that feeds off the energy, psychic or otherwise, of people close to him. Finally, there was another form of love–hate – the simultaneous appeal and horror of consumption, which made you more attractive, more interesting, and with heightened sexual desires, but which would ultimately kill you. In just the same way, the vampire's victim was simultaneously horrified by and yet attracted to the thing that would finally cause death – the vampire, but, it must be stressed, the post-folklore, Byronic vampire. The Polidori vampire.

Byron's 'Fragment' of a story had given us the noble Augustus Darvell, whose constitution is failing 'without the intervention of any apparent disease: he had neither cough nor hectic, yet he became daily more enfeebled [...] he was evidently wasting away' – the word 'hectic' here being a specific reference to the fever associated with tuberculosis.[52]

Building upon this figure, with its suggestions of a victim of vampiric exsanguination, Polidori also transposes something akin to the voyage that he and Byron had made, and even the reason for it – scandalous affairs back home – onto his Lord Ruthven, and in so doing works up the prototype that was to spawn the genuine modern vampire craze, with the typical consumptive look. His short book abounds with the physical appearance of this new, 'Byronic' vampire, including the 'deadly hue of his face' and 'appearance of something supernatural', not to mention various other tropes of vampiric evil that Ruthven lugs about with him,[53] for example, the suggestion that he falls upon almost any beautiful young woman unfortunate enough to cross his path.

We can even put our finger on the exact moment in literary history that the vampire is changed from shambling corpse to alluring killer; Aubrey, the story's hapless hero, is horrified when his Grecian love interest, Ianthe, begins to talk of vampires in the locale, and then details 'to him the *traditional appearance* of these monsters, and his horror was increased, by hearing a pretty accurate description of Lord Ruthven' [my italics].[54] It is in this sentence that the transformation of the vampire is enacted, rewriting the past, casting aside centuries of folklore; forever after, vampires shall look like Lord George Gordon Byron, and a consumptive version of the lord at that.

As I show above, commentators have sometimes struggled to explain the origins of the vampire myth because they have been trying to explain the wrong thing; the modern notion of the vampire differs in almost every respect from that of the original folkloric revenant such as the Greek *vrykolakoi* (tales of which Byron came across on his particularly Levantine Grand Tour, and which were recorded by Tournefort in his *Relation d'un voyage du Levant* (1717)).

The folkloric vampire is typically a swollen, ruddy-faced corpse, most likely of the peasantry, gorged on the blood of its victims. It makes no sense that the vampire has suddenly become thin and pale and elegant, even noble, unless one views the matter through the paradoxical lens of tuberculosis, whose victims are described as being pale, despite the rose buds in the cheeks, who are both virtuous yet wanton, sexually enhanced and yet near to death. Only by including tuberculosis in the picture does it make sense that the swollen peasant vampire of folklore became the thin white duke of the Byronic variety. As 'writers of romance' used consumption as the perfect vehicle for their noble melancholy, it became simultaneously pinned to the vampire, changing its appearance forever.[55] Conversely, just as consumption was able to achieve the extraordinary status of becoming a disease that people actually wanted (with Byron himself as one a famous example), the vampire managed a similar feat, by successfully attaching itself, parasitically, to consumption's changing face at this moment in history, thus becoming the monster we were to become most familiar with on the screen during the twentieth century, from Dracula to Lestat.

Both consumption and the vampire are dialectical unities of opposites, in which our desire for, and fear of, something are simultaneously expressed. As Stoker made heavy allusion to in his novel, the vampire is well seen as disease, while for folklore disease is a vampire. They are one and the same; the disease we are talking about, ever since John Polidori put pen to paper, is tuberculosis.

To conclude, a quote from John Murray, a writer of various scientific papers, from his *Treatise on Pulmonary Consumption* (1830), makes an explicit link between vampirism and tuberculosis:

> Consumption, like the vampire, while it drinks up the vital stream, fans with its wings the hopes that flutter in the hectic breast; the transparent colours that flit on the features like those of the rainbow on the cloud, are equally evanescent, and leave its darkness more deeply shaded. They who are the kindliest and the best it selects for its victims, while it softens the temper to an angel tone, as if it would attenuate that delicate materialism to an aërial being, in anticipation of the change it is so soon to assume.[56]

Note that this quote contains an unspoken ambiguity, to the extent that the TB victim is portrayed here as angelic, while they could also, as we have seen in this chapter, be viewed as sexual beings, and thus potentially predatory in nature. As so often with discussion of TB, we have multiple, shifting identities, just as we so often find in our explorations of the vampire.

Notes

1. William Nesbit, *An Inquiry Into the History, Nature, Causes, and Different Modes of Treatment: Hitherto Pursued, in the Cure of Scrophula and Cancer* (Edinburgh: Alex. Chapman & Co, 1795), p. 33.
2. For example, Gregory Rutecki, 'Consumption and Vampires: Metaphor and Myth before Science', *Hektoen International: A Journal of Medical Humanities*, 9:2 (spring 2017) https://hekint.org/2017/03/04/consumption-and-vampires-metaphor-and-myth-before-science/ [accessed 23 June 2022].
3. See, for example, Michael E. Bell, *Food for the Dead: On the Trail of New England's Vampires* (Middletown, CT: Wesleyan University Press, 2014); Katherine Byrne, *Tuberculosis and the Victorian Literary Imagination* (Cambridge: Cambridge University Press, 2011).
4. René Dubos and Jean Dubos, *The White Plague; Tuberculosis, Man and Society* (Boston, MA: Little, Brown, 1952).
5. Aretaeus, *De causis et signis diuturnorum morborum*, trans. by Francis Adams, in *The Extant Works of Aretaeus, The Cappadocian* (London: Sydenham Society, 1856).
6. Stacey Abbot, speaking at 'Nosferatu at 100: The Vampire as Contagion and Monstrous Outsider', OGOM online conference, March 2022.
7. Susan Sontag, *Illness as Metaphor* (New York: Farrar, Straus and Giroux, 1978).
8. Israel Hershkovitz et al., 'Detection and Molecular Characterization of 9,000-year-old Mycobacterium Tuberculosis from a Neolithic Settlement in the Eastern Mediterranean', *PLOS One*, 3:10 (15 October 2008), e3426.
9. H. D. Chalke, 'Some Historical Aspects of Tuberculosis', *Public Health*, 74:3 (December 1959), 83–95.
10. Thomas Beddoes, 'Essay Seventh, On Consumption', in *Hygëia: Or, Essays Moral and Medical on the Causes Affecting the Personal State of our Middling and Affluent Classes*, 3 vols (Bristol: Printed by J. Mills, for R. Phillips, 1802–03), ii, p. 5.
11. Sontag, *Illness as Metaphor*, p. 37.
12. William Michael Rossetti, 'Introduction', *The Diary of Dr. John William Polidori, 1816: Relating to Byron, Shelley, etc.*, ed. by William Michael Rossetti (London: Elkin Mathews, 1911), p. 2.
13. Andrew McConnell Stott, *The Poet and The Vampire: The Curse of Byron and the Birth of Literature's Greatest Monsters* (New York: Pegasus, 2014), pp. 30–33.
14. Beddoes, 'Essay Seventh', p. 64.
15. Beddoes, 'Essay Seventh', p. 8.
16. Beddoes, 'Essay Seventh', p. 7. The passage in the second ('much enlarged') edition is a little different: 'The fatality and frequency of consumption are better understood than its severity. Writers of fictitious biography (whether from ignorance or to give their narrative a seasoning of the pathetic) exhibit the slow decline of the consumptive, as a state on which the fancy may agreeably repose. The personal charms of young females have occasioned them, in all countries, to be compared to flowers. Hence a young woman, whose lungs are fatally affected, is a blossom nipped by untimely frosts.'

17 Byrne, *Tuberculosis*, p. 24; Sontag, *Illness as Metaphor*, p. 32.
18 John William Polidori, *The Diary of Dr. John William Polidori, 1816: Relating to Byron, Shelley, etc.*, ed. by William Michael Rossetti (London: Elkin Mathews, 1911), 26 April 1816, 'Bruges', p. 36.
19 Henry Herbert Southey, *Observations on Pulmonary Consumption* (London: Longman, Hurst, Rees, Brown, Orme and Brown, 1814), pp. 4–5.
20 Byrne, *Tuberculosis*, pp. 7–8.
21 Edward Delafield, *An Inaugural Dissertation on Pulmonary Consumption* (New York: John Forbes, 1816), p. 13.
22 Alire Raffeneau Delile, *An Inaugural Dissertation on Pulmonary Consumption* (New York: Columbia College, 1807), p. 29.
23 Beddoes, 'Essay Seventh', p. 2, quoting from Edme-Claude Bourru's '*des bains*'.
24 William Turton, *Observations on Consumption, Scrofula or King's Evil, Gout, Asthma, Softness and Distortion of the Bones, Rickets, Cancer, Insanity and Other Chronical Diseases* (Dublin: Graisberry and Campbell, 1813), p. 48.
25 Turton, *Observations*, p. 47,
26 Bram Stoker, *Dracula* (London: Penguin Classics, 1993), p. 82.
27 Stoker, *Dracula*, p. 174.
28 Dr James Sanders, *Treatise on Pulmonary Consumption* (Edinburgh: Walker and Grieg, 1808), pp. 3–4.
29 Review of 'Treatise on Pulmonary Consumption', *Edinburgh Medical and Surgical Journal*, 4:15 (1808), 367.
30 Clark Lawlor, *Consumption and Literature: The Making of the Romantic Disease* (Basingstoke: Palgrave, 2006), p. 116.
31 Neil Vickers, 'Coleridge, Thomas Beddoes and Brunonian Medicine', *European Romantic Review*, 8:1 (1997), 47–94.
32 John Keats, 'Ode to a Nightingale' [1819], in *The Major Works*, ed. by Elizabeth Cook (Oxford and New York: Oxford University Press, 2001), pp. 285–88, lines 52, 26.
33 Mary Shelley, 'Introduction', *Frankenstein; or, The Modern Prometheus*, ed. by M. K. Joseph (1831; Oxford: Oxford University Press, 1998), pp. 5–11 (p. 8).
34 Keats's letter to P. B. Shelley, 16 August 1820, in Maurice Buxton Forman, ed., *The Letters of John Keats* (Oxford: Oxford University Press, 1952).
35 Mario Praz, *The Romantic Agony*, trans. by A. Davidson, rvsd. edn (Oxford: Oxford University Press, 1970), p. 31.
36 Thomas Moore, *The Life of Lord Byron* (London: John Murray, 1844), p. 113.
37 Charles Pears, *Observations on the Nature and Treatment of Consumption; Addressed to Patients and Families* (London: Highley and Son, 1814), p. vii.
38 Pears, *Observations*, p. x.
39 William Shakespeare, *Much Ado About Nothing*, v. 4. 94–95.
40 Beddoes, 'Essay Seventh', p. 44.
41 Beddoes, 'Essay Seventh', pp. 44–45.
42 Paul Barber, *Vampires, Burial, and Death: Folklore and Reality* (New Haven, CT and London: Yale University Press, 1988).
43 Philip M. Boffey, 'Rare Disease Proposed as Cause for "Vampires"', *The New York Times*, 31 May 1985 www.nytimes.com/1985/05/31/us/rare-disease-proposed-as-cause-for-vampires.html [accessed 30 July 2020].

44 Marcus Sedgwick, 'The Elusive Vampire, Folklore and Fiction', *Open Graves, Open Minds: Representations of Vampires and the Undead from the Enlightenment to the Present Day*, ed. by Sam George and Bill Hughes (Manchester: Manchester University Press, 2013), pp. 264–75.
45 Sir James Frazer, *The Golden Bough*, 3rd edn, 12 vols (London: Macmillan, 1906–15), x: *Balder the Beautiful (Part I)*, p. 195; xi: *Balder the Beautiful (Part II)*, p. 187.
46 Daniel McLaughlin, 'A Village Still in Thrall to Dracula', *The Observer*, 19 June 2005, www.theguardian.com/world/2005/jun/19/theobserver [accessed 30 July 2020].
47 C. A. Fraser, 'Scottish Myths from Ontario', *Journal of American Folklore*, 6:22 (July–September 1893), 185–98 (p. 196).
48 Stott, *The Poet and the Vampire*, p. 19.
49 Stott, *The Poet and the Vampire*, p. 63.
50 Polidori, *The Diary*, 18 June 1816, 'Villa Diodati', p. 128.
51 *Fantasmagoriana, ou recueil d'histoires d'apparitions de spectres, revenans, fantômes; etc.*, trans. by Jean-Baptiste Benoît Eyriès, 2 vols (Paris: chez F. Schoell, 1812), title page.
52 Lord Byron, 'Augustus Darvell', in *The Vampyre and Other Tales of the Macabre*, ed. by Robert Morrison and Chris Baldick (Oxford: Oxford University Press, 1997), pp. 246–51 (p. 248).
53 John Polidori, *The Vampyre*, Appendix 1 in this volume, pp. 240–67 (pp. 246, 249).
54 Polidori, *The Vampyre*, p. 251.
55 Thomas Beddoes, *Essay on the Causes, Early Signs and Prevention of Pulmonary Consumption, for the Use of Parents and Preceptors* (London: printed by Biggs & Cottle, for T. N. Longman and O. Rees, 1799), p. 7.
56 John Murray, *A Treatise on Pulmonary Consumption, Its Prevention and Remedy* (London: Longman, Hurst, Rees, Brown, Orme and Brown, 1830), p. 3.

7

The Vampyre, Aubrey, and *Frankenstein*

Nick Groom

Vampire thinking runs deep in Mary Shelley's novel *Frankenstein*. The novel was conceived alongside Lord Byron's unfinished vampire tale, 'A Fragment', at the Villa Diodati during the summer of 1816 – the 'Year Without a Summer' – and *Frankenstein* has deep affinities with the vampire lore that was evidently aired during conversations between Lord Byron, Percy Shelley, Mary Godwin (later Shelley), Claire Clairmont, and of course John William Polidori.[1] When in 1819 Polidori came to write *The Vampyre*, his own development of Byron's '*ébauche*' and arguably the most influential and significant short prose tale of the Romantic period, both 'A Fragment' and *Frankenstein* echoed throughout his text. But while the relationship between 'A Fragment' (published later in 1819) and *The Vampyre* was vehemently debated at the time, the more subtle and sophisticated traces of *Frankenstein* have been generally overlooked – due primarily to an uncritical acceptance of Polidori's claim that *The Vampyre* was composed in the late summer of 1816, rather than at some point after Shelley's novel appeared on 1 January 1818.[2] I have compiled the external evidence and described in detail the publication of *The Vampyre* elsewhere, arguing that it was likely to have been written in March 1819; this supporting essay explains how *Frankenstein* unlocks latent meanings in Polidori's text through internal evidence, strongly supporting my contention that it could only have been written after he had read Shelley's novel.[3] Moreover, while the character Aubrey has often been seen as a self-portrait of Polidori himself and it is generally accepted that the vampyre [*sic*] Lord Ruthven is an audacious attack on Byron (who employed Polidori as his personal physician during the summer of 1816), I argue that these correlations are not so clear-cut, and are ultimately untenable. This essay accordingly presents a close reading of the character of Aubrey informed by Mary Shelley's presentation of Victor Frankenstein, to reveal that the relationship between Aubrey and Ruthven is far more complex and radical than has hitherto been recognised.

* * *

Frankenstein 'reverberates' with vampire thinking.[4] For the maverick scientist Victor, the Being he has fashioned from the carcasses of humans and beasts and brought to life with the blood of living creatures is akin to 'my own vampire, my own spirit let loose from the grave, and forced to destroy all that was dear to me' – his use of the word 'vampire' combining literal and figurative meanings of the word.[5] *Frankenstein* is therefore not only soaked in the imagery and ties of blood, but throbs with cardiovascular circulation: blood is felt pulsing through veins, blood is chilled or curdled or boils feverishly, and bloodthirsty revenge drives the plot – 'blood will have blood'; victims of the Being, meanwhile, are 'bloodless' (149).[6]

Such vampirology was transfused into *Frankenstein* through the late-night philosophical discussions of bioscience and readings of ghost stories and Gothic poetry at Diodati. Mary Shelley later claimed that:

> Many and long were the conversations between Lord Byron and [Percy] Shelley, to which I was a devout but nearly silent listener. During one of these, various philosophical doctrines were discussed, and among others the nature of the principle of life, and whether there was any probability of its ever being discovered and communicated.
>
> (175)

In fact, it was probably Polidori who led these symposia – he held a medical degree and had researched the psychosomatic phenomenon of somnambulism.[7] On 15 June (two days before Byron proposed they all write ghost stories), Polidori recorded in the diary he intermittently kept while at the Villa that '[Percy] Shelley and I had a conversation about principles, – whether man was to be thought merely an instrument' – which would seem to be the kernel of truth at the heart of Mary Shelley's anecdote.[8] And the risen dead, if not actual vampires, do pace through Shelley's novel in figurative language and as phantasms: the Being is a 'demoniacal corpse' (37) and a 'mummy' (38, 168), and to the hallucinating Victor 'the spirits of the dead [hover] round' (158) and the 'forms of the beloved dead flit before me' (167). Despite its rational scientific Gothicism, then, there remain crepuscular shades of the supernatural in *Frankenstein*, and reading the novel must have revived many memories of that dark and stormy summer for Polidori.

Shelley's novel consequently casts a long shadow over *The Vampyre*. From the very outset of both narratives, the poetic imagination plays a central role. In *Frankenstein*, the narrator Captain Robert Walton claims that his education was 'neglected', yet he was 'passionately fond of reading', and as a young man had entertained grand literary aspirations, reading the works of 'those poets whose effusions entranced my soul, and lifted it to heaven' (8). The result: 'I also became a poet, and for one year lived in a Paradise of my own creation' (8) – he blithely compares himself to Homer and Shakespeare (perhaps a sly dig at Polidori's own writerly ambitions voiced at Diodati) and has remained a 'fervent and vivid' day-dreamer in search of experience and the intellectual companionship he identifies in Victor (7). In *The Vampyre*, Aubrey, while not a practising poet himself, also had erratic schooling from 'mercenary subalterns'.[9] As a result, like Walton, 'he cultivated more his imagination than his judgment', he had 'that high romantic feeling of honour and candour, which daily ruins so many milliners' apprentices' (a notably feminine association), and a natural sympathy with virtue – believing 'that vice was thrown in by Providence merely for the picturesque effect of the scene, as we see in romances' (4). In short, 'He thought […] that the dreams of poets were the realities of life' (4). Although, like Walton, Aubrey becomes disillusioned by these flights of imagination, he nevertheless imagines Ruthven as 'the hero of a romance': not a person but 'the offspring of his fancy' (10) – much as Walton figures Victor.[10] For his own part, Ruthven has 'the reputation of a winning tongue' (4), his eloquence being 'the serpent's art' (22) – 'Who could resist his power?' (21) – just as Victor describes the Being as 'eloquent and persuasive […] once his words had even power over my heart' (160).

This Aubrey–Walton / Ruthven–Victor analogy subsequently develops further to identify Ruthven with the Being and then Aubrey with Victor. Tony Jackson has observed that *Frankenstein* is a novel of appearance and perception: the text is 'thick with images of eyes and elaborately described acts of seeing'.[11] There is a literally morbid fascination with the complexion and physical appearance of the Being, who is luridly figured, with 'yellow skin […] hair […] of a lustrous black […] teeth of a pearly whiteness […] watery eyes […] shrivelled complexion, and straight black lips' (37). Similarly, *The Vampyre* is a story of seeing and being seen. Lord Ruthven is straightaway noted for his 'peculiarities', for his 'dead grey eye', and 'the deadly hue of his face, which never gained a warmer tint, either from the blush of modesty, or from the strong emotion of passion' (3). His eyes are oddly unseeing – for Lady Mercer, for instance, 'though his eyes were apparently fixed upon her's, still it seemed as if they were unperceived' (3).

While the Being is of 'superhuman speed' (69), Ruthven's 'strength seemed superhuman'; both have uncanny skills of evasion – and indeed both appear to live on beyond the end of their respective narratives (12). Both ride on the wings of the storm; Victor returns to Geneva during a terrific thunderstorm in which, by flashes of lightning, he glimpses the Being for the first time since he was brought to unlife: later, the Being arrives on Victor's wedding night as a sudden storm breaks. Aubrey, meanwhile, stumbles upon the hovel in the vampyre woods 'by the glare of lightening' (11). Ruthven does not of course inspire the same sort of controversial sympathy as the Being, but he does have the same incandescent temper and is even attributed the same death toll as the Being's number of direct victims: Ianthe, the countess's daughter, and Miss Aubrey, mirroring William, Elizabeth, and Henry Clerval. Both also inspire murderous intent: Victor springs at the Being to 'extinguish the spark which I so negligently bestowed' (70), whereas Aubrey 'thought of employing his own hand to free the world from such a wretch' (19).

Throughout both texts, the moon is particularly significant for these near-humans. As Victor works 'the moon gazed on my midnight labours' (34), and the Being is animated 'by the dim and yellow light of the moon, as it forced its way through the window-shutters' (37) – he subsequently reckons time by lunar phases and finds his way by the 'lovely moon' (96). The She-Being is created on Orkney, where 'the moon was just rising from the sea' (125), the Being himself scrutinising Victor's work 'by the light of the moon' (126) from his vantage point at the casement; Victor ultimately disposes of her dismembered flesh and bone under a moonlit sky. He later glimpses the Being in the 'pale yellow light of the moon' (149), and again: 'Suddenly the broad disk of the moon arose, and shone full upon his ghastly and distorted shape, as he fled with more than mortal speed' (155).

If, for the Being, moonlight is the medium of creation, for Ruthven it appears to be the agency of recreation. In classical medical theory and practice, the moon had generative powers and was strongly linked to pregnancy and childbirth, as well as being instrumental in dispersing moisture and stimulating change. The supposed humidity of moonbeams was thought to cause both the ripening and then the rotting of fruit and vegetables, as well as associated phenomena such as fermentation, curdling, and, in meat, putrefaction. Furthermore, its effect on the 'moist' organs of the body could cause cataracts, headaches, and lunacy, and the flow of blood waxed and waned with the moon's cycles, in turn affecting the ebb and flow of fever. The moon also had long-established associations with witchcraft – particularly the 'Evil Eye' – and could be 'milked' for its potent fluid.[12] Ruthven supposedly rises from the dead through moonlight and the intervention of robbers he has already instructed (a guerrilla force that Bram Stoker was to adapt in *Dracula* as the Count's gypsy band). His corpse is exposed to the 'first cold ray of the moon that rose after his death' (16), whereupon his body disappears.

Perhaps the most telling kinship between the Being and Ruthven, however, is their shared use of the oath. For the Being, it is a repeated threat: 'remember, I shall be with you on your wedding-night' (see 127, 128, 143, 144, and 145), and for Victor, 'the words of the fiend rung in my ears like a death-knell' (128); in consequence, after the murder of Elizabeth he swears his own vengeance in an oath to pursue the Being. In *The Vampyre*, however, the dire responsibility of such an utterance has shifted from the persecutor to the persecuted. Aubrey has made an oath to Ruthven to 'save my honour, your friend's honour' (15) upon his own honour as a gentleman – something that Polidori himself valued very highly. Aubrey swears an oath not to report Ruthven's death in England (meaning that he effectively remains alive there): 'Swear! [...] whatever may happen, or whatever you may see' (15). Aubrey swears, Ruthven dies laughing, and Aubrey is henceforth unrelentingly reminded of his vow – controlled by Ruthven from beyond the grave. 'Remember your oath' (18, 19), commands the undead Ruthven, again and again, until finally: 'Remember your oath, and know, if not my bride today, your sister is dishonoured' (22). Aubrey's death-knell is his unspeakable word.

The Being's threat and Ruthven's oath both focus on the relationships of the central character with women: Victor with Elizabeth Lavenza, and Aubrey with Ianthe and with his sister (only ever referred to as 'Miss Aubrey'). Here too there are repeated motifs. Elizabeth in the 1818 text of *Frankenstein* is Victor's ethereal cousin: 'Her figure was light and airy', and 'she busied herself in following the aërial creations of the poets' (21). Ianthe too has a 'light step' (9), is a 'fairy form' (10), and is allied to the arts and even the celestial: 'so beautiful and delicate, that she might have formed the model for a painter wishing to pourtray on canvass the promised hope of the faithful in Mahomet's paradise' (8). Her guileless purity is in stark contrast to the knowing shamelessness of Ruthven's liaisons: hers is 'innocence, youth, and beauty, unaffected by crowded drawing rooms, and stifling balls' (9); despite the social gulf, Aubrey takes on the parental role of 'guardian' to this 'frank infantile being' (10). Miss Aubrey too requires the protection of Aubrey when she enters society. A 'sedate and pensive' eighteen, she is 'a soul conscious of a brighter realm' and exhibits a 'melancholy charm' rather than vivaciousness – a despondency shared by Aubrey, who 'would rather have remained in the mansion of his fathers, and fed upon the melancholy which overpowered him' (17).

Both Victor and Aubrey have deep ties to these women through blood and through marriage – fatally thwarted for Elizabeth and Ianthe, and fatally consummated for Miss Aubrey. They are also defined by the creative imagination: if Ianthe is herself a walking work of art, one of the instruments of the calamities that befall Elizabeth and Miss Aubrey (and thereby Victor and Aubrey themselves) is a miniature painting of a loved one – mother or fiancé. William persuades Elizabeth to lend him 'a very valuable miniature that she possessed of your [Victor's] mother' (49); this is understood to have brought about William's murder – although only Victor is told that it is a direct revenge visited upon his family by the Being. The miniature also affords the means by which Justine is framed for the crime, the incriminating evidence being planted on her while she sleeps; she is duly executed. In *The Vampyre*, on the eve of Miss Aubrey's wedding to the 'Earl of Marsden',

Aubrey opens a locket of hers and gazes upon a miniature that he recognises as 'the features of the monster who had so long influenced his life' (21); he straightaway destroys it. In both instances, then, the artwork not only has lethal qualities: it is transformative in that it provokes ferocious rage. This rage is homicidal in the case of the Being, but for Aubrey too it confirms that he himself has become some sort of monster. Indeed, as Patricia Skarda suggests, 'The rage [...] implies connection between the envier Aubrey and the envied vampire, who displaces Aubrey as the sister's protector and insinuates himself into the sister's affection.'[13]

Elizabeth blames herself for William's murder – 'O God! I have murdered my darling infant!' (49) – sentiments appropriated by Victor when he discovers that Clerval has been killed: 'Have my murderous machinations deprived you also, my dearest Henry, of life? Two I have already destroyed' (134, also 139). He repeats his charge against himself that 'I am the cause of this [...] William, Justine, and Henry – they all died by my hands' (141). When Aubrey returns to Ianthe's parents after her death, they 'looked at Aubrey and pointed to the corpse' (13) as if in accusation, before dying broken-hearted. Aubrey himself accepts the blame: during his convalescence he becomes delirious, calling on Ruthven to spare Ianthe, while 'At other times he would imprecate maledictions upon his head, and curse him as her destroyer' (13) – and yet the pronouns here are ambiguous and are simultaneously both an accusation against Ruthven and Aubrey's own confession of guilt. As to Ruthven's vulturine courtship of Miss Aubrey, in the mind of her brother he is certainly in some sense responsible, as Ruthven, seemingly hearing of Aubrey's relapse, hastens to his house and 'by constant attendance, and the pretence of great affection for the brother and interest in his fate, he gradually won the ear of Miss Aubrey' (21).

In the context of such catastrophes, the physical and mental collapse of both Victor and Aubrey is depicted in pathological detail. When Victor is rescued from the ice-fields, Walton writes that 'his body [was] dreadfully emaciated by fatigue and suffering' (14); moreover, 'he is generally melancholy and despairing; and sometimes he gnashes his teeth, as if impatient of the weight of woes that oppresses him'; all in all, 'I never saw a man in so wretched a condition' (15). It transpires that this is only the latest in a series of breakdowns that Victor has suffered since his fateful experiment. When he first animates the Being, he does so in a fever: 'a cold dew covered my forehead, my teeth chattered, and every limb became convulsed' (37). He paces up and down his bed chamber, 'unable to compose my mind to sleep'; eventually falling into slumber, he is 'disturbed by the wildest dreams':

> I thought I saw Elizabeth, in the bloom of health, walking in the streets of *Ingolstadt* [...] but as I imprinted the first kiss on her lips, they became livid with the hue of death [...] and I thought that I held the corpse of my dead

mother in my arms [...] and I saw the grave-worms crawling in the folds of the flannel.

(37)

Victor roams the streets, 'with irregular steps', plagued by the remembrance of lines from *The Rime of the Ancient Mariner*:

> Like one who, on a lonely road,
> Doth walk in fear and dread,
> And, having once turn'd round, walks on,
> And turns no more his head;
> Because he knows a frightful fiend
> Doth close behind him tread.

He dare not return to his chambers, 'but felt impelled to hurry on, although wetted by the rain, which poured from a black and comfortless sky' (38).

When Clerval arrives, he notices how 'very ill' Victor appears – 'so thin and pale' (39). Victor's 'nervous fever' confines him for several months: 'During all that time Henry was my only nurse [...] He knew that I could not have a more kind and attentive nurse than himself' (40). This post-traumatic condition recurs when Victor works on the abortive She-Being on Orkney: he walks about the isle 'like a restless spectre', and when he escapes to Ireland succumbs to fever and remains for two months 'on the point of death' (134). Once again he is a physical wreck – a walking cadaver of 'emaciated frame and feverish cheeks' (145) – and once again he benefits from the care of a man, Mr Kirwin, who, unlike the unsympathetic and elderly female domestic to whom Victor is entrusted, shows him 'extreme kindness' (136). Notwithstanding this, Victor is afterwards declared insane and incarcerated for some months.

Polidori replicates Shelley's accounts of Victor's distress in the states of shock experienced by Aubrey following the murder of Ianthe and then the apparent post-mortem return of Ruthven. Like Victor he is 'put to bed' and 'seized with a most violent fever, and was often delirious' (13). Like Victor he is nursed by a male companion – Ruthven, chancing to be in the same city as Aubrey and hearing of his disturbed state, 'immediately placed himself in the same house and became his constant attendant' (13). Ruthven (uncharacteristically) speaks 'kind words' and 'almost' repents for his erstwhile vices (13). Indeed, 'His Lordship seemed quite changed' (13) – more like Aubrey, in fact – but reverts to his former state once Aubrey recovers. Thus the two are paired: when Aubrey is delirious, Ruthven is compassionate: when Aubrey recovers his senses, Ruthven becomes monstrous and Aubrey perceives 'a smile of malicious exultation playing upon his lips' (13).

Aubrey is also changed by his near-death experience: his mind is 'much weakened', his 'elasticity of spirit […] now seemed to have fled for ever' (14). He is 'bound' to Ruthven 'by the tender care he had taken of him during his illness' (14); furthermore, 'He was now as much a lover of solitude and silence as Lord Ruthven' (13). The two are twinned, and there is a hint too of the homosexual desire implied in *Frankenstein* in the relationship between Victor (the pioneer of a form of reproduction confined to males) and his devoted friend Henry Clerval.[14]

After his first illness, Aubrey can no longer find solitude among the ruins or in the woods: much as Victor has a nightmare that compounds Elizabeth dying with his decomposing mother, Aubrey is haunted by Ianthe. She appears to him as the living dead, bleeding from her fatal injury – 'her pale face and wounded throat with a meek smile upon her lips' (14). When, like Victor, Aubrey falls ill a second time he again lapses into solitude, not eating. Then, much as Victor, 'he left his house, roamed from street to street, anxious to fly that image which haunted him. His dress became neglected, and he wandered, as often exposed to the noon-day sun as to the midnight damps' (19). Aubrey is no longer recognisable; he regresses, becomes feral: 'at first he returned with the evening to the house; but at last he laid him down to rest wherever fatigue overtook him' (19). Although his sister employs servants to follow him, 'they were soon distanced': Aubrey, like Victor, is in flight 'from a pursuer swifter than any' – in his case, 'from *thought*' (19, my emphasis). He speaks in disconcerting riddles – 'He only uttered a few words, and those terrified her' (19) – and is confined as insane, another incarceration and another replication of Victor's troubles. In this wretched condition, Aubrey writes a letter to his sister, but it is intercepted by his physician and judged to be 'the ravings of a maniac' (22), the diary of a madman.

Other figures also hang over Victor and Aubrey. On a handful of occasions Shelley seems to have been drawing directly on Polidori for elements of Victor and his behaviour. Both are brilliant medical students (Polidori was aged just nineteen when he graduated as a doctor of medicine from Edinburgh University), but it is Victor's solitary boat trips that remind one most of Polidori's time at Diodati, who recorded in his diary that he frequently rowed across Lake Geneva (known as Lake Leman). On one such outing he got his boat to the middle of the lake 'and there lay my length, letting the boat go its way'; another time he rowed Mary around the lake 'all night till 9; tea'd together; chatted, etc.'.[15] Although Percy Shelley had also rented his own boat during the stay, the time Polidori spent with Mary and his drifting alone on the lake is highly suggestive. Victor, back with his family at Geneva, recalled that:

> Often, after the rest of the family had retired for the night, I took the boat, and passed many hours upon the water. Sometimes, with my sails set, I was carried by the wind; and sometimes, after rowing into the middle of the lake, I left the boat to pursue its own course, and gave way to my own miserable reflections.
>
> (64)

Later still, 'I passed whole days on the lake alone in a little boat, watching the clouds, and listening to the rippling of the waves, silent and listless' (113).

Skarda suggests that Aubrey is possibly a portrait of Polidori, arguing that the name alludes to the antiquary John Aubrey (1626–97), whose celebrated memoir *Brief Lives* was first published in 1813. More generally, Skarda reads *The Vampyre* as Polidori's attempts to balance Byron's colossal literary reputation and international celebrity with his own ambitions. Hence, as Simon Bainbridge observes, Polidori's tale can be read as warning of 'the perceived threat of the Byronic text to its readers'.[16] Bainbridge goes further, treating *The Vampyre* as a story of the 'double' that presents 'a struggle between two opposing parts of the self, with Aubrey's social and moral values and his sense of the real (already weak at the opening of the story) coming increasingly under threat from the transgressive desires and appetites associated with Ruthven and (Byronic) romance'.[17]

Bainbridge's thought-provoking analysis of the 'double' certainly deserves serious attention, but the paralleling of Byron/Polidori with Ruthven/Aubrey is an easy equation that ignores other key relationships in the text that have no clear analogy in the time Polidori spent with Byron: what of Aubrey and Ianthe, Aubrey and his sister, even Aubrey and the countess? Likewise, the tensions at Diodati and subsequently between Polidori and the Byron circle are not evident in *The Vampyre* – his devotion to Mary Shelley, for example. On the very day Polidori began his ghost story (18 June), Mary called him her 'younger brother' (in fact, he was two years older than she was); he also read with her, assisted with the vaccination of her son William, and they dined together several times.[18] In contrast, he apparently quarrelled several times with Percy and 'threatened to shoot [him] one day on the water [Lake Geneva]'.[19] Moreover, he was misinformed (perhaps deliberately) about the kinship between Mary and Claire Clairmont, believing them to be sisters, and on their arrival recorded that Percy Shelley 'keeps the two daughters of Godwin, who practise his theories; one L[ord] B[yron']s' – the last phrase referring to Clairmont as the lover of Byron, pregnant with his child.[20] Such a *ménage*, and the eventful and sometimes violent summer they spent together, is part of a compelling entanglement of sexual libertinism and exhilarating poetry in which Polidori, as an employee of Byron's rather than an equal, occupied an uncomfortable and ambiguous position. All of this could have provided material for *The Vampyre*, but it actually appears to have contributed very little. Instead, Polidori took his principal inspiration from the tales of Byron and Shelley written for the ghost-story challenge. Besides, when *The Vampyre* was published in 1819 it was prefaced by a 'Letter' that idolised Byron and which, being derived almost entirely from Polidori's journal, was either written by him or with his consent and cooperation. To represent the central Ruthven/Aubrey relationship as signifying Byron/Polidori needs, then, to be re-examined.

Aubrey and Ruthven arrive in London 'About the same time' (4); they meet, and, in the opening words of the third paragraph, 'He watched him' (5): the lack of proper nouns makes the remark unsettlingly ambiguous – who is watching whom? Ruthven is a man 'entirely absorbed in himself' (5) who does not appear to perceive – and who barely even addresses – women. Aubrey, in contrast, is 'handsome, frank, and rich' – in at least the first two qualities the opposite to Ruthven – and so is courted by mothers eager to find a match for their daughters, such attention increasing his vanity and leading him into 'false notions of his talents and his merit' (4). The two men also differ in their respective wealth, Aubrey learning that 'Lord Ruthven's affairs were embarrassed' – although, once abroad, Aubrey sees that Ruthven is in fact 'profuse in his liberality' to 'the idle, the vagabond, and the beggar' (5), if his charity is cursed. Ruthven thus becomes Aubrey's alter-ego. When Aubrey resolves to undertake a tour of the Continent, which, in a sardonic aside by the narrator, 'for many generations has been thought necessary to enable the young to take some rapid steps in the career of vice' (5), that is precisely what Ruthven (as Aubrey's companion) does, seeking 'the centres of all fashionable vice' (6). With Ruthven rewarding the profligate while blasting young hopes and beggaring entire families, Aubrey resolves to speak to him on the matter – but Ruthven remains an opaque and enigmatic mystery, in contrast to the openness of Aubrey, a blank canvas on which Aubrey can begin to render his disturbing passions. Aubrey is certainly the sort of affluent young gentleman that Ruthven ostensibly delights in destroying, so Aubrey's continued companionship with the lord almost implies a death wish on his part – a fatal fascination with the diabolical entity into whose clutches he has fallen and that to Aubrey's 'exalted imagination began to assume the appearance of something supernatural' (7; see also 10). But while they are in Rome, Aubrey instead devotes himself to classical archaeology.

Following a letter from Aubrey's guardians informing him that in England Ruthven is considered an 'evil power' (7) that delights in corrupting the most virtuous and innocent, Aubrey shadows Ruthven and realises that he intends to debauch the daughter of an Italian countess. He confronts the malefactor, warns the girl's family, and then leaves his iniquitous company; Ruthven simply laughs. The conflict between Aubrey and Ruthven is therefore fought out over female bodies, each seeking to exercise control over feminine flesh – if in different ways; yet it might also be the case that Ruthven is unmasking the unacknowledged desires of Aubrey, that he is a sordid fantasy of wish-fulfilment. For Bainbridge, both Ianthe and Miss Aubrey are 'sexually unobtainable' for Aubrey because of class and social laws (although perhaps not quite true of Ianthe).[21] Nevertheless, Ruthven's domination and subjugation of Aubrey in this way leads Skarda to suggest that 'Ruthven vamps his primary victim: Aubrey', arguing that Aubrey is 'a vampire by infatuation and association with a man of his dreams' who, as previously noted, assumes some sort of responsibility for the deaths of Ianthe and Miss Aubrey. By focusing on Ruthven's female victims, then, 'Polidori obscures the more significant and more subtly incestuous seduction and death of Aubrey'.[22]

It is in fact through Ianthe that Aubrey learns of 'the living vampyre, who had passed years amidst his friends, and dearest ties, forced every year, by feeding upon the life of a lovely female to prolong his existence for the ensuing months' (9). He deems Ianthe's account of the vampyre's physical details 'a pretty accurate description of Lord Ruthven' (10) – if also risible – but in comportment Ruthven is a singularity, a lone wolf: it is actually Aubrey who has 'friends' and 'dearest ties'. Ianthe tells Aubrey of the vampyre beliefs while he researches ancient archaeological sites laced with stones bearing fragmentary inscriptions, often buried 'beneath the sheltering soil or many coloured lichen' (8). Like Ianthe's improbable Greek folklore, these chthonic monuments in fact misrepresent history: 'faded records of ancient glory [...] ashamed of chronicling the deeds of freemen only before slaves' (8) – thus exposing his antiquarian studies in both Rome and Greece as trafficking in lies. What comes out of the ground is deceit, and so Aubrey is unable to concentrate on these derelict and ill-omened places in the presence of the true innocence of Ianthe – her tresses alone cause 'the forgetfulness of the antiquary' (9; see also 10). But without Ianthe the ruins beguile Aubrey. He visits a remote site, becomes absorbed, breaks his promise to return before nightfall, and during a storm is lost in a particular wood – 'the resort of the vampyres in their nocturnal orgies' (10). Chancing on a hovel, he hears a woman shrieking and a man's laughter 'in one almost unbroken sound' (11) – as if they are one and the same, foreshadowing what is to come. Breaking in, he grapples with a being who tries to strangle him, before his assailant is interrupted by lights outside and, it seems, flees. Woodsmen enter to find Aubrey recovering, and then Ianthe – dead: 'upon her neck and breast was blood, and upon her throat were the marks of teeth having opened the vein' (12) – the victim of a vampyre. There is also a weapon at the scene: Aubrey 'held almost unconsciously in his hand a naked dagger of a particular construction, which had been found in the hut' (12).

At least that is one version of events. There are several unanswered questions here. What was Ianthe doing in the very place and at the very time she had pleaded with Aubrey to avoid? What does the vampyre mean when, wrestling with Aubrey, he proclaims 'again baffled' (12), and then laughs? Why do the woodsmen arrive so opportunely? What is the significance of the suspicious dagger in Aubrey's hand? And what precisely is Aubrey's role in all this: is he the unwitting agent of some sort of malign archaic power he has disturbed among the mysterious ruins, or a focus for Ruthven's elaborate machinations? In the immediate aftermath of this episode, Aubrey suffers a breakdown – through which he is cared for by none other than Ruthven. Returning to consciousness, Aubrey is initially horrified 'at the sight of him whose image he had now combined with that of a Vampyre' (13), but they nonetheless form a new bond. Once Aubrey has recovered, they again travel together, but during their adventures Ruthven is shot and dies, and his body is lost – or vanishes. Aubrey is understandably shocked and re-traumatised by the experience: he 'did not sleep' and is haunted by Ruthven: 'the many circumstances attending his acquaintance with this man rose upon his mind, and he knew not why' (15). Aubrey is also panicked by having sworn the dying man's oath, and whenever he recalls it is struck with cold shivering – it preys on his mind, 'as if from the presentiment of something horrible awaiting him' (15). Aubrey, deciding to leave Greece, then discovers several weapons among Ruthven's effects – including the sheath of the dagger found at the scene of Ianthe's death; there is blood on both. He then learns that the countess's daughter has now disappeared. Polidori seems unequivocally to be disclosing that Ruthven is the guilty party here: he is the vampyre who killed Ianthe, and who then attacked Aubrey. But this is a reading preoccupied by reading Ruthven as Byron: there is in fact another candidate.

Bainbridge's idea is that Polidori's text 'can be read as a story of doubling, with the vampyre Ruthven as a projection of Aubrey's repressed desires which he both enacts (in displaced form) and prevents from being enacted through his murder of the object of desire'.[23] This draws on David Punter's comment that 'Ruthven transgresses the social norms, but he does so with the collaboration of his victims; he merely acts as a catalyst for repressed tendencies to emerge into the light of day'.[24] So in such an interpretation, Ruthven murders Ianthe and Miss Aubrey in 'a displaced enactment of Aubrey's own possessive and prohibited desire and a forestalling of any actual enactment through death'.[25] Bainbridge is, I believe, half-right in this suggestion, and it is worth following the plot closely from Ianthe's death to the end of the tale as there are more – and more sensational – clues that reveal Aubrey's increasingly vampiric behaviour.

Quitting Greece, Aubrey almost breaks down again on learning about the disappearance of the countess's daughter, and becomes 'morose and silent' (17) – not unlike Ruthven.[26] He speeds back to England on 'a breeze, which seemed obedient to his will' (17; in Eastern European legend, vampires have control over the weather).[27] Back in England and in society, Aubrey appears to be concurrently occupying two times (and perhaps two places): 'standing in a corner by himself, heedless of all around him, [at the same time] engaged in the remembrance that the first time he had seen Lord Ruthven was in that very place' (18). He believes he is seized by his arm, hears the words 'Remember your oath', and then sees Ruthven in front of him 'at a little distance' in an uncanny repetition of the first time he had seen the dread lord: 'the same figure which had attracted his notice on this spot upon his first entry into society' (18). So Ruthven is speaking in Aubrey's mind, physically gripping his arm from behind, and simultaneously standing some way in front of him; Aubrey practically collapses and has to be taken home. It should hardly need emphasising – although it clearly does in light of other readings of the text – that Aubrey's account is already wholly deranged.

Fearing that 'the dead rise again!' but that it is 'impossible' that the vision of Ruthven 'could be real' (18), Aubrey makes a second visit into society. Ruthven (whose name itself suggests duality and the 'riven' self within) is already inside Aubrey – at his teeth, no less: Ruthven's name 'hung upon his lips', while Aubrey is prey to vampirically 'devouring thoughts' (18).[28] Aubrey then apparently perceives Ruthven to have fallen into company with his sister – although in fact this is an image 'conjured up' (18) by his imagination. In a repetition of Ruthven apparently seizing his arm, Aubrey seizes his sister's arm and forces her away, as if rehearsing her abduction. His oath dominates his thoughts: 'was he then to allow this monster to roam, bearing ruin upon his breath, amidst all he held dear' (19) – but again the last pronoun is ambiguous; it is Aubrey who is now the perpetrator of sexual crimes. Ruthven is – and remains – dead.

Aubrey becomes a recluse, shunning human contact: 'For days he remained in this state, shut up in his room, he saw no one' (19).[29] But then, resolving to warn against what he presumes are Ruthven's fiendish intentions, Aubrey has to face the uncomfortable truth that he himself is now regarded as aberrant and freakish, for 'when he entered into a room, his haggard and suspicious looks were so striking, his inward shudderings so visible, that his sister was at last obliged to beg of him to abstain from seeking […] a society which affected him so strongly' (19–20). Aubrey's humanity has evaporated; his guardians fear that 'his mind was becoming alienated' and engage a physician to 'reside in the house' – 'He hardly appeared to notice it' (20). Incoherent, he is eventually locked in his chamber: 'There he would often lie for days, incapable of being roused. He had become emaciated, his eyes had attained a glassy lustre' (20). Lying for days, catatonic, emaciated, corpselike, with Ruthven's blank and unseeing stare, Aubrey is like a vampyre starved of sustenance. The only person who can rouse him is, calculatingly, his sister: 'he would sometimes start, and, seizing her hands, […] he would desire her not to touch him. "Oh, so not touch him – if your love for me is aught, do not go near him!"' (20). Once more, the use of the pronouns 'he'/'him' conflates his own identity with that of his unreal demon brother. Ruthven is an abiding (if increasingly phantasmic) presence who has been allowed to possess Aubrey in order to excuse Aubrey's own excesses – which accounts for Aubrey internalising the oath and why he is therefore incapable of breaking it without ruinous psychological damage. This sanctioned assimilation of the two identities, one dead, by Aubrey himself is consensual vampirism; it is also insane.

Although Aubrey appears gradually to be recovering his senses as the year-and-a-day's silence he swore comes to an end, he in fact remains utterly mad, and it is important that his perceptions and actions are understood as such. Hearing of his sister's marriage, he is hysterical with love for her until he opens her locket: he believes he sees a miniature of Ruthven, the vehicle of his fantasies – and the medium of his own incestuous desire for his sister – but the painting is effectively a mirror in which he comprehends himself as 'the monster' (21). In a paroxysm of rage, Aubrey tramples the trinket but straightaway hears Ruthven inside his head, restating the oath; moreover, 'he turned suddenly round, thinking Lord Ruthven was near him, but saw no one' (21). Ruthven is indeed near him – as close as he can be – 'closer than an eye', as Dr Jekyll describes Mr Hyde.[30] Aubrey then fantasises that it was Ruthven's 'constant attendance' during his renewed illness (a repetition of his earlier attentiveness) that gave him access to his sister – a psychological attempt to rationalise his incestuous desire by once more blaming it on the imagined Ruthven, while at the same time admitting his own complicity.[31] There is only one person who could be so close to Aubrey at all these times: it is not Ruthven, but Aubrey himself.

As the wedding hour approaches, Aubrey grows increasingly crazed, escapes his incarceration, and comes face-to-face with 'Ruthven', who is preparing to marry. Aubrey's mania is manifested in beholding his double – in his mind – as the incarnation of his 'rage' (22). Again he imagines he is grasped by (in the grip of) 'Ruthven', again he reminds himself of his oath. Things duly end in blood: Aubrey's passion 'not finding vent, had broken a blood-vessel' (22). His sister is seemingly married and 'Aubrey's weakness increased; the effusion [emission, spilling] of blood produced symptoms of the near approach of death' (23).[32] His end is a repetition of Ruthven's last hours, and although he does not prematurely rot, Aubrey does speak – justifying himself in a fantastical, self-fashioning testimony. It is telling that Aubrey's final moments at midnight also re-enact the ghost-story challenge of the Villa Diodati and Lord Byron relating, with composure, 'A Fragment' – Polidori's guilty source for *The Vampyre*, whose influence he could neither escape nor adequately explain. In the last line of his own story, we learn that 'Aubrey's sister had glutted the thirst of a VAMPIRE!' (23): so the blood with which Aubrey is covered is not his own, but that of his Miss Aubrey. Aubrey is dead; Ruthven, already in reality dead, disappears as a figment of a dead imagination; and the duplicitous tale of *The Vampyre* has been told.[33]

Aubrey and Ruthven appear at the same time as two individuals, and they disappear at the same time as one, by which time Ruthven exists wholly within Aubrey's mind, whose delusions shape the world around him. They start to merge when Aubrey begins to slake his vicious and ultimately forbidden desires and seeks a culprit, playing on Greek superstition and the European supernatural: savagely consummating his love of Ianthe, turning his defence of the countess's daughter to rape, and suicidally committing incest with his younger sister – his own flesh and blood. This final act brings about a total psychic collapse and terminates the text by repeating the single noun of the title, as if the tale has symbolically devoured itself in a Gothic deadlock of taboo desires. Although the novel *Frankenstein* is inevitably far more sophisticated in its analysis of overlapping identity than a short tale could ever be, Polidori's *The Vampyre* is deliciously seductive in the ways in which its narrative twists and turns, disordering the perspective of its principal character. But many readers, overcome with Byronism and Polidori's claim that the tale has familial kinship with the ghost stories of the Villa Diodati, cannot see beyond interpretations derived from the author's biography.

Re-reading *The Vampyre*, it is clear at what moment Aubrey convinces himself he has been vampirised. As he recovers from his breakdown, Ruthven is unfathomable – and it is from this abyss that Aubrey dreams he casts his otherworldly moon spell. Like Victor Frankenstein's experimentation, it is brewed both from ancient alchemies and modern science – in this case heliocentric astronomy and tidal forces:

> During the last stage of the invalid's recovery, Lord Ruthven was apparently engaged in watching the tideless waves raised by the cooling breeze, or in marking the progress of those orbs, circling, like our world, the moveless sun; – indeed he appeared to wish to avoid the eyes of all.
>
> (13)

The sorcery of the moon combines with the currentless waters of the Saronic Gulf to recreate Aubrey as a cold-blooded killer. Polidori is invoking the strange, interrelating identities of Victor and the Being so intricately dissected in *Frankenstein*. Certainly, *The Vampyre* is a chamber piece variation of Shelley's symphonic novel, but Polidori, trained in science and psychology, endeavours to chart the extreme mental illness of split personality, hyper-delusion, perverted fantasy, and confabulation. So the moon is not magical – except to a madman who populates his world with vampyres.

My earlier questions can now be answered. Ianthe has gone to the woods to meet Aubrey in the one place that will verify his story – the nucleus of vampirism; she is expecting a tryst with Aubrey, but instead comes face-to-face with his unfettered lust, which literally exterminates their love. Ianthe's mother has discovered her daughter to be missing – confirming that it was her own decision to visit the woods – and has sent the woodsmen as a rescue party. Aubrey imagines he hears the words 'again baffled' (12) and a loud laugh. An obsolete meaning of the word refers not so much to being 'foiled' as being 'disgraced' – so is this Ruthven's accusation against Aubrey at having humiliated him a second time, the first time being Aubrey's disclosure to the countess about his Lordship's intentions towards her daughter?[34] No, Aubrey is not a lure to entrap Ianthe for Ruthven – Ruthven is not even there, and Aubrey is already living in his own sickening unreality, killing the thing he loves. Although he fabricates a patchy alibi of which he can convince himself, Aubrey's sanity, reconfigured by rampant carnal desire, is precarious; he knows he is disgraced by his atrocious cravings, and so every challenge to his innocence is aggressively defended. Finally, although Aubrey holds a bloodstained dagger, the locals agree that it was a vampyre attack. They are defending Aubrey – which is why these seemingly irrelevant (and indeed often ignored) details of the tale are so important. Vampirism is a metaphor for, a cover for, honour slaying: Ianthe has to die because she has brought shame upon her family – even though her shame was orchestrated by her lover, who is also her killer; so too the countess's daughter; so too Miss Aubrey. Aubrey is a femicidal maniac in a patriarchal society, intent on the disgrace of seduction and the righteousness of execution. It is through justifying his madly deviant sense of murderous justice that the serial killer Aubrey reworks the events of the narrative: the killings are real, Ruthven is dead but scapegoated as a supernatural horror, the narrative is a wildly debauched nightmare. When Aubrey discovers the bloodstained scabbard among Ruthven's effects, it is the 'smoking gun' clue that he himself placed there, just as Frankenstein's Being implicated Justine with the miniature. This fabricated evidence 'proves' to the 'reluctant' Aubrey that Ruthven is a murderer, a vampyre, and abroad. Aubrey consequently *finds himself* in Ruthven's case of lethal weapons – it is a metaphor for his state of mind, and the authorisation of his future career: a licence to kill. *The Vampyre* – like *Frankenstein* – is not a supernatural tale at all: it is perhaps the first psychological thriller, a grippingly unnerving study in psychosis and slaughter.

Notes

1. For a detailed discussion, see Nick Groom, *The Vampire: A New History* (New Haven, CT and London: Yale University Press, 2020), pp. 119–25; see also D. L. Macdonald, *Poor Polidori: A Critical Biography of the Author of 'The Vampyre'* (Toronto, ON: University of Toronto Press, 1991), pp. 85–87.
2. Fabio Camilletti was the first seriously to question this in 'A Note on the Publication History of John Polidori's *The Vampyre*', *Gothic Studies*, 22:3 (2020), 330–43; see also Patricia L. Skarda, 'Vampirism and Plagiarism: Byron's Influence and Polidori's Practice', *Studies in Romanticism*, 28:2 (1989), 249–69 (p. 250).
3. For the likely date of composition of *The Vampyre*, see my article 'Polidori's "The Vampyre": Composition, Publication, Deception', *Romanticism*, 28:1 (March 2022), 46–59.
4. Groom, *The Vampire*, p. 119.
5. Mary Shelley, *Frankenstein; or, The Modern Prometheus*, ed. by Nick Groom (1818; Oxford: Oxford University Press, 2018), p. 52; subsequent references to this edition are given parenthetically in the text.
6. William Shakespeare, *Macbeth*, III. 4. 121.
7. Mary Wollstonecraft is credited with the earliest recorded use of 'somnambulist' in 1794 (*OED*).
8. *The Diary of Dr. John William Polidori, 1816: Relating to Byron, Shelley, etc.*, ed. William Michael Rossetti (London: Elkin Mathews, 1911), 15 June 1816, 'Villa Diodati', p. 123.
9. John William Polidori, 'The Vampyre', in *The Vampyre and Other Tales of the Macabre*, ed. by Robert Morrison and Chris Baldick (Oxford: Oxford University Press, 2018), pp. 3–23 (p. 4); subsequent references to this edition are given parenthetically in the text.
10. See Skarda, 'Vampirism and Plagiarism', p. 251.
11. Tony E. Jackson, *The Technology of the Novel: Writing and Narrative in British Fiction* (Baltimore, MD: Johns Hopkins University Press, 2009), p. 70; see Shelley, *Frankenstein*, p. xlv.
12. *The Elder Pliny on the Human Animal: Natural History, Book 7*, ed. and trans. by Mary Beagon (Oxford: Clarendon Press, 2005), pp. 191–95, citing, among others, Aristotle, Galen, Hippocrates, and Plutarch.
13. Skarda, 'Vampirism and Plagiarism', p. 259.
14. See Ken Gelder, *Reading the Vampire* (London: Routledge, 1994), pp. 58–60.
15. Polidori, *The Diary*, pp. 99, 110; see also p. 107.
16. Simon Bainbridge, 'Lord Ruthven's Power: Polidori's "The Vampyre"', Doubles and the Byronic Imagination', *The Byron Journal*, 34:1 (2006), 21–34 (p. 22); see also Monica Coghen, 'Lord Byron and the Metamorphoses of Polidori's *Vampyre*', *Studia Litteraria: Universitatis Iagellonicae Cracoviensis*, 6 (2011), 29–40 (p. 36).
17. Bainbridge, 'Lord Ruthven's Power', p. 30; see also Gavin Budge, '"The Vampyre": Romantic Metaphysics and the Aristocratic Other', in *The Gothic*

Other: Racial and Social Constructions in the Literary Imagination, ed. by Ruth Bienstock Anolik and Douglas L. Howard (Jefferson, NC: McFarland, 2004), pp. 212–35 (p. 234).
18 Polidori, *The Diary*, p. 127; but see also p. 132.
19 Polidori, *The Diary*, p. 135.
20 Polidori, *The Diary*, p. 99.
21 Bainbridge, 'Lord Ruthven's Power', p. 31.
22 Skarda, 'Vampirism and Plagiarism', p. 259.
23 Bainbridge, 'Lord Ruthven's Power', p. 26; see also p. 33, n. 29, in which he points to an undeveloped hint in the 'Introduction' to *The Vampyre and Ernestus Berchtold; or, The Modern Oedipus: Collected Fiction of John William Polidori*, ed. by D. L. Macdonald and Kathleen Scherf (Toronto, ON: University of Toronto Press, 1994), pp. 9–31 (p. 7).
24 David Punter, *The Literature of Terror: A History of Gothic Fictions from 1765 to the Present Day*, 2 vols (London and New York: Longman, 1996), I: *The Gothic Tradition*, pp. 103–04.
25 Bainbridge, 'Lord Ruthven's Power', p. 31.
26 See Skarda, 'Vampirism and Plagiarism', p. 256.
27 Groom, *The Vampire*, pp. 15, 181, 183.
28 See Bainbridge, 'Lord Ruthven's Power', p. 30.
29 Punctuation revised to restore the version of the text first printed in the *New Monthly Magazine*, 11:63 (April 1819), 204.
30 Robert Louis Stevenson, *The Strange Case of Dr Jekyll and Mr Hyde and Other Tales*, ed. by Roger Luckhurst (Oxford: Oxford University Press), p. 65; the similarity between the two texts is also noted by Bainbridge, 'Lord Ruthven's Power', pp. 23, 31.
31 Alternatively, see Bainbridge, 'Lord Ruthven's Power', pp. 29–30.
32 Weltering in gore was typical of Eastern European vampires.
33 There was to be no sequel.
34 Alternatively, see Bainbridge, 'Lord Ruthven's Power', p. 30.

Part II

The legacy of *The Vampyre*

8

From lord to slave: Revolt and parasitism in Uriah Derick D'Arcy's *The Black Vampyre*

Sam George and Bill Hughes

The Black Vampyre: A Legend of St. Domingo is a short tale which features the first Black vampire in Anglophone literature, published in New York in June 1819. It was attributed to 'Uriah Derick D'Arcy'; it is probably by Richard Varick Dey (1801–37), a near anagram of that name.[1] It appeared within months of the publication of John Polidori's *The Vampyre* (in April 1819), while the latter was still thought to be Byron's work. When *The Black Vampyre*'s second edition appeared in August 1819, expanded with numerous paratexts, Polidori's authorship was known. There is a whole story of literary appropriation and plagiarism here which is also crucial to D'Arcy's text.[2] Paul Gilroy's concept of 'the Black Atlantic' allows us to see *The Black Vampyre* emerging out of a trade between Britain and the USA (as well as the rivalries of commodified literature within the American literary scene).[3] D'Arcy openly acknowledges Polidori's tale and self-consciously comments on that literary commerce. In his 'Introduction' he evokes the still-fresh memory of all who had read 'The White Vampyre' (that is, *The Vampyre*) and goes so far as to appropriate Polidori's final phrase as his own: 'to GLUT THE THIRST OF A VAMPIRE!!!' (40).[4] The tale explicitly parodies *The Vampyre* and even suggests that Lord Ruthven, Polidori's British vampire aristocrat, had his origins in the Caribbean.[5]

The Black Vampyre is a direct response to Polidori but also to those ideas of liberty proclaimed by Enlightenment thinkers and brought to practice in the French Revolution and the subsequent Haitian Revolution of 1791–1804, where slaves and free people of colour fought for abolition and then independence from France. The French Revolution had not lived up to its universalist ideas and the initial abolition of slavery in 1794 had been rescinded by Napoleon in 1802 – one of the contradictory undersides to Enlightenment.[6] Saint-Domingue, or St Domingo, now named Haiti, thus became in 1804 the first nation to truly abolish slavery.[7]

The Black Vampyre has been rarely discussed and is not widely available. The first edition of the tale itself has been anthologised in Andrew

Barger's *The Best Vampire Stories 1800–1849* (2012) and an excellent scholarly edition has been edited and presented online by Ed White and Duncan Faherty, assisted by Toni Wall Jaudon (to which we are greatly indebted).[8] Apart from Katie Bray's thoughtful article on the text (referenced above), we have not found any more substantial academic criticism of it. In an attempt to draw attention to this much-overlooked and groundbreaking narrative, we published an article in the press, 'America's First Vampire was Black and Revolutionary – It's Time to Remember Him', and made the text the central focus of our 'Being Human Festival' event 'The Black Vampyre and Other Creations: Gothic Visions of New Worlds' in 2020.[9]

What is so remarkable about this story is that it is an anti-slavery narrative from the early 1800s which also depicts America's first vampire, who is Black. It is also perhaps the first short story in English to sympathise with the emancipation of slaves, released fourteen years before Lydia Child published *An Appeal in Favor of That Class of Americans Called Africans* (1833), which is widely considered to be one of the first anti-slavery books.[10] *The Black Vampyre* is also remarkable because it explores the idea of mixed marriage at a time when interracial love was deemed taboo.

Polidori's tale reanimated Gothic fiction by introducing the vampire into its repertoire of stock figures, transforming it from bestial peasant to predatory aristocrat. The Gothic mode has always had an ambivalent relationship to Enlightenment. It has also, at times, been entangled with racial ideas and often involved with the barbaric history of slavery, particularly on the North American continent and in the Caribbean. As Maisha Wester says, 'The Gothic's mutable monsters, then, reveal panicked discourses about racial difference.'[11] We argue that *The Black Vampyre* belongs with a handful of Gothic-tinged texts which may resist this panic and subvert those discourses.[12] Bray talks of a 'hemispheric gothic' which, in the case of *The Black Vampyre*, 'demonstrate[s] how the histories that link the United States to Haiti have been hidden'.[13] This chapter situates *The Black Vampyre* amid those relationships, observing how D'Arcy further transforms Polidori, employing the motifs and tropes of Gothic bodily horror within a postcolonial context of slavery, the revolts against it, and the nascent capitalism of the USA. D'Arcy also adds to the nobility of Polidori's vampire an explicit monstrosity that may seem a return to that of Eastern European folklore but is derived also from Afro-Caribbean traditions. Other folkloric or mythical themes are also alluded to and we will touch on these briefly. The dialectical shifts between the vampire as slave, noble, and bourgeois in the text echo contradictions in US society, exposing the dubious heritage of the nation in a powerful social criticism.

The Black Vampyre

The tale, as we have said, is not at all well known, so a short precis will be helpful. It begins with a slaveowner in Saint-Domingue, a Mr Personne, killing a small slave, a ten-year-old boy, and throwing him into the sea. The corpse revives; the planter throws him back but he emerges again. Personne keeps trying to kill him, eventually ordering him to be burned, but the boy miraculously causes the planter to be flung into the fire instead. He dies of his burns but not before his wife informs him that the cradle of their unbaptised son is empty apart from his skin, bones, and nails.

The story shifts forward to when Personne's widow, Euphemia, is in mourning for her third husband. Two strangers appear: an extremely handsome Black man, dressed as a 'Moorish prince', accompanied by a 'pale European boy' (20). He charms Euphemia with his eloquence, knowledge, and 'elegance and beauty' (21). He possesses that aristocratic allure first modelled by Polidori, but here exoticised as African nobility rather than the domestic threat that Lord Ruthven represents. The Prince rapidly wins Euphemia's hand in marriage, which takes place that evening.

About midnight, the Prince takes Zembo (the boy) and his new bride to the graves of her three former husbands and 'several children' (24). The Prince and boy perform certain rites and disinter her favourite son. They tear out his heart, mix the blood with earth in a chalice, and attempt to force her to drink and swear an oath of secrecy; she refuses. He stomps on the ground in fury and the dead rise up in a terrible state. She faints, and wakes up bloodstained with a cauterised wound on her breast and the cravings of a vampire. Her first husband, Personne, tenderly embraces her. There is a comic play of duelling between her second and third husbands. The Prince and Zembo stake them, then the Prince graciously gives Personne and Euphemia money to sail to Europe with Zembo (who turns out to be the son that had been reduced to hair and bone).

On their way, they encounter an armed band in a cavern which bears the signs of witchcraft. At one end sit several Africans in 'sumptuous Moorish apparel' (32), whom Mrs Personne recognises as 'Gouls' (that is, vampires), the Prince among them. Before the throne is a band of slaves 'imperfectly armed with clubs and missiles' (33) and a band of musicians performing in 'discordant harmony' (33). The Prince addresses the crowd with fine oratory, calling in the language of revolutionary Enlightenment for 'UNIVERSAL EMANCIPATION' (36). Soldiers arrive and interrupt this celebration of 'anticipated freedom' (36) while Mrs Personne snatches a phial of potion which can restore a vampire to the human state. The slaves prudently escape and the soldiers, guided by Zembo, manage to defeat and stake the vampires.

Mr and Mrs Personne and Zembo take the potion and are restored to humanity, going on to live a happy family life, clouded only by the birth of a mulatto son (presumably the Prince's) with 'vampyrish propensities' (39), a descendent of whom, Mr Anthony Gibbons, still lives in New Jersey (presumably some unidentified contemporary satirical target of D'Arcy).

The second edition of August 1819 was supplemented by several paratexts; following the tale is appended a 'Moral', 'Vampyrism: A Poem' (with its own short preface), a 'Note', and a 'Communication'. These significantly qualify and illuminate the main narrative, increasing the ambivalence and bringing out an additional theme. We will be looking at this edition as a text in itself, paying attention to these supplementary features. First, we will highlight the Gothic aspects of this text in order to explore its relationship to Enlightenment themes of liberty and revolution.

Darkness and the Gothic body

This passage, which is the prelude to the raising of the dead and the revelation of the Prince's vampiric nature, is exemplary. It sets the scene in the language of Radcliffean Gothic, employing optical effects of light and darkness:

> The moon was on the zenith, surrounded by a pale halo of ghostly lustre. When they had crossed the plantation, they came to a place of sepulture; where the dark cypresses, and lugubrious mahogany, admitted but sparse and glimmering streaks of funereal light; which, falling on the rank foliage, the white monuments and broken ground beneath, presented a thousand dusky shapes, flitting in the dim uncertainty dear to superstition.
>
> (24)

This 'dim' irrational realm conjured up by Gothic shadow is thus dismissed with the Enlightenment contempt of 'superstition'. Yet D'Arcy will use Gothic uncertainty to question aspects of Enlightenment self-assurance.

The poem 'Vampyrism', which is appended to the tale, itself recapitulates the Gothic themes of the tale, beginning by setting out the contemporary self-satisfaction that Enlightenment has banished Gothic superstition: 'In this blest land [...] valour' (I. 1) has 'rent the vail whose darkness hid / Legitimacy's monstrous creed' (I. 4–5).[14] Here, 'reason' has 'Asserted too her conquering power' (I. 9–10) and has 'exorcised the shadowy brood' (I. 12). The following two stanzas are strewn with such Gothically tinged words as 'spectre', 'terrors', 'wraiths', 'darkness', 'ghost' (II. 3, 4, 6, 7, 12), 'elves', 'fairies', 'Genii', and 'devils' (III. 3, 4, 5), all banished by reason. And yet, still, 'The VAMPYRE host infuriate roams' (VII. 12); this persisting Gothic darkness will manifest itself as an undercurrent to various aspects of modern society.

Gothic themes are further manifested in D'Arcy's treatment of the body, particularly the enslaved body. It is illuminating to compare Stephenie Meyer's description in *Twilight* (2005) of Edward Cullen sparkling like white diamonds with the 'polished ebony' and 'moonshiney lustre' of the Black Vampyre (140).[15] Personne's repeated attempts to murder the slave boy which begin the tale introduce the motif of a Black Gothic body. As much as Personne tries to drown the boy, the corpse keeps reviving: 'he swam back with much grace and agility; parting the sparkling waves with his jet black members, polished like ebony, but reflecting no single beam of light. His complexion was a dead black […]' (16). This description shows the Black body as subject to commodification, an exotic and exchangeable item, like polished ebony or jet. (Jet and ebony can be seen as colonial plunder, like the objectified slaves themselves.) This body is also perceived to be demonic, an object of darkness, 'reflecting no single ray of light', in contrast to the angelic scintillation of Edward Cullen.

Anticipating his future vampirism, the Black boy is also associated with the moon. Like Polidori's Lord Ruthven, and one of Ruthven's aristocratic heirs, Varney, the Penny Dreadful vampire, he is something of a Lunarian, revived by the moon, yet contrasting with it – even repelling it – with his 'utter blackness':[16] 'He fell where the reflection of the moon was brightest, and sunk like lead; but immediately rose again like cork, perpendicularly, with the stone under his arm; while the radiant lustre of the planet retreated from his dark figure, exhibiting in its most striking contrast its utter blackness!' (17).

The slave boy returns some years later, appearing to Personne's widow, Euphemia, as a handsome Black prince, accompanied by Zembo, the European boy. He is 'of remarkable height, and deep jetty blackness; a perfect model of the CONGO Apollo. He was drest in the rich garb of a Moorish Prince' (20). D'Arcy invokes Euphemia's reaction to the Black body, citing Shakespeare: 'Black men are pearls in beauteous ladies eyes' (20), in a passage that seems remarkably sympathetic and unprejudiced.[17] The Prince is a Black avatar of Apollo, the Sun god – light and darkness thus held in contradiction. Euphemia casts a gaze upon the Vampyre which is both objectifying and desiring: 'fixed in immoveable contemplation of the AFRICAN'S face. What peculiar feature or lineament attracted her attention, she knew not: his eyes, though bright, did not sparkle; and the iris, though of a more vivid red than the roseate line in the rainbow, emitted no scintillations' (22). Her gaze is not met; the gentleman's eyes are dead and non-reflecting. This owes much to Polidori's description of Lord Ruthven, who has a 'dead grey eye, which […] did not seem to penetrate'.[18] Later, Euphemia will recognise the vampires in the underground chamber because of their 'remarkable eyes' (32), again recalling Ruthven.

Yet D'Arcy portrays the vampiric body as an object of desire, more explicitly so than Polidori, anticipating the vampires of paranormal romances such as *Twilight*. The gentleman charms Euphemia (who is in mourning for her third husband) with his elegance and beauty and rapidly wins her hand in marriage, which takes place that evening: 'She thought surely that in him Nature might stand up and say "This was a man!" And certainly it is only the weakness and imperfection of our human senses, which, penetrating no further than the surface, is for ever deceived by superficial shadows' (21). His humanity is illuminated by Euphemia's desire, which strips off the shadows of prejudice.

Prometheus and the devoured body

Thus, the focus on the vampiric body as alien and reified, but also desirable, is central. However, the body is also depicted as abject and othered. There is much grotesque body horror in *The Black Vampyre*. This is perpetrated on Black people by slavers and then is returned upon them as vengeance. But the tale and its paratexts are infused with imagery of mutilation, particularly disembowelment, which we will show serves as a denunciation of all realms of post-revolutionary capitalist America. In the very first paragraph, a cargo of slaves arrives in Saint-Domingue 'reduced to mere skeletons' (16) (anticipating the reduction to skin and bone of Personne's child). The purchaser, Personne, has seized the one survivor, a small boy, and, in an uncomfortably cynical and facetious tone which pervades the narrative more generally, 'charitably knocked out his brains' (16) and thrown him into the sea. The child repeatedly survives attempts to kill him and causes the slaver to fall on the fire that was built to despatch the boy, causing him pain 'as if in a Cayenne bath' (18). This, as the editors note, is the same bodily torment inflicted on slaves as a punishment (18, n. 30), so there is a sense of just vengeance in this phrase. This also forms part of Vodou ritual against the Haitian equivalents of vampires.[19]

The body of Personne's unbaptised son suffers a grotesque revenge. His wife informs him that his cradle is empty apart from his dehydrated remains: 'when she went in the morning to see her baby, whom she had left in the cradle, there was nothing to *be* seen, but the *skin, hair,* and *nails!!!* She declared that there never was such another object; except, indeed, the exsiccation in Scudder's Museum' (19). Scudder's American museum exhibited desiccated human bodies wrapped in cloth; it was eventually purchased by P. T. Barnum, famous for exhibiting the Fiji mermaid in 1842.[20] The same grisly intrigue characterises the body horror here as Personne expires on hearing of his son's death:

her husband had been made a holocaust, and served up like a broiled and peppered chicken, to feed the grim maw of death; and her interesting infant, the first pledge of her pure and perfect love, had been precociously sucked, like an unripe orange, and nothing left but its beautiful and tender skin.

(19)

Elsewhere, the horror is more earnestly Gothic (though dark humour and grotesquery are often hard to distinguish). The vampire resurrection described here is more explicit than anything in Polidori:

the ghastly dead, in uncouth attitudes, crawled from their nooks; with their hair curling in tortuous and serpent twinings; and their eyeballs of fire bursting from their heads; while, as they extended their withered arms, and tapering fingers, furnished with blood-hound claws, their gory shrouds fell in wild drapery around them, transiently revealing their forms, bloated as if to bursting, and often incarnadined with clotted blood, yet warm and dripping!!!

(27)

This recalls the grotesque folkloric vampire of Eastern Europe that is absent from *The Vampyre*, bloated with gore in contrast to the pallid Lord Ruthven.[21]

A significant amount of this body horror is centred on the recurring use D'Arcy makes of the Prometheus myth – a myth to which the Romantic-period writers Byron, Percy Shelley, and Mary Shelley attached a special significance. Any references to Prometheus in this period are likely to invoke images of rebellion. In Aeschylus' *Prometheus Bound* and elsewhere in Greek myth, he bequeaths fire and language and other skills of civilisation – the embodiment of Enlightenment rationality and human progress – and is chained by the tyrannical Zeus to a rock, where an eagle daily devours his liver, only for it to be regenerated for further perpetual torture. For Percy Shelley, in *Prometheus Unbound* (1820), Prometheus is the great liberator of humankind. In Byron's poem 'Prometheus' (1816), written at the Villa Diodati, Prometheus plays the same role as standing for human liberty against tyranny (though in a more pessimistic vein).

However, for Mary Shelley, the subtitle of her 1818 novel *Frankenstein* betrays a much darker side to rationalism, science, and rebellion. The 'Modern Prometheus' of the subtitle, creator of a new being, has no sympathy for his creation and gives him speech yet denies him liberty and exiles him from sociality, leading to a bloody revolt against his maker.[22] D'Arcy exploits a similar ambivalence with the figure of Prometheus: 'Gentlemen of colour! I appeal to yourselves; shall not the descendants of the Gods be named before the offspring of the earth-born image, whom Titan impregnated with celestial fire?—For Prometheus was the first Vampyre' (34). The Prince is invoking here a Promethean ancestry to justify a hierarchy where vampires take precedence over mortal slaves (as noted, in some variants of the myth humans were created by Prometheus, 'impregnated by celestial fire').

Yet, confusingly, the African slaves are also descendants of the Titan, and there is a utopian moment where they are promised a return to their homeland:[23]

> From Titan himself, descended the Cyclopes, and all other ancient and modern Anthropophagi; and, in lineal descent, the Moco tribe of our own EBOES, to whom I have the honour of being related. Those of you, too, are his posterity, who, after your deaths, return to your native land—the true Elysium; where the balmy bowl of the Coco, the soft bloom of the ANANA, and the coal-black beauties of the clime of love, shall for ever reward your fortitude, and steep in forgetfulness the memory of your wrongs.
>
> (34–35)

Thus, the Promethean figure is ambivalently both liberator and vampire; the Prince belongs to a lineage that has both divine ancestry and the monstrous rapacity of the Cyclops.

Prometheus himself becomes both devoured and devourer, with the vulture (in D'Arcy, rather than Aeschylus' eagle) that feeds on his entrails part of another monstrous lineage, delineated in this strange bestiary: 'from this amphibious monster have descended the Crows,—the Jackalls,—and the Bloodhounds;—the pirate Bat of Madagascar,—and the man-killing Ivunches of Chili;—the Sharks;—the Crocodiles;—the Krakens;—the Horse-leeches;—the Cape-cod Sea Serpents;—the Mermaids;—the Incubi;—and the Succubi!!!' (34). The crow, as we will see later, is affiliated to the Black Vampyre.

The slaver is named Mr Personne; as the editors say, '*Personne* can translate, from the French, as "person" or "individual," but the most common meaning would be "nobody"' (16, n. 20). This is a further allusion to the Greek myth, as Odysseus in the *Odyssey* tricks the Cyclops Polyphemus by claiming his name is 'Nobody'. It also recalls forcefully the fact that slaves had their own names erased, destroying their social interconnections and cultural ancestry. As we will see below, lineage is another crucial theme; D'Arcy exploits descent and affiliation in both their literal, bodily senses and as textuality.

Vampiric lineage

The idea of lineage is important in D'Arcy's text, particularly the hereditary nature of vampirism. Thus, the legacy of vampirism has been passed down to the present day; a note by D'Arcy's says, of Euphemia's third son, 'This Spooner Dubois having never been heard of since, it is probable that he has been roaming about the world; and it is possible, that he may be the same Lord Ruthven, whose adventures have been recently related.' (24) This alludes, of course, to D'Arcy's own literary ancestry in Polidori's *The Vampyre* as well as to the social heritage of vampirism, which D'Arcy will show permeates the society of his own times.

Bray suggests that, in bringing the slaveowner back to life, the story 'offers a family reunion' rather than revolution. However, the existence of the vampire's descendent in New Jersey unsettles this 'ostensible closure'.[24] This is an ironic reflection on *The Giaour*, with its destruction of family.[25] Though the uprising has been defeated and the family restored, the lineage has become disrupted, leaving 'a child who subverts not only the familial order but also the national US one'.[26] Thus, Euphemia's child with the Prince 'was a mulatto, and of Vampyrish propensities' (39): this is the first instance of a mixed-race vampire recorded in literature. Mr Anthony Gibbons, whom the narrative announces at the beginning, is a descendant of his but (says the narrator), his 'adventures [...] "must remain buried in the bowels of futurity"' (39). (We will see that this anticipates the contemporary vampirism that D'Arcy describes in the paratexts that supplement his tale.) Though this is deflated in D'Arcy's facetious manner, as he says the well-fed Gibbons 'has too much bowels for so diabolical a profession' as vampirism (40).

D'Arcy inverts the white-supremacist paranoia over contaminated blood that one finds in the minute classifications of degrees of mixed 'race' in Caribbean colonialism.[27] For it seems that the vampire heritage determines all activity in US society and the two vampire heirs, Dubois and Gibbons, are indistinguishable from their fellow citizens. Marlene Daut argues that those pseudo-scientific notions of race and hybridity which circulated in the 'print culture of revolutionary Saint-Domingue would wield enormous influence over nineteenth-century understandings of the Haitian Revolution' (8).[28] And *The Black Vampyre* itself took part in this circulation.

Daut finds four 'racial tropics' in texts that responded to the Haitian Revolution.[29] One of these is the '"mulatto/a" vengeance narrative', to which D'Arcy's narrative, with its African Prince, does seem to conform.[30] However, it is unclear whether it undermines the second part of that narrative, which does not recognise 'a desire on the part of slaves for the philosophical ideals of liberty and equality'.[31] It does complicate the idea that rebellion was caused by '"racial hybridity"', since the purity of white Americans is itself undermined.[32] Thus, the figure of the Black Vampyre invokes the first of Daut's four 'racial tropics', the 'monstrous hybrid', only to subvert it, together with the idea of a pure lineage that it promotes.

Folkloric and mythical descent in *The Black Vampyre*

Folkloric and mythical traces other than the Prometheus story are inscribed on the vampiric body. The slave boy is already made strange and mythical before his return as a vampire: 'His hair was neither curled nor straight; but feathery, like the plumage of a crow' (16). It is significant that the crow appears in the heterogeneous genealogy that enumerates the descendants of the Promethean vulture (34). Thus the slave's lineage is not entirely human. The crow is a symbol of transformation in myth. Its black feathers are often associated with punishment (and the fallen). When Adam and Eve were driven out of Paradise, the crows started to eat carrion, so they became black-feathered.[33] In Greek myth, Apollo sent a white raven, or crow, to spy on his lover, Coronis.[34] When the raven brought back the news that Coronis had been unfaithful to him, Apollo scorched the raven in his fury, turning the animal's feathers black.

D'Arcy's work flaunts its intertextuality: it draws on Prometheus and other Greek myths, Christian legend, and the European folkloric vampire source material, but goes farther afield. There is a deliberate confusion of cultural traditions alongside the confusion of bloodlines, notably the inclusion of Caribbean material. Bray says that the story, in confounding ghouls and vampires, which in D'Arcy 'are close cousins of the zonbi', 'seems equally interested in exploring the African and orientalist roots of its monsters'.[35] Alongside the Promethean ancestry, 'there's a definite doubleness to the cultural antecedents of the novella's vampires'.[36] Haiti does have its own vampire figures but D'Arcy has not drawn on them, adapting Polidori's metamorphosis of the European vampire instead, though with a dash of ingredients from reports on Vodou.[37]

Sarah Juliet Lauro claims that 'the incarnation of living death in the zombie represents revolutions that have not completely succeeded – an accusation that many have leveled at the Black Republic. The zombie therefore incorporates a people's history of both enslavement and political resistance.'[38] (This is the original Haitian zombie rather than that of Hollywood.) However, D'Arcy's 'zombie', fusing the calculating seducer of Polidori with Caribbean lore, has an agency that the Haitian zombie lacks. Knowingly or not, D'Arcy makes his Prince more *loa* (or 'lwa') than zombie, not a thing but a god: according to Joan Dayan's informant Mambo La Merci Benjamin, submission to the *loas* 'was *not* another form of slavery [...] "instead of being turned into a thing, you become a god"'.[39] And yet his rebellion is still overthrown by state power as the soldiers arrive and stake the vampires.

In Vodou, Dahomean, Yoruban, and Kongo myths from Africa are combined with Roman Catholic elements but transformed under the conditions of slavery in Haiti.[40] Susan Buck-Morss argues that, from these conditions, 'human universality emerges'.[41] This cultural intermingling parallels the defiance of prohibitions against mixing bloodlines that takes place in the text. Lauro further argues that 'what cannot be doubted is the role that Vadou played in the slave rebellion'.[42] The initial slave revolt in Saint-Domingue 'was led by Boukman, a priest of Vodou'.[43] Supernatural stories surround the history of the Haitian Revolution, as Joan Dayan shows. Dessalines, for example, is described as invoking magical powers and was 'believed to have been a vodou adept – and in some stories, sorcerer'.[44] So there is a tradition of revolutionary leaders with magical powers that D'Arcy may have been aware of.

The Vodou Bois-Caïman ceremony which initiated the Haitian uprising has been 'retold by nearly every historian, especially those outsiders who enjoyed linking the first successful slave revolt to a gothic scene of blood drinking and abandon'.[45] Thus there is an ambivalence in rendering the Revolution through the Gothic mode.[46] Yet the story persists in Haitian culture as a source for 'the spirit of liberation'.[47] A similar ambivalence might be discovered in D'Arcy's tale.

As zombie as much as vampire, the Prince resembles the legendary revolutionary Jean Zombie, who 'became a terrible composite power: slave turned rebel ancestor turned Lwa, an incongruous demonic spirit recognized through dreams, divination, or possession', in contrast to the contemporary zombie as 'emblem of apathy, anonymity, and loss'.[48]

The radicalism of *The Black Vampyre*

The revolutionary role of the Prince and the very subject matter of *The Black Vampyre* inevitably invites the present-day reader to consider how radical it is on the question of slavery, yet the cynical tone arouses uncertainty. As White and Faherty say, 'the tone of the narrative—as the original reviewers noted—is hard to assess, at times sympathetic to the black vampire, at times dismissive, at moments serious, at others frivolous' (7). D'Arcy's text mocks itself in an ironic characterisation of the plagiarism and intertextuality which surrounds his and Polidori's texts; in his 'Introduction', he suggests it may be 'exquisite nonsense […] simple, stupid, and unadulterated absurdity' and that sources 'fine in their original use, when garbelled by the ignorant and tasteless, become a melancholy rhapsody of nonsense' (14). This will culminate, we argue, in a denunciation of the emerging mass culture as just one more symptom of vampiric capitalism. And that vampiric exchange of goods is the fruit of a lineage rooted in the commodification of bodies as slavery.

D'Arcy's political alignment is, however, uncertain. In attacking those responsible for a bad review of *The Black Vampyre*, he 'positively referenced the well-known conservative periodical *The Port Folio*, while also attacking a leftist newspaper editor (Thomas Wooler) in Britain'. So, White and Faherty infer, it may be that D'Arcy was using the second edition to emphasise an alignment with political and cultural conservatives (7). Wooler is attacked in the mocking preface to the 'Vampyrism' poem, along with the *Quarterly Review* (45). The latter was liberal–conservative (as opposed to the more radical Whig *Edinburgh Review*), though it was anti-slavery. So, D'Arcy seems more to be dissociating himself from both sides of political controversy.

The text's sympathies are themselves uncertain, regardless of D'Arcy's allegiances. A contemporary review cited in White and Faherty's introduction claims the tale 'does not seem intended as a regular burlesque' (of Polidori's text) 'but merely to ridicule the superstition in general; and the absurdity of supposing that any sane woman could fall desperately in love with the character of a Vampyre' (one wonders what they would have thought of *Twilight*).[49] There may be an undercurrent of racism here, a suggestion that it is not just vampires but Black men that are the unlikely love objects. But this does not clarify D'Arcy's own position. The Black Vampyre's marriage to a white woman would be shocking to many contemporary readers, inverting the actuality of the many abuses of slave women by white owners. And yet there is also an uncomfortable trace of the satires on lustful widows. The text subverts the idea of racial purity since the Vampyre's descendent blends in with contemporary white American society – though how this heritage of vampirism is to be interpreted is complex, as we will show. Is the taint inherited from slavers or the enslaved? Any strict allegory collapses. Bray accounts for the vampire as shifting signifier by seeing the tale as exposing 'the projection process upon which US racial ideology depends: a vampiric capitalist slave system that casts its own monstrosity onto those it would victimise'.[50]

The dignity of the Prince's struggle when he is fighting the soldiers is undermined by the mock-epic style, which compares his swordplay to a conjuror's show where 'an old woman, children, chickens, friars, and petticoats dance about in wild confusion' (37) before invoking Don Quixote's deluded battles (38). In addition, the Prince's very royalty may be suspect, especially to a post-revolutionary American; D'Arcy's poem 'Vampyrism' denounces 'Legitimacy's monstrous creed' (l. 4). Note that, when the Prince arrives, he is (or appears to be) a slaver himself: 'he had brought out a cargo of slaves, whom his subjects had lately taken prisoners in war' (20).[51]

There are indications, however, that its author had liberal sympathies (though these are not conclusive). There is a strong sense that his sympathies lie with the Irish and thus evidence of a liberal and anticolonialist tendency. He references the novelist Sydney Owenson, whose Irish nationalist sympathies were strong (21). Likewise, Zembo urges his parents to refrain from cannibalism by quoting from 'Counsellor Phillips's harangue' on bigotry, where the intolerant Protestant is 'a wretch, whom no philosophy can humanize' and who 'would gladly feed even with a brother's blood the cannibal appetite of his rejected altar!'[52] Phillips was another Irish figure who campaigned for Catholic emancipation. He employed the figure of 'the human vampire' in a courtroom speech (1). For Phillips, it is the anti-Catholic bigot who is the vampire or ghoul figure, not the rebel. So, by citing Phillips, is Zembo warning that to succumb to vampirism is the crime of bigotry? And is that extended to racial bigotry too? 'Harangue' seems to diminish any respect for the orator. And yet, later, Phillips, Burke, and Curran are described as being preyed upon by plagiarists, disembowelled ('extenterated') as though they are avatars of the liberator Prometheus: 'the Forum Orator, who, without compunction, barbarously exenterates Burke, and Curran, and Phillips' (41). John Philpot Curran was another Irish politician who defended members of the United Irishmen after the rebellion of 1798. He also defended a Jamaican slave; he was well known in US Abolitionist circles. D'Arcy compares the Prince's oration to that of the Irish Edmund Burke (33), an ambiguous choice, since Burke opposed the French Revolution but supported the American one and Catholic emancipation and expressed, in addition, a qualified opposition to the slave trade.

Byron's *The Giaour*, which is prefixed to the text (as it is to Polidori's), has a background of the contemporary Greek subjection to the Ottoman Empire and 'was explicitly presented through the metaphor of slavery' (3). And, say White and Faherty, 'D'Arcy makes slavery central to his work, most obviously by making his titular vampire black and specifically an African brought to New World enslavement' (3). White and Faherty argue that the climate of opposition to slavery, which ripened in New York during this period, 'might have influenced the presentation of *The Black Vampyre*'s titular character as Haitian' (3). They argue, too, that if the Gothic metaphors 'are meant to reveal the truth of life in an Atlantic world driven by the profit motive, they also importantly conceal some of that truth' and that the playful text evades 'the most obvious form of financial and life-predation present in the story: the enslavement of Africans (5)'. However, the cruelty of slavery is so glaring in the text that the reader inevitably makes the connections with the 'life-predation' of slavery. In addition, Bray finds the text to be a 'pointed critique' of the tolerance towards slavery of the Knickerbocker group (one of the literary circles D'Arcy targets in his satire).[53]

D'Arcy's position on rebellion is equally ambivalent. As Euphemia, the boy Zemba, and her first husband flee to Europe, they find themselves in a cavern with a group of noble-looking vampires and a crowd of slaves. The Prince addresses the crowd eloquently in the language of revolutionary Enlightenment:

> No matter whether we were bought for calico or cotton, or for gunpowder or for shot; [...] our souls shall swell like a sponge in the liquid element; our bodies shall burst from their fetters [...] O my brethren, we shall be free!—Our fetters discarded, and our chains dissolved, we shall stand liberated,—redeemed,—emancipated,—and disenthralled by the irresistible genius of UNIVERSAL EMANCIPATION!!!
>
> (36)

We showed earlier that the Black body appears objectified like a commodity. The commodification of human bodies, their reduction to such equivalents as cotton or gunpowder, is here explicitly denounced; the paratexts will later associate commodification in general with vampirism in a powerful satire on post-revolutionary American society. It is the members of a corrupt commercial society, each sucking each other's blood, who are the vampires, rather than an oppressed people.

However, the Prince's egalitarian commitment comes under question at the very beginning of his oration:

> 'Gentlemen and Vampyres!'—but the VAMPYRES expressing their resentment against this breach of etiquette, he corrected himself: —'Vampyres and Gentlemen!'—but the NEGROES were no more willing to come last, than the Vampyres [...] 'I repeat it, Vampyres and Gentlemen? Shall not the immortal precede the mortal?'
>
> (33)

This evident hypocrisy in the hierarchical quibbling in the Prince's speech may be a caution against the disappointed democratic hopes of radicals as the French Revolution led to Terror and then to Napoleonic autocracy (a not-uncommon reaction in the period), or even disappointment with the failings of the American Revolution and its subsequent corruption. The Haitian Revolution itself soon degenerated into the tyranny of monarchical leaders over the dispossessed, just as the Prince asserts his aristocracy. Thus D'Arcy may be slyly suggesting that, even at the founding insurrectionary moment of revolution (the American one included), schisms arise and a vampiric elite dominates, as in post-revolutionary USA there is such a parasitic hierarchy.

The vampiric society

The paratexts to the tale added in the second edition evoke a vampiric world which is the contemporary capitalism of the young USA, and this weighs the balance in favour of the text being read, for all its hesitations, as a powerful denunciation of the rapacity of commodification of all things, including human flesh, reinforcing the Prince's denunciation of the exchange of people 'bought for calico or cotton'. The 'Moral' (41–42) is a sequence of excoriating attacks on various trades, professions, and activities.[54] The poem 'Vampyrism' which follows (43–56) then expands upon and versifies the same satirical points.

The 'Moral' begins with a passage that sets up an argument where contemporary literary production is both means and target of critique. The tone is undoubtedly sarcastic:

> IN this happy land of liberty and equality, we are free from all traditional superstitions, whether political, religious, or otherwise. Fiction has no materials for machinery;—Romance no horrors for a tale of mystery. Yet in a figurative sense, and in the moral world, our climate is perhaps more prolific than any other, in enchanters,—Vampyres,—and the whole infernal brood of sorcery and witchcraft.
>
> (41)

Modernity has not erased Gothic darkness; it has merely displaced it from the realm of superstition to the realistic and quotidian. D'Arcy employs the vampire as political metaphor – something already established by Voltaire and other Enlightenment writers and which would later notably appear in the writings of Karl Marx.[55] D'Arcy then enumerates the various species of contemporary parasites, each made vivid by vampiric imagery. The 'accomplished dandy' who feeds off the 'life-blood of that wealth' his father had accumulated (41). The dandy (revealed to be a 'Vampyre' (IX. 8)), with his whalebone corset, recalls the parasitic devouring of innards: 'His *bowels* other bones enclose' (VIII. 14; our emphasis). The word *bowels* appears frequently; mostly this seems accidental and yet its recurrence does remind the reader of the Promethean torture.

The medical profession, too, is condemned, invoking the imagery of viscera that we mentioned earlier again: 'The Empiric, who fills his own stomach, while he empties his shop into the *bowels* of the hypochondriac'; likewise, corrupt suppliers of military provisions, 'blistering the mouths and destroying the *intestines* of thousands' (42; our emphases). Racial stereotypes are confused, adding evidence that the text is indeed progressive, as surgeons are like '[t]he anthropophagous Caribs in Robinson Crusoe' and 'whet their blades like Shylock' (42). Here, grave-robbers steal the body of a Black woman for surgeons. Again reversing racial stereotypes, 'with a savage howl they roar! / Like cannibals [...] / Like Shakespeare's Jew [...] While all the putrid limbs excite / Their foul and Vampyre appetite' (XVIII. 9–10, 12, 14–15). The reification of modern medical science is revealed as ancestral Gothic terror, with cannibalistic torments inflicted on the bodies of the Black woman.

Commerce is equally parasitic. There is the 'fraudulent trafficker', triumphant with 'bloated villainy' (suggesting the blood-filled vampire of folklore), elated in his 'shameless resurrection' (41). The 'corrupted' clerk, 'himself exhausted to feed the appetite of sharpers, drains [...] the coffers' (41). Thus the victim of vampirism becomes vampiric in turn. Financial speculators likewise are 'monsters', 'Gorg'd with the substance of a host' (x. 2–3). Legal privileges enable the 'shameless resurrection' of the 'VAMPYRE BANKRUPT' (xi. 17–18), who feigns death, assisted by the lies of 'the money'd quack' (x. 6). He warns banks to beware, for 'secret stealth' has 'suck'd the vitals' of their wealth (xi. 5–6) by a 'Vampyre pair' (xi. 12) that escapes punishment (this may refer to a particular financial scandal). D'Arcy identifies the Gothically mystified nature of modern economic processes as speculators are cast as 'ALCHYMIST', 'magician' (xii. 3, 5), and 'conjurors' (xii. 8), where 'all the pageant fade into air' (xii. 10) like fairy gold or the masque in *The Tempest*.

D'Arcy then turns to the literary world, where: 'Amid whole herds of Vampyres small, / CRITICS, who worn out common place With / Author's pilfer'd *entrails* grace' (xiv. 3–5; our emphasis). Here, the author is the tortured Prometheus, bowels devoured by the vampiric critic.

D'Arcy now associates the vampire not with Prometheus, but with the creature that preys on him, depicting the literary sphere thus:

> The whole tribe of Plagiarists, under every denomination;—The Critic, who by *eviscerating* authors, and stuffing his own meagre show of learning with the pilfered *entrails*, ekes out his periodical fulmination against public taste;—the Forum Orator, who, without compunction, barbarously *exenterates* Burke, and Curran, and Phillips,—the Secondhanded Lawyer,—Scholar,—Theologue,—who quote from quotations, [...] what are they all but Vampyres?
>
> (41–42; our emphases)

In the poem, 'All PLAGIARISTS [...] Are GOULS' (xiv. 9, 13–14). Notably, he draws attention to his own plagiarised source, Polidori (which he in turn has fed upon): 'THOMAS who vends as Byron's own / The works of doggrelists unknown' (xv. 5–6).[56]

Finally, D'Arcy includes even himself in this cannibalistic, vampiric orgy: 'And I, who, as Johnson said of an hypochondriac Lady, "have spun this discourse out of my own *bowels*," and made as free with those of others—I am a VAMPYRE!' (42; our emphasis). Recast in verse, the confession of his own complicity reads:

> And what am I, whose spider skill
> [...]
> From my own bowels spun the lay,
> [...]
> Confess,—I AM A VAMPYRE TOO!
>
> (xix. 1, 3, 6)

With 'spider skill', the editors see a reference to Pope's *Essay on Man* (56, n. 149) but it is likely that Swift's *Battle of the Books* is also being alluded to. In Swift's satirical strike in the polemic between Ancients and Moderns, the spider, spinning hack literature from its bowels, is the paradigm of the parasitic nature of Grub Street's commodified literary production.[57] In comparison to his own production of 'honey and wax', symbolising 'sweetness and light', the bee tells the spider that he excretes 'dirt, spun out of your own entrails (the guts of modern brains)'. Swift shared with D'Arcy a similar contempt for the parasitic modern literary scene, where literature is a consumer good.

The intertextuality at the heart of the literary enterprise is vampiric, and D'Arcy freely confesses to it. There is a further complication in that D'Arcy incorporates themes from Haitian belief systems but via the distortions of a colonialist source text.[58] Thus, taken as an integral text, the tale of the Black Vampyre and its paratextual commentary serve to connect the objectification and commodification of the Gothic Black body with the circulation of commodities more generally (including Gothic texts) in a corrupt, vampiric society.

Conclusion

White and Faherty confirm our own sense of the importance of *The Black Vampyre*: 'Two hundred years later, it serves as a record of sorts of a racially charged moment of economic crisis' (8). In its confused way, *The Black Vampyre* illustrates this encounter, with even the dialogic interplay of texts portrayed as just as vampiric as commercial dealings and slavery.

D'Arcy's tone throughout is playful in an uncomfortable way. It is cynical and unclear what exactly his moral position is; it cannot be read as unambiguously anti-slavery. Euphemia's eagerness to marry the Prince may be stirred by the seductive power of the vampire, following Polidori's innovation, but it may also be a rather tired satire on women's incontinence. The Prince's call to liberty seems inspired enough yet it is preceded with an argument about the superiority of vampires to mortals, retaining hierarchical thinking. Thus, it may be read as parody, resembling contemporaneous conservative satires of demagogues where people are duped into rebellion.

Yet the depiction of the slaveowner's cruelty is unambivalent and the portrayal of the nobility and appeal of the Black Prince himself is convincing; the text does seem to show sympathy with the enslaved and is relatively free from racist caricature. However parodic and ambiguous the depiction of the Prince, he still stands out as a *Black* avatar of the seductive Romantic vampire figure. Thus, the moral charge against slavery persists amid this strange and perhaps despairingly comic vision of a world where all drain each other's blood.

The attention to lineage in the text establishes the nobility of slaves yet subverts the idea of racial purity since the Vampyre's descendent blends in with contemporary white American society. Monstrosity becomes a universal heritage. This hybrid lineage of monstrosity, slavery, and nobility confused and vampirism permeating the whole of society, with slavery as a foundational crime, destabilises the very notion of white superiority over a demonised Other. When Personne's wife and children take the potion and are restored to humanity, the bourgeois family unit is restored too. But that restoration is deceptive; their heritage still bears vampirism, not merely through the vampiric descendants of that family, but through D'Arcy's account of the endemic vampirism of US society. So patrilineal legitimacy is also undermined. Doris L. Garraway makes the point that, 'By calling all Haitians black', Dessalines's 1805 Constitution 'invalidated the biologist taxonomies through which the colonialist elites discriminated against people of color in Saint-Domingue'.[59] We argue that by calling all Americans vampires, a similar disruption of racist taxonomy is initiated.

D'Arcy dwells on the ambiguous nature of vampires: 'the terror of the living and the dead, and the participants of the nature of both [...] the emblems at once of corruption and vitality' (35). There is also a suggestion of the effaced lineage of the slave while anticipating a future redemption: 'blotted from the records of existence and replenished to repletion with circulating life [...] the chronicles of what was—the solemn and sublime mementoes of what must be!' (35).[60] These are both moments which may be described as genuinely dialectical: vampiric capitalism, as Marx observed, was both deadly and the fount of future regeneration. Gothic texts may recall a decaying past and foreshadow a transformed future, and D'Arcy's text, rooted in the foundational moments of revolution in the USA, France, and Haiti, captures this dialectical sense. *The Black Vampyre* exhibits the economic interactions and contradictions of slavery and capitalism.[61] It is no accident that Hegel's image of the dialectic between master and bondsman was directly inspired by reading accounts of rebellion in Saint-Domingue, where all the contradictions of modernity emerge: the realisation of the dialectic in this response to that event is peculiarly apt.[62] As in Hegel's master–slave dialectic, D'Arcy shows the interdependence of one and the other. The monstrous abject Other changes places and becomes the master and lord and vampiric monstrosity permeates the hegemonic culture of capitalism.

The Black Vampyre, with its concern for the circulation of texts, may also be seen as a refraction of the significant cultural cross-fertilisation between Haiti and the USA.[63] Many French planters fled to the USA during the insurrection in Saint-Domingue, to New York and elsewhere.[64] As

Dayan says, 'It is easy to forget how permeable were the borders between the young republic of the United States (which had been helped in its revolutionary struggles against the English by French and Dominguan blacks, such as Henry Christophe) and the colony of Saint-Domingue.'[65] This interaction included the diffusion of revolutionary sentiment from Haiti to elsewhere in the Caribbean and even the US mainland. Thus '[t]he revolt in Saint-Domingue left Southerners in fear of insurrection'.[66] As Margaret Prescod succinctly puts it:

> The Haitian Revolution happened decades before the Emancipation Proclamation in the United States, and there was great fear that what happened in Haiti would happen in other slaveholding countries in the Americas. Indeed, in Barbados for example, the great Bussa's Rebellion of 1816 was definitely inspired by the Haitian Revolution. [...] [P]ractically all of those islands of the Caribbean, from Granada to St. Vincent, had uprisings [...] all very much inspired by the Haitian Revolution. Some of the people who took part in and helped organize what is considered to be the largest slave revolt in the United States, the 1811 revolt in Louisiana, were Haitians brought over by their slave masters when they fled Haiti after the revolution.[67]

The vampirism that D'Arcy uncovers in Haiti's origins, and in its interaction with the USA, has left traces in Haitian literature too.[68] The Black Vampyre's ambiguous lineage from the revolt of the oppressed to tyranny appears in the acclaimed Haitian novelist Marie Vieux-Chauvet's *Anger* (1968), where she allegorises the violence of Papa Doc's dictatorship thus: 'Vampire! Vampire! I saw him sipping and getting drunk on my blood like wine.'[69] In the Haitian radical poet René Depestre's epic *Un arc-en-ciel pour l'occident chrétien, poème mystère vaudou* [*A Rainbow for the Christian West*] (1966), racism and colonialism is attacked through the 'rendition of the evil baka as a lyric fantasy combining legends of the Ku Klux Klan, the lougawou [...] and Dracula'.[70]

D'Arcy's vampiric, parasitic plagiarism feeds on a pro-slavery source to appropriate Haitian culture and yet, paradoxically, turns this against the voracious ubiquity of commodified exchange. The Gothic elements of the story undermine Enlightenment ideas, exposing their dialectical underside. Yet the Gothic horror of vampirism can also be seen as the just deserts of the cruelty of slavery and an attack on commodified society in general. Important for being the first American vampire text and for depicting the first Black vampire in literature, *The Black Vampyre* has a contemporary resonance. The racism cultivated by slavery lives on; the struggle against it and the dreams of universal humanity expressed in the Haitian Revolution continue in Black Lives Matter and such movements. The consequences of the Haitian Revolution, particularly the reaction against it, are still felt now: the long-standing debt owed to France for compensation to slaveowners, US occupation from 1915 to 1934, later neocolonial intervention by the USA such as overthrowing the democratic election of President Aristide in 2004, corruption with foreign aid after the 2010 earthquake, poverty, and the persistent racism; see the current treatment of Haitian refugees. The links *The Black Vampyre* makes between racial oppression and a vampiric, commercial society, though ambivalent, make its resurrection worthwhile.

D'Arcy takes from Polidori the figure of the vampire as aristocratic and seductive, and employed it for political satire (though the target is very different), exemplifying how Polidori instigated a template that would serve for a wide variety of perspectives. The vampire figure had already been used politically, of course, but Polidori was the first to situate it amid modernity, preparing the way for D'Arcy's savage exposure of a wide realm of vampiric activity. Polidori had transformed the vampire from peasant into lord; D'Arcy makes him a slave but then restores his nobility, then traces his progeny among the parasitic American bourgeoisie. D'Arcy's dialectical take on vampiric nobility, with the sympathetic Black Vampyre as both predator and victim, is an early and powerful instance of how multifarious Polidori's model would become.

Notes

1 A later reprinting in 1845 attributed *The Black Vampyre* to a Robert C. Sands; however, Katie Bray persuasively argues the case for Dey (Katie Bray, '"A Climate ... More Prolific ... in Sorcery": The Black Vampyre and the Hemispheric Gothic', *American Literature*, 87:1 (March 2015), 1–22 (p. 19, n. 4)).
2 See, among other accounts, Robert Morrison and Chris Baldick, 'Introduction', in *The Vampyre and Other Tales of the Macabre*, ed. by Robert Morrison and Chris Baldick (Oxford: Oxford University Press, 2008), pp. vii–xxii (pp. vii–x).
3 Paul Gilroy, *The Black Atlantic: Modernity and Double Consciousness* (London: Verso, 1993), p. 15.
4 Echoing Polidori's final line, 'Aubrey's sister had glutted the thirst of a Vampyre!' (John Polidori, *The Vampyre*, Appendix 1 in this volume, pp. 240–67 (p. 261)).
5 D'Arcy suggests in his own footnote that Spooner Dubois, the third son of the Black Vampyre's bride, Euphemia, may be Lord Ruthven. There is no further mention of this character (Uriah Derick D'Arcy, *The Black Vampyre: A Legend of St. Domingo (1819)*, ed. by Ed White, Duncan Faherty, and Toni Wall Jaudon, Just Teach One http://jto.common-place.org/just-teach-one-homepage/the-black-vampyre/ [accessed 7 June 2020], p. 24, n. 52). All further references are to this edition as page numbers in parentheses).
6 For a thorough analysis of the contradictions between Enlightenment ideals of liberty and slavery, see David Brion Davis, *The Problem of Slavery in the*

    Age of Revolution, 1770–1823 (Ithaca, NY and London: Cornell University Press, 1975).
7 The classic account is C. L. R. James, *The Black Jacobins: Toussaint L'Ouverture and the San Domingo Revolution*, ed. by James Walvin (1958; London: Penguin, 2001). Also very illuminating are: Laurent Dubois, *Avengers of the New World: The Story of the Haitian Revolution* (Cambridge, MA: Harvard University Press, 2005) and Jean Cassimir, *The Haitians: A Decolonial History*, trans. by Laurent Dubois (Chapel Hill: University of North Carolina Press, 2020).
8 *The Best Vampire Stories 1800–1849: A Classic Vampire Anthology*, ed. by Andrew Barger (n.p.: Bottletree Classics, 2012). Barger introduces *The Black Vampyre* as being the first Black vampire story, the second vampire tale in English and the first by an American author (p. 145).
9 Sam George, 'America's First Vampire was Black and Revolutionary – It's Time to Remember Him', *The Conversation*, 30 October 2020 https://theconversation.com/americas-first-vampire-was-black-and-revolutionary-its-time-to-remember-him-149044 [accessed 31 May 2023]; 'The Black Vampyre and Other Creations: Gothic Visions of New Worlds', 14 November 2020, Open Graves, Open Minds www.opengravesopenminds.com/the-black-vampyre-and-other-creations-2020/ [accessed 31 May 2023].
10 *An Appeal in Favor of that Class of Americans Called Africans*, Project Gutenberg www.gutenberg.org/ebooks/28242 [accessed 31 May 2023].
11 See Maisha L. Wester, 'The Gothic and the Politics of Race', in *The Cambridge Companion to the Modern Gothic*, ed. by Jerrold E. Hogle (Cambridge: Cambridge University Press, 2014), pp. 157–73 (p. 157). See also Tabish Khair, *The Gothic, Postcolonialism and Otherness: Ghosts from Elsewhere* (Basingstoke: Palgrave Macmillan, 2009); Tabish Khair and Johan Höglund, *Transnational and Postcolonial Vampires: Dark Blood* (Basingstoke: Palgrave Macmillan, 2012).
12 Such as John Moore's *Zeluco* (1789) and John Thelwall's *The Daughter of Adoption* (1801).
13 Bray, '"A Climate"', p. 4.
14 The poem is on pp. 47–56; we have referenced it by canto and line number.
15 'Edward in the sunlight was shocking […] his skin […] literally sparkled, like thousands of tiny diamonds were embedded in the surface' (Stephenie Meyer, *Twilight* (London: Atom Books, 2006), p. 228).
16 Polidori, p. 16; Rymer is unusual in including lunar resurrection in his descriptions of vampire lore: 'if any incident befall them, such as being shot, or otherwise killed or wounded, they can recover by lying down somewhere where the moon's rays will fall on them' (James Malcolm Rymer, *Varney the Vampyre* (Were: Wordsworth, 2010), p. 29). For 'Lunarian' vampires, see Nina Auerbach, *Our Vampires, Ourselves* (Chicago, IL: University of Chicago Press, 1995), pp. 36–38.
17 *Two Gentlemen of Verona*, v. 2. 12.
18 Polidori, *The Vampyre*, p. 246. See also Ivan Phillips's Chapter 9 in this volume.

19 These include *lougowou* (from *loup garou*) – vampires, and *soucriant*, *soucettes*, or *soucougnan* ('suckers'), which suck the blood of their victims. They are commonly female, unlike the Black Vampyre. These evil spirits are treated with the methods used in slave torture – salt, red peppers, and lemon in the skin. (Joan Dayan, *Haiti, History, and the Gods* (Berkeley: University of California Press, 1998), pp. 264–65.)
20 The Fiji mermaid had the torso and head of a juvenile monkey sewn onto the back half of a fish. For its exhibition at Scudder's Museum, see Steven C. Levi, 'P.T. Barnum and the Feejee Mermaid', *Western Folklore*, 32:2 (1977), 149–54.
21 See Paul Barber's description of the folkloric peasant vampire, *Vampires, Burials and Death* (New Haven, CT and London: Yale University Press, 1988), p. 2.
22 In some versions of the myth, notably Ovid's, Prometheus actually fashioned human beings out of clay (see *Metamorphoses*, trans. by David Raeburn (London: Penguin, 2004), I. 76–88, pp. 8–9).
23 Many slaves supposed 'that death would involve a return to Africa' (Sarah Juliet Lauro, *The Transatlantic Zombie: Slavery, Rebellion, and Living Death* (New Brunswick, NJ: Rutgers University Press, 2015), p. 52). Sorcerers, killed by cannon, believed themselves to be reborn in Africa, just as the Prince is (Dayan, *Haiti*, p. 30).
24 Bray, '"A Climate"', p. 2.
25 Bray, '"A Climate"', p. 7.
26 Bray, '"A Climate"', p. 10.
27 See, for instance, Moreau de Saint-Mérry's 1796 classification, with its 'eleven categories of 110 combinations ranked from absolute white (128 parts white blood) to absolute black (128 parts black blood)' (Dayan, *Haiti*, p. 231, and pp. 230–37).
28 Marlene L. Daut, *Tropics of Haiti: Race and the Literary History of the Haitian Revolution in the Atlantic World, 1789–1865* (Liverpool: Liverpool University Press, 2015), p. 8.
29 Daut, *Tropics of Haiti*, pp. 5–6.
30 Daut, *Tropics of Haiti*, p. 4.
31 Daut, *Tropics of Haiti*, p. 4.
32 Daut, *Tropics of Haiti*, p. 5.
33 See Venetia Newall, 'Birds in the Icon Tradition', in *Animals in Folklore*, ed. by J. R. Porter and W. M. S. Russell (Cambridge: D. S. Brewer, 1978), pp. 185–207 (p. 185–89).
34 For Apollo's nature and deeds, see Robert Graves, *Greek Myths* (London: Penguin 2011), pp. 76–83. Birds in Greek myth can be found in Newall, 'Birds', pp. 188–89.
35 Bray, '"A Climate"', p. 12.
36 Bray, '"A Climate"', p. 13.
37 The Haitian *lougawou* 'resemble the European idea of the vampire, but they remain totally separate from the lwa' (Dayan, *Haiti*, p. 67).
38 Lauro, *The Transatlantic Zombie*, p. 7.
39 Dayan, *Haiti*, p. 72.
40 Susan Buck-Morss, *Hegel, Haiti, and Universal History* (Pittsburgh, PA: University of Pittsburgh Press, 2009), pp. 128–33.

41 Buck-Morss, *Hegel*, p. 133.
42 Lauro, *The Transatlantic Zombie*, p. 55. Lauro develops this argument in detail (pp. 55–63).
43 Buck-Morss, *Hegel*, p. 36, n. 42.
44 Dayan, *Haiti*, p. 23.
45 Dayan, *Haiti*, p. 29.
46 The role of Vodou in the Revolution has also been contested as 'mythic' and the narrative of the ceremony itself seems to be a form of Gothic counter-Enlightenment that brings its own problems (see A. James Arnold, 'Recuperating the Haitian Revolution in Literature: From Victor Hugo to Derek Walcott', in *Tree of Liberty: Cultural Legacies of the Haitian Revolution in the Atlantic World*, ed. by Doris L. Garraway (Charlottesville: University of Virginia Press, 2008), pp. 179–99 (p. 192–93)).
47 Dayan, *Haiti*, p. 29.
48 Dayan, *Haiti*, p. 37.
49 *Commercial Advertiser*, 28 June 1818, p. 2, cited in Ed White and Duncan Faherty, 'Introduction', in Uriah Derick D'Arcy, 'The Black Vampyre; A Legend of St. Domingo (1819)', pp. 1–11 (p. 2), Just Teach One http://jto.common-place.org/just-teach-one-homepage/the-black-vampyre/ [accessed 7 June 2020]. p. 2.
50 Bray, '"A Climate"', p. 15.
51 There are echoes here of Aphra Behn's 1688 novel *Oroonoko; or, The Royal Slave*.
52 From Charles Phillips 'An Aggregate Meeting of the Roman Catholics of Cork' (quoted in White and Faherty, 'Introduction', p. 30, n. 31).
53 Bray, '"A Climate"', pp. 8–9.
54 White and Faherty situate this economic satire in the context of the contemporary economic crisis known as 'the Panic of 1819' ('Introduction', p. 6).
55 For the vampire as political metaphor and in Marx, see Sam George and Bill Hughes, 'Introduction', in *Open Graves, Open Minds: Representations of Vampires and the Undead from the Enlightenment to the Present Day*, ed. by Sam George and Bill Hughes (Manchester: Manchester University Press, 2013), pp. 1–23 (pp. 12–15); Chris Baldick, 'Karl Marx's Vampires and Grave Diggers', in *In Frankenstein's Shadow: Myth, Monstrosity and Nineteenth-Century Writing* (Oxford: Clarendon Press, 1987), pp. 121–40.
56 The editors' footnote here informs us that 'Moses Thomas (1787–1865) [...] published many of Byron's poems as well as an 1819 edition of Polidori's *The Vampyre*, signed with Byron's name' (54, n. 142).
57 Jonathan Swift, 'A Full and True Account of the BATTEL Fought last FRIDAY Between the *Ancient* and the *Modern* BOOKS in St. JAMES's LIBRARY' [1704], in *A Tale of a Tub and Other Works*, ed. by Angus Ross and David Wooley (Oxford: Oxford University Press, 1986), pp. 104–25 (pp. 110–13).
58 D'Arcy relies on Bryon Edwards, 'a reasoned and, for its time, relatively moderate and humane defense of a social order based on slavery' (Dayan, *Haiti*, p. 147), compared to the more virulently racist Edward Long. See Davis, *The Problem of Slavery* (pp. 184–95) for an account of the limitations of Edwards's position.

59 Doris L. Garraway, ' "Légitime Défense": Universalism and Nationalism in the Discourse of the Haitian Revolution', in Garraway, *Tree of Liberty*, pp. 63–88 (p. 82).
60 This last phrase, say White and Faherty, comes from a speech by Charles Phillips (35, n. 82).
61 Eric Williams's 1944 groundbreaking account is still relevant here: *Capitalism and Slavery* (London: Penguin, 2022).
62 See Buck-Morss, *Hegel*.
63 For the diffusion of revolutionary ideas from Haiti to the USA, see Julius S. Scott, *The Common Wind: Afro-American Currents in the Age of the Haitian Revolution* (London: Verso, 2018).
64 Dayan, *Haiti*, p. 163.
65 Dayan, *Haiti*, p. 162.
66 Dayan, *Haiti*, p. 188.
67 Margaret Prescod in interview: Pierre Labossiere, Margaret Prescod, and Camila Valle, 'The Long Haitian Revolution', *Monthly Review*, 1 October 2021 https://monthlyreview.org/2021/10/01/the-long-haitian-revolution [accessed 5 May 2023].
68 In an important article, Raphael Hoermann sees the Haitian Revolution as a central focus for early Gothic, discerning a dialectic between a demonising, hegemonic Haitian Gothic and a radical one. *The Black Vampyre* participates ambivalently in both of these (' "A Very Hell of Horrors"? The Haitian Revolution and the Early Transatlantic Haitian Gothic', *Slavery & Abolition*, 37:1 (2016), 183–205).
69 *Anger*, in Marie Vieux-Chauvet, *Love, Anger, Madness: A Haitian Triptych*, trans. by Rose-Myriam Réjouis and Val Vinokur (New York: Modern Library, 2010), pp. 167–299 (p. 260).
70 Dayan, *Haiti*, p. 266.

9

'But if thine eye be evil': Tropes of vision in the rise of the modern vampire

Ivan Phillips

There are a lot of eyes in John Polidori's *The Vampyre: A Tale* (1819). In the opening sentences, as the mysterious Lord Ruthven arrives in London society, emphasis is placed on both his *being seen* – he 'appeared at the various parties of the *ton*' – and his *looking out*: 'He apparently gazed upon the mirth around him.'[1] A pattern is established, and the ocular mathematics of the text are striking. At 8,200 words in length (long for a short story, short for a novella, but still often referred to as a novel), *The Vampyre* features twenty-two direct references to eyes, almost thirty to acts of seeing, looking, observing or watching, ten to perception, thirteen to description, five to images and seven to the imagination more generally. All in all, the story features close to 100 words drawn from the semantic field of vision, a little above 1 per cent of the overall word count. This may not sound like much but 1 per cent is, of course, 1 in 100 words, amounting to an occurrence every three or four sentences. This is surely enough to constitute a theme. The aim here is to gaze back into Ruthven's eyes to discover what they might tell us about the emergence of the modern vampire and its evolution within popular culture across the last two centuries.

Polidori's protagonist Aubrey is described as an intense observer of Ruthven from the moment he first encounters him: 'He watched him', we are told, and a little later he resolves 'to watch him more closely' (249). This effectively fixes the frame of constant mutual surveillance that is introduced in the first lines of the story, the tropological importance of eyes – of sight, seeing, observation, the gaze – being established in a way which suggests a more unnervingly sociable version of the 'power situation' discovered by Michel Foucault in Jeremy Bentham's 1791 schema for the Panopticon: 'Visibility is a trap.'[2] Ruthven's first act is to watch and his presence as a remarked watcher leads to him being watched in return: 'His peculiarities caused him to be invited to every house; *all wished to see him*' (3; my emphasis). Moreover, it is his eyes that are indicated as a possible source of the awe that he inspires:

> some attributed it to the dead grey eye, which, fixing upon the object's face, did not seem to penetrate, and at one glance to pierce through to the inward

workings of the heart; but fell upon the cheek with a leaden ray that weighed upon the skin it could not pass.

(246)

Ruthven's eye is presented as having a physical, material force, affecting the viewed object palpably, like an unwelcome touch. Implicitly, at least, a look from Ruthven is associated with the vampiric bite, its frustrated motivation being to do more than merely rest heavily upon the skin. Explicitly, it is a weapon, used to 'quell' laughter and to 'throw fear' (246).

The intrusive and predacious gaze attributed to Ruthven is open to a phallic interpretation and might lead us to Sigmund Freud's famous essay 'The Uncanny' (1919), with its assertion of 'the substitutive relation between the eye and the male member that is manifested in dreams, fantasies and myths'.[3] Although Freud is distinctly *not* concerned with a critique of the rapacious masculine sex organ – indeed, his concern is for its anxious vulnerability – his discussion can nevertheless be suggestive in the context of *The Vampyre*. Taking issue with Ernst Jentsch's earlier exploration of uncanny psychology (1906), Freud contends that the uncanny effect has 'nothing to do' with the 'intellectual uncertainty' of, for instance, 'whether an object is animate or inanimate', but is rooted instead in 'the idea of being robbed of one's eyes'.[4] Inevitably, perhaps, given his belief in the interchangeability of the ocular and the phallic (their *Ersatzbeziehung*), Freud concludes that uncanny sensations are derived from a castration complex rooted in a specific childhood terror.[5] This is exemplified by the folk myth that provides both the title and the thematic impetus for E. T. A. Hoffmann's tale 'The Sandman', written in the same year (1816) as the legendary gathering at the Villa Diodati which led to the composition of Mary Shelley's *Frankenstein; or, The Modern Prometheus* (1818) and (via Byron's 'A Fragment') Polidori's *The Vampyre*, along with his novel *Ernestus Berchtold* (1819). Freud follows Jentsch in reflecting on Hoffmann's story but shifts the focus, strategically, away from the protagonist Nathanael's love for his professor's automaton daughter Olympia and towards the grimly cautionary tale of stolen eyes told to him in childhood by his sister's nurse: '[The Sandman] puts them into a bag and carries them off to the moon to feed his children.'[6] The knowledge that Freud claims in this context – that adults often inherit from their childhood selves an anxiety about damaged or lost eyes – is not directly pertinent to Polidori's depiction of eyes in *The Vampyre*. It is, though, significant in this connection because of the strategy that Freud adopts to distract from Jentsch's interest in the living doll Olympia.

The key point of the nurse's Sandman story – from Freud's perspective, at least – is not simply that the children's eyes will be lost or damaged; it is that they will be *stolen*. A chilling enough prospect in itself, this is given an intensified charge of horror in the climax of Hoffmann's tale, with Nathanael's discovery of his professor, Spalanzani, and the sinister Coppola wrestling for possession of Olympia. As the latter drags her away with her wooden feet clacking on the stairs, her revealed status as 'a lifeless doll' is at once emphasised and complicated by the narrated fate of her eyes. Horrified by the 'pits of blackness' in her 'deathly-white face', Nathanael subsequently sees 'a pair of blood-flecked eyes [...] staring up at him' from the floor.[7] Freud finds nothing uncanny in the artificial human but everything uncanny in her empty eye sockets. For him, Jentsch's concern for the hesitation between animacy and inanimacy is a result of overvaluing 'fairy stories': 'We are told that it is highly uncanny when inanimate objects—pictures or dolls—come to life, but in Hans Andersen's stories the household utensils, the furniture and the tin soldiers are alive, and perhaps nothing is farther removed from the uncanny.'[8] Freud forgets the thrill and the potential chill of childhood reading but the implications of his reductive approach for the kinds of stories written by Polidori can be instructive.

Freud's shorthand for the uncanny – not being able to know where you are – is also a shorthand for the fear of ocular damage or loss, encapsulated in the image of Olympia's pallid, eyeless puppet face and those eyes discarded on a floor.[9] The 'dead grey eye' of Ruthven is an altogether more enigmatic symbol, but nonetheless *unheimlich*. It simultaneously reveals and obscures the processes of seeing and being seen which are fundamental not only to *The Vampyre* but also to Polidori's other work. That Freud's revision of Jentsch should enact a collision between the anxiety of eyelessness and the anxiety of soullessness (he refers to automata and the returning dead, to trance-states, to sleepwalkers) is even more significant.

In the case of Ruthven, the dead greyness of his eyes establishes a contrast from the outset with those biblical metaphors of spiritual purity that gave rise to the idiom of eyes as windows of the soul. This is Matthew 6.22–23 in the King James translation:

> The light of the body is the eye: if therefore thine eye be single, thy whole body shall be full of light.
>
> But if thine eye be evil, thy whole body shall be full of darkness. If therefore the light that is in thee be darkness, how great *is* that darkness!

An almost identical passage can be found in Luke 11.34–35. The implications for a reading of Ruthven's eyes are clear, particularly if this takes place within the kind of popular horror paradigm invoked by psychologists Chelsea Schein and Kurt Gray: 'Horror movies have discovered an easy recipe for making people creepy: alter their eyes. Instead of normal eyes, zombies' eyes are vacantly white, vampires' eyes glow with the color of blood, and those possessed by demons are cavernously black.'[10] Interestingly, against this (admittedly unsophisticated) colour coding, Ruthven would be identified as a hybrid of the zombie and demon figures rather than a vampire. This hardly matters. The thing to note is that his eyes as described in the novella, long before the paradigm could be recognised as such, identify him as 'creepy', and this creepiness is to do with a perceived absence, or corruption, of the 'soul'.

The value of Schein and Gray's approach is that they are concerned not so much with what an 'abnormal' eye denotes about an individual but what it connotes to those who perceive that individual, and what this connotation signifies at a mythic level.[11] From the perspective of Polidori's depiction of Ruthven, the suggestion that 'strange eyes are broader cues to *strange minds*' is helpful in drawing attention to his anomalous and disconnected presence within society.[12] If, as Schein and Gray argue, minds are perceived 'along two broad dimensions of agency (intending, planning, doing) and experience (feeling, sensing, consciousness)', then Ruthven's incongruous relationship to the second of these becomes important.[13] He has agency, it is clear, but what are his claims to experience, and how is this communicated by eyes that are seen as dead and grey? If 'we rely on eyes' to know whether others have the capacity for 'experience', then what might that experience be? In an age before the development of humanoid robots, an age nevertheless fascinated by humanoid automata, any questions of artificial (or 'unnatural') life must be inextricably bound up with questions of real (or 'natural') life and, by extension, real (or 'natural') death. If 'robots are creepy when they seem to feel', does it follow that humans are creepy when they seem *not* to feel?[14] And at what point do they stop being human at all? When eyes are assumed to be a window on the soul, the implications for a character whose eyes are somehow obscure are profound. This takes us back to the realms of Freud and the uncanny.

Polidori was a hundred years too early to read Freud, and it is uncertain whether he had read his contemporary Hoffmann (and, specifically, 'The Sandman'), but he had certainly read Edmund Burke.[15] His 'Essay Upon the Source of Positive Pleasure' (1818) explicitly references Burke's *A Philosophical Enquiry into the Origin of Our Ideas of the Sublime and Beautiful* (1757), and that work also informs the presentation of the natural world in his novel *Ernestus Berchtold* (1819), written at the same time as *The Vampyre* and published in the same year. This is worth considering because Burke, as well as being fascinated by processes of visual perception in his reflections on beauty and the sublime, seems to have been drawn to the image of the eye as an indicator of both aesthetic and moral integrity. In the *Philosophical Enquiry*, for example, he states that 'the beauty of the eye consists, first, in its clearness' and goes on to claim that 'none are pleased with an eye, whose water (to use that term) is dull and muddy'.[16] More explicitly, in *Reflections on the Revolution in France* (1790), he uses the figure of the eye as a measure of social stability, referring to 'passions of the human mind, which are as doubtful a colour in the moral eye, as superstition itself'.[17] It is with this in mind that Richard A. Barney has noted '[t]he eye's moral and political prominence in Burke's analysis', and a comparable symbolic status is given to the eye in Polidori's vampire tale.[18] As a thing both seen and seeing, disturbingly unknowable in both respects, the eye of Ruthven acts as a kind of moral locus for the narrative world he inhabits.

Strangely, although Ruthven is an object of close and continual scrutiny in *The Vampyre*, he seems to be impossible to see, or at least to describe. Aubrey, we are told, finds him imperceptible as a character, both physically and morally, without 'a single bright point on which to rest the eye'; at the same time, he resolves 'to watch him more closely', his 'eye follow[ing] him in all his windings' (250). Ruthven's face has 'a deadly hue' and its 'form and outline' are 'beautiful' (246), but he remains – as Sam George has noted – 'something of a blank canvas', and this is the key to his compelling enigma, both within Polidori's story and beyond it.[19] David Glover has described Dracula as being 'virtually beyond representation, an unmirrorable image', referring to him as 'physiognomy's true vanishing point', but these characteristics are clearly traceable to Ruthven as Dracula's aristocratic progenitor.[20] The enigma of invisibility is one that can also be found in *Ernestus Berchtold*.

Although it has never had the fame or influence of its slimmer companion piece (selling fewer than 200 copies on its original publication), *Ernestus Berchtold* is a more ambitious and complex work, and might even be seen as a more fully resolved piece of writing.[21] Set against a backdrop of the Napoleonic wars, the novel is avowedly a product of the ghost story competition at the Villa Diodati and its Gothic credentials are apparent throughout, with themes of identity, imprisonment, violence, wild nature, personal and public corruption, obsessive love and death (*lots* of death) to the fore. The specifically supernatural elements of the story are kept to a minimum, and Polidori's disclosure of them in his introduction is uncomfortably apologetic, yet this conscious marginalisation of the fantastical within the narrative has the curious effect of making it stand out. In particular, the mysterious forces which serve Count Doni – the Milanese aristocrat who adopts the eponymous protagonist and his sister, Julia – are noteworthy for the challenge that they present to the eye. Sitting with Julia by the river in the Count's garden, hidden in a clematis bower, Ernestus sees Doni walking and apparently speaking to himself. 'I could perceive no one near him', he remembers, but his sister insists that there is someone, or something, there:

> I could not at first see to what she directed my attention; but at last I perceived the outline of a figure, through the shape of whose body the very leaves were visible; something in the manner that I have seen in the summer, a current of heated air, accurately defined by the wavering outline of the things between which and our sight it stands, only that this was even more sensible to vision.[22]

This almost invisible presence – described by Ernestus as 'figured vapour' – has a vital role to play in the tragic unfolding of events in the novel. Julia, at a point of terrible crisis, finds herself increasingly drawn to the necromancy that enables Doni to conjure this 'transparent, all-pervading being' into existence (112). Her desperate urge to discover the secret of 'that being almost lost amidst the ambient air' leads her to observe the Count's habits and, ultimately, to hide in a closet adjoining his room so that she can spy on him through a hole in the wainscoting.

Julia's act of cupboard espionage is the scene that comes closest within Polidori's oeuvre to resembling Mary Shelley's description of his Diodati story in her introduction to the 1831 edition of *Frankenstein*: '[he] had some terrible idea about a skull-headed lady who was so punished for peeping through a key-hole – what to see I forget'.[23] The absence of this unfortunate voyeur from any of the author's surviving texts gives her an aura of infinite deferral, making her seem like a bibliographical equivalent of the elusive and not-quite-seeable Lord Ruthven. What Julia encounters during her first session of surveillance is intriguing in this sense, however, and perhaps throws some light on the character of Polidori's vampire, its relationship to his other writings and its wider influence through time:

> [T]he door slowly opened, and a figure clad in a white robe entered; its dark black eye was fixed; its grey locks seemed as if no breath of air could move their weight; no sign of life, save the moving feet belonged to it, for the face was pale, the lips blueish. It approached with an unvarying step; it was Doni! its hand took hers within its cold grasp.
>
> (113)

Dark eyes, pale face, blue lips, cold hands, a steady, relentless walk, apparently lifeless; the sleepwalking Count Doni bears a remarkable resemblance not only to Ruthven but to a subsequent lineage of literary, theatrical, cinematic and televisual vampires. There are no (overt) vampires in *Ernestus Berchtold* – as mentioned, there is relatively little of the supernatural at all, and what there is, is invisible – but there are many figures who are presented in terms that might now strike a reader as vampiric. There is the tortured villager who is found by Ernestus and his soldiers in a war-ravaged village:

> While yet speaking one of them brought before us a man, who seemed to have risen from the grave. His grey locks, thinly scattered on his head, were entangled, his eyes were sunk so deep within their sockets, that their lustre seemed the last glimmering of life before it sinks.
>
> (70)

And there is the sickly Louisa, Doni's daughter, whose bedside is visited by the love-struck Ernestus:

> There was a clear whiteness that overspread her face, where it was not tinged by the hectic flush, her eye shone with a glassy brilliancy that seemed not mortal, it was the glance of death mocking my sense through a beauteous vizor, for there were the seeds of death sown deep in her broken heart.
>
> (100)

There is a foreshadowing here of several scenes in James Malcolm Rymer's *Varney, the Vampire; or, The Feast of Blood* (1845–47), and of the relationship between Laura and the title character in Sheridan Le Fanu's *Carmilla* (1872), as well as a clear anticipation of Lucy Westenra's decline into eroticised undeath in Bram Stoker's *Dracula* (1897).

The icy, fragile, otherworldly beauty of the ailing Louisa is mirrored in that of the dying Julia later in the story, with a similar contrast being drawn between the complexion of her skin and the appearance of her eye: 'I found her health much decayed [...]. Yet there was perhaps a greater charm in that pale cheek and languid eye, than I had found in the delicate colouring of the one, or the splendour of the other' (145). What is evident here – regardless of the specific illness afflicting Julia – is the influence of the 'tubercular moment' described by Carolyn A. Day, the rise of consumption as 'a fashionable disease' in the late eighteenth and early nineteenth centuries.[24] The 'moment' has had an extended legacy, of course, not least in the 'heroin chic' of the early 1990s. It is notable how this became manifest in the translation of pallor from print to screen in film adaptations of the same period, in particular Francis Ford Coppola's *Bram Stoker's Dracula* (1992) and Neil Jordan's *Interview with the Vampire* (1994), based on Anne Rice's novel of 1976. There is a clear continuation of the 'fashion' in the pale glamour of Edward Cullen in Stephenie Meyer's *Twilight* novels (2005–08) and their subsequent film adaptations (2008–12). Back in 1819, Polidori's Ernestus is unequivocal in his attribution of *phthisis pulmonalis* to the deterioration of Laura – 'Consumption was ruining her system; she was faint and weak; her continued cough and the marked colour on her cheek, but too well denoted the power it had acquired' (127) – and it is impossible to overlook the aesthetic apotheosis of 'the great white plague' in the narration of her death. This is worth quoting in full:

> The wax tapers seemed to burn dimly, as if in unison with the solemn scene; the black walls, the felted ground, the corpse stretched out, arrayed in white, the stillness visible upon that beauteous face, stilled even the tumult in my breast. She did not seem dead but asleep, I had held her in my arms, upon my breast, looking as she then looked, I gazed upon her for moments, it seemed as if I believed the still appearance wronged my senses. I was about to press her to my heart, my lips were approaching hers, but I started; there were two flies already revelling on those lips, and she could not chase them.
>
> (131)

Louisa is not a vampire but, as displayed in her death, she anticipates so many vampires who will follow on page, stage and screen across the next two centuries. In many cultures the eyes are thumbed shut at death, and it is noticeable that (unusually, given his typical field of reference) they are not mentioned at this point by Ernestus.[25] Even so, the hesitancy of his bereaved perceptions and the necrophiliac sensuousness of his responses mean that – notwithstanding the attentions of the two flies – there can be little certainty that Louisa's eyes will remain closed. The 'atmosphere of Juliet's tomb' that pervades the scene brings with it a challenge to the supposedly absolute binaries of life and death.[26] Shakespeare's teenage heroine is, after all, only wearing the 'borrowed likeness of shrunk death' when Romeo discovers her in the vault, and the suspended condition predicted by Friar Laurence is intriguingly similar to the descriptions of consumptive fade-out in *Ernestus Bertchtold*: 'The roses in thy lips and cheeks shall fade / To wanny ashes'.[27] Louisa's death is, in some ways, no more convincing than that of Ruthven following the bandit attack in Greece, when he literally dies laughing and then disappears without a trace from the mountaintop on which he has been left (271–22).

In considering the mirroring themes and images of *The Vampyre* and *Ernestus Berchtold*, what becomes evident is the manner in which Polidori begins to generate, in his prose fiction, an anatomy of the modern vampire. This can be itemised quite simply in terms of three modes of estrangement: a 'strange' eye and accompanying 'strange' ways of seeing or being seen; a 'strange' complexion, typically (but not exclusively) one of consumptive pallor; and a 'strange' physicality, strength and motion. Taken together, these amount to an uncanny phenomenology that has been taken up and adapted through subsequent vampiric narratives, combining elements of the existential, the ontological and the political. It is epitomised in Polidori's fiction by the shadowy evasiveness of Lord Ruthven and of the 'transparent, all-pervading being' in *Ernestus Berchtold* (112), redolent in both cases of the 'darkness visible' that John Milton associates with Satan and his rebels in *Paradise Lost* (1667).[28] A paradoxical darkness that challenges empirical understandings, this also haunts the analysis of sleepwalking, or 'oneirodynia', in Polidori's medical dissertation of 1815, written when he was just twenty years old. A crucible for many of the themes that emerge in his fiction, the document establishes at the outset the epistemological obscurity of the natural sciences – 'it seems we will never learn the primary causes of things' – and the specific challenge of the subject matter, which he describes as 'quite difficult and immersed in blackest darkness'.[29] As an initial statement of the author's Gothic credentials, this could hardly be improved. It inaugurates the use of tropes of vision within Polidori's work and his explicit interest in eyes, conjuring the mise-en-scène for his most famous and influential creation while developing a thesis that would make him the youngest physician ever to receive a medical degree from Edinburgh University.

Polidori's definition of oneirodynia – although it confuses *duno*, 'dream', for *odunē*, 'pain', something raised in his oral examination – is highly suggestive in relation to his emergent imagination: 'I would say it is the habit of doing something in sleep that is usually done by those who are awake.'[30] This can be assigned straightforwardly to the night wanderings of Count Doni in *Ernestus Berchtold* but it might also be adapted quite easily as a précis of the activities of Ruthven and his kind: 'the habit of doing something in *death* that is usually done by those who are alive'. This conjoining of sleep and death is hardly an unprecedented leap of imagination, but in Polidori's medical dissertation it is conspicuously presented through a preoccupation with the sensory operations observed in sleepwalking, in particular a fascination with the ocular and motor functions. In both the preamble and the account of his two case studies, Polidori speculates on the involvement of the eyes in these actions and in any subsequent recollections of the sleepwalker, as well as on their appearance. Some sleepwalkers have their eyes open, some do not; some seem to be aware of visual stimulus, some do not; some display remarkable spatial and physical awareness, yet this is not necessarily linked to the working of the eyes. The crucial synthesis made by Polidori is between the eyes as physical organs, the sense of vision associated with them, and the mysterious impulses of the imagination. At several points, when reflecting on his case studies, he conjectures that the latter faculty is both contiguous with, and transcendent of, the mechanical operations of sight: 'the impressions caused by imagination and memory were stronger than those reaching him through his eyes'; 'he made use of his vision only when his imagination provided him with some idea that he needed vision in order to carry out properly'; 'What a vivid imagination he had may be inferred from the fact that he, without the use of his eyes, held the things depicted in his mind by force of imagination alone.'[31] Significantly, this observed fusion of seeing and imagining is situated in relation to acts of movement and spatial negotiation. This has interesting implications for the ways in which Polidori's writings can be seen to inform the represented character of the modern vampire, not least in a disconcerting passage from 'An Essay Upon the Source of Positive Pleasure': 'if the sight were perfect we should see everything in its decaying and decayed state; we should see the reptile instruments of destruction upon every leaf, the effects of the weather and time upon every blade of grass, constant decay, and irreparable destruction'.[32] The faculty of vision – so vital to the empirical operations of science within which Polidori, as a student of medicine, finds himself – is here presented as a sense that, taken apart from its excitement of the imagination, will show us nothing but death.

Anne Stiles, Stanley Finger and John Bulevich, in showing how Polidori's medical dissertation heralded 'Polidori's interest in sleep, dreams, and states of suspended animation', draw attention to both its topicality and its influence.[33] Most immediately, they point to the somnambulist aspects of his fictional vampire: 'Ruthven's uncommon physical strength, his occasional visual and tactile impairment, and his emotionless, machinelike behavior resemble the case studies presented in Polidori's medical thesis.'[34] They also resemble the kinetic traits of subsequent literary and (perhaps especially) screen vampires, anticipating the paradigm established by Max Schreck as Orlok in *Nosferatu* (dir. by F.W. Murnau, 1922) and Bela Lugosi as the Count in *Dracula* (dir. by Tod Browning, 1931). The paradigm has been challenged on many occasions in the century since Murnau's film, but the slow, relentless, trance-like walk and superhuman strength of the early cinematic vampires – and of other early cinematic 'monsters' such as the title characters in *The Golem: How He Came into the World* (dir. by Paul Wegener, 1920) and *The Mechanical Man* (dir. by André Deed, 1921), and Cesare in *The Cabinet of Dr Caligari* (dir. by Robert Wiene, 1920) – remain persistent within popular genres of the fantastic.

What connects the ocular and kinetic tropes which emerge from Polidori's writing is what also connects them with ideas of the uncanny. Freud recognises that '[t]he false semblance of death and the raising of the dead' are 'commonplace in fairy tales', but he questions their legitimacy as 'uncanny themes'.[35] Even so, his preferred locus of the uncanny, the eyes, can be related directly to understandings of animal movement. As Schein and Gray argue, eyes are essential in 'communicating emotional experience', enabling others to 'identify emotions', but they 'are also used to convey basic animacy' – signs of life, in other words.[36] The fact that 'animacy' and 'animation' are etymologically linked (via the Latin *animus*) with ideas of the soul means that Freud's anxiety about damaged or lost eyes is perhaps more relevant to those fairy tales than he allows it to be. For Schein and Gray, 'losing one's eyes is tantamount to losing one's soul—at least from the perspective of the perceiver'.[37] This returns us, by way of the gospels of Matthew and Luke, and Hoffmann's Olympia, to Ruthven and his 'dead grey eye'.

Lord Ruthven marks the point at which vampires begin to evolve, in Catherine Spooner's words, 'from the grotty living corpses of folklore to witty, sexy, super-achievers'.[38] At the same time, he retains the DNA of those folk revenants – of Peter Plogojowitz and Arnold Paole – and it is his eyes that threaten to give him away.[39] This is because they conceal rather than reveal experience, refusing connection and the reassuring sense of a life being lived. They disclose nothing that might be thought of as a soul and reflect only the limitations of the perceiver's own eyes (by narrative implication, our eyes), the impossibility of really *seeing* Ruthven. Looking into his eyes, nothing is seen, and to see him is to see nothing at all. Like the vampires that will come after him, he unsettles not simply by his blood-sucking actions but through his 'embod[iment of] the possibility that humans might be soulless automata'.[40] Given the shadowy indeterminacy of his appearance, it is ironic that it is Ruthven's depicted image, contained in his sister's locket, that Aubrey destroys when he discovers that she is to marry 'this monster' (260). The parallel invisibility of Aubrey's sister – who is never even named within the narrative – seems to add to the theme of ontological perplexity.

Tellingly, despite the early popular success of *The Vampyre*, there seem to be no contemporary (or even near-contemporary) illustrations of Ruthven. The first edition of the story in book format (1 May 1819, exactly one month after its publication in the *New Monthly Magazine*) includes no images and, notoriously, names no author. Published sixty-five years later, John Dicks's People's Edition perpetuates the myth of Byron's authorship and features a portrait of the mad, bad and dangerous lord by F. Gilbert (see Figure 9.1). The vampire himself, however, remains invisible. The illustration immediately below that of Byron shows the scene from the story in which Ianthe has been attacked in the forest by (presumably) Ruthven: a huddle of peasants with burning torches stare in horror at her neck-bitten form while a floored and anxious Aubrey recovers at their feet. The vampire himself is nowhere to be seen. He is there in his effects, though, a disturbingly present absence, and it might be argued that he is also there in his coded origins. The presiding name and countenance of Byron serve as reminders not only of the tale's extended history of authorial confusion but also of its roots in the poet's abandoned fragment from the Diodati ghost story session, and in the putatively 'vampiric' character of the poet himself. Gilbert's illustrations present the vampire *sous rature*, in Derridean terms, 'under erasure', at once crossed out and legible.[41] They seem, in this respect, to be emblematic

Figure 9.1 F. Gilbert's cover for the popular edition of *The Vampyre* (London: John Dicks, 1884).

of both the character of Ruthven himself and of the restlessly metamorphic image of the vampire as it was to develop across the next 200 years.

It is surely no coincidence that portraits were to become a recurrent element in the world-building of vampire (and related) fiction following the narrated destruction of Ruthven's locket miniature, and George has explored elsewhere the idea of 'vampire painting'.[42] A pair of portraits plays a pivotal role in the conclusion of *Ernestus Berchtold*, it should be noted, and Oscar Wilde's *The Picture of Dorian Gray* (1890) also depends on a painted, vampiric likeness. A portrait features prominently in *Varney, the Vampire*, too, appearing initially in the opening scene in which Flora Bannerworth is attacked by the vampire in her bedchamber (see Figure 9.2).[43] The figure in the portrait is described in terms that seem strikingly like Ruthven and, again, there is an emphasis on the eyes and on the challenges of perception: 'a young man, with a pale face, a stately brow, and a strange expression about the eyes, which no one cared to look on twice'.[44] Like Ruthven, then, the portrait resists observation at the same time as enacting it, 'appear[ing] to fix its eyes upon the attempting intruder'.[45] A portrait of the vampire as a young man stares, in effect, at its own subject. When Flora's brother Henry and his friend Robert Marchdale inspect the portrait in the wake of the vampire's assault, not surprisingly it is the eyes that they first remark upon.[46]

In *Carmilla*, too, a portrait plays a key role, the old, restored painting of Mircalla Karnstein providing the first intimation of the true nature of Laura's mysteriously alluring visitor. Again, the author draws attention to acts of looking and seeing in relation to the portrait, Laura's father 'seem[ing] but little struck by it' (as if it repels his attention) and Carmilla responding by watching her friend closely: 'her fine eyes under their long lashes gazing on me in contemplation'.[47] Shortly afterwards, walking in the moonlight, the two women share a moment of physical and emotional intimacy, at which point Carmilla undergoes a visible transformation that begins at the eyes: 'She was gazing on me with eyes from which all fire, all meaning had flown, and a face colourless and apathetic.'[48]

There is no explicit reference to a portrait in the original novel of *Dracula*, but Stoker's handwritten notebooks suggest a significant and intriguing reason for this: 'No looking glasses in Count's house never can see him reflected in one – no shadow?'[49] As George recognises, shadow is figured as a correlative of representational processes in some of the earliest writings on artistic practice.[50] Specifically, it is related to portraiture, so it is no surprise that Stoker extends the evasiveness of Dracula's likeness beyond reflective or tenebrous surfaces to those that support the capture of analogue images: 'painters could not paint him – their likeness always like someone else'; 'Could not codak [sic] him – come out black or like skeleton corpse.'[51] Whether he might be represented sculpturally, rendered in three dimensions, is not

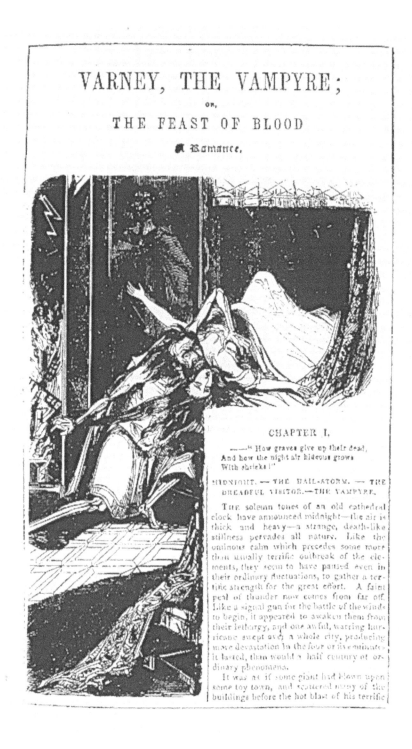

Figure 9.2 Flora Bannerworth is attacked by Sir Francis Varney on the opening page of *Varney, the Vampire* (1845), while his portrait looks on from the shadows.

indicated, but it would seem unlikely given his supposed resistance to any other form of capture, his status as, in Glover's phrase, 'physiognomy's true vanishing point'.⁵² The irony of this, given the rich history of portrayals across myriad formats since the publication of *Dracula*, is intensified by an awareness that – even before Stoker's momentous additions to the mythology – the vampire was making itself difficult to see, refusing any stable and unambiguous representation. Strikingly, Francis Ford Coppola introduces a portrait to his 1992 film adaptation of *Dracula*, an image of the Count's 'ancestor' – reminiscent of Albrecht Dürer's *Self-Portrait at Twenty-Eight* (1500) – which provides a trigger to the scene in which he rages about the pride of the Szekelys, at once drawing attention to, and deflecting away from, the truth of his identity.

Although there is no portrait painting in Stoker's novel, there is – famously, and influentially – a mirror, the 'shaving glass' of Jonathan Harker, in which his host cannot be seen. A vital innovation within modern vampire lore, this confounding of physical laws also extends its use of tropes of vision in a way that anticipates the theories and practices of screen media.⁵³ The mirror is a form of old media, enacting (in Marshall McLuhan's terms) an extension of the self which constitutes, among other things, an archetype for the digital selfie.⁵⁴ The portrait, similarly, is an archaic visual-material medium which is both embedded within, and superseded by, the technological developments that have followed the invention of photography in the 1830s. The point here is that Polidori's representation of the vampire initiates an evolution of the underlying mythology which adapts itself in distinctive ways to the visual modes of mass-entertainment technologies. From Ruthven onwards, the vampire perplexes the eyes and complicates modes of seeing and being seen, whether the mirror image, the painted portrait, the staged performance or the screened (in both senses of the verb) presence. In a way, the attempt to represent the vampire, post-Polidori, has been an attempt to represent something which is constantly moving, changing, evading, unsettling visual expectations, whether through the invention of the 'vampire trap' for James Robinson Planché's *The Vampire; or, The Bride of the Isles* at the English Opera House in 1820, the adaptation of the theatrical 'ghost glide' for Orlok's phallic rise in *Nosferatu*, the adoption of late-nineteenth-century technologies for Coppola's cinematic version or the translation to episodic web drama for Smokebomb Entertainment's *Carmilla* (2014–16).⁵⁵ From this perspective, it seems both startling and oddly appropriate that Polidori's tale, with its elusive antagonist, has never been adapted for film or television. Ruthven, in other words, has never been seen on screen (except in some filmed excerpts from Planché's play, used in Christopher Frayling's 1996 documentary series *Nightmare: The Birth of Horror*). It is similarly appropriate, however, that when he appeared on the London stage only four months after his original appearance in print, one of the more enthusiastic reviewers in the audience was the radical essayist William Hazlitt, who was also an accomplished painter, specialising in portraits. Hazlitt, one of the finest art critics of the period, compared the presentation of the play to the work of the great Baroque artists, writing that it had 'all the harmony and mellowness of the finest painting'.[56] His conclusion, that the play was 'upon the whole, the most splendid *spectacle* we have ever seen', seems to comprehend, with uncanny percipience, the ocular essence of Polidori's tale and the vampiric attractions it would bring to our senses in the years to come.[57]

Notes

1. John William Polidori, *The Vampyre*, Appendix 1 in this volume, pp. 240–67 (p. 246). All further references to this edition in parentheses in the main text.
2. Michel Foucault, *Discipline and Punish: The Birth of the Prison*, trans. by Alan Sheridan (1977; New York: Vintage, 1995), pp. 201, 200.
3. Sigmund Freud, *The Uncanny*, trans. by David McLintock (1919; Harmondsworth: Penguin, 2003), p. 140.
4. Ernst Jentsch, 'On the Psychology of the Uncanny (1906)', *Angelaki: Journal of Theoretical Humanities*, 2:1 (1997), 7–17. Freud, *The Uncanny*, p. 139.
5. For a discussion of Freud's specific use of *Ersatzbeziehung*, 'the relationship of substitution' (p. 536), see Hélène Cixous, 'Fiction and Its Phantoms: A Reading of Freud's *Das Unheimliche* (The "Uncanny")', trans. by Robert Dennomé, *New Literary History*, 7:3 (spring 1976), 525–48.
6. E. T. A. Hoffmann, *Tales of Hoffmann*, ed. by R. J. Hollingdale (Harmondsworth: Penguin, 1982), p. 87.
7. Hoffmann, *Tales*, pp. 119–20.
8. Freud, *The Uncanny*, p. 153.
9. Freud, *The Uncanny*, p. 125.
10. Chelsea Schein and Kurt Gray, 'The Eyes are the Window to the Uncanny Soul: Mind Perception, Autism and Missing Souls', *Interaction Studies*, 16:2 (2015), 173.
11. Schein and Gray, 'The Eyes', pp. 174, 179. The mythic dimension of semiotics is, for Roland Barthes, that in which signs are separated from their ideological basis – depoliticised, in other words – through the creation of a culturally innocent narrative. See Roland Barthes, *Mythologies*, trans. by Annette Lavers (London: Vintage, 1993), pp. 142–58.
12. Schein and Gray, 'The Eyes', p. 173.
13. Schein and Gray, 'The Eyes', p. 173.
14. Schein and Gray, 'The Eyes', p. 174. For accessible histories of automata and related artificial 'life forms', see Gaby Wood, *Living Dolls: A Magical History of the Quest for Mechanical Life* (London: Faber & Faber, 2002) and the television documentary *Mechanical Marvels: Clockwork Dreams*, dir. by Nic Stacey, writ. by Simon Schaffer (BBC, 2014).

15 Hoffmann's work does not seem to have become widely known in English-speaking culture until the mid- to late 1820s, following the publication of a translation of his novel *The Devil's Elixir* (1824), and 'The Sandman' was only translated into English in the 1840s. This does not preclude Polidori from having read the story in the original German, of course, but it could not have featured in the storytelling at the Villa Diodati in the summer of 1816 because it was not actually published until 1817, when it appeared in the anthology *Die Nachtstücke*.
16 Edmund Burke, *A Philosophical Enquiry into the Origin of Our Ideas of the Sublime and Beautiful* (1757; Mineola, NY: Dover Publications, 2012), p. 161.
17 Edmund Burke, *Reflections on the Revolution in France*, ed. by Conor Cruise O'Brien (1790; Harmondsworth: Penguin, 1982), p. 269.
18 Richard A. Barney, 'Burke, Biomedicine, and Biobelligerence', *The Eighteenth Century*, Special Issue: Sensational Subjects, 54:2 (Summer 2013), 231.
19 Sam George, 'Vampire's Rebirth: From Monstrous Undead Creature to Sexy and Romantic Byronic Seducer in One Ghost Story', *The Conversation*, 29 March 2019 www.theconversation.com/vampires-rebirth-from-monstrous-undead-creature-to-sexy-and-romantic-byronic-seducer-in-one-ghost-story-114382 [accessed 6 July 2021].
20 David Glover, *Vampires, Mummies, and Liberals: Bram Stoker and the Politics of Popular Fiction* (Durham, NC: Duke University Press, 1996), p. 74. See also Sam George, '"He Make In the Mirror No Reflect": Undead Aesthetics and Mechanical Reproduction – *Dorian Gray*, *Dracula* and David Reed's "Vampire Painting"', in *Open Graves, Open Minds: Representations of Vampires and the Undead from the Enlightenment to the present day*, ed. by Sam George and Bill Hughes (Manchester: Manchester University Press, 2013), pp. 56–78.
21 Anne Stiles, Stanley Finger and John Bulevich, 'Somnambulism and Trance States in the Works of John William Polidori, Author of *The Vampyre*', *European Romantic Review*, 21:6 (December 2010), 800.
22 John William Polidori, *Ernestus Berchtold; or, The Modern Oedipus: A Tale*, in *'The Vampyre' and Other Writings*, ed. by Franklin Charles Bishop (Manchester: Carcanet/Fyfield Books, 2005), pp. 47–150 (p. 103). All further references to this edition are given in parentheses in the main text.
23 Mary Shelley, 'Introduction', *Frankenstein; or, The Modern Prometheus*, ed. by M. K. Joseph (1831; Oxford: Oxford University Press, 1998), p. 7.
24 Carolyn A. Day, 'Dying to Be Beautiful: Fragile Fashionistas and Consumptive Dress in England, 1780–1820', *Journal for Eighteenth-Century Studies*, 40:4 (2017), 603.
25 See, for instance, A. D. Macleod, 'Eyelid Closure at Death', *Indian Journal of Palliative Care*, 15:2 (July–December 2009) www.ncbi.nlm.nih.gov/pmc/articles/PMC2902109/ [accessed 23 June 2022].
26 T. S. Eliot, 'Portrait of a Lady', *Collected Poems 1909–1962* (London: Faber & Faber, 1989), p. 18.
27 William Shakespeare, *The Tragedy of Romeo and Juliet*, IV. 1. 104, 99–100.
28 John Milton, *Paradise Lost*, in *The Complete Poems*, ed. by Gordon Campbell (London and Melbourne: Dent, 1986), I. 63, pp. 160–61.

29 John William Polidori, 'Inaugural Medical Dissertation Concerning Certain Aspects of the Disease Called Oneirodynia' [1815], trans. by David E. Petrain, *European Romantic Review*, 21:6 (2010), 776.
30 Polidori, 'Dissertation', p. 785 n. 7, p. 776.
31 Polidori, 'Dissertation', pp. 781, 783.
32 John William Polidori, 'From *An Essay Upon the Source of Positive Pleasure*' [1818], in Bishop, *'The Vampyre'*, pp. 37–45 (p. 41).
33 Stiles, Finger and Bulevich, 'Somnambulism', p. 790.
34 Stiles, Finger and Bulevich, 'Somnambulism', p. 790.
35 Freud, *The Uncanny*, p. 153.
36 Schein and Gray, 'The Eyes', p. 174.
37 Schein and Gray, 'The Eyes', p. 179.
38 Catherine Spooner, '*Gothic Charm School*; or, How Vampires Learned to Sparkle', in George and Hughes, *Open Graves*, p. 147.
39 For accounts of the 'peasant' Plogojowitz (Petar Blagojević), the *hajduk* Paole and others, see Paul Barber, *Vampires, Burial, and Death: Folklore and Reality* (London and New Haven, CT: Yale University Press, 1988), pp. 3–9, 15–16, 161; Christopher Frayling, ed., *Vampyres: Lord Byron to Count Dracula* (London: Faber & Faber, 1991), pp. 19–37, 100–01; and Nick Groom, *The Vampire: A New History* (London and New Haven, CT: Yale University Press, 2018), pp. 33–39, 48–49. The primary sources are perhaps best approached via the routes recommended by both Barber and Frayling: Augustine Calmet, *The Phantom World: The History and Philosophy of Spirits, Apparitions, Etc., Etc.*, 2 vols, ed. by Henry Christmas (London, 1850); and Joseph Pitton de Tournefort, *A Voyage into the Levant* (1717; London, 1741).
40 Stiles, Finger and Bulevich, 'Somnambulism', p. 790.
41 See Gayatri Spivak, 'Translator's Introduction', in Jacques Derrida, *Of Grammatology* (1967; Baltimore, MD: Johns Hopkins University Press, 1976), p. xiv.
42 George, ' "He Make In the Mirror No Reflect" ', pp. 56–78.
43 James Malcolm Rymer, *Varney, the Vampire; or, The Feast of Blood* (1845–47; Ware: Wordsworth, 2010), pp. 5–8.
44 Rymer, *Varney, the Vampire*, p. 6.
45 Rymer, *Varney, the Vampire*, p. 7.
46 Rymer, *Varney, the Vampire*, pp. 16–17.
47 Joseph Le Fanu, 'Carmilla', in *In a Glass Darkly*, ed. by Robert Tracy, World's Classics (1872; Oxford and New York: Oxford University Press, 1993), pp. 243–319 (p. 272).
48 Le Fanu, 'Carmilla', p. 274.
49 Bram Stoker, *Bram Stoker's Notes for Dracula: A Facsimile Edition*, ed. by Robert Eighteen-Bisang and Elizabeth Miller (Jefferson, NC: McFarland, 2008), p. 3.
50 George, ' "He Make In the Mirror No Reflect" ', pp. 56–57.
51 Stoker, *Bram Stoker's Notes*, p. 4.
52 Glover, *Vampires*, p. 74.

53 Bram Stoker, *Dracula*, ed. by Nina Auerbach and David J. Skal (New York and London: W. W. Norton & Company, 1996), p. 211. See also George, '"He Make In the Mirror No Reflect"', pp. 56–59, 61–62, 66–73.
54 See Marshall McLuhan, *Understanding Media: The Extensions of Man* (1964; Berkeley, CA: Gingko Press, 2014), pp. 36, 92, 144.
55 For an account of the theatrical adaptation of Polidori's story, see Sam George's Chapter 2 in this volume.
56 William Hazlitt, *Criticisms and Dramatics Essays of the English Stage* (London: Routledge, 1854), p. 138.
57 Hazlitt, *Criticisms*, p. 137.

10

'Knowledge is a fatal thing'; or, from fatal whispers to vampire songs: Breaking Polidori's oath in The Vampire Chronicles and *Byzantium*

Sorcha Ní Fhlainn

There is something altogether exciting, if not outright spellbinding, about the whispers and murmurs of vampires. While subjectivity has become a streamlined feature in the vampire narrative since the late 1960s, in film, literature, and popular culture, the musings and haunting disclosures of the vampire's voice can be sourced back to the early nineteenth century, in John Polidori's 1819 novella *The Vampyre*.[1] Polidori's tale initiates two tantalising elements in vampire fiction which continue to inform its postmodern iterations today; the first concerns the introduction of a Gothic voice whose disclosures either seduce (at best) or plague (at worst) its audience. The second feature concerns the viral nature of vampiric disclosures – like an infection, vampire secrets inevitably spill out into the wider world, threatening to undo ancient codes that keep the existence of vampires wholly separate from the mortal realm; like any virus, this form of disclosure mutates in form across popular culture, and takes on new shapes, media, and audiences. Thus, vampire stories emerge in popular fiction as documented oral histories, or as fragmented narratives gleaned and repurposed from diary entries, confessions, and biographical accounts, only to later evolve into circulated art forms including video and musical recordings, lyrics, and stage performances. Of all Gothic creatures, the vampire seems to relish in personal disclosures the most, torn between the seductive power of possessing a subjectivity that transcends the limits of time, while also fearful of the terrible consequences their disclosures may trigger; vampire confessions rarely end well. Polidori's tale is the first of many that enable vampires to amplify their voices – for this is no mere mortal's mode of communication but rather the emergence of a heteroglossia weighted with the power of Gothic time – voices from the past that disrupt the present. This essay will examine the subjective vampire voice and its haunting Gothic qualities from Polidori's *The Vampyre* to contemporary film and vampire adaptations. It will examine the infecting nature of secrets and the emotional need for vampiric disclosures in Anne Rice's subjective vampire tales and Neil Jordan's cinematic postmodern vampires in *Interview with the Vampire* (1994) and *Byzantium* (2012), through to the musical evolution of the vampiric voice in the twenty-first century.

Secret oaths and draining friendships

The discovery of a terrible secret and the forbidden, if not downright blasphemous, nature of vampirism lurking in high society is perhaps one of Polidori's greatest contributions to vampire literature. Narratives of vampirism were traditionally relegated to the peasantry. With Lord Ruthven's arrival into high society, vampirism evolved from its folk origins to the rank of an urban and educated revenant of noble birth.[2] Polidori's tale, with its twisted convoluted prose, offers tantalising glimpses of Lord Ruthven as observed by the tale's narrator, Aubrey, marking this revenant out as a distinguished and distinctly captivating social climber. The description of Ruthven's 'dead grey eye' and the 'deadly hue of his face, which never gained a warmer tint' mark him out as a dangerous Gothic interloper.[3] Lord Ruthven's strangeness, 'peculiarities [which] caused him to be invited to every house', sets the tone for Aubrey's subsequent fascination and dire psychological torment. The tale's other overriding feature, as the progenitor of a range of wonderful vampire fiction over the next 200 years, is the corrosive nature of guilt and the promise to fulfil an oath – in this case, to keep a dastardly secret – which condemns Aubrey and his sister to a terrible fate. Aubrey knows, as do most bearers of secrets in vampire fiction that follow, that this knowledge dooms him from the moment he is oath-bound to keep Ruthven's death and disappearance a secret. Ruthven implores that Aubrey fulfils this dying wish on his honour: 'Swear by all your soul reveres, by all your nature fears, swear that for a year and a day you will not impart your knowledge of my crimes and my death to any living being in any way, whatever may happen, or whatever you may see.'[4] This oath, between travelling companions and friends, unsettles Aubrey, with 'the presentiment of something horrible awaiting him'.[5] Bewildered at the disappearance of Ruthven's body and his dying wish, Aubrey *hears* Ruthven's stern warning to 'Remember your oath' as an intimate whisper without a living or visible source; this repeated whisper eventually drives Aubrey to madness.

According to Nina Auerbach, '[t]he vampire fragment Byron began at Villa Diodati in 1816 and Polidori's 1819 tale, *The Vampyre*, are symbiotic', reflecting the fractious relationship between both authors.[6] In this respect, both Byron's and Polidori's tales directly reflected their own class positions and their noted clashing worldviews. Byron, Shelley, and Mary

Godwin, revelling in the Romantic perspective that fuelled their passions, were artists, while Polidori, as Byron's travelling physician, was relegated to the position of a paid employee; Polidori's skills were more medical than poetical. This schism is evident not only in the genesis of the adaptation of Byron's fragment that followed but also transparent in the description of both Byron's and Polidori's vampires: Byron's elderly vampire Darvell, infused with brilliance, has 'no existence independent of his travelling companion's awe', while Polidori's Aubrey, in contrast, is silenced in horror, wholly at odds with the curious practices to which he bears witness as the travelling companion to the strange Lord Ruthven.[7] The weird encounters in foreign lands that incept vampiric transformation in the stories – the nocturnal bite by a snake in the mouth of a stork in Byron's fragment, and Polidori's revenant who finds restoration in the moonlight – also emphasise from the offset the shifting and variable nature in the literary evolution of vampirism (and its debates on creation and transformation) to come for the next 200 years. Polidori's subsequent rewriting and expansion of Byron's original premise repositions both the vampire and his chronicler/travelling companion in light of the souring of their relationship while abroad. As Christopher Frayling observes, 'the unstable relationship between Aubrey and Ruthven during and after their Grand Tour (admiration, disillusionment, disgust) mirrors closely what Polidori felt about Lord Byron in the summer of 1816'.[8] Byron too felt a growing frustration with Polidori's 'tracasseries […] emptiness […] ill-humour and vanity'.[9] Ruthven, then, as Polidori's vampiric projection of Byron's self-aggrandisement, fame, and seductive charm, holds his sway over Aubrey until the end of the tale – for Polidori, both Byron's and 'Ruthven's dreadful power springs from his oath of friendship'.[10] It is the lingering promise to keep Ruthven's oath of secrecy that haunts Aubrey's psyche to the brink of madness, a kind utterance between friends recast as a curse brimming with malice. While Auerbach argues that vampires sought out friendship but made for 'draining friends' in nineteenth-century fiction, this observation equally holds merit in twentieth-century considerations also.[11]

Tours of Europe, under Gothic moonlight and in search of acceptance, underpin late-twentieth-century vampire narratives too. Anne Rice's Vampire Chronicles series is a prime example wherein immortals look back to European folklore and traditions to revive themselves when friendships and family formations have failed, and abandonment seems inevitable.[12] In the same vein as Lord Ruthven and Darvell, Rice's vampires are seasoned travellers; Europe may be the ferocious continent of vampiric genesis for Rice's elder vampires, but it is also a space to revive and rediscover their cultural history and social purpose. As Auerbach and Macdonald observe, Polidori and Byron both introduce the trope of the meandering vampire whose ability to travel is 'both psychic and geographical'.[13] Earlier folkloric vampires were bound by place, like ghosts and other haunting spectres, but in Polidori's tale, Ruthven is wholly unbound by place. Stoker's Count Dracula furthers this ability to travel, desiring to infiltrate whole nations, but is burdened by the native soil he must carry in tow.[14] While Stoker's Count is unperturbed by guilt for his actions and grand ambitions, he is bound by the necessity of his restorative native earth. His solution, to buy both time and silence, is to imprison Jonathan Harker in his remote castle. An oath of honour cannot guarantee success in Stoker's tale. Rice's postmodern vampires are not bound by Dracula's laws of restoration nor the Catholic instruments that exert power over the undead, but they are profoundly haunted by the guilt of their immortal existence and produce numerous (and mostly entertaining) maundering immortal confessions. Other late-twentieth-century vampires who wander, including Chelsea Quinn Yarbro's Saint Germain, continuously seek friendship and share their tales, occasionally taking comfort with human lovers to quell their isolating sense of pain by seeking out limited moments of contentment.[15] It is only through the catharsis of subjective confession – to spill the sacred secret and break the oath of silence – that the burden of their secret histories and oaths can be truly lifted. Travel has never granted the vampire, nor his victims, a complete sense of control or closure.

The influential legacy of Polidori's tale has been somewhat undermined in popular culture, which often locates Stoker's 1897 novel *Dracula* as the fount of twentieth-century and contemporary vampiric fascination. While *Dracula*'s influence cannot be overestimated, Stoker's narrative does not facilitate the Count's subjective position in the novel; this absence, in an epistolary novel that swims with accounts from multiple points of view, limits our proximity to the Count accordingly. While Aubrey also accounts for Lord Ruthven's terrifying whisper, 'Remember your oath!', the proximity of this vampire to our troubled narrator is psychologically more claustrophobic, more insular, and distinctly more personal than Dracula's infiltration into English society in 1897.[16] Ruthven also commands the interests of high society from the offset, a vampire who, therefore, through reputation and class, cannot be banished or killed by his former friend. Less fatal forms of proximity, and our subjective reorientation with the undead, would come later in more postmodern and metatextual stories. Fred Saberhagen rewrote Stoker's *Dracula* from Dracula's subjective position in *The Dracula Tape* (1975), situating this reflective version of the tale from the Count's point of view. As a sympathetic immortal in Saberhagen's account, Dracula's brush with British society has erroneously stained his legacy in literary history as monstrous; recording his corrective disclosures on audiotape, this Dracula simultaneously becomes both postmodern subject and chronicler. It would be Anne Rice's 1976 novel *Interview with the Vampire* which would furnish a more popular subjective history of the vampire's life from the vampire's point of view. Discarding established vampire characters in favour of a new legion of the undead, Rice introduced a whole new world of immortal charismatic predators, who care little for, nor barely interact with, the human world beyond necessity. Rice's interview subject, Louis de Pointe du Lac, reveals his secret undead existence to a nameless human ('the boy', later named Daniel Malloy in the series), who records the unfolding tale on audio tape.[17] The impact of Rice's novel would give rise to a host of competing subjective vampire narratives in literature and film in its wake, inspiring a significant trend that distinctly privileges vampire subjectivity, and makes strange and seductive the lingering whispers of the undead.

Neil Jordan's postmodern vampires: 'I would like to tell you the story of my life'

Vampire cinema has been particularly keen to foreground undead disclosures and secret testimonies since the publication of Rice's novel. Neil Jordan's 1994 cinematic adaptation of Rice's novel examines the burden of *vampiric* disclosures and significantly chimes with Polidori's literary legacy of a dastardly secret that corrodes the soul.[18] However, guilt does not burden Rice's human interviewer, Malloy (Christian Slater), but rather plagues the confessing vampire, Louis (Brad Pitt), whose story takes on the tone of a Catholic confession – equal parts biography and vampire historiography – to atone for his blasphemous existence. Louis is compelled to reveal what earlier vampires such as Ruthven are keen to keep secret. Jordan's own passion as a director lies in exploring suppressed stories and feelings of guilt in his cinematic craft; according to Carole Zucker, Jordan's thematic registers notably include:

> A fascination with storytelling and how stories are told by various modes of performance; the quest for identity and wholeness; meditations on innocence; permutations of the family unit; violence and its attendant psychic and physical damage; impossible love and erotic tension; the dark and irrational aspects of the human soul; and characters who are, in some way, haunted by loss.[19]

These themes find significant purchase in both of his vampire film adaptations. Jordan's postmodern vampire tales feature gloomy and often beautiful aesthetics associated with the magic of liminal spaces, with a particular recurring motif of water. Water signals the transformation and rebirth of Jordan's vampires onscreen, whether they are bitten and discarded at the waterfront (as seen in the opening encounter between Louis and Lestat in

Interview with the Vampire) or bathed in supernatural blood-red springs to signal their rebirth in *Byzantium*. The recurring motif of waterfront spaces, captured via shots of bridges, piers and promenades, ships, and distant magical islands, signifies Jordan's vampires as transcendent liminal beings – they are islands in the streams of time. As we shall see, both films work in tandem to address anxieties about the disclosure of vampire secrets and draw their inspiration from Polidori's playful horror on the consuming nature of vampire secrets, and the vampiric compulsion to tell secret stories.

The wasteland of a remembered and traumatic past rules over both *Interview with the Vampire* and *Byzantium*. Both films ruminate on the horrid nature of immortality under the rule of brutal, insular, and masculine forms of power. Jordan's films actively deploy postmodern techniques including bricolage and metatextuality to critique the canon of vampire literature, often by citing past masters by name to announce their difference: *Interview with the Vampire* jokingly dismisses *Dracula* as 'the vulgar fictions of a demented Irishman' (and thus overwrites Stoker's overwhelming cultural legacy), while *Byzantium* is equally indebted to Polidori's tale and Byron's fragment by co-locating both Lord Ruthven and Darvell in the same narrative universe.[20] These citations function as modes of playful legitimation, signalling fluency in vampirism's complex literary and cinematic evolution. Jordan is also determined to bring his interest in Irish folklore and myths from the Irish oral tradition into both tales. As a filmmaker, he is keen to include explicit reminders of his fascination with Irish folklore and literary history, including stories of the *neamh-mhairbh* (undead in Gaelic) in *Byzantium*, while Louis's barb about *Dracula*, witty as it is, is included to openly declare Stoker and his Gothic masterpiece as Irish in no uncertain terms.

Jordan's film adaptation of *Interview with the Vampire* sets out the parameters of late-twentieth-century vampirism in the American imagination. To briefly recapitulate the tale: Jordan's film opens with Louis inviting his interviewer to record the story of his life. Louis' tale, which spans centuries, is marred by the guilt of taking life and his thirst for human blood. Transformed by Lestat (Tom Cruise), Louis's guilt defines his undead misery, while Lestat encourages him to embrace his newfound powers. Louis supplements his emotional torment and ethical 'diet of rats' to forgo human blood with the creation of a vampire child, Claudia (Kirsten Dunst), to love and raise. Kept in a doll-like stasis for over a century, Claudia turns monstrous under Louis and Lestat's charge, driven mad by the unchanging nature of her vampire body, her adult mind in distinct dissonance with her outward appearance. The eventual dissolution of this faux-nuclear family culminates in the murder of Lestat by Claudia. Both Louis and Claudia flee to Europe to discover answers to their questions about the meaning of immortality but find no solace. Encountering an ancient and barbaric coven, the Théâtre des Vampires, in Paris, Claudia is condemned to death for her killing of Lestat, while Louis, utterly disillusioned with his European brethren's ferocity, metes out retribution for Claudia's murder and eventually returns to America. He eventually chances upon Lestat, whose existence has not kept pace with the modern world, and embraces the opportunity to tell his story to the interviewer. Malloy is seduced by Louis's tale and demands that he experience vampirism for himself. Louis declares the interview a failure, as it has not provided any true sense of enlightenment or catharsis for him. In Jordan's film, diverging here from Rice's novel, Lestat returns to attack Malloy on the Golden Gate Bridge, and Lestat offers Malloy 'the choice [he] never had' to fully embrace vampirism and its mysteries.

Interview with the Vampire was noted for its deeply problematic journey to the screen. Jordan openly acknowledged that he rewrote a version of Rice's script (a script that had already been revised numerous times during its seventeen years in 'development hell') and reshaped the screenplay without a screen credit before commencing production. Rice had sold the rights before the book's publication in 1976 and had rewritten the script on several occasions, including, at one point, transforming Louis, its central narrator, into a woman to 'straighten' its queer focus. By 1993, Jordan's timely ascension in Hollywood circles and the concurrent, positive cultural shift for queer/ed and LGBT+ representations in commercial cinema revived Rice's 'problematic' script for development. Rice's script had found a director and a producer committed to her *original* vision of telling a homoerotically charged vampire tale without fear of commercial marginalisation. This shift in foregrounding marginal voices occurred in Hollywood circles at precisely the right time during the Hollywood Gothic renaissance (1990–96), a period in which several Gothic texts were greenlit for cinematic adaptation for mature audiences.[21] In Jordan, producer David Geffen had also found the right auteur for Rice's script. Jordan had successfully stormed Hollywood with his LGBT+ political thriller *The Crying Game* (1992), in a film that counterbalances potentially controversial subject matter with human warmth and catharsis; this feat secured him an Academy Award for Best Original Screenplay for *The Crying Game* in March 1993. In Jordan's hands, *Interview with the Vampire* still dealt with its various controversies – most notably its celebrated queer tone and casting process – but his deft direction and careful edge-walking enabled him to keep his vision of Rice's script intact.[22] Above all else, *Interview with the Vampire* celebrates vampire subjectivity, the power of storytelling, and the seductive, dangerous, and utterly enticing perspective of an immortal. It is a gateway for the audience, by taking the place of Polidori's Aubrey, to gain forbidden insight and to hear marginalised and fantastical voices. Echoing Polidori's creative process, Jordan's wider filmography points to his superb talents for telling familiar stories anew. One need only look to one of his earliest films, *The Company of Wolves* (1984), to see his playfulness in dialogue with the writings of Angela Carter and postmodern fairy tales. Jordan prefers to rework scripts based on fragments, echoes, drafts, ideas, and images conjured up from short stories or other forms of adaptation for the screen. Yet, in both of his vampire films, his visual style and script polishing neither eclipse nor overwrite the foundational work of his female scriptwriters; both Anne Rice and Moira Buffini retain their authorial command and sole screenwriting credits for their respective adaptations. Jordan's films tend to privilege themes concerning hidden or suppressed narrative voices that now demand to be heard. This dialogism also extends across his cinema, as *Byzantium* is positioned as an informal female companion piece to *Interview with the Vampire*; *Byzantium* inverts the narrative's emphasis on the male-centred obsession with vampirism and power in favour of female survival and emancipation from patriarchal power.[23]

'Those with knowledge have to die': *Byzantium*

Much like *Interview with the Vampire*, *Byzantium* opens with a confession by a vampire. Sixteen-year-old Eleanor (Saoirse Ronan) confides that her 'story can never be told. I write it over and over […] I write of what I cannot speak: the truth. I write all I know of it, and then I throw the pages to the wind.' Her cast-off notes intrigue an old man, Fowlds (Barry Cassin), who recognises Eleanor as a member of the *neamh-mhairbh* (undead), and soon begs her to relieve his suffering by taking his life. Eleanor takes life by consent, acting as an angel of death. Fowlds urges her to tell her story, warning her that 'there comes a time in life when secrets should be told'. Eleanor's desire to tell cannot be indulged – for Eleanor and Clara (Gemma Arterton) to divulge their existence as vampires would be fatal to them both. Both mother and daughter are being pursued by a mysterious all-male vampire Brotherhood who intend to mete out punishment for their crime of becoming vampires. Clara's transgression into the male dominion of immortality results in her banishment, but in transforming Eleanor also, to spare her life, both are marked for death, as 'women are not permitted to create'. Moving to an unnamed English coastal town to evade detection, Clara is determined to scrub the past from her memory as though it were a stain, while Eleanor's very survival is tied to her ability to remember and document the past.[24] She laments: 'I walk and the past walks with me.' Her memories are both a blessing and a burden, through which she feeds her compulsion to tell her story over and over. She is a confessing vampire that has yet to experience catharsis, caught in the repetitive cycle of telling her story to an audience who cannot survive its telling. The pair take refuge in the hotel Byzantium, hiding out from their pursuers. Eleanor's memories of her human life, and the circumstances of her turn to vampirism 200 years prior, haunt her daily walks in the town. She returns to memories of life in an orphanage in the town before her metamorphosis, the space now transformed into a local college in the twenty-first century. At the college, she befriends a sickly young man, Frank (Caleb Landry Jones), who is suffering from leukaemia, and soon divulges her origin story to him.[25]

Eleanor's account of 'the story that cannot be told' begins with the horror of Clara's life during the Napoleonic Wars, and the sexual exploitation she endured at the hands of a cruel Captain Ruthven (Jonny Lee Miller). This cinematic descendant of Polidori's vampire is twinned with the more noble midshipman Darvell (Sam Riley), another naval officer who Ruthven claimed was fatally wounded while crushing a rebellion in Ireland.[26] While in Ireland, Darvell learns the secrets of vampirism from a mysterious group of 'scholars of dead languages and ancient manuscripts', housed in Trinity College's Long Room Library. Surrounded by scholarly tomes, the library space is the written and privileged domain of male knowledge.[27] Darvell and Ruthven travel to an island as directed by the Brotherhood, but Ruthven is too frightened by the mystical island's powers. He abandons Darvell's lifeless body, who has perished in a monastic cave following his transformation, and returns to England to take his worldly possessions. Upon Darvell's return to England, to gift a map to the island to a dying and disbelieving Ruthven, he confirms to Ruthven that he has supernaturally survived the grave. In an act of emancipation, Clara steals the map and travels to the mysterious island and is reborn as a vampire. By stealing the power of immortality for herself, Clara gains privileged and distinctly patriarchal knowledge, and vows to use her immortal gift to 'curb the power of men'. Eleanor's account spills outwards into the human world as Frank shares her written account, and soon her teachers at the college investigate her circumstances. Brotherhood members Darvell and Savella (Uri Gavriel) pose as police to entrap Eleanor and Clara to finally destroy them both. In the end, Darvell chooses to spare both women from the Brotherhood's vengeance and kills Savella. Clara sets Eleanor free, realising she needs to live her immortal life beyond her mother's bonds. Eleanor ceases to tell this story, allowing another one, with Frank as an immortal, to begin.[28]

The patriarchal policing of vampirism, in the form of classism and misogyny, underpins both vampire tales quite explicitly. As Gina Wisker observes, Jordan's *Byzantium* hinges upon the 'immense inequality' between men and women, as women are decreed to have no direct access to the patriarchal power vampirism affords, particularly in the creation of vampire children.[29]

Both of Jordan's cinematic vampire children – Claudia and Eleanor – are described by vampire elders as 'aberrations' or forbidden mistakes, deviants in the patriarchal line of vampiric knowledge and kinship. Under the fierce regulation of the Brotherhood, knowledge of vampirism and its miracles is transformed into 'a fatal thing', for 'those with knowledge have to die' according to the Brotherhood's code of honour. Eleanor comes to know most of the process of her transformation but only retains incomplete memories of it. Tied to the neomyths of Irish folklore, James Aubrey notes that 'the vampires of *Byzantium* not only originate in Ireland, they are associated iconographically with the immortals of Celtic mythology', which include many fierce female warriors and queens.[30] The ancient *clochán* (beehive huts) on Skellig Michael are visually combined with the scenic waterfalls of the Beara Peninsula to create this distinctly supernatural island, a place that conceals a nonrational magical process that cannot be regulated or tamed. Once transformed into a revenant by encountering one's immortal double in a 'quasi-sacred ritual' inside the *clochán*, 'birds noisily fly overhead' and the island's waterfalls run red to signify this new 'baptism' in blood.[31] These elements deliberately underscore the ancient mysteries and beauty of natural places beyond the worlds of class and patriarchy. The island stands in sharp contrast with the unnatural exploitation of women evident on the streets of the English seaside town, replete with the grime of faded grandeur, drug addiction, and prostitution. To regulate and enslave women, the film reminds us, is an unnatural and distinctly ugly pathological practice under patriarchy. As an untameable supernatural space, knowledge of the island's gifts and its location remains the only form of patriarchal policing available to the Brotherhood. At the heart of these vampiric transformations lies a sacred bond with nature that quickens the undead: both Byron and Polidori's revenants are transformed through snakes and moonlight respectively (though the process itself remains mysterious), while in numerous vampire narratives that follow, including *Dracula* and *Interview with the Vampire*, it is the repeated draining and tasting of 'tainted' blood that anoints vampiric rebirth. Claudia is also initially denied knowledge of how vampirism is conferred. When she probes Lestat further on the transformation process, he demeans her: 'why should I tell you? It is within *my* power', reaffirming his alpha status over her. Foregoing fangs for a subtle extending thumbnail to pierce the flesh, *Byzantium*'s vampires return to another small yet significant visual echo from *Interview with the Vampire* – that of a protruding spiked thumbnail – as a predatory means to pierce the flesh when needed. Jordan trades Lestat's decorative spiked silver thimble with a more organic but equally lethal variation in *Byzantium*. Lestat's spiked thimble is a valuable phallic extension of his physical capabilities, worn as a decorative marker of acquired (or potentially stolen) wealth to drain and rob a rich fop, while Clara and Eleanor's organic nails signal their innate ability to kill, awakened by their struggle for survival. Moreover, the mystical island is itself described by Captain Ruthven as a 'sinister black thumbnail sticking out of the ocean', an untameable protrusion that is an extension of nature's mysteries.

'Must we hide from everyone?': Vampire stardom in the twenty-first century

Both of Jordan's films hinge on the possibility that lingers in Polidori's tale – what if Aubrey had broken his oath of secrecy? Polidori's Aubrey does not truly contest the limits of his oath, through either oral or written accounts, and his promise of silence consumes his every thought. This silence directly leads to the death of Ianthe – a girl who relays the oral history of vampirism to Aubrey in Greece, and for whom he felt much affection – but also his beloved sister, both of whom glut the terrible thirst of Lord Ruthven. In dialogue with this maddening form of silenced suffering, Jordan delights in enabling 'the damned' (vampires under the yoke of their small, suffocating societies) to announce their existence and cast off their guilt, a feat which Aubrey failed to accomplish under the constraints of his honour. Jordan's fascination with the telling of vampire secrets emanates from much of postmodern vampire fiction since the 1970s, hinging on the vampire's need to unburden their secrets to a (typically) human reader. Louis unburdens himself to his interviewer, Malloy, whose occupation as a documenter, a vampiric 'collector of lives', also hinges on disclosures to relay and retell the tale through the playback and eventual publication of these tape recordings. The story must live on in the retelling. Eleanor also discards her handwritten stories and confessions of her and Clara's origins, casting the pages away to the wind (and mirroring the actions of Mina Murray in Frances Ford Coppola's 1992 film *Bram Stoker's Dracula*, no less) to spread the wonders of the confessional word outward.[32] Vampires proliferate through the dissemination of their secrets.

Postmodern vampires of the late twentieth and early twenty-first centuries are an altogether different breed from Polidori's Lord Ruthven – they may be seductive and charming, refined by age and experience, and seek acceptance and friends, but they are often lonely and isolated. They evolve into highly communicative Gothic beings and are dismissive of the ancient codes of honour that silenced their predecessors. Rice's undead brood, in particular, delight in the destruction of silence; their existence comes alive with the chatter of voices. Lestat also embraces the confessional mode; his disavowal of *Interview with the Vampire* in the opening pages of *The Vampire Lestat*

(1985) situates him as both its metatextual central narrator and as a contemporary conduit for vampirism in global popular entertainment. Lestat closes the twentieth century by becoming an MTV icon, spilling the tales of the undead through song, and resurrecting Queen Akasha in retribution in Rice's *Queen of the Damned* (1988). Attempting to extend Jordan's success in adapting Rice's novel for the screen, *Queen of the Damned* also underwent a screen adaptation in 2002. The film charts Lestat's rise to global fame as a vampire and his dissemination of vampire secrets through rock songs. Despite the film's critical and commercial failure, its most interesting feature concerns Lestat's own voice: actor Stuart Townsend's vocal performance onstage and in song was re-recorded and 'ghost voiced' by Korn's lead singer Jonathan Davis to achieve a more suitable and distinctive sound and style for Rice's vampire rock star. The mixture of Gothic Rock iconography with Davis's signature nu-metal sound and deliciously dark, morose lyrics was perhaps the most successful turn for contemporary vampires as singing rock stars on screen.[33] The success of the *Queen of the Damned* soundtrack is a testament to its musical excellence as Gothic/nu-metal fusion, as distinct from the film adaptation that failed to register in critical or commercial circles, or remain coherent within the diegesis of Rice's Vampire Chronicles. Lestat delights in the playful ruse of 'performing' as a vampire on MTV while humans believe it to be a clever persona-turned-marketing ruse. He is the modern Byronic 'vampire stranger', much in the style of Polidori's Lord Ruthven – a star whose fame commands allegiance and captivates twenty-first-century audiences.

Undead culture has produced a cacophonous chorus of vampire voices in film, fiction, and onstage. Voices plague Lestat's mind in the subsequent novels of Rice's Vampire Chronicles from the offset; through the spread of voices on radio, television, and through the dissemination of popular music, each Ricean adventure privileges a subjective undead voice and seeks out new forms of communication. Lestat's undead life is soundtracked with the voices of the living, sounds that quicken him from his weary existence in the modern world. In response, his musical lyrics and songs reveal vampire histories and call out to the ancients in angst, only to be further disseminated as recordings and rock anthems. However, these sung siren calls have not always been successful, either onscreen or on the Broadway stage. Two early twenty-first-century musical productions evidence the vampire's awkward transition to the musical stage: both *Dance of the Vampires*[34] and *Lestat* are particularly infamous for their calamitous musical theatre adaptations.[35] Both productions were critically eviscerated, proving that vampire musicals are often particularly troubled and short-lived endeavours. Perhaps it is the loss of intimacy in these stage-set vampire disclosures, here too safe and too public in this format, which renders their musical secret songs unremarkable; on Broadway, these vampires are drained of Gothic's sublime powers in favour of accessible and campy, staged entertainments. These vampire afterlives in popular culture speak to the need of the undead to tell stories and to perform for our unending fascination in myriad, and occasionally unsuccessful, ways.

Contemporary vampire narratives are indebted to Polidori's short tale. *The Vampyre* provides us with two forms of personal vampiric disclosure simultaneously – the uttered oath and the written account of the vampiric secret. Rice's *Interview with the Vampire* is informed by secrets caught on tape, utterances that are so incredulous they can scarcely be believed. In *Byzantium*, while folklore and popular culture give Eleanor and her ilk a cultural register, they enable Clara to learn about vampirism from Captain Ruthven's oral account, while Eleanor feels she must document, author, and destroy her tale over and over, to legitimate the telling of the tale until it is read by another. While Rice's confessing vampires in her ever-expanding series may seem to provide confessions on paper (printed as The Vampire Chronicles, wherein Lestat metatextually addresses the reader directly), they nevertheless give voice to orally transmitted secrets via recorded disclosures: Louis's confession is captured as an audio recording, and Lestat's music (in *Queen of the Damned*) is also recorded and performed for global dissemination. Polidori's Aubrey uses both forms of disclosure – the whispered secret oath he has vowed to keep, alongside the oral traditions as told by Ianthe, and eventually writes the tale in order to warn his sister on the final day of the oath's duration. Of course, by then, the secret is worthless: Ruthven has escaped, and the disclosure has come too late. Vampire secrets, undead authorship, and immortal confessions endure in the long cultural shadow cast by *The Vampyre*, only to spread out, to be rewritten, reclaimed, and reimagined anew, across two centuries. These beautiful vulgar fictions linger on, to be shared, whispered, and (occasionally) sung, delighting in the violation of Polidori's oath of silence.

Notes

1 John Polidori, *The Vampyre*, Appendix 1 in this volume, pp. 240–67.
2 Robert Morrison and Chris Baldick, 'Introduction', *The Vampyre and Other Tales of the Macabre*, ed. by Robert Morrison and Chris Baldick (Oxford: Oxford World Classics, 1997), p. xii.
3 Polidori, *The Vampyre*, p. 246.
4 Polidori, *The Vampyre*, p. 255.
5 Polidori, *The Vampyre*, p. 255.
6 Nina Auerbach, *Our Vampires, Ourselves* (Chicago, IL: University of Chicago Press, 1995), p. 15.
7 Auerbach, *Our Vampires, Ourselves*, p. 15.

8 Christopher Frayling, ed., *Vampyres: From Lord Byron to Count Dracula* (London: Faber & Faber, 1991), p. 8.
9 Frayling, *Vampyres*, p. 12.
10 Auerbach, *Our Vampires, Ourselves*, p. 16.
11 Auerbach, *Our Vampires, Ourselves*, p. 18.
12 Looking back to the European and North African past of vampirism underpins much of Rice's Vampire Chronicles (1976–2021). The vampire historiographies feature several instalments in the series wherein characters ruminate on the *ancien régimes* of Egypt, Rome, and Constantinople, and the circumstances that led to their vampiric transformations.
13 Auerbach, *Our Vampires, Ourselves*, p. 194 n. 8, quoting D. L. Macdonald, *Poor Polidori: A Critical Biography of the Author of 'The Vampyre'* (Toronto, ON: University of Toronto Press, 1991), pp. 192–96; Auerbach, *Our Vampires*, p. 194 n. 7.
14 Auerbach, *Our Vampires, Ourselves*, p. 194 n. 7.
15 See Chelsea Quinn Yarbro, *Hôtel Transylvania* (New York: Tor, 1978). Yarbro's Saint Germain series offers glittering transhistorical subjective adventures, with her mesmerising gemologist Saint Germain as the series' heroic vampire.
16 Polidori, *The Vampyre*, p. 257.
17 Malloy is named and later turned into a vampire by the coven elder Armand in Rice's third vampire chronicle, *The Queen of the Damned* (New York: Ballantine, 1988), pp. 83–136.
18 Anne Rice, *Interview With The Vampire* (1976; London: Sphere, 2008), p. 7.
19 Carole Zucker, *The Cinema of Neil Jordan: Dark Carnival* (New York: Wallflower, 2008), p. 1.
20 Buffini's play is evidently indebted to the literary fruits of the Villa Diodati ghost story competition in 1816, as Polidori's Ruthven and Byron's Darvell are all present, alongside Franklin Stein (Eleanor's male companion, who takes his name from Shelley's *Frankenstein* [1818]).
21 Sorcha Ní Fhlainn, *Postmodern Vampires: Film, Fiction, and Popular Culture* (London: Palgrave, 2019), pp. 134–38.
22 Sorcha Ní Fhlainn, 'Cruising the Vampire: Hollywood Gothic, Star Branding, and *Interview with the Vampire*', in *Starring Tom Cruise*, ed. by Sean Redmond (Detroit, MI: Wayne State University Press, 2021), pp. 133–51 (pp. 145–50).
23 In an interview with Roger and James Deakins on the Team Deakins podcast, Jordan remarked that Moira Buffini's play was not wholly in thrall to vampirism, and was distinctly more ambivalent about its connection to vampire literature and lore. Revising the script with Jordan for *Byzantium* enabled Buffini to embrace more overt and direct vampire themes and visual cues, as her play, while steeped in literary nods to vampires, does not embrace vampirism as its narrative framework at its conclusion ('Interview with Neil Jordan', Team Deakins, podcast, 22 August 2021 https://teamdeakins.libsyn.com/neil-jordan-director [accessed 23 August 2021].
24 The coastal town featured in the film is Hastings.
25 Frank describes his illness as a 'drain' on his family's limited resources, hence their need to move to the UK. It is interesting to note that these 'draining'

qualities unite them as friends. While they both perceive themselves as hindrances to their parents, they each find and fulfil what the other lacks (blood, time) as a couple.

26 The date and specificity of which Irish rebellion is unclear in the film, as Eleanor is born in 1804, and Clara learns of the map, and Darvell's secret vampirism, after giving her daughter up for adoption. Darvell has not been seen by Ruthven for years, and thus the rebellion in question is either a reference to the rebellion of 1798 by the United Irishmen, or their renewed struggle in the Rising of 1803 in Dublin and Kildare (on 23 July 1803), the consequences of which resulted in the execution of twenty-three rebels, including Robert Emmet. For the connections between Irish rebellion and Lord Ruthven in *Glenarvon*, see Bill Hughes's Chapter 5 in this volume.

27 In a later scene, Clara is brought to Long Room Library to learn of her fate at the hands of the Brotherhood following her transformation into a vampire. Her clothes, buxom features, and sharp, 'crass' manner announce her incongruity in the space while the Brotherhood adjudicate her fate. They are ruled by reason while she is ruled by emotion and her desire for female emancipation and revenge.

28 Another interesting feature that connects Polidori's tale with both *Interview with the Vampire* and *Byzantium* concerns birthday gifts and anniversaries. While Aubrey must contain his secret about Lord Ruthven's vampirism for a year and a day, both *Interview with the Vampire* and *Byzantium* share pivotal and explosive consequences around birthday gifts. Claudia is given a doll by Lestat to mark her birthday (the day she was turned), a gesture that she feels mocks her inability to age. Her rage culminates in her planning to dispatch Lestat permanently. In *Byzantium*, Eleanor gives Frank the map as a birthday gift to take him to the island to be turned into a vampire. Eleanor's plan to leave with him climaxes in a confrontation with the Brotherhood. Both birthday gifts mark a celebration of creation with violent consequences.

29 Gina Wisker, *Contemporary Women's Gothic Fiction: Carnival, Hauntings and Vampire Kisses* (London: Palgrave, 2016), p. 202.

30 James Aubrey, 'Celtic Vampires: Neil Jordan's Film *Byzantium* as Irish Neomyth', *Journal of Literature and Art Studies*, 7:7 (July 2017), 909–15 (p. 912).

31 Aubrey, 'Celtic Vampires', p. 909.

32 *Bram Stoker's Dracula*, dir. by Francis Ford Coppola (Zoetrope, 1992).

33 Jonathan Davis of Korn performed Lestat's songs in the film *Queen of the Damned* and co-produced a superb soundtrack album which featured numerous nu-metal stars singing 'Lestat's' vampire songs, including Marilyn Manson, David Draiman, and Chester Bennington.

34 *Dance of the Vampires* had a strong stage history prior to its Broadway run. In 1997, it was adapted by Michael Kunze into a successful rock opera based on Roman Polanski's 1967 film entitled *Tanz der Vampire*. The show, according to Helen Shaw, successfully played in thirteen countries to an audience of 9.6 million people during its multiple international runs. The Broadway production

was hampered by numerous issues, including cast tensions, illogical rewrites, and staging setbacks. It had a very limited residency (December 2002–January 2003) and eventually closed due to poor reviews and sales. For more on this, see Helen Shaw, ' "Within Fifteen Minutes, It Became Unbearable": The Bloody Broadway Mess That Was Dance of the Vampires', *Vulture*, 14 August 2020 www.vulture.com/article/broadway-dance-of-the-vampires-bloody-disaster.html [accessed 13 August 2021].

35 *Lestat*, the musical, with music and lyrics by Elton John and Bernie Taupin, was directed by Robert Jess Roth at The Palace Theatre, New York. It had a very brief performance run in San Francisco (December 2005–January 2006) and on Broadway (March–May 2006), and underwent significant revisions during its short staging. It was met with critical derision in theatrical reviews and closed following thirty-three previews and thirty-nine performances. Bootleg recordings of the show still circulate online today as the official cast recording is unlikely to be released.

11

'The deadly hue of his face': The genesis of the vampiric gentleman and his deadly beauty; or, how Lord Ruthven became Edward Cullen

Kaja Franck

The pleasure elicited by the beautiful, undead object of the vampire can be observed with one of the earliest literary vampires, Lord Ruthven from John Polidori's *The Vampyre* (1816). This chapter will show how the depiction of Polidori's Ruthven informs Edward Cullen's vampirism in Stephenie Meyer's Twilight series (2005–08) by analysing the relationship between the vampire and the human, and the importance of the vampire's skin as a denominator of otherness. The term 'vampiric gaze' will be used to express the power of the gaze in these texts, and its potential to objectify and consume the individual upon whom it is turned. It can be wielded by human or vampire; at its most destructive, those who wield it deny the subjectivity of those upon whom they gaze. By acknowledging the changing status of the vampire – from a monster to be feared to an antihero to be loved (or at least actively desired), the vampiric gaze will be shown to offer pleasure as well as destruction.

In Season One of Joss Whedon's TV series *Angel*, the titular character, a vampire, steps into the sun for the first time in centuries thanks to the protective power of a magical ring. His appearance is remarked upon by the character Oz: 'You're incredibly pale […] He's very pale. Paler than most people.'[1] His remarks highlight Angel's 'otherness' as a vampire, particularly in regard to the pallor of his skin which marks him as both corpse-like and unable to withstand the sunlight. The camera rests on Angel's face, who is seemingly unaware that he is being watched, inviting the viewer to stare at his paleness. Angel is framed as a beautiful, undead object voyeuristically enjoyed by humans, both characters and audience. This depiction of vampire-as-beautiful-object finds its apotheosis in Meyer's Twilight series, in which vampires are portrayed as 'exotic, marvellous, eminently consumable – a rare and precious object'.[2] Meyer's vampires appear invulnerable, with flawless skin and excessive beauty, suggestive of celebrity culture rather than folkloric monsters. When Anne Rice writes her vampire series The Vampire Chronicles (1976–2018), her vampires have been transformed so that they are 'more than ever noticeable, astonishing, unlike a human being'; her most famous creation, Lestat, is shocked to discover on being turned that his 'chest was like a marble torso in a museum'.[3] Meyer's vampires take this a step further: in the sunlight, each is 'a perfect statue, carved in some unknown stone, smooth like marble, glittering like crystal'.[4] They are *objets d'art* to be gazed at first by the humans in the novels, then the readers of the novels, and finally the viewers of the films based on the novels. The description of them as marble-like demarcates their difference as aesthetic, first and foremost, signified by the 'deadly hue' of their skin. This pallor elicits both fear and desire in those who look upon them.[5]

The arrival and subsequent popularity of 'sparkly vampires'[6] was met with an almost immediate backlash in the media and online.[7] While many of the negative responses centred upon the perceived anti-feminism of the series, there was significant concern that the Cullens were not 'real' vampires.[8] They were too beautiful and too appealing. However, neither the vampires nor the explicit romance in the Twilight series are aberrations. Rather, they represent the textual evolution of vampiric desire and desirability, one which complicates the binary opposition of prey and predator.

Early literary vampires and vampiric entities already showed evidence of departing from their folkloric origins. Christopher Frayling writes that in 'Romantic fiction, they [vampires] tended to be fashionably pallid and clean-shaven, with seductive voices and pouting lips, and they were always sexually attractive'.[9] Thus Frayling perhaps anticipates the arrival of Edward Cullen in romantic fiction (with a small 'r') via his literary predecessor Ruthven. The publication of *The Vampyre* introduced the vampire into the modern world: 'the bloodsucker had left the graveyard and entered the drawing-room. Groomed and debonair, now he mingles within high society and is often invited into the bedroom.'[10] Like his antecedents, Ruthven is notably pale, a trait which is both repellent and attractive: 'In spite of the deadly hue of his face, which never gained a warmer tint, either from the blush of modesty, or from the strong emotion of passion, though its form and outline were beautiful, many of the female hunters after notoriety attempted to win his attentions.'[11] His paleness is a mark of his 'otherness': it is unnatural and unchanging. On a surface level, it gives the impression of inhuman coldness and immutability; he appears unmoved by passion or desire. There is an element of literary irony here as well. While professing that women are attracted to Ruthven 'in spite' of his pallor, their response equally suggests that it is *because* of it. He is not simply 'invited to every house' (246) to socialise, but to be stared at and commented upon like a piece of art. The behaviour of those around him is not motivated by disgust but desire. While explicitly a love story between the human Bella Swan and the vampire Edward Cullen, the central storyline of the Twilight series repeatedly focuses on the pleasure of viewing; the desirability and beauty of the vampire is focalised through Bella's first-person narration.

In comparison, Ruthven, a distorted reflection of Lord Byron, who had employed Polidori as his physician prior to the novel being written, is cruel and immoral yet intensely attractive to the human protagonist, Aubrey. Like the other humans at the beginning of the novel, he is intrigued and excited by his appearance. In the course of the narrative, he accompanies the mysterious Ruthven in his travels across Europe, only to discover the Lord's evil nature. Aubrey's plan to leave Ruthven fails, resulting in both the woman he loves and his sister becoming victims to the vampiric Lord. Mariam Wassif explores the relationship between the depiction of Ruthven and Lord Byron, arguing that 'Lord Ruthven is less a portrait of Byron than a portrait of Byron's portraits'.[12] These portraits were markers of a new type of celebrity in which portraiture and image creation elicited desire from the viewer through scopophilia. Ruthven's gaze is described in the novella as that of a 'dead grey eye' (246). The colour of his eye suggests a corpse-like quality. Like his unblushing skin, it suggests a blankness and lack of response to external stimulus. His gaze 'fell upon the cheek with a leaden ray that weighed upon the skin' (247). Although he is looking at a living being, he does not acknowledge this; rather, the human is regarded as an object. It is this uncanny quality which, Wassif argues, 'mediates between the ancient terror of the vampire's bite with the modern fear of the vampiric portrait's deadly gaze'.[13] In both cases, the victim of the vampire is objectified. The vampire's bite consumes the human as food; the 'vampiric portrait's deadly gaze', as demonstrated by Ruthven, precedes this violence by using looking as another method of consumption. Thus the 'vampiric gaze' is a mode of looking that denies the subjectivity of the individual upon which it is turned. It is a conscious or subconscious expression of desire, wielded by human and vampire alike.

It is Aubrey's reaction to Ruthven and his apparent desire for him which introduce the notion of inverting the power dynamic between human and vampire. Aubrey's relationship with Ruthven is introduced by the sentence 'He watched him' (247). Aubrey had gained his acquaintance and 'paid him attentions' (247), before finding out he is 'about to travel' (247). This language and behaviour exist on the boundary of admiration and obsession. Though Aubrey's death is caused, if indirectly, by Ruthven, throughout the novel his obsessive regard towards Ruthven becomes its own form of vampirism in which the object of desire is consumed through the gaze. Though Ruthven is identified as a vampire at the end of the novel, it is Aubrey who commands the vampiric gaze throughout the narrative which is focalised through him. The importance of seeing and looking at the vampiric object is made clear in the opening paragraph of Polidori's narrative. Ruthven is invited to many households because 'all wished to see him' (246). Ruthven is 'some*thing*' to be looked upon, rather than some*one* (my emphasis). When the Cullens are first seen by Bella in the school cafeteria, the objectification of the vampiric body is repeated through separation: the family are seated apart from the other students. Much like the drawing room in Polidori's novella, the cafeteria is a central focus in high school dramas: it allows for a large congregation of students to meet and observe other students in a more informal setting, where gossip can be exchanged over refreshments. Drawn to their beauty, Bella quickly learns that they do not socialise with the other students. She complains that it is 'excessive for them to have both money and looks […]. The isolation must be their desire' (27–28). Their 'money and looks' make them objects, associating them with consumerism. Bella assumes that they want to be isolated rather than acknowledging that the other students take part in creating this distance by staring at them and projecting their fantasies and desires onto them. Like Ruthven, with his unresponsive pallor, they are assumed to be incapable of desire themselves. One of the Cullens' fellow students, Jessica, tells Bella: 'He's [Edward is] gorgeous, of course, but don't waste your time. He doesn't date' (19). Ruthven and Edward both elicit a response in the human viewer as only a beautiful 'something' with no apparent subjectivity themselves. Ruthven's 'deadly hue' and Edward Cullen's 'deadly beauty' make them objects of adoration, obsession, and frustration as they fail to respond to flattery. Jessica's comments mirror Aubrey's that Ruthven 'gave few other signs of his observation of external objects, than the tacit assent to their existence' (247). Like Jessica, Aubrey's reaction to Ruthven moves from desire to frustration. On seeing him, 'he [Aubrey] soon formed this object into the hero of a romance, and determined to observe the offspring of his fancy' (247). Though the term 'romance' does not refer to the contemporary genre of romantic fiction, it is suggestive of a fantasy in which Aubrey is saved by Ruthven and provides a veneer of sexuality to their relationship. Ruthven, although older and more powerful socially, is still rendered a beautiful, undead object by Aubrey's gaze. Through this fantasy, the gaze becomes vampiric; the pleasure of consumption is visual rather than the orality of the vampire's bite. Moreover, the term 'offspring' suggests that Aubrey has made or created Ruthven, inverting the model of the vampire transforming their victim. Instead, Ruthven appears to be the victim of Aubrey. Yet Aubrey is unable to be fully satisfied in being close to and being able to observe Ruthven. On their travels, Aubrey is frustrated by his inability to engage with Ruthven. Though he is 'near the object of his curiosity, he obtained no great gratification from it than the constant excitement of vainly wishing to break that mystery' (249). The use of 'gratification' and 'constant excitement' reinforce the sense of the repressed sexuality in Aubrey's relationship with Ruthven. It is this inability to acknowledge his pleasure at viewing Ruthven and his own engagement in (re)producing a romantic fantasy that destroy him.

Simon Bainbridge argues, 'a wealthy orphan without the benefit of a proper education, Aubrey occupies the place in Gothic fiction normally filled by the heroine'.[14] Aubrey's fantasies regarding Ruthven and 'high romantic feeling of honour and candour, which daily ruin so many milliners' apprentices' (247) further 'feminises Aubrey, suggesting his own susceptibility, and his relationship with Ruthven involves a process of projection that is structured by the forms of fiction'.[15] His decision to follow Ruthven across Europe further isolates him from family protections, potentially imperilling him. (Though, unlike a female Gothic heroine, his financial independence and gender allow him to remove himself from the peril at hand.) However, though Bainbridge characterises Aubrey's susceptibility, it is possible to read this countertextually. Rather than being entirely victim to Ruthven, Aubrey actively takes on the role of Gothic heroine, projecting the role of hero onto Ruthven. This reverses Ruthven's vampiric gaze, his 'cold, dead eye'. Aubrey now views Ruthven vampirically as an object of desire. His vampiric gaze traps Ruthven into the role of hero. The narrative's repeated emphasis of Aubrey's swooning, leading to his hysterical collapse at the denouement, and Ruthven's unemotional response pastiches romantic traditions. Moreover, there is an element of masochism in Aubrey's performance of Gothic heroine. Though ostensibly Aubrey is the victim of Ruthven, his engagement in 'forming' Ruthven into a heroic role reinforces his own control in their relationship. His desire (re)creates Ruthven, enforcing Ruthven's performance in the drawing rooms of London. The revelation of Ruthven as a villain can be read as an escape from Aubrey's regard. Aubrey fails to acknowledge that Ruthven's 'deadly hue' signifies his absolute Otherness which cannot be coalesced into his own fantasy.

The performative nature of the relationship between Aubrey and Ruthven is repeated in the relationship between Meyer's Bella and Edward. However, the similarities are qualified by the twenty-first-century glorification of vampires in popular culture. The audience for the Twilight series is largely made up of teenage girls who take part in Bella's delight at Edward's pale, sparkling skin. The Cullens are 'good vampires' who perform humanness to protect their identity. Unlike Ruthven, they choose not to prey on humans – calling themselves 'vegetarians' – for ethical reasons. Though Ruthven is invested in his true nature remaining secret, it is not due to moral compunction. Rather, he protects his identity to allow him to continue to prey on and degrade his human victims, before moving on to find new prey. In comparison, the Cullens attempt to live alongside humans, staying in one location for extended periods of time. As Rosalie declares: 'We *try* to blend in' (174; italics in original). Their performance makes them both self-aware and self-regarding. Bella's father Charlie sees the children as being 'well behaved and polite', while the Cullens 'stick together the way a family should' (31). Though he acknowledges that they keep themselves separate from the community, Charlie responds to the idealised family image that the Cullens portray to the world. Joseph Crawford suggests that the Cullens are an inversion of *The Munsters* (1964–66), the Gothic nuclear family made popular in the 1960s television programme; they present to Bella and the other inhabitants of Forks 'a life of impeccable ordinariness and domesticity. It is as though an episode of *The Munsters* was being written by someone unaware that it was meant to be a comedy.'[16] If the message of that programme was to avoid judging by appearances, then the Cullens represent an inversion of this: they are painfully aware of what makes them different and wear a mask of normalcy which they hope will conceal their dark secret. Though both the Cullens and Ruthven engage with human society, the twenty-first-century vampires are conscious that popular culture is inundated with depictions of vampires as both terrifying *and* desirable, making the importance of concealing their true identity about protecting themselves and the human population. The 'deadly hue' of their skin, which means that they sparkle in direct sunlight, highlighting their otherness, forces them to live somewhere cloudy and means they do not go out in public if it is sunny.

Yet Bella continues to actively engage with the Cullens even after she is aware of their true identity, in contrast to Aubrey's shock and revulsion when he discovers that Ruthven is undead.[17] Moreover, her reaction to Edward's sparkling, marble-like skin is clearly desire rather than fear. Her character further complicates the construction of the vampires as fetishised objects. Like Aubrey, she is placed in the role of Gothic heroine as she is young, unmarried, and effectively motherless – a role she also actively adopts by choosing to leave her mother. Her father's involvement in her life is minimal, making her effectively 'unchaperoned'. Unlike Aubrey, she is already aware of such Gothic conventions as the 'rules' of vampirism when she meets Edward; on her first visit to the Cullens' house, he teases her, saying: 'Not what you expected, is it? [...] No coffins, no piles of skulls in the corners [...] what a disappointment this must be for you' (287). He is well aware that she has grown up with the 'saturation of Gothic motifs in contemporary culture', a mainstreaming of Gothic tropes that mirrors the attempts of the Cullens to lead a 'normal' life.[18] Bella's treatment of Edward, and his subsequent response, shows the objectification of the vampire in the novel. Indeed, many of the key moments in the novels are inversions of Laura Mulvey's thesis in 'Visual Pleasure and Narrative Cinema' (1975), which claims that in narrative cinema the female takes the role of the passive image onto which the active male gaze projects its fantasies.[19] As Sara Wasson and Sarah Artt argue, 'Edward as embodiment of the vampire figure becomes the symbol on to which the woman maps her desires' in the same way that Aubrey reconstructs Ruthven, another vampire figure, as a romantic hero.²⁰ It is the change in the human protagonist's gender which reveals a further subversion of the power dynamic between the vampire-as-predator and human-as-victim dynamic.

Mulvey's approach, with its disavowal of the male object and female subject, ignores the power of Bella's gaze in the relationship and Edward's pleasure in being viewed by her as a beautiful, supernatural object. Nor does it recognise that Meyer's novels, written by a female author, seem to circumnavigate the perceived threat of active masculinity by eliciting 'voyeuristic or fetishistic mechanisms' in order to objectify Edward, much as narrative cinema removes the castration threat of women by rendering them passive through the male gaze.²¹ The vampire's fangs are symbols of phallic power threatening to penetrate and consume the female protagonist, in this case Bella. Yet Bella's aggressive gaze de-fangs Edward. Bella, like Aubrey, eroticises and projects romantic fantasies onto the vampire's body. In the Twilight novels and films, the female gaze is focalised through Bella, and with the direction of Catherine Hardwick in the first film, Edward becomes 'slim and muscly, pale and defined, wearing makeup, lusciously coiffed, looking exactly like [...] a girl'.²² The description reiterates the importance of the 'deadly hue of his skin' in creating a sense of 'otherness'. Many detractors have been quick to argue that Edward is 'gay' despite his intense love for Bella; it would appear that they are reacting to his placement as the feminised object there to be viewed.²³ The reader or viewer is left in no doubt that the visual pleasure gained from Edward is entirely meant for them. It is this elision of masculine and feminine, vampiric-aggressor, and fetishised object that highlights the similarity between not only Edward and Ruthven, but also Edward and Ianthe, the alternative object of Aubrey's desire who is also objectified through Aubrey's vampiric gaze.

Having removed himself from Ruthven's malign influence, Aubrey meets a young Greek girl: Ianthe is depicted as a beautiful, 'frank infantile being' (251) who entrances Aubrey after he has split from Ruthven on his travels. She is entirely focalised through Aubrey's gaze. Where Aubrey seems almost wilfully ignorant of his desire for Ruthven and Ianthe, she is portrayed as sexually naive. She is described as 'unconscious' twice, in regard to her own beauty and Aubrey's affection (250, 252). This word choice suggests that it is Aubrey, from whose viewpoint the narrative is focalised, who is the active participant. Ianthe is an object for him to regard and onto which to project his desire – much as he attempted to do with Ruthven. He finds himself distracted by her beauty to the extent that he cannot concentrate on his 'antiquarian research' (251). Repeatedly, the narrative shows how Aubrey's gaze moves from an ancient text or relic to Aubrey, suggesting the two are conflated in his mind: 'often would the unconscious girl, [...] show the whole beauty of her form, [...] to the eager gaze of him, who forgot the letters he had just deciphered upon an almost effaced tablet' (250). The beauty of Ianthe's hair in the sunlight 'might well excuse the forgetfulness of the antiquary, who let escape from his mind the very object he had before thought of vital importance' (250). Aubrey's 'innocence' may be more convincingly interpreted as his unacknowledged desire to own her. He realises that she is a distraction to his antiquarian research, for which 'he would depart, determined not to return until his object was attained' (251), though ultimately forget in preference to thinking about Ianthe. The repeated slippage between antiquarian object and Ianthe suggests that they are of equal interest. She is conflated with the other Greek objects. Moreover, the descriptions of Ianthe reinforce the idea that she, like Ruthven, is also supernatural – an 'almost fairy form' (251) – and therefore unattainable. Ianthe replaces Ruthven as a 'good' supernatural entity in comparison to Ruthven's vampiric evil. In the Twilight novels, Edward's appearance is framed similarly by Bella.

Throughout the Twilight novels, we are continually reminded that Bella's gaze is intensely objectifying in relation to her vampire acquaintances. Indeed, the space between the Cullen clan and Bella is often created by Bella herself, almost so that she can view them better – like a piece of art. Yet it is maintained not through fear or revulsion, but Bella's idealisation of Edward's family, echoing Aubrey's sense of distance when he travels alongside Ruthven. Bella's gaze becomes vampiric when she looks at Edward; she continually views him not as a whole but as constituent parts; her gaze becomes the means by which she cuts him into pieces and the language with which she describes him a system of rhetoricised violence. Her descriptions are similar to blazon poetry, much favoured by the Elizabethan poets of love, which catalogues the physical merits of women in a manner that entirely objectifies them. On opening the door to Edward, Bella describes the way in which, 'My eyes traced over his pale white features: the hard square of his jaw, the softer curve of his full lips – twisted up into a smile now, the smooth marble span of his forehead – partially obscured by a tangle of rain-darkened bronze hair.'[24] Though Edward may be the vampire, it would seem that through Bella's gaze he is slowly being visually consumed like a beautiful piece of meat. She reiterates the paleness of his skin as the first thing she notices, the quality that marks him as a beautiful, undead object. After ravishing him visually she suggests that Edward's face is 'a face any male model in the world would trade his soul for'.[25] By evoking the image of the male model, Bella continues to concentrate on the outward appearance of Edward.

The description of Edward as a model is echoed in Aubrey's of Ianthe. She is described as being so beautiful 'that she might have formed the model for a painter, wishing to portray on canvass the promised hope of the faithful in Mahomet's paradise, save that her eyes spoke too much mind for any one to think she could belong to those who had no souls' (8). In uncritically adopting Orientalist clichés and Islamophobic sentiments, Polidori depicts absolute beauty, as does Meyer, as soulless. Or at least, potentially soulless. Both texts invoke the idea that beauty, and the object of desire, are soulless but then disavow the possibility. The emotion in Ianthe's eyes shows that she must have a soul, which can be read in comparison to Ruthven's unresponsive pallor and 'dead, grey eye', while Bella retracts her comment: 'No. I didn't believe that. I felt guilty for even thinking it.'[26] These slips in expression suggest that the first impression of Ianthe and Edward's beauty is that it is inhuman and overwhelming. It can only be expressed through metaphors of the supernatural and art. Both Edward and Ianthe's beauty invites them to be seen as portraits. Bella describes the Cullens as living art; they could have been 'painted by an old master as the face of an angel' (17). Their appearance allows them to become empty objects onto which the viewer can project their interpretation. The Cullens, like Ruthven and then Ianthe, are visual phenomena, both reflecting and absorbing the desire of those who view them. Their beauty functions for the pleasure of the viewer(s), Aubrey and Bella. Bella fetishises Edward and his vampiric nature. Her gaze on Edward maintains the gap between the viewing subject and the viewed object, even after he reciprocates her desire. The vampiric gaze denies subjectivity to the viewed object. The projection of the viewer's fantasy prevents the possibility of response. Aubrey's desire for both Ruthven and Ianthe is equally thwarted. He is unable to act on his desires, either because they are repressed, as in the first case, or entirely idealised, as in the second.

In their discussion of Gilles Deleuze's theory of masochism, Wasson and Artt claim that 'masochism is fundamentally an aesthetic, a fantasy tableau of two frozen figures, straining towards each other with consummation relentlessly deferred'.[27] The repeated depictions of Edward, Ianthe, and Ruthven certainly speak to this aesthetic: they are models and images that cannot or should not be touched. The sterility of the language 'frozen' and the notion of eternally deferred gratification is replicated in how the Cullens consume or fail to consume. Moreover, it can be seen in the sparkling nature of their skin, which calls to mind not only marble but also ice statures. Bella notes that 'they weren't eating though they each had a tray of untouched food in front of them' (16). Immediately afterwards we are told that Alice throws away an 'unopened soda, [an] unbitten apple' (17). The language evokes a frozen tableau. The image of the apple alludes to the story of Adam and Eve – indeed, the cover of *Twilight* shows a pair of female hands offering a red, shining apple – evoking the idea of loss of innocence. While the fact that the apple is unbitten promises things to come, as with the 'Plump unpecked cherries' of Christina Rossetti's 'Goblin Market', the reader is excited by the possibility that the apple may be eaten and what the consequences of this action may be.²⁸ The close correlation between the soda can and the apple continues the tension in Bella's descriptions of the Cullens, which flit from contemporary allusions about celebrity culture to fine art. The Cullens uncomfortably combine the two in their physical appearance. Meanwhile, Meyer's use of the prefix 'un-', suggesting a suspension in action, a not-quite-getting, calls to mind Keats's 'Ode on a Grecian Urn': 'Bold Lover, never, never canst thou kiss, / Though winning near the goal'.²⁹ Perfection, it would appear, comes in the constant deferment of action and maintaining of suspense.

Both *The Vampyre* and the Twilight novels make their protagonists' relationships into frozen, unconsummated tableaux. The Cullens, Ruthven, and Ianthe become like the Grecian Urn itself: exquisite objects whose meaning is written onto their surface appearance at the expense of their own subjectivity, and 'marble men and maidens' carved upon it.³⁰ While Edward and Bella strain toward each other, Aubrey is caught reaching for Ruthven and Ianthe. The pleasure that Aubrey and Bella experience in viewing their vampiric objects (Ruthven and Edward) and the fey object that is Ianthe stands in place of actual satisfaction through physical intimacy. The 'deadly hue' of Ruthven and Edward's skin reinforces this connection: their skin makes them already statue-like and beautiful, undead objects. Yet, though ostensibly both Bella and Aubrey are trapped by their own idealisation – and idolisation – of the people they desire, Meyer's texts subvert the stagnation and frustration that defines Aubrey's desire. Her narrative finishes with the consummation of Edward and Bella's relationship: they admit their love for one another, get married, and live 'happily ever after'. Moreover, where both Ruthven and Ianthe seem to be unwilling, or at least unknowing, victims of Aubrey's gaze, Edward consciously performs his role as vampiric object by setting up scenarios in which Bella is invited to look at him and, alongside his family, maintaining a distance from humans. Therefore, unlike Ruthven's reaction to Aubrey's vampiric gaze, Edward takes part in Bella's fantasy as a vampiric *objet d'art*. His telepathy allows him to be aware of the effect that his pale, marble-like beauty has on those around him.

In *Midnight Sun*, a rewriting of the first novel in the series told from Edward's point of view, Edward comments on the manner by which he is objectified by Bella and other people around him. Due to his telepathic ability he is accustomed to 'simply *watch[ing]* myself through someone's following eyes'.³¹ Edward's ability to see himself through other people's point of view means that he is able to be, simultaneously, the object being viewed and the subject viewing, the means by which he can learn to temper his appearance and actions to suit the viewing public. Since Bella is immune to Edward's telepathy, he can only be aware of the 'intangible sensation of watching eyes' which he finds 'strangely exciting'.³² This excitement suggests that he enjoys the sensation of being the passive object. Unlike Ianthe, who is 'unconscious of his [Aubrey's] love' (10), Edward is hyper-aware of how he is viewed by humans – particularly how he is desired by them. With Bella, he can only rely on the knowledge that she is watching him. Thus he utilises the seductive quality of deadly, and sparkling, hue in order to attract her gaze.

Bella's gaze, therefore, becomes a source of potential pleasure for Edward, Bella, and the reader. Edward wants her to look at him and acknowledge his vampirism, taking part in her fantasy in which he is a vampiric *objet d'art*. This differs from the oppressive quality of the Cullens' life in which they perform normality out of obligation. Thus, Edward creates a series of tableaux in which he can be viewed; these seem to be a response to his frustration at the limitations of his telepathy regarding Bella as he reasserts his position as 'viewed object'. The much-celebrated scene in the meadow is orchestrated in a manner that seems to take a great deal from striptease. Bella is placed in a central viewing position and Edward steps forward to be viewed. In the sunlight he appears only too happy to let Bella stare at him and she notes that he 'lay perfectly still in the grass, his shirt open over his sculpted, incandescent chest [while his] glistening, pale lavender lids were shut'; he is like a 'perfect statue, carved in some unknown stone' (228). Like Aubrey, Bella comments on the pallor of his skin, which attracts her. The entire pose, with his eyes shut so that Bella can gaze in peace, seems to be caught between shameless exhibitionism and an art exhibition. Focalised through Bella, the narrative allows the reader to take part in the pleasure of looking at Edward; they are able to engage in permissible voyeurism. Yet, when Bella moves closer to him, he runs back into the shade, where he looks at Bella, 'his eyes dark in the shadows' (231). Though he maintains that he is the predator in their relationship, his reaction to Bella is like a scared animal. Like both artwork and striptease, he is there to be viewed but not touched. Gratification is deferred once more but apparently to the mutual pleasure of both viewer and viewed.

Notably, Edward's pleasure at being viewed seems to be only in regard to Bella's gaze. Edward's method of intended suicide after the apparent death of Bella also involves uncovering his sparkling body in full view of people. As Wasson and Artt explain, 'what will kill him is essentially the massed gaze of hundreds of human spectators'.[33] Without Bella, the human gaze becomes destructive once more. The desire that Edward's sparkling pallor elicits in Bella is transformed into fear and violence in other humans. Despite his preternatural speed and strength, Edward vacillates between predator and prey. In comparison, Ianthe is consistently depicted as prey – of both Aubrey and Ruthven. Under Aubrey's gaze, she is compared to a prey animal: 'one would have thought the gazelle a poor type of her beauties' (8), much as Bella depicts Edward when he flies from her touch. She is given no interiority – her personality is exemplified by ignorance and naivety. In his relationship with Ianthe, Aubrey becomes the predator, pursuing her regardless of her wants. As in his relationship with Ruthven, he appears wilfully ignorant of the violence of his gaze. Her death at the hands of Ruthven can be read as an extension of Aubrey's violent desires.

Bainbridge reads the text as hinting at the possibility that Ruthven is Aubrey's double, a projection of his own violence.[34] Thus Aubrey's attempts to prevent Ruthven from killing Ianthe are 'strongly suggestive of a battle between conscience and desire [...] this time won by Ruthven, who kills Ianthe by tearing out her throat'.[35] When the stasis of unrequited desire is finally broken in *The Vampyre*, it leads to violence and death. The power imbalance between Ruthven, Aubrey, and Ianthe can only end in tragedy. The vampiric gaze in this narrative consumes the object figuratively and potentially, giving the recipients, Ruthven and Ianthe, only the options to fight back or submit. The desirability of Ruthven's 'deadly hue' and his positioning as a beautiful, undead object is undone by the death of Aubrey. Wassif argues that Aubrey is repulsed to the point of madness by what he sees when he gazes at Ruthven, a palimpsest of the celebrity of Byron: 'the celebrity's image provides a constant stimulus for self-reflection in the viewer – resulting, for Aubrey, in madness and death'.[36] His attempts to contain and understand Ruthven through his vampiric gaze are thwarted as they only reassert what he cannot consciously acknowledge: his desire for Ruthven and to be like him.

Yet Ruthven's entrance into the drawing room left an indelible mark on the vampire. The pallor which marked them as corpse-like, undead, and Other could be rendered as potentially attractive eliciting desire from the human viewer. Entering the drawing room, and then the bedroom, places the vampire in a position to be gazed upon as a piece of art. Though not every post-Polidori vampire would be alluring, the boundaries of desire and terror became increasingly blurred. The uncovering of the vampire, whether in their coffin, through the removal of clothing, or simply as they stepped into the sunlight like Angel, became a repeated motif in vampire narratives. By reading Polidori's novella through the vampiric gaze, the potential inversion of power through the act of looking is made explicit. As the vampire becomes more sympathetic, the act of looking destabilises the victim–predator dynamic of human–vampire engagement. Although Bella and Edward's relationship is equally centred on the vampiric gaze, it is reciprocal, allowing for self-aware performance. The potential for violence and harm is explicitly stated, and even expressed, such as when they first have sex and during Bella's pregnancy and labour. However, despite this, the series ends with Bella becoming a vampire, marrying her vampire lover, and having his child. Where Aubrey's desires are unacknowledged, repressed, and sublimated, Bella's are expressed and achieved. As Joseph Crawford argues, Bella's 'desires are mad, illogical, amoral, impossible, anti-social, wildly excessive – and yet, by some dream-logic by the end of the fourth book every single one of them has been fulfilled'.[37] Bella is able to admit that she both desires, sexually and romantically, her vampiric object and that she wishes to be a vampire herself. In the Twilight series, Bella's vampiric gaze leads to the fulfilment of her desires. Her 'vampirism' is defined through looking and through it she can both have Edward and become like him – she can also sparkle in the sunlight.

Notes

1. 'In the Dark', *Angel*, 1:3, writ. by Douglas Petrie, dir. by Bruce Seth Green (The WB, 19 October 1999).
2. Catherine Spooner, '*Gothic Charm School*; or, How Vampires Learned to Sparkle', in *Open Graves, Open Minds: Representation of Vampires and the Undead from the Enlightenment to the Present Day*, ed. by Sam George and Bill Hughes (Manchester: Manchester University Press, 2013), pp. 146–64 (p. 149).
3. Anne Rice, *Queen of the Damned* (London: Macdonald, 1989), p. 418.
4. Stephenie Meyer, *Twilight* (2005; London: Atom, 2006), p. 228. All further references are from this edition and are in the main text in parentheses.
5. Given the repeated use of 'whiteness' and 'paleness' in the text(s), there is a discussion to be had about the construction of 'whiteness' with regard to these vampires. However, this is beyond the scope of this essay.
6. In the novels, Meyer's vampires sparkle when in direct sunlight. This became the defining feature of her vampires; the term 'sparkly vampires' became short-hand, with derogatory overtones, for the Cullens and their ilk.
7. For further information on anti-Twilight online behaviour, see Anne Gilbert, 'Between Twi-Hards and Twi-Haters: The Complicated Terrain of Online "Twilight" Audience Communities', in *Genre, Reception, and Adaptation in the 'Twilight' Series*, ed. by Anne Morey (Farnham: Ashgate Publishing, 2012), pp. 163–79.
8. Spooner, '*Gothic Charm School*', pp. 146–47. For feminist critiques of the Twilight series, see Kristine Moruzu, 'Postfeminist Fantasies: Sexuality and Femininity in Stephenie Meyer's "Twilight" Series', in Morey, *Genre*, pp. 47–64.
9. Christopher Frayling, ed., *Vampyres: Lord Byron to Count Dracula* (London: Faber & Faber, 1991), p. 6.
10. Conrad Aquilna, 'The Deformed Transformed; or, From Bloodsucker to Byronic Hero – Polidori and the Literary Vampire', in George and Hughes, *Open Graves, Open Minds*, pp. 24–28 (p. 35).
11. John Polidori, *The Vampyre*, Appendix 1 in this volume, pp. 240–67 (p. 246). All further references are from this edition and are in the main text in parentheses.

12 Marriam Wassif, 'Polidori's *The Vampyre* and Byron's Portraits', *The Wordsworth Circle*, 49 (Winter 2018), 53–61 (p. 53).
13 Wassif, 'Polidori's *The Vampyre*', p. 60.
14 Simon Bainbridge, 'Lord Ruthven's Power: Polidori's "The Vampyre", Doubles and the Byronic Imagination', *The Byron Journal*, 34:1 (2006), 21–34 (p. 23).
15 Bainbridge, 'Lord Ruthven's Power', p. 23.
16 Joseph Crawford, *The Twilight of the Gothic? Vampire Fiction and the Rise of Paranormal Romance, 1991–2012* (Cardiff: University of Wales Press, 2014), p. 177.
17 I use the term 'undead' rather than 'vampire' as it is not clear that Aubrey explicitly makes the connection between Ianthe's stories and Ruthven's identity as a vampire, despite having witnessed him return from the grave. Instead, he becomes aware that Ruthven is not entirely human.
18 Monica Germana, 'Skulls, Skulls Everywhere: Consuming the Gothic in the 21st Century', The Gothic Imagination, 22 February 2010 www.gothic.stir.ac.uk/guests/viewblog.php?id=67 [accessed 5 September 2021].
19 Laura Mulvey, 'Visual Pleasures and Narrative Cinema', in *Visual and Other Pleasures* (Basingstoke: Macmillan, 1989), pp. 14–28 (p. 19).
20 Sara Wasson and Sarah Artt, 'The Twilight Saga and the Pleasures of Spectatorship: The Broken Body and the Shining Body', in George and Hughes, *Open Graves, Open Minds*, pp. 181–91 (p. 189).
21 Mulvey, 'Visual Pleasures', p. 25.
22 Bidisha, 'Bitten by the Female Gaze', *The Guardian*, 19 January 2009 www.guardian.co.uk/commentisfree/2009/jan/19/women-gender [accessed 14 September 2021].
23 A number of attacks on the character of Edward Cullen return to the idea that he is 'gay'. The most infamous of these slurs was summed up by the Facebook group 'You're not a vampire, you're a sparkly faggot in a tree'. The original group has 153,925 members. The group was made to change its name, swapping the word 'faggot' for 'douchebag', due to its overt homophobia. Similar groups include: 'Twilight is a good book about vampires LOL JK its about gay sparkly faries' [sic], and 'No Edward Cullen. You're not a vampire, you're a fairy. Literally.' Much has been made of the facts that, since Edward Cullen lives in a forest, does not kill humans, and sparkles in the sunlight, he is in fact a 'fairy', with the implied homophobic insult.
24 Stephenie Meyer, *Eclipse* (London: Atom, 2007), p. 17.
25 Meyer, *Eclipse*, p. 17.
26 Meyer, *Eclipse*, p. 17.
27 Wasson and Artt, 'The Twilight Saga', p. 184.
28 Christina Rossetti, 'Goblin Market', in *Selected Poems*, ed. by Dinah Roe (London: Penguin Classics, 2008), pp. 67–83, line 7. John Polidori was Christina Rossetti's uncle. David F. Morrill argues that Polidori's novella influenced the themes of transformation, consumption, and desire in Rossetti's 'Goblin Market'. See David F. Morrill, ' "Twilight is Not Good for Maidens": Uncle Polidori and the Psychodynamics of Vampirism in "Goblin Market" ', *Victorian Poetry*, 1 (Spring 1990), 1–16; and the response by Ronald D. Morrison,

'"Their Fruits like Honey in the Throat / But Poison in the Blood": Christina Rossetti and *The Vampyre*', *Weber Studies*, 14:2 (1997) www.weber.edu/weberjournal/Journal_Archives/Archive_B/Vol_14_2/RMorrisonEss.html [accessed 30 May 2023].

29 John Keats, 'Ode on a Grecian Urn', in John Keats, *The Major Works*, ed. by Elizabeth Cook (Oxford and New York: Oxford University Press, 2001), pp. 288–89, lines 17–18.
30 Keats, 'Ode on a Grecian Urn', line 42.
31 Stephenie Meyer, *Midnight Sun* (London: Atom, 2020), p. 211.
32 Meyer, *Midnight Sun*, p. 211.
33 Wasson and Artt, 'The Twilight Saga', p. 186.
34 Bainbridge, 'Lord Ruthven's Power', pp. 29–34. See also Nick Groom's Chapter 7 in this volume.
35 Bainbridge, 'Lord Ruthven's Power', p. 34.
36 Wassif, 'Polidori's *The Vampyre*', p. 61.
37 Crawford, *The Twilight of the Gothic?*, p. 172.

12

Vampensteins from Villa Diodati: The assimilation of pseudo-science in twenty-first-century vampire fiction

Jillian Wingfield

What connects the early-twenty-first-century vampire novels of Justin Cronin and Octavia Butler to two pivotal Gothic novels conceived at the Villa Diodati in Geneva, Switzerland in 1816? There is certainly no problem in advancing a critical argument that the genetically modified characters of Cronin's death row criminals-turned-vampires and Butler's amnesiac, Shori Matthews, bear generic evolutionary ties to the first work of vampire prose fiction, John Polidori's novella *The Vampyre: A Tale* (1819). However, my focus is on a 'vampenstein' *fusion* that increases the fictional plausibility of vampirism with the aid of pseudo-science; David Punter describes the exploitation of the fundamental Gothic affect of fear in raising 'anxieties about scientific progress […] if undertaken in the absence of moral guidance'.[1] This conjunction of science and the supernatural connects back to the other Gothic masterpiece brought into being at Diodati: Mary Shelley's *Frankenstein; or, The Modern Prometheus* (1818).[2] Thus, alongside the 'vamp' origins seen in the supernatural allure of Polidori's central antagonist, the suave and enigmatic Lord Ruthven, sits the 'stein' of Victor Frankenstein's pseudo-scientific undertakings.

For over 200 years, Ruthven's 'dreadfully vicious' (yet terribly refined) vampirism and the misappropriation of science in Frankenstein's 'secret toil' – core to the existence of his 'filthy creation' – have persisted side-by-side in many readers' imaginations.[3] Together, vampire and creature serve as frames of reference for the hybridised beings considered here as 'vampensteins' – vampires whose existences are crucially shaped by interpretations of the scientific. Thus, two centuries after their initial manifestation, this chapter explores the effects of the amalgamated influence of Polidori's vampire and Shelley's pseudo-science on Cronin and Butler's twenty-first-century vampires.

Returning to the summer of 1816, Polidori – then in his early twenties – became personal physician to Lord Byron, travelling with him to the Villa Diodati on the shores of Lake Geneva. Through this role, as other contributors to this volume attest, Polidori is ideally placed to be inspired to create the story that introduces to the world an enduring parasite, in the form of the vampire Lord Ruthven. Ruthven's aristocratic seductiveness and magnetism change the image of vampires from that of folkloric revenant degradation to fascinating attraction. Consequently, Polidori's *The Vampyre* introduces an evolutionary leap for the undead that remains generically central, with the enticements of Ruthven's aristocratic dead-eyed pallor initiating the propulsion of vampires to top billing within the Gothic pantheon.

However, as has been suggested above, vampire speciation within Western fiction exhibits adaptions that can be identified as developing from the stimulus of another Gothic stalwart instigated at the Villa Diodati: Shelley's *Frankenstein*. The romanticised legend of literary creation that has formed since 1816 intimates that, by the light of a piercingly 'bright, gibbous moon', a teenaged Mary Godwin (not yet Shelley) dreams forth a patchwork creature constructed from a legion of (not entirely human) dead body parts acquired from 'charnel-houses' (54), 'dissecting room[s]' and 'slaughter-house[s]' (55). Overwhelmed by the consequences of his revivification of this sordid assemblage by the undefined use of 'unhallowed arts', the obsessed scientist Victor Frankenstein himself has recourse to undead imagery, deeming his creature 'my own vampire [...] forced to destroy all' (77). With Gothic fiction's mythology citing the foundations for both vampire and creature as having been lain during an uncannily rainy summer sojourn in Switzerland, Frankenstein's creature and his glamorous undead brother-in-darkness are bonded as Gothic grandees.[4]

While Polidori's role in the creation of vampires as we now know them is difficult to dispute, these beings are constantly reinvented relative to contemporary concerns. An infection of popular vampire fiction – itself often conceived as a metaphor for disease and contagion – with pseudo-scientific shadows of contemporary advances can be traced forwards from the novels of Polidori and Shelley. The more memorable vampire tales, toying with contemporary pseudo-scientific understanding, that have been written in the two centuries since Polidori and Shelley first published their stories include what remains the most well-known vampire narrative: Bram Stoker's *Dracula* (1897). Stoker's novel displays an openness to 'science-knowledge', its human characters reliant on nineteenth-century technological advances such as rail transportation, photography, typewriting and the phonograph alongside blood transfusion, hypnosis and theories of physiognomy relating to criminality in such a way as to lend a credibility to their first-person epistolary accounts of the Count. Continuing in stride with scientific advances, by the mid-twentieth century the vampensteinian is a fundamental feature of Richard Matheson's *I Am Legend* (1954). Published amid the paranoia of early Cold War antagonism between the USA and the USSR, Matheson's reliance on incorporating novel biological jargon voices contemporaneous fears of potential mass extinction events in an era when comprehension of bacteria and viruses was still yet to become commonplace. In defining his vampirism as 'a facultative saprophyte' that 'is anaerobic and sets up a symbiosis with the [host] system', Matheson reinvents the vampire 'legend' for a readership becoming newly aware of the potential that lies in scientific advances to kill or cure *en masse*.[5]

Jumping forward to the opening years of the new millennium, this evolution of ersatz scientific explanations within vampire fiction continues to intensify in line with a broader cultural awareness of all things scientific. Alongside Cronin's and Butler's vampires, early millennial thematic alliances between science and the supernatural include the epidemiological in Guillermo del Toro and Chuck Hogan's *The Strain* (2009) – where the vampire virus 'fuses to the RNA [of human hosts]'.[6] However, in an aside to what is a biological bias within vampire fiction, Andrew Fox misappropriates mass-energy physics to reimagine supernatural shapeshifting in *Fat White Vampire Blues* (2003). In the simplicity of Fox's transgender vampire character Doodlebug's attempt to rationalise vampire transformation, readers are given an explanation of the vampiric ability to morph into anything from a dog to a dust mote: 'mass can be converted to energy, but mass can never simply disappear'.[7] Such a generalised interpretation may leave physicists unconvinced, but it lends vampires yet another layer of credibility for a nonspecialist readership ready and willing to suspend disbelief.

I turn now to the two early-twenty-first-century novels central to this discussion: Cronin's *The Passage* (2010) and Butler's *Fledgling* (2005). These two early-millennial novels – neither of which has been subject to any significant critical commentary – demonstrate distinctly differing evocations of modern cultural disquiet over essentially the same scientific field of genetic engineering. As examples of early-twenty-first-century vampensteinian tales, these stories share a thematic emphasis on the use of genetic engineering as a means of exploitation and control. Cronin's violent vampires – nicknamed 'virals' – stem from American militarily sanctioned experimentation gone wrong. In contrast, Butler's outwardly young, Black female protagonist is the product of vampire–human hybridisation and is representative of a more sympathetic narrative consideration of genetics. As such, although both assimilate the scientific language of genetics into their vampire narratives, Cronin and Butler exhibit divergent notions of vampirism. Cronin reflects on the dangers raised by deliberate interference in the process of evolution by natural selection in an attempt to produce super-soldiers, while Butler incorporates the pseudo-scientific into her vampirism to enhance the discursive centrality of otherness and prejudice within *Fledgling*.

As with other vampire storylines, including those briefly touched on above, Cronin and Butler expand the aristocratic singularity of Polidori's

Ruthven with the aid of sham science. As part of their vampensteinian storylines, Cronin and Butler attempt to account for their vampire variants via a reliance on recognisable bio-medical terminology including such phenomena as gene-splicing, RNA, DNA and mutation. Both novels address the ramifications of genetic manipulation and, thereby, propose variations of vampiric evolutionary development. Cronin uses pseudo-science to enhance a thematic emphasis on modern post-9/11 American existential fears, drawing attention to the catastrophic consequences of genetic misappropriation, here of a Bolivian chiropteran virus. The collapse of a recognisable American society into isolated pockets of fearful and (technologically) ignorant humanity sits within a globalised human-made vampiric plague. Conversely, Butler depicts vampire–human hybridity as a positive product of scientific study.[8] As an adjunct to the science, Butler's novel has her vampires nonviolently reliant on humans. In exchange for an extended life of chemically induced happiness and love, humans are co-opted to be what Butler calls 'symbionts' (or 'syms'). Science creeps in through the explanation of Ina vampire saliva or 'venom' making humans 'highly suggestible and deeply attached' (73), addicting the men and women targeted for lifetime indenture. Arguably, in this situation, Butler's vampires are *equally* enslaved to their human food sources, with symbiosis creating as strong a desire in vampire as in sym. As the Ina vampire Joan Braithwaite explains to Matthews: 'We need our symbionts […] not only their blood, but physical contact with them and emotional reassurance from them […] We either weave ourselves a family of symbionts, or we die' (270).[9] And so, Cronin and Butler transpose the Polidorian vampire narrative, with its fixation on individualised power dynamics, into modern dichotomous articulations, both reliant on science to bestow credibility: one sets forth mass human cultural disintegration through infection and an attendant global vampiric ascendency, and the other stages a largely empathetic intra-vampiric contemplation of scientific advancement.

With Shelley's *Frankenstein* subtitled *The Modern Prometheus*, the Promethean myth cannot be overlooked when considering the 'stein' in Cronin's and Butler's vampenstein fictions. In ancient Greek mythology, Prometheus was a Titan who, as well as being the creator, 'patron and champion' of humanity, defied Zeus to appropriate fire and gift it to his creations.[10] For this overreaching, Prometheus is doomed to a daily penance of having his perpetually renewing liver pecked out by an eagle. As a Promethean allegory, Shelley's culturally Christian creator, Frankenstein, is hounded for daring to play God and subsequently disowning his 'Adam', thereby condemning himself to a life overshadowed by existential trauma. Through the reduction of Frankenstein's creature's formation to one galvanically inspired sentence, Shelley philosophises upon the damaging consequences of scientific innovation: 'I collected the instruments of life around me, that I might infuse a spark of being into the lifeless thing that lay at my feet.'[11] For such (scientific) overreaching, Frankenstein must be seen to be punished, but here there is no eagle; instead, he is punished by his creation.

Cronin and Butler, like Shelley, gloss over the details of bio-technological processes. Instead, they focus on the repercussions of Promethean misadventures, creating metaphors for contemporary debates surrounding genetic manipulation out of their vampires. Like Shelley, Cronin's and Butler's 'science' remains nebulous, with culturally familiar biological terms such as cell theory or viral sequencing unexplained, reduced to passing observations. Cronin's virals experience 'A hugely accelerated rate of cellular regeneration' (41) and Butler's Matthews is the product of eldermothers who 'made genetic alterations directly to the germ line, so that [she would] be able to [...] be awake and alert during the day, able to walk in sun-light' (218).[12] For Cronin and Butler, 'science' may provide a useful means of explaining their vampirism, but it is little more than secularised magic supporting the supernatural within each story.

The Promethean script within Cronin's *The Passage* expands on Shelley's interpretation in its concentration on science as social malfeasance. Shelley's individualised Promethean penalty, where consequences such as death and misery have the greatest effect on Frankenstein and those either closely related to him or who come into direct contact with the creature, is transposed into a globally overwhelming punishment of the general population for what are political and military deceptions. This leads to a cataclysmic collapse of modern humanity in conjunction with the formation of a worldwide vampire ascendency. Cronin positions those instituting the clandestine bio-engineering project, codenamed 'NOAH', as corrupt as well as corrupting entities, vaingloriously playing God to maintain America's modern global dominance.[13] Lies about a 'terroristic threat' (223) told by authority figures from the US president downwards are part of a rapid degeneration of democracy, devolving into 'martial law' and 'curfew' (468) as an unsuspecting populace is subjected to vampiric decimation. Rather than putting the welfare of America's citizens to the fore, in what might be read as an unknowing but chillingly prescient foreshadowing of global diversionary politicking during the COVID-19 global pandemic barely a decade after initial publication, Cronin's POTUS, President Hughes, sets forth a mendacious denial of involvement. Hughes claims that 'evidence exists that this devastating epidemic is [...] the work of anti-American extremists, operating within our own borders but supported by our enemies abroad', and ends his deception with empty irony in an assurance that 'Justice will be swift' (223). Such a smoke-and-mirrors rhetorical attempt to place blame with undefined 'terroristic' others veils the truth behind a comprehensive 'punishment' of millions of unknowing – if not always innocent – civilians, multiplying the immorality associated with the manufacture of Shelley's fabulous creature to catastrophic proportions more reminiscent of the pandemic routing of civilisation in Shelley's later novel *The Last Man* (1826).[14] Unlike the narrow band of punishment meted out by Shelley's creature, the unethically bullish, yet fearful, self-righteousness running through the veins of the owners of political and military authority in Cronin's USA brings about what is feared: a tandem devastation of nationhood and global authority through 'international quarantine, forbidding any shipping or aircraft from approaching within 200 miles of the North American continent', sanctioned by the 'U.N. General Assembly' (232). In the uchronic, or 'what if', scenario of Cronin's America, the vampiric is seeded in a literally as well as figuratively infected human criminal source, with the fraudulence displayed by those in authority a demonstration of how easily despotism might masquerade as democracy and how punishment expands to affect those beyond the obviously responsible.[15]

In contrast to Cronin's tale, the Promethean in Butler's *Fledgling* stems from an intra-vampiric source: the reactionary murder of those who are directly connected to a scientifically manipulated evolutionary leap towards the hybridising of vampires with human genetic material to enable them to survive and operate diurnally. The vampire Ina female Matthews, as the only surviving 'product' of a bio-engineering project, brings the scale in Butler's story closer to that encountered by Shelley's and Polidori's victims than Cronin's. Butler's tale of scientific enterprise places the hybridised vampire Matthews in a nuanced role closer to that of Shelley's creature, while her three '350 years old, and biology fascinated' (77–78) vampire eldermothers can be jointly considered in the creative Frankensteinian role. Paralleling Frankenstein's initially benevolent intentions, Matthews' eldermothers create a photo-resistant species variant able to function in daylight, their research in genetic science 'integrat[ing] […] human DNA with [their] own' (77). Consequently, Matthews functions as the focus for violent animosity on the part of particular unhybridised Ina vampires: she is 'burned and shot' (77), just as Shelley's creature is 'dashed […] and struck' (135). Although both hybrid vampire and creature are portrayed as persecuted beings, where Shelley's narrative is determined by the creature's personalised grievances (aimed, as they are, squarely at his creator-father Victor Frankenstein), Butler's tale climaxes in an intra-vampiric judicial questioning of the violence initiated against her, as well as those associated with her, because of her chromosomally customised status. Shelley's creature and Butler's vampire may both be considered as aberrant entities but, where Shelley's creature appears driven by an outsider's extralegal self-determination, Butler's location of Matthews *within* a community allows for a lawfully navigated redress of prejudicial behaviours extended towards her. Ultimately, Butler's positioning of Matthews as nearer creature than creator affords her a crucial narrative escape route from the deadly punishment exacted on her eldermothers.

Returning to Cronin's *The Passage*, the novel offers an open-ended reinterpretation of vampirism that moves away from a Polidorian reliance on uncanny and alluring individuality. No longer human but far from the supernatural of Polidori's Ruthven, Cronin's vampires are products of experimentation and, as with Butler's Ina, no longer immortal but extremely long-lived. For Cronin, mass infection is not only thematically pervasive but also firmly associates his vampires – dehumanised as a 'bunch of ugly bastards' (69) – with the downfall of a global human dominance. Cronin's vampires are 'a roiling mass' (532) of semi-zombified parasites with chiropteran and insectoid characteristics. Their behaviours, including 'hanging upside down' (532) and making 'a wet clicking from deep in their throats' (69), are indicative of their vampirism as well as suggestive of their status as unnatural vectors of infection (these behaviours linking the 'roiling mass' back to the characteristics of those Bolivian bats exploited as sources for the infection of a multitude of test subjects).[16] These vampires, as the animalistic byproducts of scientific miscalculation, are intended to be prototypes for indefatigable, fast and self-repairing super-soldiers, aligning them with Shelley's creature, whose design results from Frankenstein's crafting of a 'new species' of creature to 'renew life where death had apparently devoted the body to corruption' (54). Cronin's list of guinea pigs for covert laboratory testing, including death-row criminals and a kidnapped young girl as the latest in a line of host subjects for 'an experimental drug therapy' (40), is a litany of corpses, nonchalantly catalogued as 'about three hundred dead monkeys, who knew how many dogs and pigs, [and] half a dozen dead homeless guys' (87).[17]

The endeavours of Cronin's scientific characters lead to a destruction that consigns America to little more than academic source material. The 'A.V.' (After Vampires) years are examined as mere historical artefacts at the 'Third Global Conference on the North American Quarantine Period' (250) a millennium after the first vampires escape their incarceration at a covert military laboratory. Just as Frankenstein's creature is intended to bring hope but brings about misery and death, what is intended to solidify US global (military) authority gives rise to rapid quarantining and a nation's downfall.

This Frankensteinian contagion central to Cronin's vampire pandemic stems from the fictional scientific research of Jonas Lear, a professor in the 'Department of Molecular and Cellular Biology [at] Harvard University' (18). Cronin's tale of flawed experimentation echoes that of Shelley's

Frankenstein in its motivation: an emotive reaction to personal loss. For Cronin's story, this is the early death, after a 'long battle with lymphoma' (87), of Professor Lear's wife, Dr Elizabeth Macomb Lear. In contrast to Frankenstein's secret 'toils', Lear goes on to publish a paper in the '*Journal of Paleovirology*' identifying an obscure 'family of viruses, hidden away [...] that could, with the proper refinements, restore the thymus gland to its full and proper function' (18). This does not naturally suggest a preclusion to vampirically induced global catastrophe. Just as Frankenstein's monomaniacal imperative sees him work tirelessly to create a 'new species [that] would bless me as its creator' (54), Lear reasons, anthropocentrically, that 'an agent [...] etched over eons into human DNA' might hold a 'power that could be reactivated, refined, brought under control' (86), and ultimately cheat the problematics of human entropy. But, as with many scientific advances throughout human history, the benefits of this bat virus are quickly considered for military use and Professor Lear's scientific conjecturing is a stimulus for a deceitful politico-martial attempt to usurp vampirism for the continuation of American worldwide authority.

Cronin's vampirism taps into an early-twenty-first-century reality that sees America's 'watchdog' armed forces stretched to capacity by attempts to retain US authority in the face of global unrest, courtesy of clandestine experimentation instigated by a fictionalised, but quite plausible-sounding, branch of American military forces, the Special Weapons Division (233). Cronin constructs a speculative narrative based on the unethical commandeering, by a fictionalised version of the 'United States Army Medical Research Institute of Infectious Diseases (USAMRIID)' (18), of the work of a team of paleovirologists while they are on a research mission in Bolivia. A viral agent that can 'significantly lengthen human life span and increase physical robustness' (86), as well as slow ageing and prompt a 'hugely accelerated rate of cellular regeneration [...] curing *everything*' (41, 42), is misused for state-sanctioned violence. As self-appointed governor of global morality, Cronin's fictional USAMRIID demonstrates an innate hypocrisy in its creation of invincible soldiers to shore up America's global authority.

As part of his recourse to the pseudo-scientific, Cronin employs descriptions that include the necessity of safety protocols such as the use of biohazard suits, rigorous decontamination, and constant monitoring as forebodingly predictive acknowledgements that these 'test subjects' are 'just crawling with virus' (87). This increased accessibility to scientific advances emphasises that Cronin's military characters are hubristically exploiting the 'bunker bust[ing]' (183) potential of 'risky [...] vampire stuff' (86). Therefore, readers may not be surprised when this 'Special Weapons' operation to combine 'vampire stuff' with death-row criminals creates uncontrollable creatures intent on 'eat[ing] the very world' (182). However, the deliberate viral infection of a prepubescent girl, Amy Harper Bellafonte, takes the exploitation even further into the unpalatable.

The callousness of the character Colonel Sykes' request for a child on whom to experiment sees the prepubescent Bellafonte objectified, reduced to a neuter pronoun as the latest in a line of sentient 'expendables' for vivisection: 'The younger it was [...] the better it could fight off the virus, to bring it to a kind of stasis' (88–89). Unlike the virally enhanced death-row criminals, who kill millions of humans, Bellafonte's siding with what remains of (America's) humankind belies the frequently simplistic pigeon-holing of vampires as monstrous beings: she is the enigmatic 'Girl from Nowhere' character that, in Cronin's words, 'saves the world' and, in doing so, prevents a complete global routing of humans.[18] Thus, the manmade vampire pandemic central to *The Passage* unifies science and the supernatural, amplifying the Frankensteinian in a tale of catastrophic fallout from biological interference.

Like *Frankenstein*, *The Passage* is unmistakably censorious of vivisection. Experimentation on death-row criminals who, as with the reduction of Bellafonte to an 'it', are coldly dismissed as 'human recyclables' (88) is a reminder that the manipulation of vulnerable citizens in Cronin's tale, where it is 'easy [...] to make a human being disappear' (46), draws on a history of eugenics in America that dates from the early twentieth century. Harry H. Laughlin's *Eugenical Sterilization in the United States* (1922) was foundational for decisions regarding sterilisation of 'defective' humans, listed as including the mentally subnormal, the clinically insane, criminals, the blind, the deaf, and epileptics.[19] Cronin's military scientists continue these eugenic assumptions, with 'sub-human' criminals deemed suitable for experimentation. Institutionalised with no chance of being released, these characters are, to all intents, already socially undead.

Following the rise of these vampensteins, any remaining humans in Cronin's novel subsist in a state of perpetual hyper-vigilance, where only 'the combination of [...] lights and walls' (289) offer any security, and primitive routines display a social disruption brought about by the abject forms of these vampires.[20] The disruption of the known world by Cronin's vampenstein creations quickly turns tens of millions of US citizens into vampires, with the virus going on to mutate and kill billions of humans globally (aided by migratory birds as unwitting secondary vectors of infection). This is loosely hypothesised as 'One person taken up for every nine that died' (305). Despite this, after a vampirocene millennium, the third book in this series – *The City of Mirrors* (2016) – sees a cycling round to reset the social clock, with vampiric devastation leaving behind enough humans to allow for the possibility of a redemptive recolonisation of the former USA.[21]

As with the vampensteinian in Cronin's *The Passage*, Butler's *Fledgling* is a tale driven by a scientific impetus, but here it is the expansion of vampirism from the nocturnal norm into the human dominated daytime: 'Shori's families were experimenting with ways of using human DNA to enable us to walk in daylight' (294). Matthews represents a literal assimilation of humanity into the vampiric. Alongside her dependence on the pseudo-science of vampire–human genetic assimilation, Butler also defies the supernatural generic predominance of creating vampires from bitten humans that is commonplace in vampire fiction from Polidori onwards. As Matthews's vampire 'father' Iosif Petrescu makes clear, while apparently close enough to benefit from the integration of human genetic material, Butler's Ina vampires firmly remain 'another species' (67). Thus, as near-humans, Butler's Ina – even the genetically modified Matthews – are *born* as long-lived haemovores rather than *created* beings, as is Shelley's patchwork creature. This is reinforced by Matthews's clarification of the Ina vampiric condition. Despite a symbiotic co-dependence, she responds to her human sym Celia's musing that 'It doesn't seem fair that you can't convert [humans] like all the stories say' with a logical argument: 'If a dog bit a man, no one would expect the man to become a dog' (123). If Matthews can give birth to fertile offspring in line with fellow Ina females, then she carries the potential to become the source of a new subspecies of vampires, able to function during the day as easily as they do during the night.

This dovetailing of speculative science fiction and vampire fantasy is underlined in Butler's recourse to the biological term 'mutualistic symbiosis' to describe the reciprocal interaction between her vampires and their chosen humans. As the evolutionary biologist Nancy Moran describes, in symbiosis, 'both host and symbiont often evolve to accommodate one another [...] Many symbionts provide [...] their hosts with nutrients or defenses [and] may evolve to conserve or even to benefit [...] host[s].'[22] Until Matthews, Butler's human syms are necessary not only as food sources but also as intermediaries between vampire and human worlds – functioning during the day, the syms can safely conduct business on behalf of the Inas.

Such reasoning about what it means to be a modern Western vampire, specifically incorporating the biological through gene splicing, has Butler's interpretation of vampirism continuing a departure from supernatural authority in favour of the pseudo-scientific. Once again, a traditionally understood Gothic opposition between rationality and irrationality is collapsed into the vampenstein. Butler's absorption of traits from both *The Vampyre* and *Frankenstein* into a tale that revolves around Matthews's amnesiacal questioning and (re)learning of who and what she is finds an echo in Punter's characterisation of Frankenstein's creature as not 'inherently evil' but 'a *tabula rasa*, a being who will have [their] psyche formed by [their] contacts with circumstance'.[23] The amnesiac Matthews is an all-too-literal 'tabula rasa' whose burgeoning self-awareness is shown in her statement, 'I think I'm an experiment' (31). Matthews's situation as a hybridised being incites intra-vampiric persecution for embodying modifications that also speak of Butler's development of the wider vampire genre. In Matthews's (re)learning about her history and, through it, a wider cultural comprehension of vampirism, Butler rewrites the history of vampire fiction, placing her Ina as 'probably responsible for most vampire legends' (123). Matthews's consideration that vampires are traditionally 'undead [...] drink blood [...] have no reflection in mirrors [...] can become bats or wolves [...] turn other people into vampires' leads to a single question that also governs the existence of Shelley's creature: 'what was I?' (123). Even in its acknowledgement of a generic continuum, with references to the ur-text *Dracula* alongside the folkloric, Butler's narrative pushes at the boundaries of what it means to be part of a wider post-Polidorian vampiric mythos. Beginning with Butler opening her story from the confused position of Matthews's amnesia as she restarts her existence, Butler's narrative demonstrates her central character's need to understand (generic) history as well as her place within it.

Matthews's status as a vampire carrying African American human DNA is not only crucial to her personal journey from amnesia to understanding but pivotal to a narrative interrogation of racially motivated reactions and hostilities. These are made evident in three words uttered by the intra-vampiric antagonist Russell Silk; to him, Matthews is reduced to being a 'black mongrel bitch' (300). Race and racism are integral to *Fledgling* and central to Butler's primary focus on Matthews and her family as victims of extreme prejudice in their attempted eradication. Butler's novel is thematically dominated by Matthews's skin colour: 'Shori is black, and racists – probably Ina racists – don't like the idea that a good part of the answer to [vampiric] daytime problems is melanin' (147). As with Shelley's creature, Matthews is treated as a monstrous entity predominantly because of physical difference. The hostility directed towards Matthews comes from those who position themselves as 'pure' vampires such as the Silks (who are physically representative of the Ruthvenesque, being 'tall, ultrapale, lean, [and] wiry' (130) males). This extreme animosity is indicative of vampire fiction in a wider context: it is, to borrow from Butler, a 'mongrel' (173) genre, constantly adapted and repositioned to represent or critique contemporary cultural dominants.

In contrast to more traditional vampire narratives, such as Stoker's novel *Dracula*, where human perspectives are dominant, Matthews's first-person voice acts as the focus for readers. All that is known in the novel is communicated through Matthews's window of understanding. Matthews, who is first encountered as apparently powerless, alone and unknowing as she nihilistically acknowledges there is 'nothing in [her] world but hunger and pain, no other people, no other time, no other feelings' (1), contrasts with Polidori's Ruthven, who is, from the outset, *observed* and *discussed* as a 'nobleman', possessing the power to 'throw fear into [...] breasts' (246). Like Frankenstein's creature, Matthews starts from an unknowing, almost innocent, point where she is driven only by will and necessity, with no comprehension beyond the immediate. Thus, Butler's story revolves around Matthews as subject to mental, physical, and cultural darknesses that echo those suffered by Shelley's creature as he attempts to map out an existence as a unique entity within an unsympathetic (and often hostile) environment.

Butler's representation of Matthews's vampirism features violations perpetrated *against* rather than *by* a character who is initially portrayed as the antithesis of the mesmeric attractiveness of Polidori's Lord Ruthven. Where Matthews's first-person self-awareness, even at her most physically damaged, is couched in positivity, both Shelley's and Polidori's central antagonists are subject to negative human scrutiny. The daunting appearance of Frankenstein's creature testifies to his creator's repulsion for 'the wretch whom with such infinite pains and care [he] had endeavoured to form' (57), and Polidori's 'nobleman' Ruthven invites attention 'for his singularities', proximity to whom 'quell[s]' mirth (246). Matthews is only initially aware that she is 'burned – all over' (19), and it 'hurt[s] to move [...] even to breathe' (1), but quickly adopts a pragmatic perspective upon first viewing herself: she dispassionately observes she is 'scarred over every part of [her] body', with a head where 'the flesh had been damaged and the skull broken' (14). Where Frankenstein reacts to his creation with 'breathless horror and disgust' (57), Matthews's self-examination results in an objective self-assessment of 'a lean, sharp-faced, large-eyed, brown-skinned person', 'look[ing] like a child of about ten or eleven' but possessing 'canine teeth [...] longer and sharper than [any human's]' (18). Despite most elements of Matthews's appearance aligning with those traditionally understood as vampiric, her self-evaluation raises in her an uncharacteristic concern among vampires, namely that she might 'frighten people' (18).

Those Ina who encounter Matthews mainly react positively, and she even raises a frisson of excitement as a genetically engineered carrier of 'potentially life-saving human DNA that has [...] given her [...] the ability to walk in sunlight' (272). Diverging from this positivity, the self-serving hostility of the Silks (an all-male Ina clan) is aligned with that of Ruthvenesque vampires such as Stoker's Dracula, del Toro and Hogan's Master, or even Cronin's first death-row inmate to survive experimentation, the 'bullshit crazy' Giles Babcock (87). The Silks' archaic ideas, attitudes and behaviour patterns see them resorting to such actions as exploiting and expending their human syms in a manner much closer to that of Polidori's vampire than to that of their cohort. Alongside this conformity to more traditional vampiric characterisations, the Silks' intransigence towards Matthews corresponds to Frankenstein's symbolic abortion of his female creature as a coda to his creativity. Matthews's procreative potential, as well as her gradually returning self-awareness, evokes a reactionary response in the Silks which echoes the argument used by Frankenstein to justify the eradication of his female creation. What Shelley portrays as anxiety concerning 'a race of devils [that] would be propagated upon the earth' (165) reverberates in the somewhat less erudite Silks' argument for retaining species integrity used to excuse their murderous behaviour towards Matthews and her kin: 'What will she give us all? Fur? Tails?' (300).

The Silks' unwavering attachment to retaining an unmodified vampiric lineage is, through the rhetorical device of a courtroom trial and judgment, shown to be a dead end. Butler employs a courtroom interrogation to highlight the Silks' despicable behaviour, mimetic as it is of right-wing extremist irrationality in its perception of Matthews's existence as a hybrid. The Silks' irrationality leads to the massacre of eighty of Matthews's family and symbionts, alongside their unsuccessful attempts on her own life. Yet, despite a judicial decision falling in her favour, Matthews's narrative arc 'does not resolve [...] antagonism': she, too, ultimately fails to find a definite answer to the terrors she encounters and recognises the retention of a potential for irrational violence within herself; when facing Russell Silk at the Ina Council of Judgement, Matthews surmises, 'I could kill him [...] joyfully' (299).[24] Just as Shelley's creature is born from an act of scientific endeavour and lives an existence full not only of growing bitterness and aggression but, more importantly, of philosophical questioning and understanding, the vampire Matthews is *reborn* from an act of bigoted and irrational hostility stemming from her genetic alteration. But, as a vital departure from Shelley's narrative, Matthews finds acceptance among more enlightened Ina and human symbionts, allowing for a legitimate prosecution of her persecutors' prejudices towards the potential for change that endures within her body. Consequently, Matthews is a truly vampenstein creation, carrying traits that might be considered as both good and evil.

Combining the traits of predator and prey, Matthews's vampire–human hybridity might style her as a new Eve for a genre begun in earnest with Polidori's *The Vampyre* two centuries ago, demonstrating a generic mutability that reminds readers that vampire fiction is forever greater than the sum of its parts. Matthews is indeterminately positioned on a spectrum running from benevolence to monstrosity. Her questioning – 'I wonder how you can be honorable and still kill the innocent?' (309) – highlights the ambivalence of Matthews's status, her hybrid physical being, behaviour, thoughts, and morality at odds with traditional perceptions of vampirism. And so, although Ruthven may maintain an enduring fascination, vampire fiction, like Matthews, will continue to necessarily assimilate other generic and contextual DNA to preserve the species.

Consequently, two centuries after the romanticised individualism of Polidori's Gothic creation Lord Ruthven was conjured into being alongside Shelley's creature, the vampire genre has soundly assimilated a secular 'faith' in science as a means of lending plausibility to what once belonged wholly in the realm of the supernatural. Vampires are those supernatural creatures who remain driven by what Byron, in his fragment of a vampire tale that was to inspire Polidori, describes as an ever-changing 'cureless disquiet'.[25] It is, without doubt, thanks to the progenitory 1816 stormy summer holiday of Polidori *et al.* that we have the varied vampire fictions that have, over the intervening centuries, made us fearful as well as thoughtful.

Since Polidori introduced the 'peculiarities' (246) of Lord Ruthven, vampire fiction has adapted to reflect contemporaneous characteristics of Western culture, which has become increasingly dependent on, if not always trusting of, scientific advances. Modern readers, even if not *au fait* with what lies behind it, are familiar with much scientific terminology and, thus, are ready to suspend disbelief when faced with the use of jargon as a pseudo-rational bolster to superstitions that allow for the existence of vampires. Vampenstein fiction shows that, while the roots of vampire fiction may lie in Polidori's tale, narratives of the supernatural need to assimilate its presumed opposite, science, in order to flourish in a secularised and sophisticated modern Western culture. As Cronin's and Butler's stories reveal, the modification of superstition in vampire fiction by the introduction of scientific underpinning injects plausibility for a modern readership.

Just as Polidori's *The Vampyre* shifted popular conceptions of vampires away from the folkloric to socially sophisticated parasites, so too do vampires such as Cronin's and Butler's advance a continuing process of speciation. Modified through a genetic absorption of pseudo-science, Cronin's and Butler's vampires, whether 'virals' or 'Ina', belong to a vampire genre that incorporates changes that are more than just nominal. With stories such as Cronin's and Butler's abiding by an ever-increasing annexation of science, it would seem that a revision of Gothic taxonomy is needed, amalgamating the Polidorian paradigm and Shelley's pseudo-science into the novel subspecies of the vampenstein. As vampenstein examples, Cronin's and Butler's protagonists are double helixes twisting cod science and the supernatural around each other to draw on the contemporary alongside generic inheritances traceable to both Polidori and Shelley.

Notes

1 David Punter, *The Literature of Terror: A History of Gothic Fictions from 1765 to the Present Day*, 2 vols (London and New York: Longman, 1996), II: *The Modern Gothic*, p. 3.
2 John Polidori was a nineteenth-century would-be literato and personal medical doctor to George Gordon, Lord Byron. The association of these two even affected the original publication of *The Vampyre*, which was (possibly deliberately) misattributed to Byron. Also, not entirely coincidentally, the name of Polidori's vampire, Lord Ruthven, is borrowed from Lady Caroline Lamb's *Glenarvon* (1816). As Byron's rejected lover, Lamb based her central protagonist, Clarence de Ruthven (Lord Glenarvon), on Lord Byron.
3 John Polidori, *The Vampyre*, Appendix 1 in this volume, pp. 240–67 (p. 249); Mary Shelley, *Frankenstein; or, The Modern Prometheus*, ed. by M. K. Joseph (1831; Oxford: Oxford University Press, 1998), pp. 54, 55. All further references are to these editions in parentheses.
4 Polidori's vampire novella was inspired by the tale Byron told at the Villa Diodati (that came to his attention during their holiday in Switzerland, later published as 'A Fragment' (Appendix 2 in this volume)).
5 Richard Matheson, *I Am Legend* (1954; London: Gollancz, 2001), p. 135.
6 Guillermo del Toro and Chuck Hogan, *The Strain* (London: Harper Collins, 2009), p. 277.
7 Andrew J. Fox, *Fat White Vampire Blues* (New York: Ballantine Books, 2003), p. 204.
8 Matthews's vampire hybridity, with its incorporation of Black human DNA, updates the dynamics of the nineteenth-century tale *The Black Vampyre: A Legend of St Domingo* (1819), attributed to Uriah Derick D'Arcy and discussed in Chapter 8 in this volume. Butler integrates technology into a narrative that continues what is, almost two centuries after D'Arcy's tale, a necessary positioning of slavery and predation as thematically central.
9 Octavia E. Butler, *Fledgling* (2005; New York: Warner Books, 2007). All references are to this edition as page numbers in parentheses in the text.
10 Just as Shelley positions Frankenstein as falsely assuming the role of creator-god in his gifting of life to his creature, according to Hope Moncrieff, Prometheus may be considered a usurper of creator-god status in 'kneading' humans out of clay before 'gifting' them fire (A. R. Hope Moncrieff, *Classical Mythology* (London: Senate, 1994), p. 17).
11 Frankenstein leaves readers in no doubt that the knowledge he possesses cannot be shared: in recounting his tale to Robert Walton, Frankenstein realises the folly of disseminating his scientific knowledge as he states, 'you expect to be informed of the secret with which I am acquainted; that cannot be' (53).
12 As an aside, in *Lost Souls* (1992), Poppy Z. Brite's vampires are also able to function beyond the night, with characters such as the vampire Molochai 'pictur[ing] himself gliding through shadowy afternoon halls' (p. 35). Brite evokes vampire–human hybridity from the outset in *Lost Souls*, not by way of

Butler's clinical genetic manipulation but by way of the sexually conventional ejaculation of potent vampire sperm into the fertile bodies of human women. The vampire Zillah impregnates the human Jessy with 'sperm [that] smelled like altars', resulting in a hybridised birth (Poppy Z. Brite, *Lost Souls* (1992; London and New York: Penguin, 1994), pp. 8–9).

13 Justin Cronin, *The Passage* (London: Orion, 2010), p. 33. All further references are to this edition as page numbers in parentheses in the text.

14 After *Frankenstein*, Shelley went on to write *The Last Man* (1826). This apocalyptic narrative, originally set over 250 years into an imagined future of 2092, presents a uchronic situation that goes beyond the dystopian to the point of evoking the final moments before the planet becomes post-Anthropocene. When read in light of the global damage meted out by COVID-19 since 2020, *The Last Man* might even be considered as prophetic (if exaggerated) in its descriptions of pandemic and societal breakdown.

15 'Uchronia has been defined in science-fiction criticism as "that amazing theme in which the author imagines [...] the representation of "an alternative present"' (Alessandro Portelli, *The Death of Luigi Trastulli and Other Stories: Form and Meaning in Oral History* (New York: SUNY Press, 1991), pp. 99–100).

16 Cronin's pseudo-scientific dependence on bats as vectors of contagion merges the influences of post-Polidorian vampire lore and the Frankensteinian in this vampenstein generic remodelling. The hubris of Cronin's military goes beyond social irresponsibility. Their placing of global martial hegemony above any degree of social accountability results, as with Frankenstein's creature, in an escape of index cases, here marking a catastrophic near-total devastation of assumed global anthropocentrism.

17 Cronin's link to bats as vectors of globally catastrophic infection again reads as a foreshadowing of COVID-19, with consideration during 2020's pandemic seeing academics such as Professor David Robertson suggesting more attention should be given to the monitoring of 'generalist virus[es] circulating in bats' (Helen Briggs, 'Covid-19: Infectious Coronaviruses "Circulating in Bats for Decades"', BBC News, 29 July 2020 www.bbc.co.uk/news/science-environment-53584936 [accessed 29 July 2020]).

18 '*The Passage*: Q & A with Justin Cronin', Justin Cronin Books http://enterthepassage.com/the-passage-q-a-with-justin-cronin/ [accessed 3 January 2013].

19 Harry H. Laughlin, *Eugenical Sterilization in the United States* (Chicago, IL: Psychopathic Laboratory of the Municipal Court of Chicago, 1922).

20 For discussion of the abject, see Julia Kristeva, *Powers of Horror: An Essay on Abjection*, trans. by Leon S. Roudiez (New York: Columbia University Press, 1982), p. 4.

21 Cronin's *The Passage* is the first in a series of three, the sequels being *The Twelve* (2012) and *The City of Mirrors* (2016).

22 Nancy A. Moran, 'Symbiosis', *Current Biology*, 16:20 (2006), 866–71 (p. 867).

23 Punter, *The Literature of Terror*, I: *The Gothic Tradition*, p. 108.

24 Jean Baudrillard, *The Spirit of Terrorism and Other Essays*, trans. by Chris Turner (London and New York: Verso, 2003), p. 58.

25 Byron, 'A Fragment', Appendix 2 in this volume, pp. 268–72 (p. 268).

Afterword: St Pancras Old Church and the mystery of Polidori's grave

Sam George

St Pancras Old Church has withstood the Industrial Revolution, Victorian improvements, wartime damage and an attack by Satanists in 1985. In 1847, the church was derelict and virtually in ruins until Victorian architects Robert Lewis Roumieu (1814–77) and Hugh Roumieu Gough (1843–1904) transformed the medieval building. They replaced the original West Tower with a large extension and added the Clock Tower to the south. It underwent further restorations of its ancient building in 1888 and 1925 (see Figure A.1).

If you enter through the magnificent wrought-iron gates you will find yourself at the entrance to St Pancras Old Church. The high altar, carved panels and old pulpit are ascribed to a pupil of Grinling Gibbons (1648–1721). The church appears mostly Victorian Neo-Norman in style. A remarkable *memento mori*, a reminder of death and the shortness of life, can be seen on the Offley family monument, which dates back to the 1660s and includes winged angel heads. The winged skull allows visitors to muse on the immortal soul's flight following its release from the dying body (see Figure A.2). On leaving the church, if you follow the uncanny path made up of broken headstones, you will find the church's undead motto, written by Jeremy Clarke: 'I am here in a place beyond desire or fear' (see Figure A.3). The motto suggests the transcending of death through visions of new worlds (though this is mysterious and ambiguous). From this you can head into the unsettled graveyard, John William Polidori's final resting place.

The churchyard ceased to be used as a graveyard in 1854, by which time it had accommodated centuries of burials. Records indicate that between 1689 and 1854, 88,000 burials took place, with over 32,000 in the final twenty-three years.[1] The picturesque and leafy setting is offset by beautiful gardens surrounding the church which were opened in 1877, the remains of two graveyards, St Pancras and an extension to the churchyard of St Giles in the Fields. Twice in the late 1800s the St Pancras Railway sought to acquire the land. Graves were subsequently disturbed and dismantled and the bodies exhumed. A great many unidentified human fragments were placed in a

Figure A.1 St Pancras Old Church exterior. © Sam George.

Figure A.2 *Memento mori*, St Pancras Old Church. © Sam George.

Figure A.3 Church motto, St Pancras Old Church. © Sam George.

deep pit and covered over. The architect at this time was Arthur Blomfield (1829–99) and his assistant was none other than the Victorian novelist Thomas Hardy (1840–1928), then a young man. Many of the disturbed gravestones were stacked under an ancient ash tree, which has become known as 'The Hardy Tree', an uncanny fusion of abandoned gravestones and the roots of a living tree (see Figure A.4).

The ash is associated in plant lore with death and resurrection. It has stood serene in divination and in folk medicine from the time of the Norse god Odin. The roots and branches of the ash Yggdrasil, the mighty world tree of Scandinavian mythology, united heaven, earth and hell. From its wood, after the death of the old gods, a new race would arise.[2] The ash tree in England has Gothic credentials: folklore has it that a failed crop of ash seeds or 'keys' portends a death within a year.[3] In Gothic circles it has become associated with witchcraft, hauntings and demonic curses, due to M. R. James's ghost story 'The Ash Tree' (1904).[4]

The unsettled, darkly beautiful ash tree at St Pancras has fascinated artists and writers down the years. What is remarkable is that John William Polidori's tomb is rumoured to be one of many unsettled graves under this uncanny tree. 'Poor Polidori', uncelebrated in life and unmemorialised in

Figure A.4 The Hardy Tree, St Pancras Old Church. © Sam George.

death, lies somewhere here in an unmarked grave. His death at the age of twenty-six is often considered a suicide, but the coroner's verdict of death 'by visitation of God' allowed a churchyard burial to take place (suicides were still being buried at crossroads as late as 1823).[5] Musing on Murgoci's study of the folkloric vampire, where dying unmarried, dying unforgiven by one's parents or dying a suicide or a murder victim can lead to a person returning as a vampire, I can't help but wonder if Polidori himself, in an act of revenge, his grave disturbed, could have returned a revenant to wander here.[6] Speculation on Polidori's afterlife dates back to William Michael Rossetti, who recorded his contact with Polidori's spirit in his seance diary of 25 November 1865.[7]

The church's theme of bloodsucking and mystery can be traced back to William Blake, another writer who has associations with this place. He placed the site of St Pancras Old Church at the centre of his mystical map of London. *The Ghost of a Flea*, a miniature painting by Blake, is an image of vampirism; the flea holds a cup for blood drinking and stares eagerly towards it. Surprisingly, it was created in 1819–20, thus around the very same year as Polidori's *Vampyre*.

Sadly, the tomb that has inspired the most Gothic tourism at the church is not Polidori's (which is forgotten); it belongs instead to Mary Wollstonecraft. Wollstonecraft, author of *A Vindication of the Rights of Woman*, published 1792, died on 10 September 1797, just ten days after giving birth to her daughter, Mary Godwin, who went on to write *Frankenstein* (1818). The poet Percy Bysshe Shelley was drawn to the teenage Mary due to her melancholy habit of reading on her mother's grave. The graveyard was the scene of their courtship and Mary is rumoured to have succumbed to Shelley, an advocate of free love, in this very spot (see Figure A.5).

Figure A.5 Mary Wollstonecraft Godwin's tomb, St Pancras Old Church. © Sam George.

The monument can still be seen but the remains of Mary's parents, William Godwin and Wollstonecraft, are no longer buried here; with the disruption of the railway, the family removed them to Bournemouth.[8] The Gothic history of the church had only just begun, however; Dickens set his body-snatching scene in *A Tale of Two Cities* (1859) in this churchyard. Even today, there is a contemporary fiction set in 1901 amid the graveyard which features the Hardy Tree, the site of Polidori's grave.[9] In this story, John Tweed, the newly installed vicar at St Pancras Old Church, writes to his wife Charlotte, complaining that:

> Every thief, vagabond and ne'er-do-well in London seems to have wound up buried at St P. Which would be all well and good, except that the digging up of late seems to have unearthed more than just bones. Judging by the number of lost souls drifting about the place in one spirit form or another, I would offer that many of my guests are far from welcome in Heaven.

The ash tree is again the focus of Tweed's letter of December 1859:

> More missing headstones. Increasingly certain of connection with my guests. Today I traced strange lines of disturbed earth across the graveyard. Each lead to the ash tree. Are they being dragged there? And then where? The ash tree itself is looking increasingly unhealthy, possibly diseased. I don't like to get too close to it.

> If I hadn't seen such as I have seen these past months, I may not have trusted my eyes, but trust them I must. I shall record it in as plain a manner as I know how: By the light of the moon last night, I saw a gravestone, moving with some speed, and quite of its own accord, across the graveyard. It hurtled towards the ash tree, at the base of which it disappeared, as if plunging into the very bowels of the tree.

The ash tree, it seems, has become a portal for the restless dead, a veritable hell mouth!! Tweed's descendants are driven to bury a large Bible among the roots of the disturbed tree in an attempt to stave off its demonic curse.

This same tree, the St Pancras ash tree, the Hardy Tree, holds the secret to Polidori's grave. In December 2022, just over 200 years after his burial, it collapsed suddenly in a storm; the stacked gravestones remained entirely intact.[10] The turbulent Gothic history of St Pancras Old Church and Polidori's lost remains serve as a metaphor for his life and work; this volume unearths his unjustly buried legacy.

(With thanks to Father James Elston.)

Notes

1 See *A Walk in the Past* (London: St Pancras Old Church, no date), p. 4.
2 The mighty ash tree Yggdrasil is discussed widely in Neil Gaiman's *Norse Mythology* (London: Bloomsbury, 2017), pp. 23–31.
3 It is reported that no ash tree in England bore keys in 1648, the year before the execution of Charles I. See Margaret Baker, *The Folklore of Plants* (Oxford: Shire, 1969), p. 19.
4 M. R. James, 'The Ash Tree' [1904], in *Collected Ghost Stories*, ed. by Darryl Jones (Oxford: Oxford University Press, 2011), pp. 35–48.
5 See my research on the folklore of crossroads, 'Vampire at the Crossroads', Open Graves, Open Minds, 2 July 2018 www.opengravesopenminds.com/ogom-research/vampire-at-the-crossroads/ [accessed 7 May 2023]. For Polidori's death, see Henry R. Viets, '"By the Visitation of God": The Death of John William Polidori', *British Medical Journal* (1961), 1773–75. D. L. Macdonald argues that the jurors had known Polidori at Ampleforth School and that the coroner acted out of sympathy for the family (*Poor Polidori: A Critical Biography of the Author of 'The Vampyre'* (Toronto, ON: University of Toronto Press, 1991), p. 237).
6 Agnes Murgoci, 'The Vampire in Roumania', *Folklore*, 86 (1926), 320–49.
7 See Macdonald, *Poor Polidori*, pp. 240–41, and Chapter 2 in this volume.
8 Mary Shelley was buried with the remains of Shelley's heart in St Peter's Churchyard, Bournemouth. The remains of her parents, William Godwin and Mary Wollstonecraft, were moved to the same plot in 1851 when St Pancras Churchyard was broken up for the railway. See Sam George, 'Gothic Hearts: A Love Story', Open Graves, Open Minds, 14 February 2023 www.opengravesopenminds.com/ogom-research/lost-hearts-a-gothic-love-story/ [accessed 7 May 2023].
9 'Exit Strategy for a Restless Dead: The Hell Tree of St Pancras', Portals of London, 20 January 2017 https://portalsoflondon.com/2017/01/20/the-hell-tree-of-st-pancras/ [accessed 7 May 2023].
10 See John Sutherland and Kevin Rawlinson, 'Gravestone-Encircled "Hardy Tree" Falls in London', *The Guardian*, 27 December 2022 www.theguardian.com/uk-news/2022/dec/27/historic-hardy-tree-falls-in-london [accessed 7 May 2023].

Appendix 1

John William Polidori, *The Vampyre*

The Vampyre; A Tale. By John William Polidori

Extract of a Letter from Geneva

'I breathe freely in the neighbourhood of this lake; the ground upon which I tread has been subdued from the earliest ages; the principal objects which immediately strike my eye, bring to my recollection scenes, in which man acted the hero and was the chief object of interest. Not to look back to earlier times of battles and sieges, here is the bust of Rousseau[1]—here is a house with an inscription denoting that the Genevan philosopher first drew breath under its roof.[2] A little out of the town is Ferney, the residence of Voltaire;[3] where that wonderful, though certainly in many respects contemptible, character, received, like the hermits of old, the visits of pilgrims, not only from his own nation, but from the farthest boundaries of Europe. Here too is Bonnet's[4] abode, and, a few steps beyond, the house of that astonishing woman Madame de Stael:[5] perhaps the first of her sex, who has really proved its often claimed equality with, the nobler man. We have before had women who have written interesting novels and poems, in which their tact at observing drawing-room characters has availed them; but never since the days of Heloise[6] have those faculties which are peculiar to man, been developed as the possible inheritance of woman. Though even here, as in the case of Heloise, our sex have not been backward in alledging the existence of an Abeilard[7] in the person of M. Schlegel[8] as the inspirer of her works. But to proceed: upon the same side of the lake, Gibbon, Bonnivard, Bradshaw,[9] and others mark, as it were, the stages for our progress; whilst upon the other side there is one house, built by Diodati, the friend of Milton,[10] which has contained within its walls, for several months, that poet whom we have so often read together, and who—if human passions remain the same, and human feelings, like chords, on being swept by nature's impulses shall vibrate as before—will be placed by posterity in the first rank of our English Poets. You must have heard, or the Third Canto of Childe Harold[11] will have informed you, that Lord Byron resided many months in this neighbourhood.

I went with some friends a few days ago, after having seen Ferney, to view this mansion. I trod the floors with the same feelings of awe and respect as we did, together, those of Shakespeare's dwelling at Stratford. I sat down in a chair of the saloon, and satisfied myself that I was resting on what he had made his constant seat. I found a servant there who had lived with him; she, however, gave me but little information. She pointed out his bed-chamber upon the same level as the saloon and dining-room, and informed me that he retired to rest at three, got up at two, and employed himself a long time over his toilette; that he never went to sleep without a pair of pistols and a dagger by his side, and that he never ate animal food. He apparently spent some part of every day upon the lake in an English boat. There is a balcony from the saloon which looks upon the lake and the mountain Jura; and I imagine, that it must have been hence, he contemplated the storm so magnificently described in the Third Canto; for you have from here a most extensive view of all the points he has therein depicted. I can fancy him like the scathed pine, whilst all around was sunk to repose, still waking to observe, what gave but a weak image of the storms which had desolated his own breast.

> The sky is changed!—and such a change; Oh, night!
> And storm and darkness, ye are wond'rous strong,
> Yet lovely in your strength, as is the light
> Of a dark eye in woman! Far along
> From peak to peak, the rattling crags among,
> Leaps the live thunder! Not from one lone cloud,
> But every mountain now hath found a tongue,
> And Jura answers thro' her misty shroud,
> Back to the joyous Alps who call to her aloud!
> And this is in the night:—Most glorious night!
> Thou wert not sent for slumber! let me be
> A sharer in thy far and fierce delight,—
> A portion of the tempest and of thee!
> How the lit lake shines a phosphoric sea,
> And the big rain comes dancing to the earth!
> And now again 'tis black,—and now the glee
> Of the loud hills shakes with its mountain mirth,
> As if they did rejoice o'er a young earthquake's birth,
> Now where the swift Rhine cleaves his way between
> Heights which appear, as lovers who have parted
> In haste, whose mining depths so intervene,
> That they can meet no more, tho' broken hearted;
> Tho' in their souls which thus each other thwarted,
> Love was the very root of the fond rage
> Which blighted their life's bloom, and then departed—
> Itself expired, but leaving them an age
> Of years all winter—war within themselves to wage.[12]

I went down to the little port, if I may use the expression, wherein his vessel used to lay, and conversed with the cottager, who had the care of it. You may smile, but I have my pleasure in thus helping my personification of the individual I admire, by attaining to the knowledge of those circumstances which were daily around him. I have made numerous enquiries in the town concerning him, but can learn nothing. He only went into society there once, when M. Pictet took him to the house of a lady to spend the evening. They say he is a very singular man, and seem to think him very uncivil. Amongst other things they relate, that having invited M. Pictet and Bonstetten[13] to dinner, he went on the lake to Chillon, leaving a gentleman who travelled with him to receive them and make his apologies. Another evening, being invited to the house of Lady D —— H ——,[14] he promised to attend, but upon approaching the windows of her ladyship's villa, and perceiving the room to be full of company, he set down his friend, desiring him to plead his excuse, and immediately returned home. This will serve as a contradiction to the report which you tell me is current in England, of his having been avoided by his countrymen on the continent. The case happens to be directly the reverse, as he has been generally sought by them, though on most occasions, apparently without success. It is said, indeed, that upon paying his first visit at Coppet,[15] following the servant who had announced his name, he was surprised to meet a lady carried out fainting; but before he had been seated many minutes, the same lady, who had been so affected at the sound of his name, returned and conversed with him a considerable time—such is female curiosity and affectation! He visited Coppet frequently, and of course associated there with several of his countrymen, who evinced no reluctance to meet him whom his enemies alone would represent as an outcast.

Though I have been so unsuccessful in this town, I have been more fortunate in my enquiries elsewhere. There is a society three or four miles from Geneva, the centre of which is the Countess of Breuss,[16] a Russian lady, well acquainted with the *agrémens de la Société*,[17] and who has collected them round herself at her mansion. It was chiefly here, I find, that the gentleman who travelled with Lord Byron, as physician, sought for society. He used almost every day to cross the lake by himself, in one of their flat-bottomed boats, and return after passing the evening with his friends, about eleven or twelve at night, often whilst the storms were raging in the circling summits of the mountains around. As he became intimate, from long acquaintance, with several of the families in this neighbourhood, I have gathered from their accounts some excellent traits of his lordship's character, which I will relate to you at some future opportunity. I must, however, free him from one imputation attached to him—of having in his house two sisters as the partakers of his revels. This is, like many other charges which have been brought against his lordship, entirely destitute of truth. His only companion was the physician I have already mentioned. The report originated from the following circumstance: Mr. Percy Bysshe Shelly, a gentleman well known for extravagance of doctrine, and for his daring, in their profession, even to sign himself with the title of ἄθεος in the Album at Chamouny,[18] having taken a house below, in which he resided with Miss M. W. Godwin and Miss Clermont, (the daughters of the celebrated Mr. Godwin)[19] they were frequently visitors at Diodati, and were often seen upon the lake with his Lordship, which gave rise to the report, the truth of which is here positively denied.[20]

Among other things which the lady, from whom I procured these anecdotes, related to me, she mentioned the outline of a ghost story by Lord Byron. It appears that one evening Lord B., Mr. P. B. Shelly, the two ladies and the gentleman before alluded to, after having perused a German work, which was entitled Phantasmagoriana,[21] began relating ghost stories; when his lordship having recited the beginning of Christabel,[22] then unpublished, the whole took so strong a hold of Mr. Shelly's mind, that he suddenly started up and ran out of the room. The physician and Lord Byron followed, and discovered him leaning against a mantle-piece, with cold drops of perspiration trickling down his face. After having given him something to refresh him, upon enquiring into the cause of his alarm, they found that his wild imagination having pictured to him the bosom of one of the ladies with eyes (which was reported of a lady in the neighbourhood where he lived) he was obliged to leave the room in order to destroy the impression. It was afterwards proposed, in the course of conversation, that each of the company present should write a tale depending upon some supernatural agency, which was undertaken by Lord B., the physician, and Miss M. W. Godwin.[23] My friend, the lady above referred to, had in her possession the outline of each of these stories; I obtained them as a great favour, and herewith forward them to you, as I was assured you would feel as much curiosity as myself, to peruse the *ebauches*[24] of so great a genius, and those immediately under his influence.'

The Vampyre

Introduction

THE superstition upon which this tale is founded is very general in the East.[25] Among the Arabians it appears to be common: it did not, however, extend itself to the Greeks until after the establishment of Christianity; and it has only assumed its present form since the division of the Latin and Greek churches; at which time, the idea becoming prevalent, that a Latin body could not corrupt if buried in their territory, it gradually increased, and formed the subject of many wonderful stories, still extant, of the dead rising from their graves, and feeding upon the blood of the young and beautiful. In the West it spread, with some slight variation, all over Hungary, Poland, Austria, and Lorraine, where the belief existed, that vampyres nightly imbibed a certain portion of the blood of their victims, who became emaciated, lost their strength, and speedily died of consumptions; whilst these human blood-suckers fattened—and their veins became distended to such a state of repletion, as to cause the blood to flow from all the passages of their bodies, and even from the very pores of their skins.

In the London Journal, of March, 1732, is a curious, and, of course, *credible* account of a particular case of vampyrism, which is stated to have occurred at Madreyga, in Hungary. It appears, that upon an examination of the commander-in-chief and magistrates of the place, they positively and unanimously affirmed, that, about five years before, a certain Heyduke, named Arnold Paul,[26] had been heard to say, that, at Cassovia, on the frontiers of the Turkish Servia, he had been tormented by a vampyre, but had found a way to rid himself of the evil, by eating some of the earth out of the vampyre's grave, and rubbing himself with his blood. This precaution, however, did not prevent him from becoming a vampyre[27] himself; for, about twenty or thirty days after his death and burial, many persons complained of having been tormented by him, and a deposition was made, that four persons had been deprived of life by his attacks. To prevent further mischief, the inhabitants having consulted their Hadagni,[28] took up the body, and found it (as is supposed to be usual in cases of vampyrism) fresh, and entirely free from corruption, and emitting at the mouth, nose, and ears, pure and florid blood. Proof having been thus obtained, they resorted to the accustomed remedy. A stake was driven entirely through the heart and body of Arnold Paul, at which he is reported to have cried out as dreadfully as if he had been alive. This done, they cut off his head, burned his body, and threw the ashes into his grave. The same measures were adopted with the corses of those persons who had previously died from vampyrism, lest they should, in their turn, become agents upon others who survived them.

This monstrous rodomontade is here related, because it seems better adapted to illustrate the subject of the present observations than any other instance which could be adduced. In many parts of Greece it is considered as a sort of punishment after death, for some heinous crime committed whilst in existence, that the deceased is not only doomed to vampyrise, but compelled to confine his infernal visitations solely to those beings he loved most while upon earth – those to whom he was bound by ties of kindred and affection.—A supposition alluded to in the 'Giaour'.[29]

But first on earth, as Vampyre sent,
Thy corse shall from its tomb be rent;
Then ghastly haunt the native place,
And suck the blood of all thy race;
There from thy *daughter, sister, wife*,
At midnight drain the stream of life;
Yet loathe the banquet, which perforce
Must feed thy livid living corse,
Thy victims, ere they yet expire,
Shall know the demon for their sire;
As cursing thee, thou cursing them,
Thy flowers are withered on the stem.
But one that for *thy crime* must fall,
The youngest, best beloved of all,
Shall bless thee with a *father*'s name—
That word shall wrap thy heart in flame!
Yet thou must end thy task and mark
Her cheek's last tinge—her eye's last spark,
And the last glassy glance must view
Which freezes o'er its lifeless blue;
Then with unhallowed hand shall tear
The tresses of her yellow hair,
Of which, in life a lock when shorn
Affection's fondest pledge was worn –
But now is borne away by thee
Memorial of thine agony!
Yet with thine own best blood shall drip;
Thy gnashing tooth, and haggard lip;
Then stalking to thy sullen grave,
Go – and with Gouls and Afrits[30] rave,
Till these in horror shrink away
From spectre more accursed than they.[31]

Mr. Southey has also introduced in his wild but beautiful poem of 'Thalaba',[32] the vampyre corse of the Arabian maid Oneiza, who is represented as having returned from the grave for the purpose of tormenting him she best loved whilst in existence. But this cannot be supposed to have resulted from the sinfulness of her life, she being pourtrayed throughout the whole of the tale as a complete type of purity and innocence. The veracious Tournefort[33] gives a long account in his travels of several astonishing cases of vampyrism, to which he pretends to have been an eyewitness; and Calmet,[34] in his great work upon this subject, besides a variety of anecdotes, and traditionary narratives illustrative of its effects, has put forth some learned dissertations, tending to prove it to be a classical, as well as barbarian error.

Many curious and interesting notices on this singularly horrible superstition might be added; though the present may suffice for the limits of a note, necessarily devoted to explanation, and which may now be concluded by merely remarking, that though the term Vampyre is the one in most general acceptation, there are several others synonymous with it, made use of in various parts of the world: as Vroucolocha, Vardoulacha, Goul, Broucoloka, &c.

The Vampyre

IT happened that in the midst of the dissipations attendant upon a London winter, there appeared at the various parties of the leaders of the *ton*[35] a nobleman, more remarkable for his singularities, than his rank. He gazed upon the mirth around him, as if he could not participate therein. Apparently, the light laughter of the fair only attracted his attention, that he might by a look quell it, and throw fear into those breasts where thoughtlessness reigned. Those who felt this sensation of awe, could not explain whence it arose: some attributed it to the dead grey eye, which, fixing upon the object's face, did not seem to penetrate, and at one glance to pierce through to the inward workings of the heart; but fell upon the cheek with a leaden ray that weighed upon the skin it could not pass.[36] His peculiarities caused him to be invited to every house; all wished to see him, and those who had been accustomed to violent excitement, and now felt the weight of ennui, were pleased at having something in their presence capable of engaging their attention. In spite of the deadly hue of his face,[37] which never gained a warmer tint, either from the blush of modesty, or from the strong emotion of passion, though its form and outline were beautiful, many of the female hunters after notoriety attempted to win his attentions, and gain, at least, some marks of what they might term affection: Lady Mercer,[38] who had been the mockery of every monster shewn in drawing-rooms since her marriage, threw herself in his way, and did all but put on the dress of a mountebank,[39] to attract his notice:—though in vain:—when she stood before him, though his eyes were apparently fixed upon her's, still it seemed as if they were unperceived;—even her unappalled impudence was baffled, and she left the field. But though the common adultress could not influence even the guidance of his eyes, it was not that the female sex was indifferent to him: yet such was the apparent caution with which he spoke to the virtuous wife and innocent daughter, that few knew he ever addressed himself to females. He had, however, the reputation of a winning tongue; and whether it was that it even overcame the dread of his singular character, or that they were moved by his apparent hatred of vice, he was as often among those females who form the boast of their sex from their domestic virtues, as among those who sully it by their vices.

About the same time, there came to London a young gentleman of the name of Aubrey:[40] he was an orphan left with an only sister in the possession of great wealth, by parents who died while he was yet in childhood. Left also to himself by guardians, who thought it their duty merely to take care of his fortune, while they relinquished the more important charge of his mind to the care of mercenary subalterns, he cultivated more his imagination than his judgment. He had, hence, that high romantic feeling of honour and candour, which daily ruins so many milliners' apprentices. He believed all to sympathise with virtue, and thought that vice was thrown in by Providence merely for the picturesque effect of the scene, as we see in romances:[41] he thought that the misery of a cottage merely consisted in the vesting of clothes, which were as warm, but which were better adapted to the painter's eye by their irregular folds and various coloured patches. He thought, in fine, that the dreams of poets were the realities of life. He was handsome, frank, and rich: for these reasons, upon his entering into the gay circles, many mothers surrounded him, striving which should describe with least truth their languishing or romping favourites: the daughters at the same time, by their brightening countenances when he approached, and by their sparkling eyes, when he opened his lips, soon led him into false notions of his talents and his merit. Attached as he was to the romance of his solitary hours, he was startled at finding, that, except in the tallow and wax candles that flickered, not from the presence of a ghost, but from want of snuffing, there was no foundation in real life for any of that congeries of pleasing pictures and descriptions contained in those volumes, from which he had formed his study. Finding, however, some compensation in his gratified vanity, he was about to relinquish his dreams, when the extraordinary being we have above described, crossed him in his career.

He watched him; and the very impossibility of forming an idea of the character of a man entirely absorbed in himself, who gave few other signs of his observation of external objects, than the tacit assent to their existence, implied by the avoidance of their contact: allowing his imagination to picture every thing that flattered its propensity to extravagant ideas, he soon formed this object into the hero of a romance, and determined to observe the offspring of his fancy, rather than the person before him. He became acquainted with him, paid him attentions, and so far advanced upon his notice, that his presence was always recognised. He gradually learnt that Lord Ruthven's affairs were embarrassed,[42] and soon found, from the notes of preparation in ——— Street, that he was about to travel. Desirous of gaining some information respecting this singular character, who, till now, had only whetted his curiosity, he hinted to his guardians, that it was time for him to perform the tour,[43] which for many generations has been thought necessary to enable the young to take some rapid steps in the career of vice towards putting themselves upon an equality with the aged, and not allowing them to appear as if fallen from the skies, whenever scandalous intrigues are mentioned as the subjects of pleasantry or of praise, according to the degree of skill shewn in carrying them on. They consented: and Aubrey immediately mentioning his intentions to Lord Ruthven, was surprised to receive from him a proposal to join him. Flattered by such a mark of esteem from him, who, apparently, had nothing in common with other men, he gladly accepted it, and in a few days they had passed the circling waters.

Hitherto, Aubrey had had no opportunity of studying Lord Ruthven's character, and now he found, that, though many more of his actions were exposed to his view, the results offered different conclusions from the apparent motives to his conduct. His companion was profuse in his liberality;—the idle, the vagabond, and the beggar, received from his hand more than enough to relieve their immediate wants. But Aubrey could not avoid remarking, that it was not upon the virtuous, reduced to indigence by the misfortunes attendant even upon virtue, that he bestowed his alms;—these were sent from the door with hardly suppressed sneers; but when the profligate came to ask something, not to relieve his wants, but to allow him to wallow in his lust, or to sink him still deeper in his iniquity, he was sent away with rich charity. This was, however, attributed by him to the greater importunity of the vicious, which generally prevails over the retiring bashfulness of the virtuous indigent. There was one circumstance about the charity of his Lordship, which was still more impressed upon his mind: all those upon whom it was bestowed, inevitably found that there was a curse upon it, for they were all either led to the scaffold, or sunk to the lowest and the most abject misery. At Brussels and other towns through which they passed, Aubrey was surprized at the apparent eagerness with which his companion sought for the centres of all fashionable vice; there he entered into all the spirit of the faro table:[44] he betted, and always gambled with success, except where the known sharper was his antagonist, and then he lost even more than he gained; but it was always with the same unchanging face, with which he generally watched the society around: it was not, however, so when he encountered the rash youthful novice, or the luckless father of a numerous family; then his very wish seemed fortune's law—this apparent abstractedness of mind was laid aside, and his eyes sparkled with more fire than that of the cat whilst dallying with the half-dead mouse. In every town, he left the formerly affluent youth, torn from the circle he adorned, cursing, in the solitude of a dungeon, the fate that had drawn him within the reach of this fiend; whilst many a father sat frantic, amidst the speaking looks of mute hungry children, without a single farthing of his late immense wealth, wherewith to buy even sufficient to satisfy their present craving. Yet he took no money from the gambling table; but immediately lost, to the ruiner of many, the last gilder he had just snatched from the convulsive grasp of the innocent: this might but be the result of a certain degree of knowledge, which was not, however, capable of combating the cunning of the more experienced. Aubrey often wished to represent this to his friend, and beg him to resign that charity and pleasure which proved the ruin of all, and did not tend to his own profit;—but he delayed it—for each day he hoped his friend would give him some opportunity of speaking frankly and openly to him; however, this never occurred. Lord Ruthven in his carriage, and amidst the various wild and rich scenes of nature, was always the same: his eye spoke less than his lip; and though Aubrey was near the object of his curiosity, he obtained no greater gratification from it than the constant excitement of vainly wishing to break that mystery, which to his exalted imagination began to assume the appearance of something supernatural.

They soon arrived at Rome, and Aubrey for a time lost sight of his companion; he left him in daily attendance upon the morning circle of an Italian countess, whilst he went in search of the memorials of another almost deserted city. Whilst he was thus engaged, letters arrived from England, which he opened with eager impatience; the first was from his sister, breathing nothing but affection; the others were from his guardians, the latter astonished him; if it had before entered into his imagination that there was an evil power resident in his companion, these seemed to give him sufficient reason for the belief. His guardians insisted upon his immediately leaving his friend, and urged, that his character was dreadfully vicious, for that the possession of irresistible powers of seduction, rendered his licentious habits more dangerous to society. It had been discovered, that his contempt for the adultress had not originated in hatred of her character; but that he had required, to enhance his gratification, that his victim, the partner of his guilt, should be hurled from the pinnacle of unsullied virtue, down to the lowest abyss of infamy and degradation: in fine, that all those females whom he had sought, apparently on account of their virtue, had, since his departure, thrown even the mask aside, and had not scrupled to expose the whole deformity of their vices to the public gaze.

Aubrey determined upon leaving one, whose character had not yet shown a single bright point on which to rest the eye. He resolved to invent some plausible pretext for abandoning him altogether, purposing, in the mean while, to watch him more closely, and to let no slight circumstances pass by unnoticed. He entered into the same circle, and soon perceived, that his Lordship was endeavouring to work upon the inexperience of the daughter of the lady whose house he chiefly frequented. In Italy, it is seldom that an unmarried female is met with in society; he was therefore obliged to carry on his plans in secret; but Aubrey's eye followed him in all his windings, and soon discovered that an assignation had been appointed, which would most likely end in the ruin of an innocent, though thoughtless girl. Losing no time, he entered the apartment of Lord Ruthven, and abruptly asked him his intentions with respect to the lady, informing him at the same time that he was aware of his being about to meet her that very night. Lord Ruthven answered, that his intentions were such as he supposed all would have upon such an occasion; and upon being pressed whether he intended to marry her, merely laughed. Aubrey retired; and, immediately writing a note, to say, that from that moment he must decline accompanying his Lordship in the remainder of their proposed tour, he ordered his servant to seek other apartments, and calling upon the mother of the lady, informed her of all he knew, not only with regard to her daughter, but also concerning the character of his Lordship. The assignation was prevented. Lord Ruthven next day merely sent his servant to notify his complete assent to a separation; but did not hint any suspicion of his plans having been foiled by Aubrey's interposition.

Having left Rome, Aubrey directed his steps towards Greece, and crossing the Peninsula, soon found himself at Athens. He then fixed his residence in the house of a Greek; and soon occupied himself in tracing the faded records of ancient glory upon monuments that apparently, ashamed of chronicling the deeds of freemen only before slaves, had hidden themselves beneath the sheltering soil or many coloured lichen. Under the same roof as himself, existed a being, so beautiful and delicate, that she might have formed the model for a painter wishing to pourtray on canvass the promised hope of the faithful in Mahomet's paradise, save that her eyes spoke too much mind for any one to think she could belong to those who had no souls.[45] As she danced upon the plain, or tripped along the mountain's side, one would have thought the gazelle[46] a poor type of her beauties; for who would have exchanged her eye, apparently the eye of animated nature, for that sleepy luxurious look of the animal suited but to the taste of an epicure. The light step of Ianthe[47] often accompanied Aubrey in his search after antiquities, and often would the unconscious girl, engaged in the pursuit of a Kashmere butterfly,[48] show the whole beauty of her form, floating as it were upon the wind, to the eager gaze of him, who forgot the letters he had just decyphered upon an almost effaced tablet, in the contemplation of her sylph-like figure. Often would her tresses falling, as she flitted around, exhibit in the sun's ray such delicately brilliant and swiftly fading hues, it might well excuse the forgetfulness of the antiquary, who let escape from his mind the very object he had before thought of vital importance to the proper interpretation of a passage in Pausanias.[49] But why attempt to describe charms which all feel, but none can appreciate?—It was innocence, youth, and beauty, unaffected by crowded drawing-rooms and stifling balls. Whilst he drew those remains of which he wished to preserve a memorial for his future hours, she would stand by, and watch the magic effects of his pencil, in tracing the scenes of her native place; she would then describe to him the circling dance upon the open plain, would paint, to him in all the glowing colours of youthful memory, the marriage pomp she remembered viewing in her infancy; and then, turning to subjects that had evidently made a greater impression upon her mind, would tell him all the supernatural tales of her nurse. Her earnestness and apparent belief of what she narrated, excited the interest even of Aubrey; and often as she told him the tale of the living vampyre, who had passed years amidst his friends, and dearest ties, forced every year, by feeding upon the life of a lovely female to prolong his existence for the ensuing months,[50] his blood would run cold, whilst he attempted to laugh her out of such idle and horrible fantasies; but Ianthe cited to him the names of old men, who had at last detected one living among themselves, after several of their near relatives and children had been found marked with the stamp of the fiend's appetite; and when she found him so incredulous, she begged of him to believe her, for it had been, remarked, that those who had dared to question their existence, always had some proof given, which obliged them, with grief and heartbreaking, to confess it was true. She detailed to him the traditional appearance of these monsters, and his horror was increased, by hearing a pretty accurate description of Lord Ruthven; he, however, still persisted in persuading her, that there could be no truth in her fears, though at the same time he wondered at the many coincidences which had all tended to excite a belief in the supernatural power of Lord Ruthven.

Aubrey began to attach himself more and more to Ianthe; her innocence, so contrasted with all the affected virtues of the women among whom he had sought for his vision of romance, won his heart; and while he ridiculed the idea of a young man of English habits, marrying an uneducated Greek girl, still he found himself more and more attached to the almost fairy form[51] before him. He would tear himself at times from her, and, forming a plan for some antiquarian research, he would depart, determined not to return until his object was attained; but he always found it impossible to fix his attention upon the ruins around him, whilst in his mind he retained an image that seemed alone the rightful possessor of his thoughts. Ianthe was unconscious of his love, and was ever the same frank infantile being he had first known. She always seemed to part from him with reluctance; but it was because she had no longer any one with whom she could visit her favourite haunts, whilst her guardian was occupied in sketching or uncovering some fragment which had yet escaped the destructive hand of time. She had appealed to her parents on the subject of Vampyres, and they both, with several present, affirmed their existence, pale with horror at the very name. Soon after, Aubrey determined to proceed upon one of his excursions, which was to detain him for a few hours; when they heard the name of the place, they all at once begged of him not to return at night, as he must necessarily pass through a wood, where no Greek would ever remain, after the day had closed, upon any consideration. They described it as the resort of the vampyres in their nocturnal orgies, and denounced the most heavy evils as impending upon him who dared to cross their path. Aubrey made light of their representations, and tried to laugh them out of the idea; but when he saw them shudder at his daring thus to mock a superior, infernal power, the very name of which apparently made their blood freeze, he was silent.

Next morning Aubrey set off upon his excursion unattended; he was surprised to observe the melancholy face of his host, and was concerned to find that his words, mocking the belief of those horrible fiends, had inspired them with such terror. When he was about to depart, Ianthe came to the side of his horse, and earnestly begged of him to return, ere night allowed the power of these beings to be put in action;—he promised. He was, however, so occupied in his research, that he did not perceive that day-light would soon end, and that in the horizon there was one of those specks which, in the warmer climates, so rapidly gather into a tremendous mass, and pour all their rage upon the devoted country.—He at last, however, mounted his horse, determined to make up by speed for his delay: but it was too late. Twilight, in these southern climates, is almost unknown; immediately the sun sets, night begins: and ere he had advanced far, the power of the storm was above—its echoing thunders had scarcely an interval of rest—its thick heavy rain forced its way through the canopying foliage, whilst the blue forked lightning seemed to fall and radiate at his very feet. Suddenly his horse took fright, and he was carried with dreadful rapidity through the entangled forest. The animal at last, through fatigue, stopped, and he found, by the glare of lightning, that he was in the neighbourhood of a hovel that hardly lifted itself up from the masses of dead leaves and brushwood which surrounded it. Dismounting, he approached, hoping to find some one to guide him to the town, or at least trusting to obtain shelter from the pelting of the storm. As he approached, the thunders, for a moment silent, allowed him to hear the dreadful shrieks of a woman mingling with the stifled, exultant mockery of a laugh, continued in one almost unbroken sound;—he was startled: but, roused by the thunder which again rolled over his head, he, with a sudden effort, forced open the door of the hut. He found himself in utter darkness: the sound, however, guided him. He was apparently unperceived; for, though he called, still the sounds continued, and no notice was taken of him. He found himself in contact with some one, whom he immediately seized; when a voice cried, 'Again baffled!' to which a loud laugh succeeded; and he felt himself grappled by one whose strength seemed superhuman: determined to sell his life as dearly as he could, he struggled; but it was in vain: he was lifted from his feet and hurled with enormous force against the ground:—his enemy threw himself upon him, and kneeling upon his breast, had placed his hands upon his throat—when the glare of many torches penetrating through the hole that gave light in the day, disturbed him;—he instantly rose, and, leaving his prey, rushed through the door, and in a moment the crashing of the branches, as he broke through the wood, was no longer heard. The storm was now still; and Aubrey, incapable of moving, was soon heard by those without. They entered; the light of their torches fell upon the mud walls, and the thatch loaded on every individual straw with heavy flakes of soot. At the desire of Aubrey they searched for her who had attracted him by her cries; he was again left in darkness; but what was his horror, when the light of the torches once more burst upon him, to perceive the airy form of his fair conductress brought in a lifeless corse. He shut his eyes, hoping that it was but a vision arising from his disturbed imagination; but he again saw the same form, when he unclosed them, stretched by his side. There was no colour upon her cheek, not even upon her lip; yet there was a stillness about her face that seemed almost as attaching as the life that once dwelt there:—upon her neck and breast was blood, and upon her throat were the marks of teeth having opened the vein:—to this the men pointed, crying, simultaneously struck with horror, 'A Vampyre! a Vampyre!' A litter was quickly formed, and Aubrey was laid by the side of her who had lately been to him the object of so many bright and fairy visions,[52] now fallen with the flower of life that had died within her. He knew not what his thoughts were—his mind was benumbed and seemed to shun reflection, and take refuge in vacancy—he held almost unconsciously in his hand a naked dagger of a particular construction, which had been found in the hut. They were soon met by different parties who had been engaged in the search of her whom a mother had missed. Their lamentable cries, as they approached the city, forewarned the parents of some dreadful catastrophe.—To describe their grief would be impossible; but when they ascertained the cause of their child's death, they looked at Aubrey, and pointed to the corse. They were inconsolable; both died broken-hearted.

    Aubrey being put to bed was seized with a most violent fever, and was often delirious; in these intervals he would call upon Lord Ruthven and upon Ianthe—by some unaccountable combination he seemed to beg of his former companion to spare the being he loved. At other times he would imprecate maledictions upon his head, and curse him as her destroyer. Lord Ruthven, chanced at this time to arrive at Athens, and, from whatever motive, upon hearing of the state of Aubrey, immediately placed himself in the same house, and became his constant attendant. When the latter recovered from his delirium, he was horrified and startled at the sight of him whose image he had now combined with that of a Vampyre; but Lord Ruthven, by his kind words, implying almost repentance for the fault that had caused their separation, and still more by the attention, anxiety, and care which he showed, soon reconciled him to his presence. His lordship seemed quite changed; he no longer appeared that apathetic being who had so astonished Aubrey; but as soon as his convalescence began to be rapid, he again gradually retired into the same state of mind, and Aubrey perceived no difference from the former man, except that at times he was surprised to meet his gaze fixed intently upon him, with a smile of malicious exultation playing upon his lips: he knew not why, but this smile haunted him. During the last stage of the invalid's recovery, Lord Ruthven was apparently engaged in watching the tideless waves raised by the cooling breeze, or in marking the progress of those orbs, circling, like our world, the moveless sun;—indeed, he appeared to wish to avoid the eyes of all.

Aubrey's mind, by this shock, was much weakened, and that elasticity of spirit which had once so distinguished him now seemed to have fled for ever. He was now as much a lover of solitude and silence as Lord Ruthven; but much as he wished for solitude, his mind could not find it in the neighbourhood of Athens; if he sought it amidst the ruins he had formerly frequented, Ianthe's form stood by his side—if he sought it in the woods, her light step would appear wandering amidst the underwood, in quest of the modest violet; then suddenly turning round, would show, to his wild imagination, her pale face and wounded throat, with a meek smile upon her lips. He determined to fly scenes, every feature of which created such bitter associations in his mind. He proposed to Lord Ruthven, to whom he held himself bound by the tender care he had taken of him during his illness, that they should visit those parts of Greece neither had yet seen. They travelled in every direction, and sought every spot to which a recollection could be attached: but though they thus hastened from place to place, yet they seemed not to heed what they gazed upon. They heard much of robbers, but they gradually began to slight these reports, which they imagined were only the invention of individuals, whose interest it was to excite the generosity of those whom they defended from pretended dangers. In consequence of thus neglecting the advice of the inhabitants, on one occasion they travelled with only a few guards, more to serve as guides than as a defence. Upon entering, however, a narrow defile, at the bottom of which was the bed of a torrent, with large masses of rock brought down from the neighbouring precipices, they had reason to repent their negligence; for scarcely were the whole of the party engaged in the narrow pass, when they were startled by the whistling of bullets close to their heads, and by the echoed report of several guns. In an instant their guards had left them, and, placing themselves behind rocks, had begun to fire in the direction whence the report came. Lord Ruthven and Aubrey, imitating their example, retired for a moment behind the sheltering turn of the defile: but ashamed of being thus detained by a foe, who with insulting shouts bade them advance, and being exposed to unresisting slaughter, if any of the robbers should climb above and take them in the rear, they determined at once to rush forward in search of the enemy. Hardly had they lost the shelter of the rock, when Lord Ruthven received a shot in the shoulder, which brought him to the ground. Aubrey hastened to his assistance; and, no longer heeding the contest or his own peril, was soon surprised by seeing the robbers' faces around him—his guards having, upon Lord Ruthven's being wounded, immediately thrown up their arms and surrendered.

By promises of great reward, Aubrey soon induced them to convey his wounded friend to a neighbouring cabin; and having agreed upon a ransom, he was no more disturbed by their presence—they being content merely to guard the entrance till their comrade should return with the promised sum, for which he had an order. Lord Ruthven's strength rapidly decreased; in two days mortification ensued, and death seemed advancing with hasty steps. His conduct and appearance had not changed; he seemed as unconscious of pain as he had been of the objects about him: but towards the close of the last evening, his mind became apparently uneasy, and his eye often fixed upon Aubrey, who was induced to offer his assistance with more than usual earnestness—'Assist me! you may save me—you may do more than that—I mean not my life, I heed the death of my existence as little as that of the passing day; but you may save my honour, your friend's honour.' — 'How? tell me how? I would do any thing,' replied Aubrey. —'I need but little—my life ebbs apace—I cannot explain the whole—but if you would conceal all you know of me, my honour were free from stain in the world's mouth—and if my death were unknown for some time in England—I—I—but life.'—'It shall not be known.'—'Swear!' cried the dying man, raising himself with exultant violence, 'Swear by all your soul reveres, by all your nature fears, swear that, for a year and a day you will not impart your knowledge of my crimes or death to any living being in any way, whatever may happen, or whatever you may see.'[53]—His eyes seemed bursting from their sockets: 'I swear!' said Aubrey; he sunk laughing upon his pillow, and breathed no more.

Aubrey retired to rest, but did not sleep; the many circumstances attending his acquaintance with this man rose upon his mind, and he knew not why; when he remembered his oath a cold shivering came over him, as if from the presentiment of something horrible awaiting him. Rising early in the morning, he was about to enter the hovel in which he had left the corpse, when a robber met him, and informed him that it was no longer there, having been conveyed by himself and comrades, upon his retiring, to the pinnacle of a neighbouring mount, according to a promise they had given his lordship, that it should be exposed to the first cold ray of the moon that rose after his death.[54] Aubrey astonished, and taking several of the men, determined to go and bury it upon the spot where it lay. But, when he had mounted to the summit he found no trace of either the corpse or the clothes, though the robbers swore they pointed out the identical rock on which they had laid the body. For a time his mind was bewildered in conjectures, but he at last returned, convinced that they had buried the corpse for the sake of the clothes.

Weary of a country in which he had met with such terrible misfortunes, and in which all apparently conspired to heighten that superstitious melancholy that had seized upon his mind, he resolved to leave it, and soon arrived at Smyrna. While waiting for a vessel to convey him to Otranto,[55] or to Naples, he occupied himself in arranging those effects he had with him belonging to Lord Ruthven. Amongst other things there was a case containing several weapons of offence, more or less adapted to ensure the death of the victim. There were several daggers and ataghans.[56] Whilst turning them over, and examining their curious forms, what was his surprise at finding a sheath apparently ornamented in the same style as the dagger discovered in the fatal hut—he shuddered—hastening to gain further proof, he found the weapon, and his horror may be imagined when he discovered that it fitted, though peculiarly shaped, the sheath he held in his hand. His eyes seemed to need no further certainty—they seemed gazing to be bound to the dagger; yet still he wished to disbelieve; but the particular form, the same varying tints upon the haft and sheath were alike in splendour on both, and left no room for doubt; there were also drops of blood on each.

He left Smyrna, and on his way home, at Rome, his first inquiries were concerning the lady he had attempted to snatch from Lord Ruthven's seductive arts. Her parents were in distress, their fortune ruined, and she had not been heard of since the departure of his lordship. Aubrey's mind became almost broken under so many repeated horrors; he was afraid that this lady had fallen a victim to the destroyer of Ianthe. He became morose and silent; and his only occupation consisted in urging the speed of the postilions, as if he were going to save the life of some one he held dear. He arrived at Calais; a breeze, which seemed obedient to his will, soon wafted him to the English shores; and he hastened to the mansion of his fathers, and there, for a moment, appeared to lose, in the embraces and caresses of his sister, all memory of the past. If she before, by her infantine caresses, had gained his affection, now that the woman began to appear, she was still more attaching as a companion.

Miss Aubrey had not that winning grace which gains the gaze and applause of the drawing-room assemblies. There was none of that light brilliancy which only exists in the heated atmosphere of a crowded apartment. Her blue eye was never lit up by the levity of the mind beneath. There was a melancholy charm about it which did not seem to arise from misfortune, but from some feeling within, that appeared to indicate a soul conscious of a brighter realm. Her step was not that light footing, which strays where'er a butterfly or a colour may attract—it was sedate and pensive. When alone, her face was never brightened by the smile of joy; but when her brother breathed to her his affection, and would in her presence forget those griefs she knew destroyed his rest, who would have exchanged her smile for that of the voluptuary? It seemed as if those eyes,—that face were then playing in the light of their own native sphere. She was yet only eighteen, and had not been presented to the world, it having been thought by her guardians more fit that her presentation should be delayed until her brother's return from the continent, when he might be her protector. It was now, therefore, resolved that the next drawing-room, which was fast approaching, should be the epoch of her entry into the 'busy scene.' Aubrey would rather have remained in the mansion of his fathers, and fed upon the melancholy which overpowered him. He could not feel interest about the frivolities of fashionable strangers, when his mind had been so torn by the events he had witnessed; but he determined to sacrifice his own comfort to the protection of his sister. They soon arrived in town, and prepared for the next day, which had been announced as a drawing-room.

The crowd was excessive—a drawing-room had not been held for a long time, and all who were anxious to bask in the smile of royalty, hastened thither. Aubrey was there with his sister. While he was standing in a corner by himself, heedless of all around him, engaged in the remembrance that the first time he had seen Lord Ruthven was in that very place—he felt himself suddenly seized by the arm, and a voice he recognized too well, sounded in his ear—'Remember your oath.'[57] He had hardly courage to turn, fearful of seeing a spectre that would blast him, when he perceived, at a little distance, the same figure which had attracted his notice on this spot upon his first entry into society. He gazed till his limbs almost refusing to bear their weight, he was obliged to take the arm of a friend, and forcing a passage through the crowd, he threw himself into his carriage, and was driven home. He paced the room with hurried steps, and fixed his hands upon his head, as if he were afraid his thoughts were bursting from his brain. Lord Ruthven again before him—circumstances started up in dreadful array—the dagger—his oath.—He roused himself, he could not believe it possible—the dead rise again!—He thought his imagination had conjured up the image his mind was resting upon. It was impossible that it could be real—he determined, therefore, to go again into society; for though he attempted to ask concerning Lord Ruthven, the name hung upon his lips, and he could not succeed in gaining information. He went a few nights after with his sister to the assembly of a near relation. Leaving her under the protection of a matron, he retired into a recess, and there gave himself up to his own devouring thoughts. Perceiving, at last, that many were leaving, he roused himself, and entering another room, found his sister surrounded by several, apparently in earnest conversation; he attempted to pass and get near her, when one, whom he requested to move, turned round, and revealed to him those features he most abhorred. He sprang forward, seized his sister's arm, and, with hurried step, forced her towards the street: at the door he found himself impeded by the crowd of servants who were waiting for their lords; and while he was engaged in passing them, he again heard that voice whisper close to him—'Remember your oath!'—He did not dare to turn, but, hurrying his sister, soon reached home.

    Aubrey became almost distracted. If before his mind had been absorbed by one subject, how much more completely was it engrossed, now that the certainty of the monster's living again pressed upon his thoughts. His sister's attentions were now unheeded, and it was in vain that she intreated him to explain to her what had caused his abrupt conduct. He only uttered a few words, and those terrified her. The more he thought, the more he was bewildered. His oath startled him;—was he then to allow this monster to roam, bearing ruin upon his breath, amidst all he held dear, and not avert its progress? His very sister might have been touched by him. But even if he were to break his oath, and disclose his suspicions, who would believe him? He thought of employing his own hand to free the world from such a wretch; but death, he remembered, had been already mocked. For days he remained in this state; shut up in his room, he saw no one, and ate only when his sister came, who, with eyes streaming with tears, besought him, for her sake, to support nature. At last, no longer capable of bearing stillness and solitude, he left his house, roamed from street to street, anxious to fly that image which haunted him. His dress became neglected, and he wandered, as often exposed to the noon-day sun as to the midnight damps. He was no longer to be recognized; at first he returned with the evening to the house; but at last he laid him down to rest wherever fatigue overtook him. His sister, anxious for his safety, employed people to follow him; but they were soon distanced by him who fled from a pursuer swifter than any—from thought. His conduct, however, suddenly changed. Struck with the idea that he left by his absence the whole of his friends, with a fiend amongst them, of whose presence they were unconscious, he determined to enter again into society, and watch him closely, anxious to forewarn, in spite of his oath, all whom Lord Ruthven approached with intimacy. But when he entered into a room, his haggard and suspicious looks were so striking, his inward shudderings so visible, that his sister was at last obliged to beg of him to abstain from seeking, for her sake, a society which affected him so strongly. When, however, remonstrance proved unavailing, the guardians thought proper to interpose, and, fearing that his mind was becoming alienated, they thought it high time to resume again that trust which had been before imposed upon them by Aubrey's parents.

Desirous of saving him from the injuries and sufferings he had daily encountered in his wanderings, and of preventing him from exposing to the general eye those marks of what they considered folly, they engaged a physician to reside in the house, and take constant care of him. He hardly appeared to notice it, so completely was his mind absorbed by one terrible subject. His incoherence became at last so great, that he was confined to his chamber. There he would often lie for days, incapable of being roused. He had become emaciated, his eyes had attained a glassy lustre;—the only sign of affection and recollection remaining displayed itself upon the entry of his sister; then he would sometimes start, and, seizing her hands, with looks that severely afflicted her, he would desire her not to touch him. 'Oh, do not touch him—if your love for me is aught, do not go near him!' When, however, she inquired to whom he referred, his only answer was, 'True! true!' and again he sank into a state, whence not even she could rouse him. This lasted many months: gradually, however, as the year was passing, his incoherences became less frequent, and his mind threw off a portion of its gloom, whilst his guardians observed, that several times in the day he would count upon his fingers a definite number, and then smile.

The time had nearly elapsed, when, upon the last day of the year, one of his guardians entering his room, began to converse with his physician upon the melancholy circumstance of Aubrey's being in so awful a situation, when his sister was going next day to be married. Instantly Aubrey's attention was attracted; he asked anxiously to whom. Glad of this mark of returning intellect, of which they feared he had been deprived, they mentioned the name of the Earl of Marsden. Thinking this was a young Earl whom he had met with in society, Aubrey seemed pleased, and astonished them still more by his expressing his intention to be present at the nuptials, and desiring to see his sister. They answered not, but in a few minutes his sister was with him. He was apparently again capable of being affected by the influence of her lovely smile; for he pressed her to his breast, and kissed her cheek, wet with tears, flowing at the thought of her brother's being once more alive to the feelings of affection. He began to speak with all his wonted warmth, and to congratulate her upon her marriage with a person so distinguished for rank and every accomplishment; when he suddenly perceived a locket upon her breast; opening it, what was his surprise at beholding the features of the monster who had so long influenced his life. He seized the portrait in a paroxysm of rage, and trampled it under foot. Upon her asking him why he thus destroyed the resemblance of her future husband, he looked as if he did not understand her—then seizing her hands, and gazing on her with a frantic expression of countenance, he bade her swear that she would never wed this monster, for he—. But he could not advance—it seemed as if that voice again bade him remember his oath—he turned suddenly round, thinking Lord Ruthven was near him but saw no one. In the meantime the guardians and physician, who had heard the whole, and thought this was but a return of his disorder, entered, and forcing him from Miss Aubrey, desired her to leave him. He fell upon his knees to them, he implored, he begged of them to delay but for one day. They, attributing this to the insanity they imagined had taken possession of his mind, endeavoured to pacify him, and retired.

Lord Ruthven had called the morning after the drawing-room, and had been refused with every one else. When he heard of Aubrey's ill health, he readily understood himself to be the cause of it; but when he learned that he was deemed insane, his exultation and pleasure could hardly be concealed from those among whom he had gained this information. He hastened to the house of his former companion, and, by constant attendance, and the pretence of great affection for the brother and interest in his fate, he gradually won the ear of Miss Aubrey. Who could resist his power? His tongue had dangers and toils to recount—could speak of himself as of an individual having no sympathy with any being on the crowded earth, save with her to whom he addressed himself;—could tell how, since he knew her, his existence, had begun to seem worthy of preservation, if it were merely that he might listen to her soothing accents;—in fine, he knew so well how to use the serpent's art,[58] or such was the will of fate, that he gained her affections. The title of the elder branch falling at length to him, he obtained an important embassy, which served as an excuse for hastening the marriage, (in spite of her brother's deranged state,) which was to take place the very day before his departure for the continent.

Aubrey, when he was left by the physician and his guardians, attempted to bribe the servants, but in vain. He asked for pen and paper; it was given him; he wrote a letter to his sister, conjuring her, as she valued her own happiness, her own honour, and the honour of those now in the grave, who once held her in their arms as their hope and the hope of their house, to delay but for a few hours that marriage, on which he denounced the most heavy curses. The servants promised they would deliver it; but giving it to the physician, he thought it better not to harass any more the mind of Miss Aubrey by, what he considered, the ravings of a maniac. Night passed on without rest to the busy inmates of the house; and Aubrey heard, with a horror that may more easily be conceived than described, the notes of busy preparation. Morning came, and the sound of carriages broke upon his ear. Aubrey grew almost frantic. The curiosity of the servants at last overcame their vigilance, they gradually stole away, leaving him in the custody of an helpless old woman. He seized the opportunity, with one bound was out of the room, and in a moment found himself in the apartment where all were nearly assembled. Lord Ruthven was the first to perceive him: he immediately approached, and, taking his arm by force, hurried him from the room, speechless with rage. When on the staircase, Lord Ruthven whispered in his ear—'Remember your oath, and know, if not my bride to day, your sister is dishonoured. Women are frail!' So saying, he pushed him towards his attendants, who, roused by the old woman, had come in search of him. Aubrey could no longer support himself; his rage not finding vent, had broken a blood-vessel, and he was conveyed to bed. This was not mentioned to his sister, who was not present when he entered, as the physician was afraid of agitating her. The marriage was solemnized, and the bride and bridegroom left London.

Aubrey's weakness increased; the effusion of blood produced symptoms of the near approach of death. He desired his sister's guardians might be called, and when the midnight hour had struck, he related composedly what the reader has perused—he died immediately after.

The guardians hastened to protect Miss Aubrey; but when they arrived, it was too late. Lord Ruthven had disappeared, and Aubrey's sister had glutted the thirst of a VAMPYRE!

Notes

1 'Rousseau': Jean-Jacques Rousseau (1712–78). Genevan *philosophe*, educationalist, novelist, and composer. Much concerned with the relationship between nature and culture and the origins of language and society.
2 In the original publication of *The Vampyre* in the *New Monthly Magazine* (April 1819), the 'Extract of a Letter', which preceded the tale, was preceded by a statement by the sub-editor, Alaric Watts. In addition, the tale was followed by 'An Account of Lord Byron's Residence' which is patently fictitious and most agree that it is not by Polidori (we have not included this here). The 'Extract of a Letter' itself has been attributed to various authors, including (by Byron among others) Polidori himself, though D. L. Macdonald thinks this unlikely (see Robert Morrison and Chris Baldick, eds, 'Preliminaries for *The Vampyre*', in *The Vampyre and Other Tales of the Macabre* (Oxford: Oxford University Press, 2008), p. 235). The *New Monthly Magazine* allegedly received the 'Extract' in a package that included *The Vampyre* itself 'from a friend travelling on the Continent', according to a prefatory note probably by the editor Alaric Watts (Morrison and Baldick, 'Preliminaries', p. 235). Patricia L. Skarda assumes without question that all the paratextual material published with the story is by Polidori and bases a dubious psychological reading on that ('Vampirism and Plagiarism: Byron's Influence and Polidori's Practice', *Studies*

in Romanticism, 28:2 (1989), 249–69 (p. 258 n. 19)). Henry R. Viets asserts that it is by Henry Colburn, the publisher ('The London Editions of Polidori's *The Vampyre*', *The Papers of the Bibliographical Society of America*, 63:2 (1969), 83–103 (pp. 96–97)). Fabio Camilletti argues that Polidori wrote it as part of a strategy to promote his literary career and gives a later date for the composition as 1818 ('A Note on the Publication History of John Polidori's *The Vampyre*', *Gothic Studies*, 22:3 (2020), 330–43; and Chapter 3 in this volume).

We are indebted to the notes in the editions by Morrison and Baldick, and D. L. Macdonald and Kathleen Scherf (John William Polidori, *The Vampyre and Ernestus Berchtold; or, the Modern Oedipus: Collected Fiction of John William Polidori*, ed. by D. L. Macdonald and Kathleen Scherf (Peterborough, ON and Orchard Park, NY: Broadview Press, 2007)).

3 'Voltaire': pen-name of François-Marie Arouet (1694–1778). French *philosophe*, dramatist, poet, historian, and writer of philosophical tales. Known for his hostility to established religion and defence of liberty.
4 'Bonnet': Charles Bonnet (1720–93). Genevan naturalist and philosopher.
5 'Madame de Stael': Anne Louise Germaine de Staël-Holstein (1766–1817). French novelist, dramatist, and essayist on political and literary matters. Proto-feminist, a friend of Byron, and important in the development of the idea of Romanticism.
6 'Heloise': Héloïse d'Argenteuil or Héloïse du Paraclet (*c*. 1100–01?–1163–64?). French nun, philosopher, and scholar. Famous for her passionate love affair and intellectual collaboration with the philosopher Pierre Abélard (see n. 7 to this appendix), both were punished for their clandestine marriage. The affair and their correspondence have inspired many literary works, including Rousseau's *Julie, ou la nouvelle Héloïse* (1761).
7 'Abeilard': Pierre Abélard (*c*. 1079–1142). French philosopher and scholar. Husband of Héloïse d'Argenteuil (see n. 6 to this appendix). Castrated on the orders of Héloïse's uncle for their secret affair.
8 'M. Schlegel': August Wilhelm Schlegel (1767–1845). German poet, translator (of Shakespeare, in particular), and critic. He and his brother, Friedrich, were the leading theoreticians of the Jena Romanticism movement. A friend of, and influence upon, Madame de Staël (see n. 5 to this appendix).
9 'Gibbon, Bonnivard, Bradshaw': Edward Gibbon (1737–94). English historian, known principally for *The History of the Decline and Fall of the Roman Empire* (1776–88). François Bonivard (1493–1570). Genevan historian and prior, a republican activist who fought against the Duke of Savoy, who imprisoned him in the Castle of Chillon. This would inspire Byron's poem *The Prisoner of Chillon* (1816). Bradshaw is not known.
10 'Diodati, the friend of Milton': the Villa Diodati was, in fact, built by Gabriel Diodati, distantly related to Giovanni Diodati, whom the poet John Milton (1608–74) visited in 1639.
11 'Childe Harold': *Childe Harold's Pilgrimage*, a narrative poem by Byron, published in four cantos between 1812 and 1818. This account of the travels

through Europe of a melancholic, disillusioned, and introspective young man was a significant moment in the creation and ascendency of the Byronic hero. It was hugely popular and influential throughout Europe.

12 Lord Byron, *Childe Harold's Pilgrimage*, in *Lord Byron: The Major Works*, ed. by Jerome J. McGann (Oxford and New York: Oxford University Press, 2008), III. 92–94, pp. 131–32.

13 'M. Pictet and Bonstetten': Marc-August Pictet (1752–1825). Genevan natural philosopher. Charles Victor von Bonstetten (1745–1832). Genevan liberal writer who associated with Madame de Staël (see n. 5 to this appendix) and was influenced by Rousseau and Bonnet (see n. 2 and n. 4 to this appendix). Apparently, Polidori invited Pictet to dinner, not Byron, and the latter snubbed him (Morrison and Baldick, 'Preliminaries', pp. 275–76). The 'gentleman who travelled with him' is presumably Polidori.

14 'Lady D —— H ——': Lady Jane Dalrymple-Hamilton (c. 1780–1852). Eldest daughter of Adam, 1st Viscount Duncan of Camperdown. In 1800, she married Sir Hew Dalrymple-Hamilton.

15 'Coppet': a municipality in the canton of Vaud, Switzerland.

16 'Countess of Breuss': Countess Catherine Bruce, born in St Petersburg. She lived for a while near Geneva, in the Maison D'Abraham Gallatin, 'where Polidori spent so much of his time'. According to Viets, this is most likely the woman with whom Polidori left his manuscript (p. 87). The misspelling of 'Breuss' for 'Bruce' appears in Polidori's diary, transcribed wrongly, claims Viets, by his sister Charlotte (Viets, 'The London Editions', p. 88). For Camilletti, that 'Breuss' is used in both documents indicates that Polidori wrote this preliminary piece; this, of course, is not compatible with the misspelling being due to the posthumous transcription (Camilletti, 'A Note', pp. 338–39; see n. 2 to this appendix).

17 '*agrémens de la Société*': 'charms of the society', where 'society' means something like a salon.

18 'the title of ἄθεος in the Album at Chamouny': ἄθεος = 'atheist'. In July 1816, in the register at the Hotel de Villes de Londres, Chamonix, Shelley had declared in Greek his occupation as 'democrat, lover of humanity, and atheist'. Chamonix, or Chamonix-Mont-Blanc, is a French commune to the north of Mont Blanc. Shelley wrote his ode *Mont Blanc: Lines Written in the Vale of Chamouni* there when he visited in 1816 with Mary Godwin and Claire Clairmont.

19 'Miss M. W. Godwin and Miss Clermont, (the daughters of the celebrated Mr. Godwin)': Mary Wollstonecraft Godwin (later Shelley) (1797–1851). Daughter of the feminist philosopher and novelist Mary Wollstonecraft (1759–97) and William Godwin. Novelist, author of *Frankenstein* (1818). Claire Claremont, or Clara Mary Jane Clairmont (1798–1879). Daughter of Mary Claremont and stepdaughter of Godwin. Writer. William Godwin (1756–1836). Political philosopher, journalist, publisher, and novelist.

20 These insinuations of sexual 'revels' with Mary Godwin and Clare Clairmont were excised in the third issue of the book edition (Viets, 'The London Editions', p. 97).

21 'Phantasmagoriana': *Fantasmagoriana* (1812) was the collection of German ghost stories that the group read together at the Villa Diodati in 1816 and which allegedly inspired Byron's 'A Fragment' (the basis of *The Vampyre*) and Mary Shelley's *Frankenstein*. This was a French translation by Jean-Baptiste Benoît Eyriès from German tales in *Gespensterbuch* (1810–11) by Johann August Apel and Friedrich Laun, and others by Johann Karl August Musäus and Heinrich Clauren.

22 'Christabel': Samuel Taylor Coleridge's narrative poem *Christabel* was probably written in 1797, with a second part in 1800; it was first published in 1816. The poem has vampiric undercurrents.

23 Since published under the title of 'Frankenstein; or, The Modern Prometheus' [note in original].

24 '*ebauches*': *ébauches* – preliminary sketches.

25 This section on vampire folklore is probably by Watts or John Mitford, whom Macdonald suggests also wrote the first part.

26 'Arnold Paul': the story of Arnold Paul appeared in various accounts as well as in, as noted here, the *London Journal* (11 March 1732). Calmet recounts the story in his *Dissertation Concerning Vampires* (1746) (see n. 34 to this appendix), as does Southey in his notes to *Thalaba the Destroyer* (1801) (see n. 32 to this appendix).

27 The universal belief is, that a person sucked by a vampyre becomes a vampyre himself, and sucks in his turn [note in original]. Note that this motif, common in subsequent vampire narratives, is not followed through by Polidori.

28 Chief bailiff [note in original].

29 *The Giaour: A Fragment of a Turkish Tale* (1813) was the first of a series of Oriental romances by Byron that became immensely popular. It is set in Greece under Ottoman rule and shows Byron's philhellenism and concerns with Greek independence (fighting for which led to his death). In the poem, Hassan drowns Leila, a woman from his harem who loves the giaour. 'Giaour' was a derogatory Turkish name for a non-Muslim and the titular character kills Hassan to avenge Leila's death. For this, he is cursed to become a vampire and prey on his own family. Byron's detailed notes to the poem reference vampire lore, acknowledging Southey's notes to *Thalaba the Destroyer* (see n. 32 to this appendix).

30 'Gouls and Afrits': ghouls (Arabic *ghūl*) are demonic beings, originally pre-Islamic, who haunt graveyards and eat the flesh of corpses. The afrit (Arabic *ifrit*) in Islamic culture is a powerful Jinn or spirit of the dead.

31 Byron, *The Giaour: A Fragment of a Turkish Tale* [1813], in *The Major Works*, pp. 207–47 (pp. 227–28), ll. 755–86.

32 'Thalaba': Robert Southey's long narrative poem *Thalaba the Destroyer* (1801) is likely the first poem in English to feature vampires. It was accompanied by copious notes on the mythical and folkloric material it draws on, including vampirism.

33 'Tournefort': Joseph Pitton de Tournefort (1656–1708). French botanist who, in the journal of his travels *Relation d'un voyage du Levant* (1718), observed the Greek superstitions around the vampire-like *vrykolakas* (Greek βρυκόλακας).

34 'Calmet': Antoine Augustin Calmet (1672–1757). French theologian. He wrote much biblical commentary but is known now for his *Dissertations sur les apparitions des anges, des démons et des esprits, et sur les revenants et vampires de Hongrie, de Bohême, de Moravie et de Silésie* (1746). This treatise attempts to investigate the phenomena of vampires in a rational way yet is also somewhat uncritical, deferring to clerical tradition and thus prompting the mockery of Enlightenment thinkers such as Voltaire. It does, however, record a great many vampire incidents.

35 '*ton*': Polite society in the late eighteenth and early nineteenth centuries.

36 'the dead grey eye [...] could not pass': The strangeness of Ruthven's gaze is discussed by Ivan Phillips in Chapter 9 in this volume.

37 'the deadly hue of his face': Polidori, with Ruthven's pallor, makes a significant innovation in vampire lore, sharply in contrast to the excessive ruddiness of the folkloric vampire. Chapters 5, 6, 9, and 11 in this volume all discuss this theme.

38 'Lady Mercer': most likely a caricature of Lady Caroline Lamb, whose affair with Byron and, more importantly, her fictionalising of that and her social circle in her *roman à clef*, *Glenarvon* (1816), was seen as scandalous. The Byronic hero Lord Glenarvon, Clarence de Ruthven supplied the name for Polidori's vampire. See Bill Hughes's Chapter 5 in this volume for *Glenarvon*.

39 'put on the dress of a mountebank': a mountebank is a charlatan or deceiver; Lady Caroline Lamb had on occasions dressed up as a pageboy to impress Byron and even to gain access to his lodgings.

40 'Aubrey': 'Aubrey' can mean 'elf king', suggesting that he, too, has something of the supernatural about him. The name also recalls the antiquarian John Aubrey (1626–97), who, as James Uden notes, was famously credulous ('Gothic Fiction, the Grand Tour, and the Seductions of Antiquity: John Polidori's "The Vampyre" (1819)', in *Illusions and Disillusionment: Travel Writing in the Modern Age*, ed. by R. Micallef (Boston, MA: ILEX Foundation, 2018), pp. 60–79 (pp. 71–72)). Aubrey here has antiquarian interests (and the Greek setting is important) and is gullible.

41 'romances': this sense of 'romance' is that of fiction, where the sense of the marvellous predominates, in contrast to the realist novel. This encompasses such genres as the medieval romance (for example, Arthurian tales), the Gothic novel, the historical novels of Sir Walter Scott, and, quite possibly, Byron's metrical romances such as *The Giaour* (see Harriet Fletcher's Chapter 4 in this volume). Aubrey's susceptibility to romance is repeatedly stressed as: 'that high romantic feeling'; 'the dreams of poets'; 'the romance of his solitary hours'; 'the hero of a romance'.

42 'Lord Ruthven's affairs were embarrassed': 'Ruthven' takes his name from the Byronic Clarence de Ruthven in Lady Caroline Lamb's *Glenarvon* (see n. 33 to this appendix). Simon Bainbridge points out that Ruthven is pronounced 'Riven', suggesting a 'divided self' ('Lord Ruthven's Power: Polidori's "The Vampyre", Doubles, and the Byronic Imagination', *The Byron Journal*, 34:1 (2006), 21–34 (p. 30)). In his drafts towards a second edition, Polidori changes the name to 'Strongmore'. Byron, too, had left England because of financial (and other) embarrassments.

43 'the tour': it was usual for young upper-class men to undertake the Grand Tour – an educational journey round Europe with a tutor, particularly viewing art of the Renaissance and visiting the sites of classical antiquity. Polidori is acidly satirical here about the benefits of the tour, thus invoking the prevalent genre of satires on the Grand Tour (see Uden, 'Gothic Fiction', pp. 63–68).
44 'faro table': faro was a gambling card game, originally from seventeenth-century France, popular among the upper classes in this period. Cheating at faro was rife.
45 'those who had no souls': it was a common Orientalist misconception that Muslims believed that women had no souls.
46 'gazelle': a sly allusion to Byron's images of women as gazelles in 'To Ianthe' (prefatory stanzas added in 1814 to *Childe Harold's Pilgrimage*) and *The Giaour* (see Skarda, 'Vampirism and Plagiarism', pp. 254–55; Bainbridge, 'Lord Ruthven's Power', p. 29; Byron, *The Major Works*, pp. 21–23 (ll. 28–29), 207–47 (ll. 473–74)).
47 'Ianthe': there are classical allusions, but Ianthe was also the name given to Lady Charlotte Mary Harley by Byron and used in 'To Ianthe' (see Skarda, 'Vampirism and Plagiarism', pp. 253–54). Ianthe also appears in Shelley's *Queen Mab*, where she is fairy-like – a suitable pairing for Aubrey the elf king (see n. 40 to this appendix); she has a 'fairy form' and incites 'fairy visions' (see Skarda, 'Vampirism and Plagiarism', p. 254 n. 12; Percy Bysshe Shelley, *Queen Mab*, in *The Major Works*, ed. by Zachary Leader and Michael O'Neill (Oxford and New York: Oxford University Press, 2009), pp. 10–88).
48 'a Kashmere butterfly': another reworking of Byron's imagery in *The Giaour* (ll. 387–99; see Skarda, 'Vampirism and Plagiarism', p. 255).
49 'Pausanias': Pausanias (c. 110–c. 180) was a Greek geographer whose *Hellados Periegesis* [*Description of Greece*] served as a valuable guide for antiquarians, linking topographical features to classical literature.
50 'forced every year [...] to prolong his existence for the ensuing months': this is an addition to traditional vampire lore which Polidori seems to have invented.
51 'fairy form': emphasises the fay nature of Ianthe that her name suggests (see n. 47 to this footnote).
52 'fairy visions': Ianthe's fairy nature again, also illustrating Aubrey's propensity for romance narratives.
53 This oath to conceal both Ruthven's death and any crimes he may be guilty of echoes that in Byron's 'A Fragment'. There are similar oaths in the tales in *Fantasmagoriana*.
54 'the first cold ray of the moon that rose after his death': this revivifying power of moonlight is not in vampire folklore and again seems Polidori's invention. It appears again in James Malcolm Rymer's Penny Dreadful *Varney, the Vampire* (1845–47) (see Sam George's Chapter 2 in this volume).
55 'Otranto': a town on the east coast of the Salento Peninsula in Italy. Horace Walpole's *The Castle of Otranto* (1764) may be said to have inaugurated the Gothic novel.

56 'ataghans': the ataghan (Turkish: *yatağan*) is a Turkish sword with a curved blade; Byron mentions one in his 'A Fragment'.
57 'Remember your oath': Macdonald and Scherf suggest Polidori is recalling the oath of silence from Sir Walter Scott's *Guy Mannering* (1815), which Byron had also read; they also point to the line 'Lady Margaret reminded him of his vow' in *Glenarvon* (p. 15).
58 'the serpent's art': Ruthven's persuasive rhetoric, like that of Milton's Satan, is part of his uncanny allure, something Polidori bequeaths to subsequent vampire narratives.

Appendix 2

George, Lord Byron, 'A Fragment'

In the year 17—, having for some time determined on a journey through countries not hitherto much frequented by travellers I set out, accompanied by a friend, whom I shall designate by the name of Augustus Darvell. He was a few years my elder, and a man of considerable fortune and ancient family—advantages which an extensive capacity prevented him alike from undervaluing or overrating. Some peculiar circumstances in his private history had rendered him to me an object of attention, of interest, and even of regard, which neither the reserve of his manners, nor occasional indications of an inquietude at times nearly approaching to alienation of mind, could extinguish.

I was yet young in life, which I had begun early; but my intimacy with him was of a recent date: we had been educated at the same schools and university; but his progress through these had preceded mine, and he had been deeply initiated into what is called the world, while I was yet in my noviciate. While thus engaged, I had heard much both of his past and present life; and although in these accounts there were many and irreconcileable contradictions, I could still gather from the whole that he was a being of no common order, and one who, whatever pains he might take to avoid remark, would still be remarkable. I had cultivated his acquaintance subsequently, and endeavoured to obtain his friendship, but this last appeared to be unattainable; whatever affections he might have possessed seemed now, some to have been extinguished, and others to be concentred: that his feelings were acute, I had sufficient opportunities of observing; for, although he could control, he could not altogether disguise them: still he had a power of giving to one passion the appearance of another in such a manner that it was difficult to define the nature of what was working within him; and the expressions of his features would vary so rapidly, though slightly, that it was useless to trace them to their sources. It was evident that he was a prey to some cureless disquiet; but whether it arose from ambition, love, remorse, grief, from one or all of these, or merely from a morbid temperament akin to disease, I could not discover: there were circumstances alleged, which might have justified the application to each of these causes; but, as I have before said, these were so contradictory and contradicted, that none could be fixed upon with accuracy. Where there is mystery, it is generally supposed that there must also be evil: I know not how this may be, but in him there certainly was the one, though I could not ascertain the extent of the other—and felt loth, as far as regarded himself, to believe in its existence. My advances were received with sufficient coldness; but I was young, and not easily discouraged, and at length succeeded in obtaining, to a certain degree, that common-place intercourse and moderate confidence of common and every day concerns, created and cemented by similarity of pursuit and frequency of meeting, which is called intimacy, or friendship, according to the ideas of him who uses those words to express them.

Darvell had already travelled extensively; and to him I had applied for information with regard to the conduct of my intended journey. It was my secret wish that he might be prevailed on to accompany me: it was also a probable hope, founded upon the shadowy restlessness which I had observed in him, and to which the animation which he appeared to feel on such subjects, and his apparent indifference to all by which he was more immediately surrounded, gave fresh strength. This wish I first hinted, and then expressed: his answer, though I had partly expected it, gave me all the pleasure of surprise—he consented; and, after the requisite arrangements, we commenced our voyages. After journeying through various countries of the south of Europe, our attention was turned towards the East, according to our original destination; and it was in my progress through those regions that the incident occurred upon which will turn what I may have to relate.

The constitution of Darvell, which must from his appearance have been in early life more than usually robust, had been for some time gradually giving way, without the intervention of any apparent disease: he had neither cough nor hectic, yet he became daily more enfeebled: his habits were temperate, and he neither declined nor complained of fatigue, yet he was evidently wasting away: he became more and more silent and sleepless, and at length so seriously altered, that my alarm grew proportionate to what I conceived to be his danger.

We had determined, on our arrival at Smyrna,[1] on an excursion to the ruins of Ephesus[2] and Sardis,[3] from which I endeavoured to dissuade him in his present state of indisposition—but in vain: there appeared to be an oppression on his mind, and a solemnity in his manner, which ill corresponded with his eagerness to proceed on what I regarded as a mere party of pleasure, little suited to a valetudinarian; but I opposed him no longer—and in a few days we set off together, accompanied only by a serrugee[4] and a single janizary.[5]

We had passed halfway towards the remains of Ephesus, leaving behind us the more fertile environs of Smyrna, and were entering upon that wild and tenantless track through the marshes and defiles which lead to the few huts yet lingering over the broken columns of Diana[6]—the roofless walls of expelled Christianlty, and the still more recent but complete desolation of abandoned mosques—when the sudden and rapid illness of my companion obliged us to halt at a Turkish cemetery, the turbaned tombstones of which were the sole indication that human life had ever been a sojourner in this wilderness. The only caravansera[7] we had seen was left some hours behind us, not a vestige of a town or even cottage was within sight or hope, and this 'city of the dead' appeared to be the sole refuge for my unfortunate friend, who seemed on the verge of becoming the last of its inhabitants.

In this situation, I looked round for a place where he might most conveniently repose:—contrary to the usual aspect of Mohometan[8] burial-grounds, the cypresses were in this few in number, and these thinly scattered over its extent: the tombstones were mostly fallen, and worn with age:—upon one of the most considerable of these, and beneath one of the most spreading trees, Darvell supported himself, in a half-reclining posture, with great difficulty. He asked for water. I had some doubts of our being able to find any, and prepared to go in search of it with hesitating despondency—but he desired me to remain; and turning to Suleiman, our janizary, who stood by us smoking with great tranquillity, he said, 'Suleiman, verbana su,' (i.e. bring some water,) and went on describing the spot where it was to be found with great minuteness, at a small well for camels, a few hundred yards to the right: the janizary obeyed. I said to Darvell, 'How did you know this?'—He replied, 'From our situation; you must perceive that this place was once inhabited, and could not have been so without springs: I have also been here before.'

'You have been here before!—How came you never to mention this to me? and what could you be doing in a place where no one would remain a moment longer than they could help it?

To this question I received no answer. In the mean time Suleiman returned with the water, leaving the serrugee and the horses at the fountain. The quenching of his thirst had the appearance of reviving him for a moment; and I conceived hopes of his being able to proceed, or at least to return, and I urged the attempt. He was silent—and appeared to be collecting his spirits for an effort to speak. He began.

'This is the end of my journey, and of my life—I came here 'to die: but I have a request to make, a command—for such my 'last words must be— You will observe it?'

'Most certainly; but have better hopes.'

'I have no hopes, nor wishes, but this—conceal my death from every human being.'

'I hope there will be no occasion; that you will recover, and——'

'Peace!—it must be so: promise this.'

'I do.'

'Swear it, by all that'—He here dictated an oath of great solemnity.

'There is no occasion for this—I will observe your request; and to doubt me is——'

'It cannot be helped,—you must swear.'

I took the oath: it appeared to relieve him. He removed a seal ring from his finger, on which were some Arabic characters, and presented it to me. He proceeded—

'On the ninth day of the month, at noon precisely (what month you please, but this must be the day), you must fling this ring into the salt springs which run into the Bay of Eleusis: the day after, at the same hour, you must repair to the ruins of the temple of Ceres, and wait one hour.'

'Why?'

'You will see.'

'The ninth day of the month, you say?'

'The ninth.'

As I observed that the present was the ninth day of the month, his countenance changed, and he paused. As he sate, evidently becoming more feeble, a stork, with a snake in her beak, perched upon a tombstone near us; and, without devouring her prey, appeared to be stedfastly regarding us. I know not what impelled me to drive it away, but the attempt was useless; she made a few circles in the air, and returned exactly to the same spot. Darvell pointed to it, and smiled: he spoke—I know not whether to himself or to me—but the words were only, ''Tis well!'

'What is well? what do you mean?'

'No matter: you must bury me here this evening, and exactly where that bird is now perched. You know the rest of my injunctions.'

He then proceeded to give me several directions as to the manner in which his death might be best concealed. After these were finished, he exclaimed, 'You perceive that bird?'

'Certainly.'

'And the serpent writhing in her beak?'

'Doubtless: there is nothing uncommon in it; it is her natural prey. But it is odd that she does not devour it.'

He smiled in a ghastly manner, and said, faintly, 'It is not yet time!' As he spoke, the stork flew away. My eyes followed it for a moment, it could hardly be longer than ten might be counted. I felt Darvell's weight, as it were, increase upon my shoulder, and, turning to look upon his face, perceived that he was dead!

I was shocked with the sudden certainty which could not be mistaken—his countenance in a few minutes became nearly black. I should have attributed so rapid a change to poison, had I not been aware that he had no opportunity of receiving it unperceived. The day was declining, the body was rapidly altering, and nothing remained but to fulfil his request. With the aid of Suleiman's ataghan[9] and my own sabre, we scooped a shallow grave upon the spot which Darvell had indicated: the earth easily gave way, having already received some Mahometan tenant. We dug as deeply as the time permitted us, and throwing the dry earth upon all that remained of the singular being so lately departed, we cut a few sods of greener turf from the less withered soil around us, and laid them upon his sepulchre.

Between astonishment and grief, I was tearless.

Notes

1 'Smyrna': ancient Greek city of Anatolia, now İzmir in Turkey.
2 'Ephesus': ancient Greek city, its remains now lie in Turkey. Famous for its ruins and lost splendour, particularly the Temple of Artemis (Diana; one of the Seven Wonders of the Ancient World), it would be a prominent feature of the Grand Tour undertaken by young British aristocrats in the eighteenth and early nineteenth centuries.
3 'Sardis': capital of ancient Lydia, destroyed by Persian Emperor Cyrus, c. 547 BCE. Site located in Turkey.
4 'serrugee': (Turkish, *Sürücü*) driver who manages the post-horses.
5 'janizary': (often 'janissary'; Turkish *yeniçeri*) member of elite troops of soldiers in the Ottoman Empire.
6 'Diana': Roman equivalent of the Greek goddess Artemis, who presided over the moon, hunting and virginity; she had a temple at Ephesus.
7 'caravansera': ('caravanserai'; Persian *kārvān, sara*; Turkish suffix *-yi*) inn for the refreshment of travellers on trade routes in the Islamic world.
8 'Mohometan': 'Islamic'; objectionable to Muslims and not used by them.
9 'ataghan': (Turkish: *yatağan*) Turkish sword with curved blade.

References

Books and articles

Aaronovitch, Ben, *Rivers of London*, Rivers of London, 1 (London: Orion, 2011)

Abbott, Stacey, 'The Cinematic Spectacle of Vampirism', in *Celluloid Vampires* (Austin: University of Texas Press, 2000), pp. 42–60

Abraham, Nicolas, 'Notes du séminaire sur l'unité duelle et le fantôme', in Nicolas Abraham and Maria Torok, *L'Écorce et le noyau* (Paris: Flammarion, 1987), pp. 393–425

——— 'Notes on the Phantom: A Complement to Freud's Metapsychology', in Nicolas Abraham and Maria Torok, *The Shell and the Kernel: Renewals of Psychoanalysis*, ed. by Nicholas T. Rand (Chicago, IL: University of Chicago Press, 1994), pp. 171–76

Aldiss, Brian, *Frankenstein Unbound* (London: Cape, 1973)

Aldridge, A. Owen, 'The Vampire Theme, Dumas Père and the English Stage', *Revue des Langues Vivants*, 39 (1974), 312–24

Ann, Brooklyn, *Bite Me, Your Grace* (Naperville, IL: Sourcebooks, 2013)

Aquilina, Conrad, 'The Deformed Transformed; or, From Bloodsucker to Byronic Hero – Polidori and the Literary Vampire', in *Open Graves, Open Minds: Representation of Vampires and the Undead from the Enlightenment to the Present Day*, ed. by Sam George and Bill Hughes (Manchester: Manchester University Press, 2013), pp. 24–28

Aretaeus, *De causis et signis diuturnorum morborum*, trans. by Francis Adams, in *The Extant Works of Aretaeus, The Cappadocian* (London: Sydenham Society, 1856)

Arnold, A. James, 'Recuperating the Haitian Revolution in Literature: From Victor Hugo to Derek Walcott', in *Tree of Liberty: Cultural Legacies of the Haitian Revolution in the Atlantic World*, ed. by Doris L. Garraway (Charlottesville: University of Virginia Press, 2008), pp. 179–99

Astle, Richard Sharp, 'Ontological Ambiguity and Historical Pessimism in Polidori's *The Vampyre*', *Sphinx: A Magazine of Literature and Society*, 8 (1977), 8–16

Aubrey, James, 'Celtic Vampires: Neil Jordan's Film *Byzantium* as Irish Neomyth', *Journal of Literature and Art Studies*, 7:7 (July 2017), 909–15 (p. 912)

Auerbach, Nina, *Our Vampires, Ourselves* (Chicago, IL: University of Chicago Press, 1995)

Bachardy, Don and Christopher Isherwood, *Frankenstein: The True Story* (New York: Avon Books, 1973)

Bainbridge, Simon, 'Lord Ruthven's Power: Polidori's "The Vampyre", Doubles, and the Byronic Imagination', *The Byron Journal*, 34:1 (2006), 21–34
Baker, Margaret, *The Folklore of Plants* (Oxford: Shire, 1969)
Barber, Paul, *Vampires, Burial, and Death: Folklore and Reality* (New Haven, CT and London: Yale University Press, 1988)
Barger, Andrew, ed., *The Best Vampire Stories 1800–1849: A Classic Vampire Anthology* (n.p.: Bottletree Classics, 2012)
Barney, Richard A., 'Burke, Biomedicine, and Biobelligerence', *The Eighteenth Century*, Special Issue: Sensational Subjects, 54:2 (Summer 2013), pp. 231–43
Barthes, Roland, *Mythologies*, trans. by Annette Lavers (London: Vintage, 1993)
Bartley, Mark, 'In Search of Robertson's Fantasmagorie', *The New Magic Lantern Journal*, 7:3 (November 1995), 1–5
Baudrillard, Jean, *The Spirit of Terrorism and Other Essays*, trans. by Chris Turner (London and New York: Verso, 2003)
Beddoes, Thomas, *Essay on the Causes, Early Signs and Prevention of Pulmonary Consumption, for the Use of Parents and Preceptors* (London: printed by Biggs & Cottle, for T. N. Longman and O. Rees, 1799)
—— 'Essay Seventh, On Consumption', in *Hygëia: or, Essays Moral and Medical on the Causes Affecting the Personal State of our Middling and Affluent Classes*, 3 vols (Bristol: Printed by J. Mills, for R. Phillips, 1802–03), II
Bell, Michael E., *Food for the Dead: On the Trail of New England's Vampires* (Middletown, CT: Wesleyan University Press, 2014)
Bérard, Cyprien, *Lord Ruthwen ou les vampires* (Paris: Ladvocat, 1820)
—— *The Vampire Lord Ruthwen*, trans. by Brian Stableford (Encino, CA: Black Coat Press, 2011)
Beresford, Matt, 'The Lord Byron/John Polidori Relationship and the Development of the Early Nineteenth-Century Literary Vampire' (unpublished doctoral thesis, University of Hertfordshire, 2019)
Bidisha, 'Bitten by the Female Gaze', *The Guardian*, 19 January 2009 www.guardian.co.uk/commentisfree/2009/jan/19/women-gender [accessed 14 September 2021]
Blyth, Henry, *Caro the Fatal Passion: The Life of Lady Caroline Lamb*, ed. by Frances Wilson (New York: Coward, McCann & Geoghegan, 1973)
Boffey, Philip M., 'Rare Disease Proposed as Cause for "Vampires"', *The New York Times*, 31 May 1985 www.nytimes.com/1985/05/31/us/rare-disease-proposed-as-cause-for-vampires.html [accessed 30 July 2020]
Booth, Michael R., *English Melodrama* (London: Herbert Jenkins, 1965)
Boone, Troy, 'Mark of the Vampire: Arnod Paole, Sade, Polidori', *Nineteenth-Century Contexts*, 18:4 (1995), 349–66
Botting, Fred, *Limits of Horror: Technology, Bodies, Gothic* (Manchester: Manchester University Press, 2013)
—— *Gothic*, 2nd edn (New York: Routledge, 2014)
Braccini, Tommaso, *Prima di Dracula. Archeologia del vampiro* (Bologna: Il Mulino, 2011)
Bray, Katie, '"A Climate … More Prolific … in Sorcery": The Black Vampyre and the Hemispheric Gothic', *American Literature*, 87:1 (2015), 1–21
Brenton, Howard, *Bloody Poetry* [1989], in *Plays 2* (London: Methuen Drama, 1990)
Briggs, Helen, 'Covid-19: Infectious Coronaviruses "Circulating in Bats for Decades"', BBC News, 29 July 2020 www.bbc.co.uk/news/science-environment-53584936 [accessed 29 July 2020]
Brite, Poppy Z., *Lost Souls* (1992; London and New York: Penguin, 1994)

Brontë, Emily, *Wuthering Heights*, ed. by Pauline Nestor (1847; London: Penguin, 1995)
Broughton, Lord [John Hobhouse], *Recollections of a Long Life*, ed. by Lady Dorchester, 2 vols (New York: Scribner's Sons, 1909)
Bruffee, Kenneth A., 'Elegiac Romance', *College English*, 32:4 (1971), 465–76
Buck-Morss, Susan, *Hegel, Haiti, and Universal History* (Pittsburgh, PA: University of Pittsburgh Press, 2009)
Budge, Gavin, '"The Vampyre": Romantic Metaphysics and the Aristocratic Other', in *The Gothic Other: Racial and Social Constructions in the Literary Imagination*, ed. by Ruth Bienstock Anolik and Douglas L. Howard (Jefferson, NC: McFarland, 2004), pp. 212–35
Burke, Edmund, *A Philosophical Enquiry into the Origin of Our Ideas of the Sublime and Beautiful* (1757; Mineola, NY: Dover Publications, 2012)
―――― *Reflections on the Revolution in France*, ed. by Conor Cruise O'Brien (1790; Harmondsworth: Penguin, 1982)
Burwick, Frederick, 'Vampires in Kilts', in *The Romantic Stage: A Many-Sided Mirror*, ed. by Lilla Maria Crisafulli and Fabio Libeto (Amsterdam: Rodopi, 2014), pp. 199–224
Butler, Erik, *Metamorphoses of the Vampire in Literature and Film: Cultural Transformations in Europe, 1732–1933* (Rochester, NY: Camden House, 2010)
Butler, Octavia E., *Fledgling* (2005; New York: Warner Books, 2007)
Byrd, Brandon R., *The Black Republic* (Philadelphia, PA: University of Pennsylvania Press, 2019)
Byrne, Katherine, *Tuberculosis and the Victorian Literary Imagination* (Cambridge: Cambridge University Press, 2011)
Byron, Lord George Gordon, *The Giaour, Fragment of a Turkish Tale* (London: John Murray, 1813)
―――― *Letters and Journals of Lord Byron: With Notices of His Life*, ed. by Thomas Moore (New York: Harper & Brothers, 1855)
―――― 'Augustus Darvell', in *The Vampyre and Other Tales of the Macabre*, ed. by Robert Morrison and Chris Baldick (Oxford: Oxford University Press, 1997), pp. 246–51
―――― *Lord Byron: The Major Works*, ed. by Jerome J. McGann (Oxford and New York: Oxford University Press, 2008)
―――― *Childe Harold's Pilgrimage*, in *Lord Byron: The Major Works*, ed. by Jerome J. McGann (Oxford: Oxford University Press, 2008), pp. 19–206
―――― *The Giaour*, in *Lord Byron: The Major Works*, ed. by Jerome J. McGann (Oxford: Oxford University Press, 2008), pp. 207–47
Calmet, Augustine, *The Phantom World: The History and Philosophy of Spirits, Apparitions, Etc., Etc.*, ed. by Henry Christmas, 2 vols (London: Richard Bentley, 1850) [translation of *Dissertations sur les apparitions des anges, des demons at des esprits* (1746)]
Camilletti, Fabio, *Classicism and Romanticism in Italian Literature* (London: Pickering and Chatto, 2013)
―――― 'On This Day in 1816: Polidori Finds a Book', BARS Blog, 12 June 2016 www.bars.ac.uk/blog/?p=1214 [accessed 24 May 2023]
―――― 'Fantasmagoriana: The German Book of Ghost Stories that Inspired *Frankenstein*', *The Conversation*, 29 October 2018 https://theconversation.com/fantasmagoriana-the-german-book-of-ghost-stories-that-inspired-frankenstein-105236 [accessed 29 November 2020]

—— 'A Note on the Publication History of John Polidori's *The Vampyre*', *Gothic Studies*, 22:3 (2020), 330–43

—— 'Phantasmagoria: Creating the Ghosts of the Enlightenment', *History Extra*, 17 August 2021 www.historyextra.com/period/stuart/phantasmagoria-creating-the-ghosts-of-the-enlightenment/ [accessed 24 May 2023]

Carlson, Marvin, *The French Stage in the Nineteenth Century* (Metuchen, NJ: Scarecrow Press, 1972)

Carrère, Emmanuel, *Gothic Romance* (1984; New York: Charles Scribner's Sons, 1990)

Cassimir, Jean, *The Haitians: A Decolonial History*, trans. by Laurent Dubois, Latin America in Translation (Chapel Hill: University of North Carolina Press, 2020)

Castle, Terry, 'Phantasmagoria: Spectral Technology', *Critical Enquiry* (autumn 1988), 26–61

Chalke, H. D., 'Some Historical Aspects of Tuberculosis', *Public Health*, 74:3 (December 1959), 83–95

Child, Lydia Maria, *An Appeal in Favor of that Class of Americans Called Africans*, Project Gutenberg www.gutenberg.org/ebooks/28242 [accessed 31 May 2023]

Chubbe, John, 'Glenarvon Revised – and Revisited', *The Wordsworth Circle*, 10:2 (1979), 205–17

Cixous, Hélène, 'Fiction and Its Phantoms: A Reading of Freud's *Das Unheimliche* (The "Uncanny")', trans. by Robert Dennomé, *New Literary History*, 7:3 (Spring 1976), 525–48

Coghen, Monica, 'Lord Byron and the Metamorphoses of Polidori's *Vampyre*', *Studia Litteraria: Universitatis Iagellonicae Cracoviensis*, 6 (2011), 29–40

Coleman, John, *Fifty Years of an Actor's Life*, 2 vols (London: Hutchinson, 1904)

Crawford, Joseph, *The Twilight of the Gothic? Vampire Fiction and the Rise of Paranormal Romance, 1991–2012*, Gothic Literary Studies (Cardiff: University of Wales Press, 2014)

Cronin, Justin, *The Passage* (London: Orion, 2010)

—— *The Twelve* (London: Orion, 2012)

—— *The City of Mirrors* (London: Orion, 2016)

—— '*The Passage*: Q & A with Justin Cronin', Justin Cronin Books http://enterthepassage.com/the-passage-q-a-with-justin-cronin/ [accessed 3 January 2013]

D'Arcy, Uriah Derick, *The Black Vampyre: A Legend of St. Domingo* (New York: Printed for the author, 1819)

—— 'The Black Vampyre', in *The Best Vampire Stories 1800–1849: A Classic Vampire Anthology*, ed. by Andrew Barger (n.p.: Bottletree Classics, 2012)

—— 'The Black Vampyre; A Legend of St. Domingo (1819)', ed. by Ed White, Duncan Faherty, and Toni Wall Jaudon, Just Teach One http://jto.common-place.org/just-teach-one-homepage/the-black-vampyre/ [accessed 7 June 2020]

—— *The Black Vampyre: A Legend of St. Domingo*, ed. by Panton Plasma (Edinburgh: Gothic World Literature Editions, 2020)

Daut, Marlene L., *Tropics of Haiti: Race and the Literary History of the Haitian Revolution in the Atlantic World, 1789–1865* (Liverpool: Liverpool University Press, 2015)

Davis, David Brion, *The Problem of Slavery in the Age of Revolution, 1770–1823* (Ithaca, NY and London: Cornell University Press, 1975)

Day, Carolyn A., *Consumptive Chic: A History of Beauty, Fashion and Disease* (London: Bloomsbury Academic, 2017)

―――― 'Dying to Be Beautiful: Fragile Fashionistas and Consumptive Dress in England, 1780–1820', *Journal for Eighteenth-Century Studies*, 40:4 (2017), pp. 603–20
Dayan, Joan, *Haiti, History, and the Gods*, rpt. edition (Berkeley: University of California Press, 1998)
Deane, Hamilton and John L. Balderston, *Dracula, The Vampire Play in Three Acts, Dramatized by Hamilton Deane and John L. Balderston, from the Novel by Bram Stoker* (New York: Samuel French, 1933)
Del Toro, Guillermo and Chick Hogan, *The Strain*, The Strain Trilogy, 1 (London: Harper Collins, 2009)
―――― *The Fall*, The Strain Trilogy, 2 (London: Harper Collins, 2010)
―――― *The Night Eternal*, The Strain Trilogy, 3 (London: Harper Collins, 2011)
Delafield, Edward, *An Inaugural Dissertation on Pulmonary Consumption* (New York: John Forbes, 1816)
Delile, Alire Raffeneau, *An Inaugural Dissertation on Pulmonary Consumption* (New York: Columbia College, 1807)
Depestre, Rene, *A Rainbow for the Christian West*, trans. by Joan Dayan (Amherst: University of Massachusetts Press, 1977)
Derrida, Jacques, *Of Grammatology* (1967; Baltimore, MD: Johns Hopkins University Press, 1976)
―――― *Mal d'archive: Une impression freudienne* (Paris: Galilée, 1995)
Dickson, Leigh Wetherall, 'Authority and Legitimacy: The Cultural Context of Lady Caroline Lamb's Novels', *Women's Writing*, 13:3 (2006), 369–91
Dirks, P. T., 'Planché and the English Burletta Tradition', *Theatre Survey*, 17 (1976), 68–81
Douglass, Paul, 'The Madness of Writing: Lady Caroline Lamb's Byronic Identity', *Pacific Coast Philology*, 34:1 (1999), 53–71
―――― *Lady Caroline Lamb: A Biography* (New York: Palgrave Macmillan, 2004)
―――― 'Twisty Little Passages: The Several Editions of Lady Caroline Lamb's "Glenarvon"', *The Wordsworth Circle*, 40:2/3 (2009), 77–82
Dubois, Laurent, *Avengers of the New World: The Story of the Haitian Revolution* (Cambridge, MA: Harvard University Press, 2005)
Dubois, Laurent, Kaiama L. Glover, Nadève Ménard, Millery Polyné and Chantalle F. Verna, eds, *The Haiti Reader: History, Culture, Politics* (Durham, NC: Duke University Press Books, 2020)
Dubos, René and Jean Dubos, *The White Plague: Tuberculosis, Man and Society* (Boston, MA: Little, Brown, 1952)
Duffett, Mark, *Understanding Fandom: An Introduction to the Study of Media Fan Culture* (New York: Bloomsbury, 2013)
Dumas, Alexandre, 'A Visit to the Theatre', in Christopher Frayling, *Vampyres: Lord Byron to Count Dracula* (London: Faber & Faber, 1991), pp. 131–44
―――― *The Return of Lord Ruthven the Vampire* [*Le Vampyre*], trans. by Frank J Morlock (Encino, CA: Black Coat Press, 2004)
Edmundson, Mark, *Nightmare on Main Street: Angels, Sadomasochism, and the Culture of Gothic* (Cambridge, MA: Harvard University Press, 1997)
Edwards, Anne, *Haunted Summer* (1972; London: Coronet, 1974)
Eliot, T. S., *Collected Poems 1909–1962* (London: Faber & Faber, 1989)
Eminem, 'Stan (Long Version) ft. Dido', YouTube www.youtube.com/watch?v=gOMhN-hfMtY&ab_channel=EminemVEVO [accessed 28 February 2022]

'Exit Strategy for a Restless Dead: The Hell Tree of St Pancras', Portals of London, 20 January 2017 https://portalsoflondon.com/2017/01/20/the-hell-tree-of-st-pancras/ [accessed 7 May 2023]

'Extract of a Letter from Geneva, with Anecdotes of Lord Byron, &c', *The New Monthly Magazine*, 11:63 (1 April 1819), 193–95

Fantasmagoriana, ou recueil d'histoires d'apparitions de spectres, revenans, fantômes; etc., trans. by Jean-Baptiste Benoît Eyriès, 2 vols (Paris: F. Schoell, 1812)

Fantasmagoriana: Tales of the Dead, ed. by A. J. Day and C. Vorwerk (St Ives: Fantasmagoriana Press, 2005)

Fhlainn, Sorcha Ní, *Postmodern Vampires: Film, Fiction, and Popular Culture* (London: Palgrave Macmillan, 2019)

—— 'Cruising the Vampire: Hollywood Gothic, Star Branding, and *Interview with the Vampire*', in *Starring Tom Cruise*, ed. by Sean Redmond (Detroit, MI: Wayne State University Press, 2021), pp. 133–51

Fincher, Max, *Queering Gothic in the Romantic Age* (London: Palgrave Macmillan, 2007)

Forman, Maurice Buxton, ed., *The Letters of John Keats* (Oxford: Oxford University Press, 1952)

Foucault, Michel, *Discipline and Punish: The Birth of the Prison*, trans. by Alan Sheridan (1977; New York: Vintage, 1995)

Fox, Andrew J., *Fat White Vampire Blues* (New York: Ballantine Books, 2003)

Fraser, Lady Antonia, *Lady Caroline Lamb: A Free Spirit* (London: Weidenfeld & Nicolson, 2023)

Fraser, C. A., 'Scottish Myths from Ontario', *Journal of American Folklore*, 6:22 (July–September 1893), 185–98

Frayling, Christopher, *Nightmare: The Birth of Horror* (London: BBC Books, 1996)

—— *Inside the Bloody Chamber: On Angela Carter, the Gothic, and Other Weird Tales* (London: Oberon Books, 2016)

Frayling, Christopher, ed., *Vampyres: Lord Byron to Count Dracula*, 2nd edn (London: Faber & Faber, 1991)

—— *Vampyres: Genesis and Resurrection from 'Count Dracula' to 'Vampirella'* (London: Thames & Hudson, 2016)

Frayling, Christopher and Robert Wokler, 'From the Orang-utan to the Vampire: Towards an Anthropology of Rousseau', in *Rousseau After 200 Years*, ed. by R. A. Leigh (Cambridge: Cambridge University Press, 1982)

Frazer, Sir James, *The Golden Bough*, 3rd edn, 12 vols (London: Macmillan, 1906–15), x: *Balder the Beautiful (Part I)*

—— *The Golden Bough*, 3rd edn, 12 vols (London: Macmillan, 1906–15), xi: *Balder the Beautiful (Part II)*

Fredeman, William E., 'The Letters of Pictor Ignotus: William Bell Scott's Correspondence with Alice Boyd, 1859–1884. Part II', *Bulletin of the John Rylands Library*, 58:2 (1976), 306–52

Freud, Sigmund, *The Uncanny*, trans. by David McLintock (1919; Harmondsworth: Penguin, 2003)

Gaiman, Neil, *Norse Mythology* (London: Bloomsbury, 2017)

Garcia Marín, Álvaro, ' "The Son of the Vampire": Greek Gothic, or Gothic Greece?', in *Dracula and the Gothic in Literature, Pop Culture and the Arts*, ed. by Isabel Ermida (Leiden and Boston, MA: Brill Rodopi, 2016), pp. 21–44

Garraway, Doris L., ' "Légitime Défense": Universalism and Nationalism in the Discourse of the Haitian Revolution', in *Tree of Liberty: Cultural Legacies* of the Haitian Revolution in the Atlantic World, ed. by Doris L. Garraway (Charlottesville: University of Virginia Press, 2008), pp. 63–88

———, ed., *Tree of Liberty: Cultural Legacies of the Haitian Revolution in the Atlantic World* (Charlottesville: University of Virginia Press, 2008)

Garver, Joseph, 'Gothic Ireland: Lady Caroline Lamb's "Glenarvon"', *Irish University Review*, 10:2 (1980), 213–28

Gelder, Ken, *Reading the Vampire* (London: Routledge, 1994)

George, Sam, '"He Make In the Mirror No Reflect": Undead Aesthetics and Mechanical Reproduction – *Dorian Gray*, *Dracula* and David Reed's "Vampire Painting"', in *Open Graves, Open Minds: Representations of Vampires and the Undead from the Enlightenment to the Present Day*, ed. by Sam George and Bill Hughes (Manchester: Manchester University Press, 2013), pp. 56–78

——— 'America's First Vampire Was Black and Revolutionary – It's Time to Remember Him', *The Conversation*, 30 October 2020 http://theconversation.com/americas-first-vampire-was-black-and-revolutionary-its-time-to-remember-him-149044 [accessed 4 December 2020]

——— 'Vampire at the Crossroads', Open Graves, Open Minds, 2 July 2018 www.opengravesopenminds.com/ogom-research/vampire-at-the-crossroads/ [accessed 7 May 2023]

——— 'Gothic Hearts: A Love Story', Open Graves, Open Minds, 14 February 2023 www.opengravesopenminds.com/ogom-research/lost-hearts-a-gothic-love-story/ [accessed 7 May 2023]

George, Sam and Bill Hughes, 'Introduction', *Open Graves, Open Minds: Representations of Vampires and the Undead from the Enlightenment to the Present Day*, ed. by Sam George and Bill Hughes (Manchester: Manchester University Press, 2013), pp. 1–23

George, Sam and Bill Hughes, eds, *Open Graves, Open Minds: Representations of Vampires and the Undead from the Enlightenment to the Present Day* (Manchester: Manchester University Press, 2013)

Germana, Monica, 'Skulls, Skulls Everywhere: Consuming the Gothic in the 21st Century', The Gothic Imagination, 22 February 2010 www.gothic.stir.ac.uk/guests/viewblog.php?id=67 [accessed 5 September 2021]

Gilbert, Anne, 'Between Twi-Hards and Twi-Haters: The Complicated Terrain of Online "Twilight" Audience Communities', in *Genre, Reception, and Adaptation in the 'Twilight' Series*, ed. by Anne Morey (Farnham: Ashgate Publishing, 2012), pp. 163–79

Gilroy, Paul, *The Black Atlantic: Modernity and Double Consciousness* (London: Verso, 1993)

Glover, David, *Vampires, Mummies, and Liberals: Bram Stoker and the Politics of Popular Fiction* (Durham, NC: Duke University Press, 1996)

Graham, Peter, 'Fictive Biography in 1816: The Case of *Glenarvon*', *The Byron Journal* (1991), 53–68

Groom, Nick, 'The Celtic Century and the Rise of Scottish Gothic', in *Scottish Gothic: An Edinburgh Companion*, ed. by Carol Margaret Davison and Monica Germana (Edinburgh: Edinburgh University Press, 2017), pp. 14–41

——— *The Vampire: A New History* (New Haven, CT and London: Yale University Press, 2018)

——— 'Thomas Chatterton and the Death of John William Polidori: Copycat or Coincidence?', *Notes and Queries*, 67:4 (2020), 534–36

—— 'Polidori's "The Vampyre": Composition, Publication, Deception', *Romanticism*, 28:1 (March 2022), 46–59
Hall Caine, Thomas, *Recollections of Dante Gabriel Rossetti* (London: Elliot Stock, 1882)
Harse, Katie, 'Melodrama Hath Charms: Planche's Theatrical Domestication of Polidori's "The Vampyre"', *Journal of Dracula Studies*, 3:1 (2001) https://research.library.kutztown.edu/dracula-studies/vol3/iss1/1 [accessed 22 April 2023]
Hawksley, Lucinda, *Lizzie Siddal: The Tragedy of a Pre-Raphaelite Supermodel* (London: André Deutsch, 2004)
Hay, Daisy, *Young Romantics: The Shelleys, Byron and Other Tangled Lives* (London: Bloomsbury, 2011)
Hazlitt, William, *Criticisms and Dramatic Essays of the English Stage* (London: Routledge, 1854)
Hellekson, Karen and Kristina Busse, 'Introduction: Why a Fan Fiction Studies Reader Now?', in *The Fan Fiction Studies Reader*, ed. by Karen Hellekson and Kristina Busse (Iowa City: University of Iowa Press, 2014), pp. 1–19
Hershkovitz, Israel *et al.*, 'Detection and Molecular Characterization of 9,000-Year-Old Mycobacterium Tuberculosis from a Neolithic Settlement in the Eastern Mediterranean', *PLOS One*, 3:10 (15 October 2008), e3426
Higgins, David, 'Celebrity, Politics and the Rhetoric of Genius', in *Romanticism and Celebrity Culture 1750–1850*, ed. by Tom Mole (Cambridge: Cambridge University Press, 2009), pp. 41–60
Hoermann, Raphael, '"A Very Hell of Horrors"? The Haitian Revolution and the Early Transatlantic Haitian Gothic', *Slavery & Abolition*, 37:1 (2016), 183–205
Hoffmann, E. T. A., *Tales of Hoffmann*, ed. by R. J. Hollingdale (Harmondsworth: Penguin, 1982)
Hogle, Jerrold E., 'The Rise of the Gothic Vampire: Disfiguration and Cathexis from Coleridge's "Christabel" to Nodier's *Smarra*', in *Gothic N.E.W.S., Volume I: Literature*, ed. by Max Duparray (Paris: Michel Houdiard, 2004), pp. 48–70
—— 'Gothic and Second-Generation Romanticism: Lord Byron, P. B. Shelley, John Polidori and Mary Shelley', in *Romantic Gothic: An Edinburgh Companion*, ed. by Angela Wright and Dale Townshend (Edinburgh: Edinburgh University Press, 2015), pp. 112–28
Hughes, Bill, 'Genre Mutation in YA Gothic: The Dialectics of Dystopia and Romance in Holly Black's *The Coldest Girl in Coldtown*', in *Young Adult Gothic Fiction: Monstrous Selves/Monstrous Others*, ed. by Michelle J. Smith and Kristine Moruzi, Gothic Literary Studies (Cardiff: University of Wales Press, 2021), pp. 37–59
Hughes, William, *That Devil's Trick: Hypnotism and the Victorian Popular Imagination* (Manchester: Manchester University Press, 2018)
Hutchings, Peter, *Hammer and Beyond* (Manchester: Manchester University Press, 1991)
Jackson, Tony E., *The Technology of the Novel: Writing and Narrative in British Fiction* (Baltimore, MD: Johns Hopkins University Press, 2009)
James, C. L. R., *The Black Jacobins: Toussaint L'Ouverture and the San Domingo Revolution*, ed. by James Walvin, new edn (London: Penguin, 1958)
James, M. R., 'The Ash Tree' [1904], in *Collected Ghost Stories*, ed. by Darryl Jones (Oxford: Oxford University Press, 2011), pp. 35–48
Jenkins, Elizabeth, *Lady Caroline Lamb* (London: Cardinal Books, 1974)

Jenkins, Henry, *Fans, Bloggers, and Gamers: Exploring Participatory Cuture* (New York: New York University Press, 2006)
—— *Textual Poachers: Television Fans and Participatory Culture* (London: Routledge, 2013)
Jentsch, Ernst, 'On the Psychology of the Uncanny (1906)', *Angelaki: Journal of Theoretical Humanities*, 2:1 (1997), 7–17
Johnson, Samuel, *The Rambler*, ed. by Alex Chalmers, 4 vols (Philadelphia, PA: E. Earle, 1812)
Jones, David J., *Gothic Machine: Textualities, Pre-Cinematic Media and Film in Popular Visual Culture, 1670–1910* (Cardiff: University of Wales Press, 2011)
Jordan, Neil, 'Interview with Neil Jordan', Team Deakins podcast, 22 August 2021 https://teamdeakins.libsyn.com/neil-jordan-director [accessed 23 August 2021]
Judson, Barbara, 'Roman à Clef and the Dynamics of Betrayal: The Case of *Glenarvon*', *Genre*, 33:2 (2000), 151–69 (p. 151)
Keats, John, *The Major Works*, ed. by Elizabeth Cook (Oxford and New York: Oxford University Press, 2001)
Kelly, Gary, 'Amelia Opie, Lady Caroline Lamb, and Maria Edgeworth: Official and Unofficial Ideology', *Ariel: A Review of International English Literature*, 12:4 (1981), 3–24
—— *English Fiction of the Romantic Period 1789–1830*, Longman Literature in English Series (London and New York: Routledge, 1989)
Kelly, James and Thomas Bartlett, eds, *The Cambridge History of Ireland: Volume 3, 1730–1880* (Cambridge: Cambridge University Press, 2020)
Kelsall, Malcolm, 'The Byronic Hero and Revolution in Ireland: The Politics of *Glenarvon*', *The Byron Journal*, 9 (1981), 4–19
—— *Byron's Politics* (Brighton and Totowa, NJ: Prentice Hall/Harvester Wheatsheaf, 1987)
—— 'Byron's Politics', in *The Cambridge Companion to Byron*, ed. by Drummond Bone, Cambridge Companions to Literature (Cambridge and New York: Cambridge University Press, 2004), pp. 44–55
Khair, Tabish, *The Gothic, Postcolonialism and Otherness: Ghosts from Elsewhere* (Basingstoke and New York: Palgrave Macmillan, 2009)
Khair, Tabish and Johan Höglund, eds, *Transnational and Postcolonial Vampires: Dark Blood* (Basingstoke and New York: Palgrave Macmillan, 2012)
Kourakine, Théodore, ed., *Souvenirs des voyages de la princesse Natalie Kourakine 1816–1830* (Moscow: Grosman, 1903)
Kristeva, Julia, *Powers of Horror: An Essay on Abjection*, trans. by Leon S. Roudiez (New York: Columbia University Press, 1982)
Kubiesa, Jane M., 'The Many Lives of Lord Ruthven: Somatic Adaptation, Reincarnation and (Mass) Consumption of Polidori's *The Vampyre*', *Revenant*, Special Issue: Vampires: Consuming Monsters and Monstrous Consumption, 9 (2023), 59–70
Labossiere, Pierre, Margaret Prescod, and Camila Valle, 'The Long Haitian Revolution', *Monthly Review*, 1 October 2021 https://monthlyreview.org/2021/10/01/the-long-haitian-revolution [accessed 5 May 2023]
Lamb, Lady Caroline, *Glenarvon*, intr. by Frances Wilson (1818; London: Everyman, 1995)
—— *Ada Reis: A Tale*, 3 vols (London: John Murray, 1823)
[Lamb, Lady Caroline], *A New Canto* (London: William Wright, 1819)

Lang, Andrew, *The Book of Dreams and Ghosts* (London: Longman, Green, and Co., 1897)
Laughlin, Harry H., *Eugenical Sterilization in the United States* (Chicago, IL: Psychopathic Laboratory of the Municipal Court of Chicago, 1922)
Lauro, Sarah Juliet, *The Transatlantic Zombie: Slavery, Rebellion, and Living Death*, American Literatures Initiative (New Brunswick, NJ: Rutgers University Press, 2015)
Lawlor, Clark, *Consumption and Literature: The Making of the Romantic Disease* (Basingstoke: Palgrave, 2006)
Le Fanu, Joseph, 'Carmilla', in *In a Glass Darkly*, ed. by Robert Tracy, World's Classics (1872; Oxford and New York: Oxford University Press, 1993), pp. 243–319
Leigh Hunt, James Henry, *Lord Byron and Some of His Contemporaries; with Recollections of the Author's Life, and of His Visit to Italy* (London: Colburn, 1828)
Loving, Matthew, 'Charles Nodier: The Romantic Librarian', *Libraries & Culture*, 38:2 (2003), 166–68
Lutz, Deborah, *The Dangerous Lover: Gothic Villains, Byronism, and the Nineteenth-Century Seduction Narrative* (Columbus: Ohio State University Press, 2006)
MacCarthy, Fiona, *Byron: Life and Legend* (London: Faber & Faber, 2003)
McConnell Stott, Andrew, *The Poet and the Vampyre: The Curse of Byron and the Birth of Literature's Greatest Monster* (New York: Pegasus Books, 2014)
—— *Summer in the Shadow of Byron* (Edinburgh: Canongate Books, 2015)
McCoy, Lauren, 'Literary Gossip: Caroline Lamb's *Glenarvon* and the Roman à Clef', *Eighteenth-Century Fiction*, 27:1 (2014), 127–50
McDayter, Ghislaine, 'Conjuring Byron: Byromania, Literary Commodification and the Birth of Celebrity', in Frances Wilson, *Byromania: Portraits of the Artist in Nineteenth- and Twentieth-Century Culture* (Basingstoke: Palgrave Macmillan, 1998), pp. 43–62
—— 'Hysterically Speaking: Lady Caroline Lamb's *Glenarvon* and the Revolutionary Voice', in *Romantic Generations: Essays in Honor of Robert F. Gleckner*, ed. by Barry Milligan and Ghislaine McDayter (Lewisburg, PA: Bucknell University Press, 2001), pp. 155–77
—— *Byromania and the Birth of Celebrity Culture* (Albany, NY: SUNY Press, 2010)
Macdonald, D. L., *Poor Polidori: A Critical Biography of the Author of 'The Vampyre'* (Toronto, ON: University of Toronto Press, 1991)
Macdonald, D. L. and Kathleen Scherf, 'Introduction', in *The Vampyre and Ernestus Berchtold; or, the Modern Oedipus*, by John William Polidori, ed. by D. L. Macdonald and Kathleen Scherf (Peterborough, ON: Broadview Press, 2008), pp. 8–31
McFarland, Ronald E., 'The Vampire on Stage: A Study in Adaptations', *Comparative Drama*, 21:1 (1987), 19–33
McGann, Jerome, 'Byron, George Gordon Noel, Sixth Baron Byron (1788–1824), Poet', in *Oxford Dictionary of National Biography*, ed. by Henry Colin Gray Matthew and Brian Howard Harrison (Oxford: Oxford University Press, 2004), pp. 1–32
McLaughlin, Daniel, 'A Village Still in Thrall to Dracula', *The Observer*, 19 June 2005 www.theguardian.com/world/2005/jun/19/theobserver [accessed 30 July 2020]
Macleod, A. D., 'Eyelid Closure at Death', *Indian Journal of Palliative Care*, 15:2 (July–December 2009) www.ncbi.nlm.nih.gov/pmc/articles/PMC2902109/ [accessed 23 June 2022]

McLuhan, Marshall, *Understanding Media: The Extensions of Man* (1964; Berkeley, CA: Gingko Press, 2014)
Macmillan, Dougald, 'Planché's Early Classical Burlesques', *Studies in Philology*, 25 (1928), 340–45
—— 'Planché's Fairy Extravaganzas', *Studies in Philology*, 25 (1928), 790–98
Macpherson, James, *Poems of Ossian* (London: A. Strahan & T. Cadell, 1796)
Maddison, Anna Francesca, 'Conjugal Love and the Afterlife: New Readings of Selected Works by Dante Gabriel Rossetti in the Context of Swedenborgian-Spiritualism' (unpublished doctoral thesis, Edge Hill University, 2013)
Mannoni, Laurent, *The Great Art of Light and Shadow*, ed. and trans. by Richard Crangle (Exeter: University of Exeter Press, 2000)
Mannoni, Laurent and Ben Brewster, 'The Phantasmagoria', *Film History*, 8:4 (1996), 390–415
Matheson, Richard, *I Am Legend* (1954; London: Gollancz, 2001)
Medwin, Thomas, *The Life of Percy Bysshe Shelley*, ed. by Harry Buxton Forman (London: Oxford University Press, 1913)
Mee, Jon, *Romanticism, Enthusiasm, and Regulation: Poetics and the Policing of Culture in the Romantic Period* (Oxford: Oxford University Press, 2003)
Meyer, David, *Harlequin in His Element: The English Pantomime, 1806–1836* (Cambridge, MA: Harvard University Press, 1969)
Meyer, Stephenie, *Twilight*, The Twilight Saga, 1 (2005; London: Atom, 2006)
—— *Eclipse*, The Twilight Saga, 3 (London: Atom, 2007)
—— *Midnight Sun* (London: Atom, 2020)
Milton, John, *Paradise Lost*, in *The Complete Poems*, ed. by Gordon Campbell (London and Melbourne: Dent, 1986)
Mitford, John, 'Account of Lord Byron's Residence in the Island of Mitylene', *The New Monthly Magazine*, 10:58 (1 November 1818), 309–11
Mole, Tom, *Byron's Romantic Celebrity: Industrial Culture and the Hermeneutic of Intimacy* (London: Palgrave Macmillan, 2007)
Moncrieff, A. R. Hope, *Classical Mythology* (London: Senate, 1994)
Moore, John, *Zeluco*, ed. by Pam Perkins (Kansas City, MO: Valancourt Books, 2012)
Moore, Thomas, *The Life of Lord Byron* (London: John Murray, 1844)
Moran, Nancy A., 'Symbiosis', *Current Biology*, 16:20 (2006), 866–71
More, Henry, *An Antidote against Atheism*, Book III, Chapter IX (London: printed by Roger Daniel, 1653) https://en.wikisource.org/wiki/An_Antidote_Against_Atheism/Book_III/Chapter_IX [accessed 21 July 2020]
Morin, Christina, *The Gothic Novel in Ireland, c. 1760–1829* (Manchester: Manchester University Press, 2021)
Morrill, David F., '"Twilight Is Not Good for Maidens": Uncle Polidori and the Psychodynamics of Vampirism in "Goblin Market"', *Victorian Poetry*, 28:1 (1990), 1–16
Morrison, Robert and Chris Baldick, 'Introduction', *The Vampyre and Other Tales of the Macabre*, ed. by Robert Morrison and Chris Baldick (Oxford: Oxford University Press, 2008), pp. vii–xxiii
Morrison, Ronald D., '"Their Fruits like Honey in the Throat / But Poison in the Blood": Christina Rossetti and *The Vampyre*', *Weber Studies*, 14:2 (1997) www.weber.edu/weberjournal/Journal_Archives/Archive_B/Vol_14_2/RMorrisonEss.html [accessed 30 May 2023]

Moruzu, Kristine, 'Postfeminist Fantasies: Sexuality and Femininity in Stephenie Meyer's "Twilight" Series', in *Genre, Reception, and Adaptation in the 'Twilight' Series*, ed. by Anne Morey (Farnham: Ashgate Publishing, 2012)

Mulvey, Laura, 'Visual Pleasures and Narrative Cinema', in *Visual and Other Pleasures* (Basingstoke: Macmillan, 1989), pp. 14–28

Murgoci, Agnes, 'The Vampire in Roumania', *Folklore*, 37:4 (1926), 324–26

Murray, John, *A Treatise on Pulmonary Consumption, Its Prevention and Remedy* (London: Longman, Hurst, Rees, Brown, Orme and Brown, 1830)

Nesbit, William, *An Inquiry Into the History, Nature, Causes, and Different Modes of Treatment: Hitherto Pursued, in the Cure of Scrophula and Cancer* (Edinburgh: Alex. Chapman & Co, 1795)

Newall, Venetia, 'Birds in the Icon Tradition', in *Animals in Folklore*, ed. by J. R. Porter and W. M. S. Russell (Cambridge: D. S. Brewer, 1978), pp. 185–207

Nicoll, Allardyce, *The World of Harlequin* (Cambridge: Cambridge University Press, 1963)

Nodier, Charles, *The Vampire*, trans. by Frank J. Morlock, in *Lord Ruthven the Vampire*, ed. by Frank J. Morlock (Encino, CA: Black Coat Press, 2014), pp. 80–161

Normington, Susan, *Lady Caroline Lamb, That Infernal Woman* (London: House of Stratus, 2001)

O'Brien, Harvey, 'Creation Myth: The Imagining of the Gothic Imagination in the Diodati Tryptych: *Gothic* (1986), *Haunted Summer* (1988), and *Remando al viento* (1988)', *Gothic Studies*, 24:2 (2022), 118–36

Oliver, Alfred Richard, *Charles Nodier: Pilot of Romanticism* (Syracuse, NY: Syracuse University Press, 1964)

Olsen, Gregory, 'Rewriting the Byronic Hero: "I'll Try the Firmness of a Female Hand"', *European Romantic Review*, 25:4 (2014), 463–77

Ovid, *Metamorphoses*, trans. by David Raeburn (London: Penguin, 2004), I. 76–88

Paraschas, Sotirios, 'The Vampire as a Metaphor for Authorship from Polidori to Charles Nodier', *Compar(a)ison*, 1–2 (2015), 83–97

Pears, Charles, *Observations on the Nature and Treatment of Consumption; Addressed to Patients and Families* (London: Highley and Son, 1814)

Petrain, David E., 'An English Translation of John William Polidori's (1815) Medical Dissertation on Oneirodynia (Somnambulism)', *European Romantic Review*, 21:6 (2010), 775–88

Planché, James Robinson, *The Vampire; or, The Bride of the Isles* [1820], in *Plays by James Robertson Planché*, ed. by Donald Roy (Cambridge: Cambridge University Press, 1986), pp. 45–68

—— *The Recollections and Reflections of J. R. Planché*, 2 vols (London: Tinsley Brothers, 1872; rpt. Cambridge: Cambridge University Press, 2011)

Pliny the Elder, *The Elder Pliny on the Human Animal: Natural History, Book 7*, ed. and trans. by Mary Beagon (Oxford: Clarendon Press, 2005)

Podmore, Frank, *Modern Spiritualism: A History and a Criticism*, 2 vols (London: Methuen & Co., 1902)

Polidori, Gaetano, *La Magion del Terrore con note che contengono le memorie di quattro anni nei quali l'autore fu segretario del Conte Alfieri*, ed. by Roberto Fedi (Palermo: Sellerio, 1997)

Polidori, John William, 'Letter', *Morning Chronicle* (24 September 1819), 4

—— *The Diary of Dr. John William Polidori, 1816: Relating to Byron, Shelley, etc.*, ed. by William Michael Rossetti (London: Elkin Mathews, 1911)

―― *The Vampyre and Ernestus Berchtold; or, The Modern Oedipus: Collected Fiction of John William Polidori*, ed. by D. L. Macdonald and Kathleen Scherf (Toronto, ON: University of Toronto Press, 1994)
―― 'The Vampyre', in *The Vampyre and Other Tales of the Macabre*, ed. by Robert Morrison and Chris Baldick (Oxford: Oxford University Press, 1998), pp. 3–23
―― *'The Vampyre' and Other Writings*, ed. by Franklin Charles Bishop (Manchester: Carcanet/Fyfield Books, 2005)
―― *The Vampyre and Ernestus Berchtold; or, The Modern Oedipus*, ed. by D. L. Macdonald and Kathleen Scherf (Peterborough, ON: Broadview Press, 2008)
―― 'The Vampyre', in *Visions of the Vampire: Two Hundred Years of Immortal Tales*, ed. by Sorcha Ní Fhlainn and Xavier Aldana Reyes (London: British Library, 2020), pp. 1–21
Portelli, Alessandro, *The Death of Luigi Trastulli and Other Stories: Form and Meaning in Oral History* (New York: SUNY Press, 1991)
Powers, Tim, *The Stress of Her Regard* (1989; London: Grafton, 1993)
Prantera, Amanda, *Conversations with Lord Byron on Perversion, 163 Years After His Lordship's Death* (1987; London: Abacus, 1988)
Praz, Mario, *The Romantic Agony*, trans. by Angus Davidson, rev. edn (Oxford: Oxford University Press, 1970)
'Preliminaries for *The Vampyre*', in *The Vampyre and Other Tales of the Macabre*, ed. by Robert Morrison and Chris Baldick (Oxford: Oxford University Press, 2008), pp. 235–43
Punter, David, *The Literature of Terror: A History of Gothic Fictions from 1765 to the Present Day*, 2 vols (London and New York: Longman, 1996)
Reinhardt, Paul, 'The Costume Designs of James Robinson Planché (1796–180)', *Educational Theatre Journal*, 20 (1968), 524–44
'Review of "Treatise on Pulmonary Consumption"', *Edinburgh Medical and Surgical Journal*, 4:15 (1808), 367
Rice, Anne, *Interview with the Vampire*, The Vampire Chronicles, 1 (1976; London: Sphere, 2008)
―― *Queen of the Damned*, The Vampire Chronicles, 3 (New York: Ballantine, 1988)
―― *Queen of the Damned*, The Vampire Chronicles, 3 (London: Macdonald, 1989)
Rieger, James, 'Dr. Polidori and the Genesis of *Frankenstein*', *Studies in English Literature, 1500–1900*, 3:4 (Winter 1963), 461–72
Rigby, Mair, '"Prey to Some Cureless Disquiet": Polidori's Queer Vampyre at the Margins of Romanticism', *Romanticism on the Net*, 36–37 (2004) doi:10.7202/011135ar
Robertson, Etienne Gaspard, *Mémoires: récréatifs, scientifiques et anecdotiques* (Paris: Chez l'auteur et à la Librairie de Wurtz, 1831–33), online at Harry Houdini Collection, Library of Congress www.loc.gov/resource/rbc0001.2009houdini06148/ [accessed 29 November 2020]
Rogers, Samuel, *Table Talk* (New York: Appleton, 1856)
Rojek, Chris, *Fame Attack: The Inflation of Celebrity and Its Consequences* (London: Bloomsbury Academic, 2012)
'Romance', in *The Oxford Dictionary of Literary Terms* [online], www.oxfordreference.com/view/10.1093/acref/9780198715443.001.0001/acref-9780198715443-e-997 [accessed 4 February 2022]

Rossetti, Christina, 'Goblin Market', in *Selected Poems*, ed. by Dinah Roe (London: Penguin Classics, 2008), pp. 67–83

Rossetti, Dante Gabriel, *His Family Letters with a Memoir by William Michael Rossetti*, ed. by William Michael Rossetti, 2 vols (Boston, MA: Roberts Brothers, 1895)

Rossetti, William Michael, *Rossetti Papers 1862 to 1870* (London: Sands & Co, 1903)

—— 'Introduction', *The Diary of Dr. John William Polidori, 1816: Relating to Byron, Shelley, etc.*, ed. by William Michael Rossetti (London: Elkin Mathews, 1911)

Roy, Donald, 'Introduction', in *Plays by James Robinson Planché* (Cambridge: Cambridge University Press, 1986), pp. 1–35

Rutecki, Gregory, 'Consumption and Vampires: Metaphor and Myth before Science', *Hektoen International: A Journal of Medical Humanities*, 9:2 (spring 2017) https://hekint.org/2017/03/04/consumption-and-vampires-metaphor-and-myth-before-science/ [accessed 23 June 2022]

Rymer, James, *Varney the Vampire, or the Feast of Blood*, 2 vols (1845–47; London: Dover, 1972)

—— *Varney, the Vampire; or, The Feast of Blood* (1845–47; Ware: Wordsworth, 2010)

Salgues, Jacques-Barthèlemy, *Des Erreurs et des préjugés répandus dans la société*, 3 vols (Paris: F. Buisson, 1810–13)

Sanders, James, *Treatise on Pulmonary Consumption, in Which a New View of the Principles of Its Treatment is Supported by Original Observations on Every Period of the Disease. To Which Is Added, an Inquiry, Proving, That the Medicinal Properties of the Digitalis, or Foxglove, Are Diametrically Opposed to What They Are Believed to Be* (Edinburgh: Walker and Grieg, 1808)

Sandvoss, Cornel, *Fans: The Mirror of Consumption* (Cambridge: Polity Press, 2005)

Sansay, Leonora, *Secret History; or, The Horrors of St. Domingo and Laura*, ed. by Michael J. Drexler (Peterborough, ON: Broadview Press, 2007)

Schein, Chelsea and Kurt Gray, 'The Eyes are the Window to the Uncanny Soul: Mind Perception, Autism and Missing Souls', *Interaction Studies*, 16:2 (2015), pp. 173–79

Scott, Julius S., *The Common Wind: Afro-American Currents in the Age of the Haitian Revolution* (London: Verso, 2018)

Sedgwick, Marcus, 'The Elusive Vampire, Folklore and Fiction', in *Open Graves, Open Minds: Representations of Vampires and the Undead from the Enlightenment to the Present Day*, ed. by Sam George and Bill Hughes (Manchester: Manchester University Press, 2013), pp. 264–75

Senf, Carol A., 'Polidori's "The Vampyre": Combining the Gothic with Realism', *North Dakota Quarterly*, 56:1 (1988), 197–208

—— *The Vampire in Nineteenth-Century English Literature* (Bowling Green, OH: Bowling Green State University Popular Press, 1988)

Shakespeare, William, *The Norton Shakespeare*, ed. by Stephen Greenblatt *et al.* (New York and London: W. W. Norton, 1997)

Shaw, Helen, '"Within Fifteen Minutes, It Became Unbearable": The Bloody Broadway Mess That Was Dance of the Vampires', *Vulture*, 14 August 2020, www.vulture.com/article/broadway-dance-of-the-vampires-bloody-disaster.html [accessed 13 August 2021]

Shelley, Mary, *Frankenstein; or, The Modern Prometheus*, ed. by Nick Groom (1818; Oxford: Oxford University Press, 2018)

―――― *Frankenstein; or, The Modern Prometheus*, ed. by M. K. Joseph (1831; Oxford: Oxford University Press, 1998)
―――― *The Last Man*, ed. by Morton D. Paley (Oxford: Oxford University Press, 1998)
Shelley, Percy Bysshe, *The Major Works*, ed. by Zachary Leader and Michael O'Neill (Oxford and New York: Oxford University Press, 2009)
Skal, David J., '"His Hour Upon the Stage": Theatrical Adaptations of Dracula', in Bram Stoker, *Dracula*, ed. by Nina Auerbach and David J. Skal (New York and London: W. W. Norton, 1997), pp. 371–81
Skarda, Patricia L., 'Vampirism and Plagiarism: Byron's Influence and Polidori's Practice', *Studies in Romanticism*, 28:2 (1989), 249–69
Soderholm, James, *Fantasy, Forgery, and the Byron Legend* (Lexington: University Press of Kentucky, 1995)
Sontag, Susan, *Illness as Metaphor* (New York: Farrar, Straus and Giroux, 1978)
Southey, Henry Herbert, *Observations on Pulmonary Consumption* (London: Longman, Hurst, Rees, Brown, Orme and Brown, 1814)
Spooner, Catherine, *Fashioning Gothic Bodies* (Manchester: Manchester University Press, 2004)
―――― '*Gothic Charm School*; or, How Vampires Learned to Sparkle', in *Open Graves, Open Minds: Representations of Vampires and the Undead from the Enlightenment to the Present Day*, ed. by Sam George and Bill Hughes (Manchester: Manchester University Press, 2013), pp. 146–64
―――― *Post-Millennial Gothic: Comedy, Romance and the Rise of Happy Gothic* (London: Bloomsbury Academic, 2017)
Stauffer, Andrew, 'Speaking with the Dead: The Séance Diary of William Michael Rossetti, 1865–68', *The Journal of Pre-Raphaelite Studies*, 24 (Spring 2015), 35–43
Stevenson, Robert Louis, *The Strange Case of Dr Jekyll and Mr Hyde and Other Tales*, ed. by Roger Luckhurst (Oxford: Oxford University Press, 2008)
Stiles, Anne, Stanley Finger, and John Bulevich, 'Somnambulism and Trance States in the Works of John William Polidori, Author of *The Vampyre*', *European Romantic Review*, 21:6 (2010), 789–807
Stoker, Bram, *The Primrose Path* (1875; Westcliff-on-Sea: Desert Island Books, 1999)
―――― 'The Secret of the Growing Gold', *Black and White*, 3 (23 January 1892), 118–21
―――― *Dracula*, ed. by Nina Auerbach and David J. Skal (1897; New York and London: W. W. Norton, 1997)
―――― *Snowbound: The Record of a Theatrical Touring Party* (London: Collier & Co, 1908)
―――― 'The Star Trap' [1908], in *The Bram Stoker Bedside Companion* (London: Victor Gollancz, 1973), pp. 102–14
―――― *Bram Stoker's Notes for Dracula: A Facsimile Edition*, ed. by Robert Eighteen-Bisang and Elizabeth Miller (Jefferson, NC: McFarland, 2008)
Stott, Andrew McConnell, *The Poet and the Vampire: The Curse of Byron and the Birth of Literature's Greatest Monsters* (New York: Pegasus, 2014)
Stuart, Roxana, *Stage Blood: Vampires of the 19th-Century Stage* (Bowling Green, OH: Bowling Green State University Press, 1994)
Süner, Ahmet, 'The Gothic Horrors of the Private Realm and the Return to the Public in John Polidori's *The Vampyre*', *Moderna Språk*, 1 (2018), 187–200
Summers, Montague, *The Vampire in Europe* (London: Kegan Paul, 1929)

―――― *The Vampire, His Kith and Kin* (London: E. P. Dutton, 1929; rpt. as *Vampires and Vampirism* (Mineola, NY: Dover, 2005))

'Summary Bibliography: E. T. A. Hoffmann', Internet Speculative Fiction Database www.isfdb.org/cgi-bin/ea.cgi?19492 [accessed 8 August 2022]

Sutherland, John and Kevin Rawlinson, 'Gravestone-Encircled "Hardy Tree" Falls in London', *The Guardian*, 27 December 2022 www.theguardian.com/uk-news/2022/dec/27/historic-hardy-tree-falls-in-london [accessed 7 May 2023]

Swift, Jonathan, *A Tale of a Tub and Other Works*, ed. by Angus Ross and David Woolley (Oxford and New York: Oxford University Press, 2008)

Switzer, Richard, 'Lord Ruthwen and the Vampires', *The French Review*, 29:2 (December 1955), 107–11

Telotte, J. P., 'A Parasitic Perspective: Romantic Participation and Polidori's *The Vampyre*', in *The Blood Is the Life: Vampires in Literature*, ed. by Leonard G. Heldreth and Mary Pharr (Bowling Green, OH: Bowling Green State University Popular Press, 1999), pp. 9–18

Thorslev, P. L., *The Byronic Hero: Types and Prototypes* (Minneapolis: University of Minnesota Press, 1962)

Throsby, Corin, 'Byron, Commonplacing and Early Fan Culture', in *Romanticism and Celebrity Culture 1750–1850*, ed. by Tom Mole (Cambridge: Cambridge University Press, 2009), pp. 227–45

Tisseron, Serge, *Secrets de famille, mode d'emploi* (Paris: Ramsay, 1996)

Tournefort, Joseph Pitton de, *A Voyage into the Levant* (London: Midwinter, Ware, Rivington, Ward, and Knapton, Longman, Hett, Hitch, Austen, Wood and Woodward, and Pemberton, 1741) [Translation of *Relation d'un voyage du Levant* (1717)]

Tuite, Clara, 'Tainted Love and Romantic Literary Celebrity', *ELH*, 74:1 (2007), 59–88

―――― *Lord Byron and Scandalous Celebrity* (Cambridge: Cambridge University Press, 2015)

Turton, William, *Observations on Consumption, Scrofula or King's Evil, Gout, Asthma, Softness and Distortion of the Bones, Rickets, Cancer, Insanity and Other Chronical Diseases: With Reasonings on Their Remote Origin, Probably Affinity, and Means of Prevention and Cure: In Six Consultations* (Dublin: Graisberry and Campbell, 1813)

Twitchell, James B., *The Living Dead: A Study of the Vampire in Romantic Literature* (Durham, NC: Duke University Press, 1981)

Thelwall, John, *The Daughter of Adoption: A Tale of Modern Times*, ed. by Michael Scrivener, Yasmin Solomonescu, and Judith Thompson (Peterborough, ON: Broadview Press, 2013)

Uden, James, 'Gothic Fiction, the Grand Tour, and the Seductions of Antiquity: John Polidori's "The Vampyre" (1819)', in *Illusions and Disillusionment: Travel Writing in the Modern Age*, ed. by R. Micallef (Boston, MA: ILEX Foundation, 2018), pp. 60–79

[Utterson, Sarah Elizabeth], ed., *Tales of the Dead* (London: White, Cochrane, and Co., 1813)

Vickers, Neil, 'Coleridge, Thomas Beddoes and Brunonian Medicine', *European Romantic Review*, 8:1 (1997), 47–94

Viets, Henry R., 'By the Visitation of God: The Death of John William Polidori, M.D. in 1821', *British Medical Journal* (1961), 1773–75

―――― 'The London Editions of Polidori's *The Vampyre*', *The Papers of the Bibliographical Society of America*, 63:2 (1969), 83–103

Vieux-Chauvet, Marie, *Love, Anger, Madness: A Haitian Triptych*, trans. by Rose-Myriam Réjouis and Val Vinokur (New York: Modern Library, 2010)

A Walk in the Past (London: St Pancras Old Church, no date)

Warner, Marina, *Phantasmagoria: Spirit Visions, Metaphors, and Media into the Twenty-First Century* (Oxford: Oxford University Press, 2006)

Wassif, Marriam, 'Polidori's *The Vampyre* and Byron's Portraits', *The Wordsworth Circle*, 49 (Winter 2018), 53–61

Wasson, Sara and Sarah Artt, 'The Twilight Saga and the Pleasures of Spectatorship: the Broken Body and the Shining Body', in *Open Graves, Open Minds: Representations of Vampires and the Undead from the Enlightenment to the Present Day*, ed. by Sam George and Bill Hughes (Manchester: Manchester University Press, 2013), pp. 181–91

Watson, Nicola J., 'Trans-Figuring Byronic Identity', in *At the Limits of Romanticism: Essays in Cultural, Feminist, and Materialist Criticism*, ed. by Mary A. Favret and Nicola J. Watson (Bloomington: Indiana University Press, 1994), pp. 185–206

[Watts, Alaric], editorial note to 'The Vampyre', *The New Monthly Magazine*, 11:63 (1 April 1819), 195–96

Wester, Maisha L., 'The Gothic and the Politics of Race', in *The Cambridge Companion to the Modern Gothic*, ed. by Jerrold E. Hogle (Cambridge: Cambridge University Press, 2014), pp. 157–73

White, Ed and Duncan Faherty, 'Introduction', in Uriah Derek D'Arcy, 'The Black Vampyre; A Legend of St. Domingo (1819)', ed. by Ed White, Duncan Faherty, and Toni Wall Jaudon, pp. 1–11, Just Teach One, http://jto.common-place.org/just-teach-one-homepage/the-black-vampyre/ [accessed 7 June 2020].

Wilde, Oscar, *The Picture of Dorian Gray*, ed. by Joseph Bristow (1891; Oxford: Oxford University Press, 2006)

Williams, Eric, *Capitalism and Slavery* (London: Penguin, 1944)

Wilson, Frances, '"An Exaggerated Woman": The Melodramas of Lady Caroline Lamb', in *Byromania: Portraits of the Artist in Nineteenth- and Twentieth-Century Culture*, ed. by Frances Wilson (Basingstoke: Palgrave Macmillan, 1998), pp. 195–220

―――― 'Introduction: Byron, Byronism and Byromaniacs', in *Byromania: Portraits of the Artist in Nineteenth- and Twentieth-Century Culture*, ed. by Frances Wilson (Basingstoke: Palgrave Macmillan, 1998), pp. 1–23

Wilson, Frances, ed., *Byromania: Portraits of the Artist in Nineteenth- and Twentieth-Century Culture* (Basingstoke: Palgrave Macmillan, 1998)

Wisker, Gina, *Contemporary Women's Gothic Fiction: Carnival, Hauntings and Vampire Kisses* (London: Palgrave, 2016)

Wood, Gaby, *Living Dolls: A Magical History of the Quest for Mechanical Life* (London: Faber & Faber, 2002)

Wu, Duncan, 'Appropriating Byron: Lady Caroline Lamb's "A New Canto"', *The Wordsworth Circle*, 26 (1995), 140–46

Wynne, Catherine, *Bram Stoker, Dracula and the Victorian Gothic Stage* (London: Palgrave, 2013)
Yarbro, Chelsea Quinn, *Hôtel Transylvania* (New York: Tor, 1978).
Zucker, Carole, *The Cinema of Neil Jordan: Dark Carnival* (New York: Wallflower, 2008)

Film

Bram Stoker's Dracula, dir. by Frances Ford Coppola (Zoetrope, 1992)
Byzantium, dir. by Neil Jordan (StudioCanal, 2012)
The Cabinet of Dr Caligari, dir. by Robert Wiene (UFA GmbH/Decla-Bioscop AG, 1920)
Dracula, dir. by Tod Browning (Universal Pictures, 1932)
The Golem: How He Came into the World, dir. by Paul Wegener (PAGU, 1920)
Gothic, dir. by Ken Russell (MGM, 1986)
Haunted Summer, dir. by Ivan Passer (Cannon Films, 1988)
Interview with the Vampire, dir. by Neil Jordan (The Geffen Film Company, 1994)
Mary Shelley, dir. by Haifaa Al-Mansour (HanWay Films, 2017)
The Mechanical Man, dir. by André Deed (Società Anonima Milano Films, 1921)
Nosferatu: Eine Symphonie des Grauens, dir. by F. W. Murnau (Film Arts Guild, 1922)
Queen of the Damned, dir. by Michael Rymer (Warner Bros, 2002)
Remando al viento [*Rowing with the Wind*], dir. by Gonzalo Suárez (Ditirambo Films, 1988)
Twilight, dir. by Catherine Hardwicke (Summit Entertainment, 2009)
Ultraviolet, dir. by Kurt Wimmer (Screen Gems, Ultravi Productions, 2006)

Television

Dracula, dir. by Derek Towers, writ. by Christopher Frayling, 1:1 (BBC, 1996)
Frankenstein: The True Story, dir. by Jack Smight, writ. by Don Bachardy and Christopher Isherwood (BBC, 1973)
'The Haunting of Villa Diodati', *Doctor Who*, 12:8, dir. by Emma Sullivan, writ. by Maxine Alderton (BBC, 16 February 2020)
'In the Dark', *Angel*, 1:3, writ. by Douglas Petrie, dir. by Bruce Seth Green (The WB, 19 October 1999)
Mechanical Marvels: Clockwork Dreams, dir. by Nic Stacey, writ. by Simon Schaffer (BBC, 2014)
Nightmare: The Birth of Horror, created by Christopher Frayling (BBC, 1996)

Web series

Carmilla, created by Jordan Hall, Steph Ouaknine, and Jay Bennett (Smokebomb Entertainment, 2014–16) www.youtube.com/watch?v=3uPd3g5wi1A [accessed 4 July 2022]

Stage performances

Dance of the Vampires, dir. by John Rando, music by Jim Steinman, lyrics by Jim Steinman, book by David Ives, Jim Steinman, and Michael Kunze (New York: Minskoff Theatre, December 2002–January 2003)

Lestat, dir. by Robert Jess Roth, music and lyrics by Elton John and Bernie Taupin, book by Linda Woolverton (New York: Palace Theatre, March–May 2006)

Index

Note: literary works can be found under author's names; some key texts are also itemised for easy reference. Page numbers in *italic* refer to illustrations.

9/11 *see* terrorism

Aaliyah 69
Abbott, Stacey 18, 45
abject, the 148, 160, 225
Abraham, Nicolas and Maria Torok 14, 49, 57–8
    see also psychoanalysis
agency 25, 38–9, 90, 152, 170
    see also determinism; free will
allegory 11, 13, 154, 220
    see also genre
American revolution 156
    see also revolution
Angel (1999–2004 TV series)
angels 25, 27, 38, 59, 88, 119, 147, 193, 210, 233
    fallen 85, 88
anti-imperialism 93
    see also colonialism; imperialism; postcolonialism
anti-Jacobin novel 15, 93, 96
    see also genre
antiquarianism 10, 11, 133
aristocracy; aristocrat; aristocratic 3–4, 8, 10–12, 14, 15, 17–18, 19–20, 23–4, 25, 36, 51, 64–5, 70, 96–8, 143, 144, 145, 147, 156, 162, 171, 218, 219–20
    see also class; vampires, aristocratic
Artt, Sarah *see* Wasson, Sara, and Sarah Artt
Astle, Richard Sharpe 13

Aubrey, John 11, 131
Auerbach, Nina 10–11, 34, 70, 76, 187, 188–9
autobiography 21n45, 52, 67–8, 81–2, 83
    see also biography; genre
automata 103–4n59, 169–70, 171
    see also agency; determinism; free will

Bainbridge, Simon 12, 97, 131, 133, 134, 206, 213
Bakhtin, Mikhail 33–5
    see also heteroglossia
Baldick, Chris *see* Morrison, Robert, and Chris Baldick
Barber, Paul 24, 115
Beddoes, Thomas 106–7, 109, *109*, 110, 112, 114, 120n16
Bérard, Cyprien, *Lord Ruthwen ou les Vampires* (1820) 23, 25, 38
    see also Polidori, John William, *Vampyre, The*, sequels
biography 21n45, 83, 120n16, 190
    see also autobiography; genre; *roman á clef*
Black, Holly, *The Coldest Girl in Coldtown* (2013) 100
Black Vampyre, The (1819) *see* D'Arcy, Uriah Derick
Blake, William 236
body horror *see* horror, body
Boone, Troy 11
Botting, Fred 70

Boucicault, Dion *The Phantom* (1857) 24
  see also Polidori, John William, *The Vampyre*, stage adaptations
bourgeoisie 11–12, 13, 96–7, 144, 160, 182
  see also aristocracy; class
Bowie, David 69
Bram Stoker's Dracula (1992 film) 98, 173, 181, 196
  see also Bram Stoker, *Dracula*; Count Dracula; vampires, as lovers
Bray, Katie 144, 151, 152, 154, 155
Brazier, Nicholas, Gabriel De Lurieu, and Armand d'Artois *Les trois vampires ou le clair de la lune* (1820) 28
  see also Polidori, John William, *Vampyre, The,* stage adaptations
Brenton, Howard 9
Brontë, Emily, *Wuthering Heights* (1847) 97–8
Brontës, the 25, 86, 98
Buck-Morss, Susan 153
Budge, Gavin 12
Buffini, Moira, *Byzantium* (2012) 193, 199n20, 199n23
Burke, Edmund 155, 158, 170–1
burlesque 28, 29, 154
  see also theatre
Butler, Erik 11
Butler, Octavia, *Fledgling* (2005) 18, 217, 219–20, 221, 222–3, 225–30
Byrne, Katherine 109
Byromania 9, 15, 64–80, 83, 91, 102n33
  see also fan culture; fan fiction; fan studies
Byron, Lord George 3, 4, 5, 6–8, 9–11, 12, 14, 15–16, 17, 20n24, 23, 24, 26, 28, 36, 38, 49, 50, 51, 53–7, 64–9, 70–1, 72, 73–7, 81–2, 82, 83, 85–6, 87–8, 89, 90–2, 94–5, 96, 97–8
  Childe Harold's Pilgrimage (1812–18) 67, 68, 71, 72, 74–5, 97
  Corsair, The (1814) 102n34
  Don Juan (1819–24) 87
  'A Fragment' (1819) 23, 52, 76, 82, 90
    Darvell 23, 90
    see also *Byzantium* (film)
  Giaour, The (1813) 52, 71, 74
  Lara (1814) 86
Byronic hero 24, 75, 90, 94, 96, 97, 104n65
  see also Byron, Lord George Gordon
Byronic persona 64, 77, 86, 87–90, 91
  female 87–90, 91, 102n28, 102n34
  see also Byron, Lord George Gordon
Byronic romance 72, 74–5
  see also genre; Romance (genre)
Byronic vampire see vampire, Byronic
Byronism 12, 15, 81, 86–8, 90, 91, 92, 94–5, 97, 137
  see also Byromania; Byron, Lord George Gordon
Byzantium (2012 film) 17, 186–7, 191, 193–6, 199n23, 200n28
  see also Jordan, Neil

capitalism 144, 153, 156–7, 160
  see also commercial society; commodification; consumer culture
Caribbean 143, 144, 151, 152, 161
Carmilla (2014–16 TV series) 181
  see also Le Fanu, Sheridan, *Carmilla*
Carmilla (novella) see Le Fanu, Sheridan
Carter, Angela 193
celebrity 14–15, 17, 64–80, 81, 83, 85, 88, 92, 131, 202, 204, 211, 213
  see also fan culture
Christian legend 152
  see also folklore; myth
Clairmont, Claire 3, 5, 7, 16, 55, 100, 123, 131
class 10–11, 12, 13, 64, 66, 72, 96–7, 133, 187–8, 189, 194, 195
Cold War 218–19
Coleridge, Samuel Taylor 13, 112, 117
  Christabel (1797–1800) 117
  Rime of the Ancient Mariner, The (1798) 117, 129

colonialism 147, 151, 159, 160, 161, 162
    see also anti-imperialism; colonialism; postcolonial
commercial society 16, 97, 156, 162
    see also consumer culture, consumerism
commodification 66–7, 83, 143, 147, 153, 156, 157, 159, 161
    of bodies 147, 153, 156, 157, 159
        see also slavery
    of literature 66–7, 83, 143, 159
confession 17, 128, 186, 189, 190, 193, 196–7, 198
consumer culture; consumerism 17, 64, 66–7, 68, 70, 159, 205
    see also commercial society; commodification
consumption (tuberculosis) 106–22, 173–4, 15
contagion; infection 13, 81–2, 86–7, 88–9, 90–1, 92, 93, 95, 96, 97, 106–22, 123–4, 186, 218, 220, 222, 223–5, 232n16, 232n17
    see also disease; illness; vampires, as contagious
Count Dracula 4, 5, 17, 24, 39–40, 47n82, 49, 92, 98, 106, 119, 161, 171, 176, 179–81, 189, 218, 228
    see also Stoker, Bram, *Dracula*
Covid-19 221, 232n14, 232n17
    see also contagion; disease; illness
Crawford, Joseph 207, 214
Cronin, Justin 17–18, 217, 219–22, 223–5, 230
    City of Mirrors, The (2016) 225
    Passage, The (2010) 223–5
cross-dressing 83, 90
    see also gender

Dance of the Vampires (stage musical) 197–8, 200–01n34
D'Arcy, Uriah Derick, *The Black Vampyre* (1819) 4, 16, 143–66, 231n8
    see also Polidori, John William, *Vampyre, The*, sequels
Daut, Marlene 151

Deleuze, Gilles 210
    see also psychoanalysis
demon lovers 97–8
    see also vampires, as lover
Depestre, René 161
Derrida, Jacques 59
desire 10, 17, 65, 67–9, 70, 74, 75, 76, 83, 85, 97, 102n28, 114, 118, 119, 1310, 131, 134, 136, 137, 138, 148, 202, 203, 204, 207–14
    female 85, 97, 102n28, 148, 207–14
determinism 14, 91
    see also agency; free will
Dey, Richard Varick (1801–1837) *see* D'Arcy, Uriah Derick
dialectics 13, 85, 91, 119, 144, 160, 161, 162, 166n68
diathesis 109–11
Dickens, Charles, *A Tale of Two Cities* (1859) 238
Dickson, Leigh Wetherall 86
disease 90–1, 92, 93, 96, 196–22, 218, 224–5
    see also contagion; illness
Doctor Who (1963–1989; 2005–present TV series)
domestic sphere, domesticity 39, 72, 82–3, 86, 89, 93, 207
Don Juan 87
    see also Byron, Lord George Gordon, *Don Juan*
Double, the 12, 74, 131, 136, 195, 213
Dracula (1931 film) 176
Dracula (1897) *see* Stoker, Bram
Du Maurier, Daphne 85, 86, 98
Dumas, Alexandre *Le Vampire* (1851) 27
Dürer, Albrecht 181
dystopia 100, 232n14

Eastern Europe 23, 36, 40, 97, 106, 115, 135, 144, 149
    see also vampires, Eastern European
Edgeworth, Maria 83, 92
    see also national tale
Edward Cullen 4, 17, 24, 41n12, 90, 98, 106, 147, 173, 202–16
    see also Meyer, Stephenie, *Twilight*

effeminacy 118, 206, 208
  see also gender
Emil, B. L. *Encore un Vampire* (1820) 28
  see also Polidori, John William, *Vampyre, The*, stage adaptations
enchantment 31, 35, 70, 71, 90–1, 157
Englishness 14, 25
  see also national identity
Enlightenment 97, 143, 144, 145, 146, 149, 156, 157, 161, 165n46
  see also modernity
eyes *see* vision

Faherty, Duncan *see* White, Ed, Duncan Faherty, and Toni Wall Jaudon
fairy tales 26, 29, 44n38, 169, 176–7, 193
  see also folklore; genre
family 32, 49, 50, 57–8, 86, 116, 117, 138, 146, 151, 160, 188, 190, 191, 206–7, 209, 220
fan culture 14–15, 64–80
  see also celebrity; parasociality
fan fiction 64, 67, 71, 74–6, 77
  see also fan culture; fan studies
fan studies 14–15
  see also fan culture
Fantasmagoriana (1812) 7, 32, 117
fantasmagorie see phantasmagoria
fantasy 68, 93, 133, 138, 161, 205, 206, 210
fantasy fiction 8, 226
  see also genre
femicide 138
feminism 12, 89, 203
  see also gender; misogyny; patriarchy
feudalism 13, 100
  see also aristocracy
folklore 2, 4, 11, 12, 15, 23, 24, 36, 37, 81, 97, 106, 118–19, 144, 152–3, 158, 177, 198, 202, 203, 218, 227, 230, 235, 236
  Caribbean 144, 152–3
  Celtic 36, 37, 195
  European 95, 106, 115, 144, 149, 188, 189

Greek 95, 118, 133
Irish 11, 195
  see also fairy tales; myth; vampires, folkloric
Foucault, Michel 167
Fox, Andrew, *Fat White Blues* (2003) 219
Frankenstein see Shelley, Mary
Frayling, Sir Christopher 3, 4, 10, 54, 181, 188, 203
free will 14, 25, 38, 39, 51, 69, 90, 152, 170
  see also agency; determinism
French Revolution 10, 13, 50, 56, 143, 155, 156, 160, 171
  see also revolution
Freud, Sigmund 16, 168–9, 170, 176–7
  see also psychoanalysis
Fuseli, Henry, *The Nightmare* (1781) 5, 114

gaze, the 11, 13, 147, 167–85, 202–16
Gelder, Ken 10, 11, 12
gender 17, 83, 91, 114, 208
genetic manipulation 219–21, 222, 225–6, 228, 229, 231n12
  see also science
genre 4, 11–12, 13, 17, 33, 83–5, 86, 96, 97–8, 100, 176, 205, 227, 229–30
Georgiana, Duchess of Devonshire 66
ghost stories 14, 26, 49, 56, 117, 131, 235
  see also genre
ghost story competition *see* Villa Diodati
Gilroy, Paul 143
Glenarvon see Lamb, Lady Caroline
Godwin, Mary Wollstonecraft *see* Shelley, Mary
Godwin, William 18, 56, 131, 238
Gothic 3, 4, 5, 9, 11, 12–13, 14–15, 17–18, 23, 24, 26, 27, 28, 39, 40, 56, 64–5, 69, 70–1, 73–4, 83, 85–7, 88, 90, 92, 95, 96, 117, 124, 137, 144, 146–8, 149, 153, 155, 157, 158, 159, 160–1, 165n46, 166n68, 171, 175, 186, 192, 196, 197, 198, 207, 218, 226, 230, 235, 238

Gothic (*continued*)
    hemispheric 144
    heroine 206
    fiction; novel; romance 7, 24, 31, 56,
        57, 58, 64, 69, 70, 71, 73,
        81, 83, 85, 86, 97–8, 100,
        114, 206, 207, 217
        see also genre
    tourism 236
    villain 36, 65, 187
Gothic (1986 film) 9
Gothic Romance (twentieth-century
        genre) 24, 85, 86, 97, 98, 99
    see also genre; paranormal romance
Greece 12, 13, 26, 38, 53, 133, 134,
        135, 174, 196
    see also Hellenism
Groom, Nick 65

Haiti 16, 143–66
Haitian Revolution 143, 151, 153, 156,
        161, 166n68
    see also revolution
Hammer Horror 40
Hardy Tree, the 235, *236*, 238
Hardy, Thomas 235
harlequinade 33, 34, 46n58
    see also theatre
Hazlitt, William 182
Hegel, G. W. F. 160
Hellenism; Philhellenism 10
    see also Greece; national identity
heteroglossia 186
    see also Bakhtin, Mikhail
historical novel; historical
        romance 8, 83
    see also genre
Hoffmann, E. T. A. 26, 168–70,
        177, 183n15
Hogan, Chuck *see* Toro, Guillermo del,
        and Chuck Hogan, *The
        Strain* (2009)
Hogle, Jerrold 13
homosexuality 10, 120
    see also queerness; sexuality
horror 3, 97, 144, 157, 161,
        169–70, 191
    body 144, 188–9
        see also genre; Gothic
Hungary 28, 29, 38
    see also Eastern Europe

Hunger, The (1985 film) 69
hybridity 33, 85, 100, 151, 160,
        170, 217–32
hypnosis 8, 24, 85, 86, 92, 96, 97, 98,
        103–4n59, 218, 228

illness 90, 106–22, 130, 136,
        138, 173
    see also disease
immortality 17, 114, 156, 188,
        189–90, 191–2, 193–5,
        198, 223, 233
imperialism 93
    see also colonialism
incest 7, 56, 133, 136, 137
infection *see* contagion
intertextuality 10, 11, 12, 16, 81–2,
        152, 153, 159
Interview with the Vampire (1994 film)
        17, 69, 70, 173, 186–7,
        190–3, 195–6, 200n28
    see also Jordan, Neil
intimacy 64, 67–9, 71, 74–6, 179,
        197, 211
Ireland 81–105, 129, 191, 194–5
    see also nationalism, Irish
Irish Rebellion 15, 85, 200n26
    see also revolution
Isherwood, Christopher 9
Islamophobia 210
    see also Orientalism; race
Italianness 49, 50–1
    see also national identity

James, M. R., 'The Ash Tree'
        (1904) 235
    see also ghost stories
Jaudon, Toni Wall *see* White, Ed,
        Duncan Faherty, and Toni
        Wall Jaudon
Jordan, Neil 17, 70, 173, 187,
        190–1, 199n23
Judson, Barbara 81, 83, 92, 94

Keats, John 112, 113, 115, 211
    'Ode on a Grecian Urn'
        (1819) 211
Kelly, Gary 83
King, Stephen, *Misery* (1987) 73
Kipling, Rudyard, 'The Vampire'
        (1897) 69

Lady Gaga 69
Lamb, Lady Caroline 4, 7, 15, *84*, 86, 73–4, 61–105
  Ada Reis (1823) 87
  Glenarvon (1816) 4, 7, 15, 36, 73, 81–105, 99
  'New Canto, A' (1819) 87
  see also Byron, Lord George Gordon
Lauro, Sarah Juliet 152, 153
Le Fanu, Sheridan *Carmilla* (1871) 5, 173, 179, 181
Lestat 4, 69, 70, 77, 90, 98, 100, 106, 119, 190–2, 195–6, 197, 198, 202–3
  see also Rice, Anne, *Interview With the Vampire* (1976); Rice, Ann, *The Vampire Lestat* (1985)
Lestat (2005–06 stage musical) 10
Lewis, Matthew 88
  see also Gothic novel
libertinism 24, 84–5, 92, 131
  see also sexuality
liminality 190, 191
Lyceum, The 14, 23, 28–9, 31, 38, 39, 40, 45n48
  see also theatre

McDayter, Ghislaine 68, 71, 73, 83, 91, 102n28, 102n33, 100n44, 103n57
Macdonald, D. L. 4, 5, 9, 50, 54, 188–9, 239n5
Macpherson, James, *Ossian* (1796) 26, 37
magic lantern 29, 31
  see also phantasmagoria; stage effects
male beauty 207–8, 209, 211–13
  see also desire. female
Marschner, Heinrich, *Der Vampyre* (1829 opera) 38
Martineau, Harriet 16
Marx, Karl 102n28, 157, 160, 165n55
masculinity 17, 24, 52, 89, 91, 168, 191, 208
  see also gender
Matheson, Richard, *I Am Legend* (1954) 218

melodrama 8, 20n24, 23, 252–9 , 36, 38, 44n40
  see also theatre
memento mori 233, *234*
mesmerism *see* hypnosis
metatextuality 180, 191, 197, 198
Meyer, Stephenie 17, 202–16
  Midnight Sun (2020) 211–13
  Twilight (2005) 147, 202–16
    reaction against 214n6, 215n23
    see also Twilight (film)
  Twilight series 17, 173, 202–16
middle class *see* bourgeoisie
Milbanke, Annabella 67, 85, 87, 90
  see also Byron, Lord George Gordon
Milton, John 19, 85, 88, 175, 240
  see also angels, fallen
Miltonic revolt *see* angel (fallen)
mimicry 5, 15, 85, 87
  see also plagiarism
Misery (1990 film) 73
  see also King, Stephen, *Misery* (1987)
misogyny 92, 194
  see also feminism; patriarchy
modernity 10, 11, 12, 15, 16, 65, 66, 137, 146, 157, 158, 159, 160, 162, 197, 219, 220, 230
  see also Enlightenment
Mole, Tom 65, 68, 72, 74
monsters 3, 4, 23, 24, 26, 27, 71, 98, 102, 115, 18, 119, 128, 144, 158, 176, 202
  see also vampires; zombies
moon, the; moonlight 6, 34, 35, 98, 126, 127, 138, 146, 147, 163n16, 168, 179, 188, 195, 218
Morgan, Lady *see* Owenson, Sydney
Morrison, Robert, and Chris Baldick 64–5
Mulvey, Laura 207–8
  see also gaze, the
Munsters, The (1964–66 TV series) 207
Murray, John 6, 12, 54, 66
music 197–8
myth 23, 96, 116, 144, 152–3, 165n46, 168, 190, 182n11

myth (*continued*)
  African 152–3
  Greek 7, 26, 147, 148–50, 152, 220–1
  Irish 171, 195
  Scandinavian 235
  see also folklore

national identity *see* Englishness, Hellenism, Irishness, Italianness, Scottishness
national tale 83, 92
  see also Edgeworth, Maria; genre; national identity; nationalism, Irish; Owenson, Sydney
nationalism, Irish 92, 94, 194–5
  see also national identity
neamh-mhairbh 191, 193
  see also folklore, Irish
neoliberalism 100
Newman, Kim, *Anno Dracula* (1992) 70
Ní Fhliann, Sorcha 70
Nodier, Charles, *Lord Ruthwen ou les vampires* (1820) 25, 26, 42n17, 42n21, 42n22, 44n40
  see also Polidori, John William, *The Vampyre*, stage adaptations
Nosferatu (1922 film) 35, 108, 176, 131
novel, the; novelism 11–13, 56
  see also genre; realism

objectification 147, 156, 159, 202, 204, 205, 207–11, 285
  see also reification
oneirodynia *see* somnambulism
opera 29, 28
Orientalism 210
  see also Islamophobia; otherness
Orlok *see Nosferatu* (1922)
otherness 12, 17, 18, 148, 160, 202–3, 206, 207, 208, 213, 219
Owenson, Sydney 83, 92, 155
  see also national tale

pallor (of complexion) 8, 24, 37, 59, 81, 85, 86, 90–1, 97, 106–7, 111, 112–13, 117, 119, 129, 172–4, 202–3, 208, 210, 212, 213, 214n5, 218, 227

paranormal romance 4, 15, 24, 85, 98, 100, 148
  see also romance; romance fiction; vampire, as lover
parasociality 64, 68, 71–6
  see also fan culture
patriarchy 138, 193–6
  see also feminism; masculinity; misogyny
phantasmagoria 14, 23–4, 29–32, *32, 33, 34*, 38, 43n46
phantoms 32, 35, 49, 57, 58
plagiarism 10, 12, 16, 52–3, 143, 153, 155, 158–9, 161
  see also intertextuality; mimicry; Polidori, John William, as plagiarist
Planché, James Robinson 8, 14, 20n24, 23, 26, 33, 34, 35, 44n38
  Giovanni the Vampire (1821) 29
  The Vampire; or, The Bride of the Isles (1820) 8, 14, 28–9, *30, 33, 35*, 36–9, *37*, 181
  see also Polidori, John William, *Vampyre, The*, stage adaptations
Polidori, Charlotte 58
Polidori, John William
  as Byron's employee 5, 6–7, 123, 188, 204, 217
  as character (in book or film) 8–9
  death 6, 48–9, 50, 57–9, 235–6
  diary 14, 52, 55–6, 57, 58, 110, 124, 130, 263n16
  dissertation 5, 16, 51, 103–4n59, 108, 175–6
    see also somnambulism
  Ernestus Berchtold; or, The Modern Oedipus (1821) 5, 7, 16, 51–2, 56–8, 168, 171–6
  Fall of Angels: A Sacred Poem, The (1821) 6
  life 5–7, 9–10, 50–1, 116–17
  medical career; as physician 3, 5, 7, 123, 124, 175, 188, 204, 217
  as plagiarist 10, 12, 53, 142, 261–2n2
    see also mimicry; plagiarism

Vampyre, The (1819) 3, 4, 6–8, 10–18, *178*
   attribution to Byron 3, 7, 10, *178*
   Aubrey
      as image of Polidori 16, 123, 137
      oath, his 126–7, 134, 135, 136, 187–9, 196, 198
   composition 7–8, 23, 52, 53–6, 123, 131–2, 168, 217
   editions 8
   Lord Ruthven
      as image of Byron 15, 16, 53, 64–5, 70–1, 123, 187–8, 204
      see also *Byzantium* (film)
   publication 7–8, 52, 53–6, 57
   sequels 8, 24–5
   stage adaptations 8, 14, 23–47
   translations 8
Ximenes and Other Poems (1819) 5–6, 112
Pope, Alexander 159
popular culture 64–80, 167, 176, 186, 189, 197, 198, 206
porphyria 115
   see also disease
postcolonialism 144
   see also anti-imperialism; colonialism; imperialism
postmodernism 5, 17, 70, 186, 187, 189–90, 191, 193, 196–7
Praz, Mario 113
Prometheus 57, 97, 148–50, 152, 155, 157, 158, 220–1, 231n10
   see also myth, Greek
pseudo-science 17, 151, 217–32
   see also science
psychoanalysis 10, 14, 49, 57–9
   see also Freud, Sigmund
psychological thriller 38
   see also genre
psychosis 138
public sphere 89
Punter, David 11, 64, 96–7, 134, 217, 226

Queen of the Damned (2002 film) 69, 197, 198
   see also Rice, Anne
queerness; queer theory 10, 192
   see also homosexuality; queer theory

race; racism 51, 154–5, 227, 159–60, 161–2
Radcliffe, Ann 56, 88, 146
   see also Gothic novel
realism 11–13, 83, 265n41
   see also genre; novel
Regency society 65, 72, 73, 75, 76
reification 11–13, 98, 148, 157
   see also alienation; capitalism; commodification
revolution 4, 5, 10, 13, 16, 50, 56, 86, 91–6, 100, 143, 145, 146, 148, 151, 152–4, 155, 156, 160, 161–2
   see also American Revolution; French Revolution; Haitian Revolution; Irish Rebellion
Rice, Anne 4, 17, 69, 70, 98, 100, 173, 188, 190, 193, 196, 198, 202–3
   Interview With the Vampire (1976) 69, 90, 173, 187, 190, 192, 195, 196–7, 198
      see also *Interview With the Vampire* (film)
   Queen of the Damned (1988) 69, 197
   Vampire Chronicles, The 188, 197, 198, 186–201, 199n12, 202–3
   Vampire Lestat, The (1985) 196–7
Richardson, Samuel, *Clarissa* (1748) 93
Rigby, Mair 10
Robertson, Etienne Gaspard 31–2, 32, 34
roman à clef 81, 83
   see also biography; genre
romance 4, 8, 24, 85, 93, 97–8, 100, 203, 205
   see also paranormal romance; romance fiction; vampire, as lover
Romance (genre) 11–13, 71–2, 73, 74–6, 83, 91, 98, 109, 119, 125, 131, 157, 205
   see also genre; novel
romantic fiction 8, 12, 74, 100, 203, 205
   see also genre; paranormal romance; romance; vampire, as lover

Romanticism 1, 4, 6, 8, 10, 13
Romkey, Michael, *I, Vampire* (1990) 70
Rossctti, Christina 6
  'Goblin Market' (1862) 210
Rossetti, Dante Gabriel 6, 14, 48–9, 57, 58
Rossetti, William Michael 6, 14, 48–9, 50, 54, 57, 58, 108, 236
Rousseau, A., *Les Etrennes d'un Vampire* (1820) 28
  see also Polidori, John William, *Vampyre, The*, stage adaptations
Rousseau, Jean-Jacques 28, 44n35
Rymer, James Malcolm, *Varney the Vampire; or, The Feast of Blood* (1845–47) 5, 8, 24, 35, 147, 173, 179, *180*

Saberhagen, Fred, *The Dracula Tape* (1975) 189
Sade, Marqui de, *Justine* (1791) 11
St Domingo *see* Haiti
Saint-Domingue *see* Haiti
St Pancras Old Church 6, 10, 18, 233–9
satire 4, 10, 12, 16, 83, 87, 97, 100, 154, 155, 156, 157n62, 246n43
  political 4, 10, 87, 97, 100, 156, 157, 162
  see also genre; vampire as political metaphor
science 17–18, 56, 124, 137, 138, 149, 157, 175, 176, 217–32
  see also genetic manipulation; pseudo-science
science fiction 8, 226
  see also genre
Scotland; Scottishness 26–36, 39, 43n25, 116
  see also national identity
Scribe, Eugène, and Mélesville, *Le Vampire Amoureux* (1820) 228
  see also Polidori, John William, *Vampyre, The*, stage adaptations
seduction 7, 24, 35, 97, 133, 138, 249
  see also seduction narrative; vampires, seductive

seduction narrative 10, 15, 93
  see also genre; seduction; vampires, seductive
Senf, Carol 18
sentimental fiction 15, 81, 85
  see also genre
sexuality 10, 11, 15, 24, 69, 113, 205
  see also desire; homosexuality; queerness
Shakespeare, William 114, 125, 147, 157, 174
Shelley, Mary 3, 5, 6, 7, 16, 18, 51, 55, 56, 112, 123, 124, 131, 149, 172, 187–8, 218, 236–7
  Frankenstein (1818) 3, 7, 9, 15, 17, 42n21, 49, 52, 56, 112, 123–42, 149, 168, 217–32
  Last Man, The (1826) 222, 232n14
Shelley, Percy Bysshe 3, 5, 6, 7, 9, 16, 18, 50, 55, 56, 97, 112–13, 115, 117, 123, 124, 149, 187–8, 220, 236–7
Siddal, Elizabeth 48, 57, 59
silverfork novels 83, 96
  see also genre
Skarda, Patricia 10, 12, 97, 128, 131, 133
slavery 16, 75, 143, 144, 152–3, 154, 155, 159–60, 161, 221n8
sleepwalking *see* somnambulism
somnambulism 5, 14, 16, 51, 57, 108, 124, 169, 172, 175, 176
Sontag, Susan 107, 108, 109, 115
Spiritualism 14, 48–63
Spooner, Catherine 24, 65, 70, 177
stage effects 23–47
  see also theatre
star trap 33–4
  see also stage effects; Stoker, Bram; theatre; vampire trap
Stoker, Bram 14, 31, 33, 49, 59, 179–81
  Dracula (1897) 5, 39, 40, 52, 69, 111, 115, 119, 126, 173, 181, 189, 191, 218, 227
  Primrose Path, The (1875) 33
  'Secret of the Growing Gold, The' (1892) 59, 63n56
  'Star Trap, The' (1908) 33–4

sublime, the 86, 102n28, 170–1, 198
  see also Burke, Edmund
suicide see Polidori, John
    William, death
Summers, Montague 26, 28, 34, 40
Süner, Ahmet 11
Swift, Jonathan 159
syphilis 113
  see also contagion; disease; illness;
    vampires, as contagious

TB see consumption (tuberculosis)
Telotte, J. P. 13
terrorism 156, 220, 221–2
theatre 23–47, 69, 177–8
  see also stage effects
Todorov, Tzvetan 13
Toro, Guillermo del, and Chuck Hogan,
    The Strain (2009) 219
Torok, Maria see Abraham, Nicolas,
    and Maria Torok
Tournefort, Pittton de 38, 42n16, 118
transgender 219
  see also gender
travel narratives 12, 56
  see also genre; vampires, as travellers
tuberculosis (TB) see consumption
    (tuberculosis)
Tuite, Clara 83, 85, 90, 96
Twilight (2005 novel) see Meyer,
    Stephenie
Twilight (2008 film) 173, 208
  see also Meyer, Stephenie
Twitchell, James B. 13

uchronia 222, 232n15
Uncanny, the 16, 26, 34, 135, 168–70,
    174, 176, 204
  see also Freud, Sigmund
utopian; utopianism 95, 150

vampensteins 18, 217–32
vampire lore 16, 24, 35, 76, 115, 118,
    123, 163n16, 181, 232n14,
    265n37, 266n50
  sunlight, effect of 35, 48n70, 202–3,
    207, 212, 213, 228
vampire slaying kits 39–40, 47n88
  see also stage effects; vampires,
    slaying of

vampire trap 29, 31, 33–5, 38,
    39, 181
  see also stage effects; star trap
vampires
  aristocratic 4, 8, 10, 11, 15, 17, 18,
    23, 24, 25, 36, 70, 97, 98,
    143, 144, 145, 147, 162,
    171, 218, 219
    see also aristocracy; class
  and betrayal of kin 95, 117
  their bite 168, 204, 205, 205, 208
  Black 4, 16, 143–66, 219, 225–30
  Byronic 4, 15, 90, 115, 119
    see also vampires, Romantic
  Caribbean 148, 164n19
  child 191, 194–5
  contagious nature of 15, 90, 97,
    218, 223–5, 232n16, 92,
    97, 186, 220, 222, 232n17
    see also contagion
  Eastern European 23, 24, 36, 97,
    106, 115–16, 135, 144, 149
  female 5, 25
  folkloric 15, 24, 25, 81, 106, 115,
    118, 119, 135, 149, 152,
    158, 177, 189, 218, 236
  hypnotic 24, 92
    see also hypnosis
  immortality of 186, 190, 193
  as lovers 70, 98–100
    see also demon lovers;
      paranormal romance;
      romance; romance fiction
  in New England 116
  peasant see vampires, folkloric
  as political metaphor 12, 17, 94, 94,
    97, 100, 156–9, 161, 162
    see also satire, political
  postmodern 187, 189, 190–3, 196
    see also vampires,
      twenty-first-century
  Romantic 4, 13, 14, 24, 40, 65, 69,
    70, 77, 93, 118, 159
  rules of see vampire lore
  seductive 15, 17, 24, 70, 106, 159,
    162, 186, 203, 207
    see also seduction; seduction
      narrative
  slaying of 25, 39, 40
    see also vampire slaying kits

vampires (*continued*)
   sparkly 17, 203, 206, 207, 214n6, 215n23
     see also Meyer, Stephenie, *Twilight*
   subjectivity of 17, 186, 187, 189–96
   sympathetic 85, 98, 189, 196, 202
   as travellers 12, 189
   see also monsters; zombies
Varney the Vampire see Rymer, James Malcolm
Vieux-Chauvet, Marie, *Anger* (1968) 161
Villa Diodati 3, 7, 8, 10, 15, 17, 23, 32, 51, 112, 123, 137, 149, 168, 171, 187, 217, 218
   ghost story competition 3, 7, 23, 32, 137, 183n15
Vodou 148, 152–3, 165n46
   see also folklore, Caribbean
voyeurism 9, 172, 202, 208, 212
   see also gaze
vrykalokas, vrykalokoi 38, 142n16, 118
   see also Greece; vampires, folkloric

Walpole, Horace, *The Castle of Otranto* (1764) 13, 69
   see also Gothic novel
Wassif, Marlam 204, 213

Wasson, Sara, and Sarah Artt 207, 210, 212
Watson, Nicola 81
Wester, Maisha 144
Whedon, Joss 98, 100, 202
   see also Angel
Whigs 11, 83, 97, 134
   see also Regency society
White, Ed, Duncan Faherty, and Toni Wall Jaudon 144, 158, 154, 155, 159
Wilde, Oscar, *The Picture of Dorian Gray* (1890) 179
Wilson, Frances 64, 83, 87
Wisker, Gina 194
Wollstonecraft, Mary 18, 83, 112, 236, 237, 238
women *see* Byronic persona, female; desire, female; femicide; feminism; gender; Gothic heroine; misogyny; patriarchy
Wordsworth, William 13

Yarbro, Chelsea Quinn 189

zombies 98, 106, 152, 153, 168, 170, 223
   see also folklore, Caribbean; monster; vampires

Milton Keynes UK
Ingram Content Group UK Ltd.
UKHW021258191124
2962UKWH00006B/49